Nick. It was really him.

Sidney couldn't see his face, but she knew it was him.

She took off running. She crashed into the glass wall. Her palms splayed against it. "Nick."

He turned. His hands met hers against the glass.

Sweet Lord, was this possible? She stared, unblinking. If she closed her eyes, she was afraid he'd disappear.

He came around the wall through the door and reached toward her. She latched on to his hand, laced her fingers through his. He was thinner than the last time she'd seen him. His complexion was pale as though he'd been ill, but this was definitely her fiancé.

She lifted her hand toward his face and touched the V-shaped scar on his jaw.

"Oh, Nick, I missed you so much."

"It's okay. I'm here. I'm back."

But there was something different. When she peered into his eyes, she didn't see the man she had once loved with all her heart.

Nick Corelli looked back at her with the eyes of a stranger.

MOUNTAIN RETREAT

USA TODAY Bestselling Author

CASSIE MILES

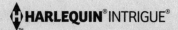

To my kids and friends and docs and
therapists and everybody who made it
possible for me to be sitting here at my
computer. And, as always, to Rick.

ISBN-13: 978-0-373-74861-7

Mountain Retreat

Recycling programs
for this product may
not exist in your area.

Copyright © 2015 by Kay Bergstrom

Printed in U.S.A.

™ www.Harlequin.com

Cassie Miles, a *USA TODAY* bestselling author, lives in Colorado. After raising two daughters and cooking tons of macaroni and cheese for her family, Cassie is trying to be more adventurous in her culinary efforts. She's discovered that almost anything tastes better with wine. When she's not plotting Harlequin Intrigue books, Cassie likes to hang out at the Denver Botanical Gardens near her high-rise home.

Books by Cassie Miles

Harlequin Intrigue

Visit the Author Profile page at Harlequin.com for more titles

CAST OF CHARACTERS

Sidney Parker—Her eidetic memory tortures her with painful details about her kidnapped fiancé.

Nick Corelli—He never purposely wanted to hurt Sidney. But as a Marine, duty comes first.

Tomas Hurtado—The dictator of the oil-rich South American country of Tiquanna.

Elena Hurtado—The exotic and beautiful wife of the dictator.

Rico Suarez—He works for Dictator Hurtado. Or does he?

Miguel Avilar—The dashing leader of the rebel forces is determined to overthrow Hurtado.

Victoria Hawthorne—The CIA special-agent-in-charge struggles to control the situation.

Sam Phillips—The CIA special agent helps Sidney. What does he want in return?

Randall Butler—As a Marine Corps intelligence officer, he keeps a close eye on Nick.

Chapter One

Working as a barmaid at the Silver Star Saloon in Austin put Sidney Parker's eidetic memory to good use. She could easily remember the drink orders for this table of twelve. With thumbs hooked in the belt loops of her thigh-high jean skirt, she faced the group of well-dressed young people who were still wearing their security badges from the state capitol.

"What'll it be?" she asked.

They could have answered in one voice: beer. But the Silver Star was a designer brewery with products ranging from Amber Angel to Zoo Brew. Sidney mentally recorded the order and gave a nod.

"Wait a minute," said a woman with platinum blond curls. "Change mine from Chantilly Lace to Raspberry Rocket."

"Got it."

"Are you sure? You didn't write anything down."

Sidney inhaled a breath and repeated their

order. "We're starting over here with two Pale Tigers, then a Blue Moon, a Lucky Ducky, Thor's Hammer Lite..." She continued around the table and ended with the redhead. "And you'll be having the Raspberry Rocket."

The gang applauded, and she swept a bow before heading to the huge central bar to fill her tray.

Keeping her brain occupied wasn't the greatest benefit of Sidney's part-time night job. The country-and-western sound track, the conversation and general clamor at the Silver Star provided her with a much-needed distraction during those lonely hours before dawn when tears swamped her pillow.

Behind the bar, Celia Marshall ducked down so the customers couldn't see her adjust the red gingham uniform shirt to better contain her cleavage. "I swear, I'm about to have a wardrobe malfunction."

"That's a problem I don't have." Sidney never needed to worry about her cup running over; her breasts were small and well behaved.

"I'd trade my chest in a minute for your mile-long legs."

"No deal." Sidney liked being tall. In her cowgirl boots, she was almost six feet. She gave her friend a closer look and noticed the puffiness around her eyes. "Something wrong?"

"Ray and I are fussing at each other again." Celia shook her head and frowned. "I always feel like a class-A whiner talking to you about man problems. Nobody has worse luck than you."

"It's not a contest." Sidney tucked a strand of her long, straight blond hair behind her ear. "And there's nothing I can do about my situation. You have options."

"Any word on Nick?"

"Not yet." She couldn't bear to think of Nick Corelli, her fiancé. The mere mention of his name conjured up a mental image of a tall, handsome marine with thick black hair and deep-set eyes the color of fine cognac. Her perfect memory filled in all the blanks as she recalled his wide grin, high cheekbones and strong jawline.

If she allowed herself to think about him, she'd be sobbing in a minute. So she pushed his image aside and asked, "What's up with you and Ray?"

"It's all about his stupid hunting plans."

Sidney listened while she loaded her tray. It was going to take a couple of trips to serve her big table, and the domestic drama of Celia and Ray gave her something else to think about. They were both good people, understandable people with normal relationship issues. Not like her and Nick.

As she stood behind the bar, she spotted two men with impeccable posture and serious expressions enter the saloon. They weren't in uniform, but they might as well have been marching shoulder to shoulder, wearing their marine dress blues.

She set her tray on the bar. "Celia, you'll have to take over for me."

After a quick explanation to the shift manager, she fell into step between the two marines. She knew the drill. They were here to escort her to an interview with a CIA agent or someone high up in Marine Intelligence. She'd taken part in sixteen of these interrogations during the past six months after her fiancé went missing in a South American dictatorship. She always hoped that her marine escorts would be bringing good news.

They never did.

In a dull beige room at the local CIA field offices, Sidney paced back and forth behind the table. The heels of her boots clunked on the tile floor. In her barmaid uniform with the short denim skirt and gingham top, she felt a little ridiculous but not intimidated.

The first time she'd been sequestered in a room like this, her anxiety level was off the charts. The shock of possibly losing Nick had been staggering, and she'd been desperate for information. She'd begged, wept and pleaded.

The only facts she'd been able to pry from the case officer, CIA Special Agent Sean Phillips, were that her fiancé was MIA in the South American country of Tiquanna, his body hadn't been found and he was probably being held by the rebels. There had been no ransom demands.

That was in early May, six months and four days ago. Nothing much had changed in the details she'd been given, but her attitude had transformed. When she first came here, she was a nervous kitty cat. Now, a lioness.

She was half a tick away from going to Tiquanna herself, marching into the palace compound of dictator Tomas Hurtado and demanding an army to storm the rebel camps. She'd met Hurtado three years ago when he consulted with the oil company she worked for in the engineering department. Along with her boss at Texas Triton, she had actually traveled to the small country that was intent on developing its natural resources.

Sometimes, she wondered if that trip was the reason Nick had been selected for the assignment. When he told her that his platoon was being sent to Tiquanna, she'd given him all the inside information on Hurtado and his stunning wife, Elena.

The door opened and Special Agent Phillips entered. Sidney had heard that CIA agents liked to look anonymous so they could fade into crowds. If true, that meant Phillips was a CIA superstar. He was the most average-looking guy she'd ever met. With his thinning brown hair, brown eyes and average build, he was as plain as a prairie chicken.

"Why am I here?" she asked.

"Nice to see you, Sidney."

"Do you have news?"

A second person entered the room. Special Agent Victoria Hawthorne was higher in rank than Phillips, always dressed in black and as thin as a greyhound. Her dark hair was slicked back in a tight bun. She pulled out a chair on the opposite side of the table and sat. "Have a seat, Sidney."

"Am I being interrogated?" Still standing, she purposely kept her anger going. "This looks like an interrogation room with the closed door and the table and the big two-way mirror on the wall."

Special Agent Hawthorne scowled. Her thin lips pulled into an upside-down U. "You've been in this room before."

"And I've answered a million questions," she said. "I've been totally cooperative, and I think it's time I got an upgrade to a comfortable chair and, maybe, a room with windows."

Ignoring Sidney's demands, she asked, "Have you been in contact with anyone from Tiquanna?"

"Of course not. If somebody contacted me, I'd tell you immediately."

Hawthorne regarded Sidney through slitted eyes. "I have information if you're ready to hear it."

Hope flickered inside her like a pilot light that refused to be extinguished. "I'm ready. Tell me."

"On one condition. You must promise not to act on this information. Trust us to do our jobs without your interference. Is that clear?"

"Crystal."

"Hurtado and his wife will be in Austin next week along with several other South American leaders."

This was big news. Sidney might have a chance to hear firsthand what was happening to Nick. "I want to see them."

"I can't promise," the thin-lipped agent said. "We'll do everything in our power to make that happen."

"Where will they be staying? How long will they be here?"

"You don't need to know." As she rose from her chair, Special Agent Hawthorne maintained steady eye contact. Her gaze was a warning. "If they agree to meet with you, we'll be in touch."

She turned on her heel and stalked from the room, leaving Sidney with a complicated tangle of anger, frustration and fear. She was afraid to expect too much, but she couldn't give up. It would be foolish to antagonize Hawthorne, but Sidney's anger demanded release.

Special Agent Phillips took Hawthorne's seat at the table, opened a folder and took out four photographs of men in camouflage fatigues. Three of them had beards. "Recognize anyone?"

"Do you think she'll let me talk to Hurtado?"

"I can't rightly say," he said in a Texan drawl.

Over the months, she and Phillips had developed a bit of rapport. He'd seen her at her worst when she broke down into hysterical tears, and she sensed that he was more sympathetic toward her than the other agents.

"I could negotiate with the rebels," she said. "I know it's against CIA policy, but I could—"

"C'mon now, Sidney girl." He poked at the photos. "Let's do this thing."

She didn't want to be a good girl. A lioness would tear these photos to scraps and throw them in his face. She was too docile. Nothing was getting done.

But what choice did she have? Could she single-handedly take on the whole intelligence community? She huffed a frustrated sigh before picking up the photos. This was part of their routine. Because of her memory, the CIA used her to identify men whom she might have met when she visited the country. Thus far, there had been only four familiar faces.

These unposed pictures had been taken in a forested setting. "It's hard to tell with the beards. I don't think I know them. Who are they?"

"Rebels," he said.

"When I was in Tiquanna, I never left the palace grounds. Why would you think I'd know rebels?" She didn't expect him to answer. "Is it because the palace guards are defecting? Are they joining the rebels?"

"Let's just say that Señor Hurtado ain't exactly winning any popularity contests."

And the CIA wanted to keep Hurtado on their side. Though the dictator had a terrible record on civil rights for his impoverished people, he supported US programs and happily accepted our aid. More important, he was working with neighboring countries to form an oil and natural gas distribution system functioning with US companies.

When Phillips pulled out several aerial photographs of the palace grounds, she groaned. "Not again," she said. "I've told you everything I could about the palace."

"Focus on this area." He pointed to a far corner in the walled compound.

She stared. "It looks like the wall is broken. Was it an explosion?"

"Yep."

A wave of guilt washed over her. In a similar

tactic, Nick had disappeared. Six months and four days ago, there had been an explosion targeting the front gates. Two marines had been injured. The last anyone had seen of Nick was when he was trying to rescue them.

Before he left on this deployment, she'd told him not to be a hero, which was impossible advice for a marine. The man lived to protect others. His courage was as much a part of him as his arms and legs. Oh, God, she missed him so much. Without him, her life was empty.

Her fingers gripped the back of the chair. Her knees were weak. Though she wanted to be fierce, the weight of her sadness dragged her down. She sank into the chair.

"Please," she said, "you've got to tell me something about Nick. Those pictures you showed me are snapshots. They were taken from surveillance at the rebel camp, weren't they? Your people have infiltrated the camp."

The corner of his mouth twitched. For Phillips, that slight change of expression was more than she'd seen from him in weeks. Sensing a possible crack in the stone wall that kept information from her, she asked, "Do you have photos of Nick?"

"You know how this works, Sidney. I'm here to get intel from you."

"I just want to know if he's all right."

"There's reason to believe that your fiancé is well."

The tiny flicker of hope burst into full flame. Something was different about Phillips. He knew something.

She asked, "Is Nick well enough to be rescued? What do you CIA people call it? Extracted. Can he be extracted?"

He pushed the aerial photo toward her. "We need to know about this part of the compound."

There was nothing to tell. She hadn't visited that part of the palace grounds, hadn't noticed anything about the far corner. For the first time, she wondered if it would serve her better to lie and build up the importance of that corner in the hope that she could get more information. But she wasn't about to play games with the CIA. They were on the same side. She needed to cooperate.

"I was never near that part of the grounds." She rose from her chair. "I've got nothing against you, Phillips. But I need more. Is there anybody else I should talk to? Anything else I can do?"

He leaned back in the chair and folded his arms across his chest. "If you left the room right now and went down the corridor to your left, I wouldn't stop you."

"Why? What does that mean?"

"You heard me."

She took the cue, not knowing what she'd find.

Hoping for the best and fearing the worst, her fingers closed on the doorknob and she yanked the door open. Had it always been unlocked? She didn't know; she'd never tried it before.

After hours, there was no one else in the hallway. One side was all windows, and the other was closed doors. The route she'd always followed when escorted into the building was in the opposite direction. She'd never been this way before.

Moving fast before Phillips changed his mind, she rushed down the carpeted corridor. At the far end, a double doorway opened into a honeycomb of cubicles encircled by offices with glass walls. She heard voices to her left and turned.

In the farthest office, Special Agent Hawthorne stood behind a desk and spoke to four men. One stood apart from the others. His left hand was in the pocket of his gray suit jacket. He was tall with black hair and wide shoulders. Sidney couldn't see his face, but she knew him.

She took off running. Dodging around file cabinets and desks, she flew across the room. Her feet barely touched the floor. She crashed into the glass wall. Her palms splayed against it. "Nick."

He turned. His hands met hers against the glass.

Sweet lord, was this possible? She stared, unblinking. If she closed her eyes, she was afraid he'd disappear.

He came around the wall through the door and reached toward her. She latched on to his hand, laced her fingers through his. He was thinner than the last time she'd seen him. His complexion was pale, as though he'd been ill, but this was definitely her fiancé. She lifted her hand toward his face and touched the V-shaped scar on his jaw.

"Oh, Nick, I missed you so much."

"It's okay. I'm here. I'm back."

But there was something different. When she peered into his eyes, she didn't see the man she had once loved with all her heart. Nick Corelli looked back at her with the eyes of a stranger.

Chapter Two

Nick folded his arms around her and held her in a warm embrace. Tucking her head beneath his chin, Sidney gasped, trying to suck oxygen into lungs that felt paralyzed. She was frozen in time. Her world had stopped spinning.

"You're trembling," he said.

"I know."

She desperately wanted to kiss him, but she was afraid to look into his eyes again. What if he'd changed? What if he was no longer the Nick she'd built her life around? She needed reassurance, needed to know that this was *her* Nick, *her* fiancé, *her* lover.

"They told me it was better to wait," he whispered in her ear. "They said it would be easier for you."

"They were wrong."

And he should have known that. He should have realized how much she had needed to know that he was safe. Every moment he'd been missing, she had feared the worst.

"I'm sorry," he said.

"Don't say that." It wasn't right for him to apologize. He'd been through hell. "It's not your fault."

"You know I'd never do anything to hurt you."

"I know."

"Forgive me, Sidney."

A burst of anger shattered her fear. Her blood surged. Her muscles tensed. She pushed away from him, whirled and stalked into the office to face the CIA agents, who had been joined by Phillips. "I blame them."

Special Agent Hawthorne had lied to her only minutes ago. The woman was a monster. If Sidney truly had been a lioness, she would have pounced on the skinny agent, thrown her to the carpet and torn out her throat. Why had they kept Nick from her? What was their plan?

She didn't really care, didn't want to know. She'd happily leave spying to the professionals. All that mattered was Nick. He was alive. Everything else was water under the bridge.

"We're leaving now," she informed them. "Nick and I are leaving. Together."

"I'm afraid that's not possible," Hawthorne said. "Nick will be staying in a safe house until after the visit from Hurtado and his wife."

"Is he in danger?"

"I don't owe you an explanation." Hawthorne's tone was brisk. "Captain Corelli is a marine. He has his orders."

"Ma'am." A man with a thick neck and a body builder's shoulders stepped forward and shook Sidney's hand. "I'm Lieutenant Randall Butler. I want you to know that we appreciate what you've gone through."

"Is that so?" Anger pumped molten lava through her veins. "You knew he was safe. I should have been informed."

"Marine Intelligence has been working with the CIA on this mission. Special Agent Hawthorne is taking the lead."

In spite of her searing fury, she understood what he was saying. "It was Hawthorne's decision to keep me uninformed. Why?"

Hawthorne unbuttoned the black jacket of her severe pantsuit and leaned against the edge of her desk. The plain office suited her dull, uncluttered personality. The bookshelves were arranged in order, a few diplomas—including one from Harvard—hung on the walls, and nothing seemed out of place.

Hawthorne's eyes narrowed to slits. "Part of my job is to assess your psychological profile. Though you're an intelligent woman who is capable of logic—"

"An engineer," Sidney said. "It doesn't get much more logical than that."

"Your behavior—especially when it pertains to your fiancé—is highly irrational. Therefore, I concluded that you would not be brought into the loop until after Captain Corelli's assignment is over."

Clenching her jaw to keep from screaming, Sidney replied, "I resent your assumptions."

"They aren't meant as criticism." Hawthorne arched an eyebrow. "It's clear that you care so much about Captain Corelli that you aren't capable of behaving in a dispassionate manner."

No one had ever accused Sidney of being too passionate. Her engineering work put her in contact with all-male crews who never showed emotion, and Nick was the only man she'd ever had a serious, long-term relationship with. In her twenty-eight years, there had been two other men she'd fallen for, but she had ultimately ended things with them.

Sidney wasn't going to waste time arguing with Hawthorne, who thought she was doing the right thing. Instead, she pointed out the obvious. "The situation has changed."

"Yes, it has." Hawthorne scowled.

"Keeping me in the dark is no longer an option. I'm here. What are you going to do about it?"

"You leave me no choice but to take you into protective custody."

"You're arresting me?"

"There's no need to be melodramatic. The only restriction is that you won't be allowed to talk to anyone. You'll be kept in comfortable accommodations, and it will only be for about a week."

Overwhelmed by rage, she saw red. "You can't do that."

"Actually, I can."

"What about my work?"

"We'll handle it," Hawthorne said. "This is inconvenient for all of us. It would have been easier if you'd just stayed in the interrogation room." She shot an accusing glance toward Phillips.

"Don't blame him," Sidney said. "After I saw the photos you took in the rebel camp, I took off running. I had a question for you."

"Go ahead and ask."

"I wanted to know if you'd seen my fiancé." She turned toward Nick, who had remained silent throughout this exchange. "The answer is obvious."

He came toward her and slipped his arm around her waist, a familiar gesture. Leaning against his chest, she was more comfortable than she'd been in half a year. Their bodies fit together so nicely.

His deep voice rumbled. "There's no reason for Sidney to be detained. She doesn't know anything about my assignment, except that I'm back in town. Hurtado and the rebels are aware of that fact."

"I don't want her talking to anyone."

"A simple instruction," Nick said. "She can handle it."

"Unacceptable," Hawthorne said. "I don't believe she can be trusted. She's a civilian."

"Which is why you can't take her into custody against her will," Nick said. "You're right about me. I'm obligated to follow orders. But Sidney wants to be home."

She appreciated the way he was taking care of her, putting her comfort ahead of his own. She tilted her head back so she could see him. "I haven't done much with the house."

Before he'd left, they'd purchased a bungalow together. She had intended to use the time while he was on deployment to do some decorating, but when he'd gone missing, she couldn't bear to make any new purchases. Cardboard boxes still packed with their belongings were stacked in every room of the house. In spite of a lovely walk-in closet, she was living out of a suitcase.

"I've been dreaming about our house," he whispered, "coming home and finding you waiting for me in the bedroom."

The tone of his voice hit precisely the right chords inside her. His words were music that touched her soul. She knew there was only one way she could be certain that everything was all right between them. She needed to kiss him.

"Try to understand," the lieutenant said. "The CIA is running this show. We need to do all we can to help them."

"Yes, sir," Nick said, "and I'm not refusing. But I want Sidney to be comfortable. She's been through enough."

"I agree," the lieutenant said. "It's important to be sensitive to the needs of the family."

"What if she's in danger?" Phillips asked. "The rebels could kidnap her and use her to influence you."

"If that's true," Nick said, "why wasn't she under protection before?"

She listened with half an ear to their discussion. The rest of her mind focused on one goal: *kiss him, kiss him, kiss him.* If she could feel his lips on hers and know their relationship was okay, she could handle anything.

Special Agent Hawthorne stomped around her desk and took a position behind it. The only overt signs of her anger were the flaring of her nostrils and a sharp gleam in her flinty eyes. Her voice was low, monotone. "I will agree to send Ms. Parker home while Captain Corelli stays in protective custody. There will be no communication between them unless it's cleared through me. Phillips will accompany her and keep an eye on her. Is that satisfactory?"

"It works for me," Nick said.

"And for me," she said.

She shifted her position within his embrace, turned toward him and tilted her head upward. Her eyelids closed, and her lips parted. The office wasn't an appropriate place for their first kiss, but she couldn't take the chance that Hawthorne would tear Nick away from her.

When his mouth joined with hers, a sweet rush of warmth spread through her body. His lips were firm. His taste always reminded her of honeysuckle. His scent was a pine forest after a rain. He held her with a perfect balance of strength and gentleness.

Even on a bummer day when he wasn't in the mood, Nick was the most irresistible kisser she'd ever known. Though his lips pressed against hers and invited her to respond, he seemed...detached. This kiss wasn't exactly right.

Silently, she cursed her eidetic memory that had recorded every nuance of their lovemaking in indelible detail. She missed the light scrape of his teeth against her lower lip, the quick stroke of his tongue and the fire.

Embarrassed, she pulled away. What had she been expecting? He certainly wasn't going to give her the kind of kiss she wanted while standing in an office surrounded by intelligence agents. This was no basis for judgment.

IN THE BACKSEAT of an unmarked SUV, Sidney sat beside Nick on their way to drop her off at their house. An agent she'd never met before was driving, and Phillips sat beside him in the passenger seat.

"Special Agent Phillips," she said, leaning forward to speak to him. "Thank you."

"It didn't feel right to keep you in the dark," he said. "I'm surprised y'all got Hawthorne to make a concession."

"She's a hard nut to crack."

"Just doing her job," Phillips drawled.

Though wearing her seat belt, her shoulder rubbed against Nick's and her naked thigh grazed the fabric of his trousers. She could feel him watching her.

"Interesting outfit," he said, "I never thought you went in for gingham."

"I have a new job at the Silver Star Saloon, night shift."

"Why?"

"It's kind of fun," she said, avoiding the sad truth. "The place is a microbrewery with ninety-nine different brands of beer, and I like to take big orders and show off by remembering every last one of them."

"You wanted to keep yourself busy," he said. "My God, Sidney, I'm so damn sorry."

There were so many things she wanted to know but was afraid to talk about. What had happened to him while he was held captive? Was he hurt? How was he rescued? Instead, she kept the topic light.

"I should warn you about the house." Quickly, she glanced up at him and then looked away. His nearness was also having a sensual effect on her. Did she dare to try another kiss? "I haven't done much with it, with the house."

"But you had such big plans for decorating."

"I wanted you to help me make up my mind. I haven't even painted the disgusting turquoise in the kitchen."

"What colors are you thinking about?"

Decisions that had seemed impossible yesterday became clear. "I like a soft beige with dark gold and brown granite countertops."

"And in the bedroom?"

"Blue," she said.

"Like the Colorado skies you grew up with."

He knew her so well. At this time of the year, in early November, they usually took a ski vacation in Colorado, where her parents had a vacation cabin. "I don't mind Austin, but I love my mountains."

"Tell me about this bar where you're working."

"Should I recite the ninety-nine varieties of beer?"

"Please don't."

Their conversation was cozy and natural and deliberately avoided dangerous topics. She felt as if she was walking through a minefield. They talked until they pulled up to the curb outside the one-story, redbrick bungalow with shrubs under the windows and a live oak in the front yard. The grass was a little raggedy in winter.

"It's even cuter than I remembered," Nick said as he unfastened his seat belt.

"Whoa," Phillips said. "My orders are for you to stay in the vehicle while I escort Sidney inside."

"You're going to have to hog-tie me to keep me from going into my own house." Nick clapped him on the shoulder. "I'll just be a minute."

Hand in hand, they walked up the sidewalk together. Being separated from him again would be hard, but she was willing to put up with a few days now that she knew he was safe. "You'll call me, won't you?"

"Every day."

"I wish you could stay here."

"Me, too."

She noticed that the porch lamp was dark. She thought she'd turned it on before she'd left for work. The bulb must have burned out. But there were two bulbs in the fixture. What were the odds of both burning out at the same time? "I must have forgotten to turn on the porch lamp."

As she reached toward the lock with her key, the front door yanked inward. A barrage of gunfire erupted.

Chapter Three

Before the bullets flew, Nick had suspected trouble. His beautiful, brilliant Sidney never forgot anything, especially not the locking-up procedures when she left the house. She knew to leave a light burning.

His right arm flung around her slender waist. He scooped her off her feet and pulled her against him as he flattened his back against the brick wall beside the front door. Bullets tore through the opened door and cut into the night.

Still holding Sidney, he stepped off the concrete stoop and ducked into the space between the shrubbery and the red brick wall. "Stay down," he said as he drew a Glock 9 from his ankle holster. He fired two shots toward the open door to let the intruders know he was armed.

It had taken a lot of negotiation to convince Hawthorne to allow him to carry a firearm, and his talk had been worth every minute. The gun felt good in his hand. When it came to survival, Nick trusted himself more than anyone else.

Special Agent Phillips and the other Fed who had been the driver were out of the vehicle and moving toward them.

"You good?" Phillips called out.

Nick gave him a silent okay signal and then motioned him toward the live oak at the far left side of the front yard. He assumed the two agents would know enough to avoid the sight line from the front window. After he turned Sidney over to their protection, he'd go back to the house and catch the sons of bitches who set up this ambush. Shielding her with his body, he crept under the window ledge toward the corner of the house.

"Where are we going?" she whispered.

"I'm taking you to Phillips. He'll get you to safety."

She balked. "I'm not going anywhere without you."

He hadn't expected resistance. "It's better if you're out of the way."

"Not if I'm armed. I can help."

His attitude shifted from mild surprise to downright shock. Six months ago, Sidney hadn't known how to handle a weapon.

A fresh blast of gunfire exploded behind them. Shards of glass from the shattered front window rained over them. He looked down at the delicate, pale oval of her face. Her jaw was set. Her clear blue eyes showed no fear.

"You don't know how to shoot," he said.

"I learned," she said, cool as ice. "It's not a difficult skill, and I have excellent hand-eye coordination."

"Why?"

"I thought I might have to go to Tiquanna and rescue you. Learning to handle weaponry seemed prudent."

The idea of Sidney charging into the palace of a Third World dictator gave him pause, but he didn't dismiss the notion. She was a remarkable woman. "For now, let's do it my way."

"I'm tired of people telling me what to do," she said, "and that includes you, Nick. I'm part of this operation."

"I won't let you risk your life."

"Ditto."

"We can't stay where we are." He nudged her forward. "Stay low and run toward the live oak where Phillips and the other agent are waiting. I'll cover you."

"And you'll follow me," she said. "Promise that you'll be right behind me. If you aren't, I'll come back for you."

"Just go."

As she stepped out from the shrubbery, he dodged to the right and fired into the house through the shattered front window. From the corner of his eye, he saw her make it to the tree. Though he would have preferred heading to the rear of the house, he ran behind her.

Sheltered by the shade tree, Nick took command. "Phillips, you stay here and keep them pinned down. I'll go around to the back door and do the same. I want to take these guys alive."

"I assume that Special Agent Phillips has already called for backup," Sidney said, again surprising him with her savvy comprehension of a dangerous situation. "If we keep the gunmen contained in the house until the others arrive, we'll have the manpower to take them."

Phillips gaped at her, and then stared at Nick. "What the hell's going on with y'all?"

Nick didn't have time to explain. "Get her to safety."

"I can help," she said. "Give me a weapon."

In her short denim skirt and gingham shirt with her blond hair tucked behind her ears, she looked about as dangerous as Cowgirl Barbie. But he knew better than to doubt her abilities. "There's no reason for you to take any risks."

"I could say the same to you."

But this was his job. He'd been trained for combat. He knew how to handle himself. "I'll stay safe."

After another burst of gunfire from the house,

Nick separated from the others and emptied the bullets from his Glock 9 into the front of the house. He loaded a fresh clip and ran, returning to the left side of the house, where he ducked down. Remembering the floor plan of their little bungalow, he knew that the windows above him opened onto a dining room that attached to the kitchen. The only exits from the house were the front entry and the kitchen door. He eased toward the rear of the house.

Stark, silvery moonlight glistened across the backyard patio and the waist-high chain link fence. Nick was painfully aware that he wasn't in a simple village in Tiquanna, where danger was a way of life. The complications of being in Austin were wide and varied. When lights went on in the house next door, he prayed that his neighbors had the good sense to stay inside. From down the street, he heard dogs barking. If this firefight continued, there were sure to be casualties.

Scanning the yard, he decided that the best vantage point for watching the kitchen door would be at the far side of the backyard, but that area offered little in the way of cover, and he wasn't carrying another ammunition clip. Every shot had to count. His best option was to stay where he was and fire at anyone who came through the door. He wanted to take these men alive, to find out why they were coming after him.

If this attack had been arranged by the underfunded Tiquanna rebels, he didn't expect sophisticated weaponry. They'd wear bulletproof vests but not body armor. How many of them were there in the house? He'd seen flashes from at least two weapons.

He heard more gunfire at the front of the house. The longer he waited for the gunmen to make their move, the greater the risk that somebody was going to get shot. Nick had to take the fight to the rebels.

Ignoring the chronic ache from a sprained ankle that hadn't healed correctly, he vaulted the chain link fence and approached the kitchen door. The interior of the house was dark. There were shouts from inside and more gunfire.

From the street at the front of the house, he heard a police siren and winced. He could have handled the situation with two other marines. Now he'd be dealing with cops, Texas Rangers and backup from the CIA…and Sidney. He couldn't help being proud of her. She'd learned to shoot and had been planning to take on the whole country of Tiquanna to engineer his rescue. He regretted every minute he'd been away from her and every lie he'd ever told her.

Red and blue cop lights flashed like fireworks through the branches of the trees, lighting up the neighborhood. There were shouts and more chaotic gunfire. The situation was slipping out of control. If he hoped to take these guys alive, he needed to rein it in.

A young, fresh-faced Texas Ranger with a handgun appeared at the back gate.

"Don't shoot," Nick said. "I'm on your side."

"Put down your gun."

Nick couldn't blame the kid. If they'd traded places, he would have done the same. Another Ranger joined the first. Now there were two of them, yelling at him to disarm himself.

"Stand down." The order was barked with the authority of a marine. Lieutenant Butler had joined the Rangers. "He's on our side, boys."

There was an explosion at the front of the house. It sounded like a grenade, but Nick guessed it was a flash-bang device that made a lot of noise and fired off thick smoke to drive the gunmen from the house.

The kitchen door flung open and two men wearing balaclavas rushed through. Nick was caught between the Rangers and the masked men. He pivoted and aimed at the rebels.

Bracing himself, he shouted, "Drop your guns." He repeated the command in Spanish. For a moment, it looked as if they might obey. Then three other armed cops came around from the front and opened fire. Nick dropped to the ground.

When the smoke cleared, the two masked

men were sprawled facedown on the concrete patio. Two of the Rangers had also been shot. Their cries and moans struck a familiar chord in Nick's memory. The stink of blood and gunpowder dragged him back in time to other battles, other attacks. Adrenaline pumped up his senses. He staggered to his feet.

He didn't seem to be injured. By some miracle, he had been spared. Stumbling, he approached one of the downed rebels and yanked the mask from his face. He'd been shot in the head, but enough of his features remained for Nick to identify him. His name was Rico.

Agent Phillips dashed into view. "I don't want you to worry, Nick. She's going to be all right."

Sidney. If anything happened to her, he would never forgive himself.

SIDNEY WASN'T HAPPY about the blatantly obvious police presence in front of her house. Most of her neighbors were still strangers, and this wasn't how she wanted to be introduced. Still, making a bad first impression might be the least of her worries. Number one was, of course, that she and Nick had been targeted, which validated Special Agent Hawthorne's insistence on safe houses. Number two, Sidney had been injured. She sat on the rear step bumper of one of the two ambulances with a bandage wrapped around her upper left arm.

A bullet had grazed her. Though the EMT told her she needed stitches, he also assured her that the wound wasn't serious. She clenched her jaw, telling herself that it didn't hurt even though the straight slash across her biceps stung like hellfire. The EMT had given her something for the pain, but it hadn't kicked in yet. If only the bleeding would stop… Her bandage was already soaked through. Nick was going to be upset.

When she saw him plowing through the mob of law enforcement officers like a running back crashing toward the goalposts, she stood and adjusted the black POLICE windbreaker draped over her shoulders so he couldn't see the bandage.

His thick black hair—though neatly trimmed—stuck out in spikes. The lines in his face seemed to be etched more deeply, and he looked much older than his thirty years. This was a part of her fiancé that she didn't know. She'd never seen him in action. The battle-tested marine who had experienced the devastation of war and who risked his life on a daily basis was a good, brave, admirable man. She wanted to be closer to him, but he kept his warrior spirit hidden.

As he approached, she could tell that he intended to embrace her, which was really going to hurt her arm. She held up a hand, bringing him to a halt.

"This wasn't my fault," she said. "Phillips wouldn't give me a weapon, and I was trying to obey orders and go back to the vehicle, but others kept arriving and—"

"Were you wounded?"

"It's nothing serious." She turned away from him, hoping to hide the bandage. "A couple of stitches and I'll be good as new."

Gently, he removed the windbreaker. When he saw the bandage, he inhaled a sharp gasp. "You need medical attention."

"Several other people have been wounded. The EMTs have their hands full."

"You're pale, Sidney. Have you lost a lot of blood?"

"I don't think so." But she did feel a bit dizzy and unsure on her feet. "I took a pill."

"You could be going into shock." He wrapped the windbreaker around her again and held her against his chest in such a way that her left arm was untouched. "I'm sorry, baby. I'm so damn sorry."

"It's not your fault."

"I never should have left you alone."

Agent Victoria Hawthorne, wearing her own

black windbreaker with CIA stenciled across the back, charged toward them. "Get in the back of the ambulance, both of you."

Glaring at her, Nick gestured toward the battlefield on their front lawn. "How the hell did this happen?"

"A misjudgment," she snapped. "Do what I say. I need to get you both out of here."

"Where are we going?"

Angrily, she gestured to the back of the ambulance. "Let's move. We'll talk on the way."

After Sidney refused to lie on the gurney, Hawthorne shoved it out of the way and they sat on plastic-cushioned seats with minimal seat belts. Wall space and drawers held an array of medical equipment, including oxygen tanks, defibrillators and stethoscopes. She reached for a blanket to cover her bare legs and settled back on the seat as they pulled away with the siren blaring.

Hawthorne barked into her cell phone, snapping out instructions to her staff. Sidney figured that if anyone should be offering an apology, it was the thin, angry senior agent. She was the one who gave the okay for Sidney to go home without having her house checked out first.

Her skeletal hand, holding the phone, dropped to her lap. She spoke loudly so they could hear her over the siren. "The only way this operation could be arranged so quickly was with prior knowledge. We have a leak, a mole."

"At the CIA," Nick said.

"I don't know. Several other agencies are involved in this operation, including Marine Intelligence." With a disgusted snort, she shook her head. "I never should have allowed you to come to the house with your fiancée."

"Thank God you made that misjudgment." His voice was cold, hard and angry. Sidney had never heard him speak so harshly. "If I hadn't been along, she would have walked into this ambush by herself, defenseless and vulnerable."

Hawthorne pinched her lips together. "Not necessarily."

"They would have taken Sidney hostage, used her to get what they wanted."

The ambulance careened around a corner, and she was thrown against his shoulder. Her wound still ached, but she appreciated the warmth of the blanket over her knees and the jacket around her shoulders. A comfortable heat spread through her, and she felt her eyelids begin to droop. Though she had plenty to say to Hawthorne, it was a struggle to merely stay alert.

"There's been a change in plans," Hawthorne said. "We'll swap vehicles shortly, and you will be taken to the safe house."

"I'm not going anywhere without Sidney," he said.

"Understood." She gave a terse nod. "For now, you'll be staying together."

Chapter Four

Propped up against several pillows, Sidney wakened slowly, cautiously. She peered through heavy-lidded eyes at a dimly lit bedroom with pine furniture. *Where am I?* Her legs stretched out straight in front of her on a king-size bed with a dark blue comforter. *Not my bed.*

Wiggling her butt to get comfortable, she winced at the sharp pain from her left arm. *I was wounded.*

Her memory began to kick in. She heard the echo of an ambulance siren. She remembered being moved into the backseat of a car, looking out the window. And there had been horses and open fields and moonlight. *And Nick, she'd been with Nick.*

"Not possible," she whispered. Her throat was dry and scratchy. Her tongue felt swollen. She couldn't have been with Nick because he was in Tiquanna.

Carefully, she turned on her side so her arm

wouldn't rub against anything. Nick wasn't here, and she had to accept that fact. All the denial in the world wouldn't make a difference. She closed her eyes. If the only way she could see him was in her dreams, she wanted to sleep forever.

In her mind, she sorted through her memories as though picking from a jewelry box to choose the shiniest bauble. She selected the day they'd met at the mountain cabin that her friend and colleague, Marissa Hughes, and her new husband had purchased in the mountains outside Deckers in Colorado.

A year and a half ago, it was the summer solstice, June 21, when magic was in the air and young maidens performed candle rituals to see the faces of the men who would be their lovers. Though Sidney didn't believe in all that mystical stuff, her heart leaped when she was introduced to Nick Corelli, and she went all gooey inside when she gazed into his golden eyes. He shook her hand; the connection between them was palpable. They were meant to be together.

Eight other people had been staying at Marissa's cabin over the weekend. Sidney could recite all their names and could report on what they were wearing and what they had for lunch, but her attention focused on Nick. They paired up, and she found herself talking more to him than she did with others. She was positively chatty, which was very unlike her. She tended to be quiet and reserved and a little bit shy. An only child, she grew up mostly in the company of her parents, who were both scientists. Sidney had learned from an early age to amuse herself.

Nick invaded her quiet world with his gentle baritone, his laughter and his intelligence. Of course, she appreciated his physically imposing presence. No red-blooded female could ignore those muscular shoulders and tree-trunk thighs. His torso was lean and well-built and begging to be stroked. But she was also attracted to his mind.

Not only did he listen to her, but he actually seemed to care about what she was saying. Her engineering work was too technical to discuss with people who weren't in the field, and she'd expanded her interests into studies of the lands her firm chose for development, learning the history of the people who lived there and the geological development of these unique places.

During that first afternoon when she and Nick were getting to know each other, the group went tubing. In big rubber inner tubes, they bobbed along a stretch of the North Fork of the South Platte River. The summer sun baked her bare arms and legs while the sparkling, cool water refreshed her senses.

Such a shiny, perfect memory! This brilliant day was meant to be treasured forever.

Lying in the grass beside the river, she and Nick talked about the rock formations and glacial shifts and volcanic activity. Her memory replayed parts of their conversation. She could accurately recall every word, but his nearness distracted her. For long, blissful moments, her overactive brain shut down as she admired this tall man with his easygoing charm. His life experiences intrigued her. Being in the military, he'd seen much of the world.

That night, the group had built a campfire to celebrate the solstice—a night for lovers. At midnight, she and Nick had kissed for the first time. *That kiss, that perfect kiss.*

She jolted awake and struggled to sit up on the unfamiliar bed. Her memory filled in the events of what had happened to her in the past few hours.

She'd been at the CIA office, and Nick was there. He was safe. But he was different. And when they kissed, it wasn't the same. A decent enough kiss, that was for sure, but it wasn't earth-shattering. She had to know why. She had to save the precious connection with the man she loved.

Throwing off the comforter, she swung her legs off the side of the bed. Sitting up, she was overcome by vertigo and had to lie back down.

They were at a safe house, a ranch outside Austin, being protected by the CIA. Shortly after they arrived, she had been seen by a doctor who stitched up the wound on her arm and gave her meds for the pain. No doubt, the sedatives were making her woozy.

But she couldn't relax, not while Nick was back and she was unable to comprehend what was happening. She had to regain control.

Struggling, she forced herself to sit up again and waited until the room stopped spinning. Though the curtains were drawn, enough moonlight spilled around the edges of the window that she could see a dresser with a mirror, an overstuffed chair and a bedside table. A digital clock showed the time: 2:37. On a typical Friday night, her shift at the saloon would have ended. She'd be off work and on her way home. Would those intruders have been waiting for her?

If Nick hadn't been there to shove her out of the way, she would have walked into a blast of gunfire. Or not. If she'd been alone, they wouldn't have needed guns to subdue her. She could have been taken hostage.

Leaning forward, she balanced on the soles of her bare feet. Her toes were cold. As soon as she shed the comforter, she shivered. All she was wearing was an oversize T-shirt that hung halfway to her knees. The white bandage on her upper arm gleamed in the moonlight.

She practiced taking one step forward and one step back, not wanting to be far away from the bed in case her knees buckled. As she straightened her shoulders, pain from her wound radiated across the upper half of her body. Fighting it, she clenched her jaw.

Her mouth was parched. She reached for a half-full water glass on the bedside table and wetted her lips. The liquid revived her. She drank it all, set down the glass and cleared her throat. Better, she felt better.

Calling out for help was one option, but she didn't want to be seen as helpless. As an engineer, she worked mostly with men, and she knew they tended to see women as the weaker gender, easily pacified and disregarded. *Not this time.* Maybe she wasn't as fierce as a lioness, but she meant to be taken seriously.

At the lower edge of her bedroom door, she saw an outline of light. Outside this room, other people were awake and probably making plans. She would join them and become part of the team.

Easier said than done. Obviously, she had to change clothes. Stumbling into a cabal of intelligence agents in her oversize T-shirt and bare feet wouldn't gain her any respect. She shuffled to the closet and opened the door. The total darkness inside the closet dissipated when she flipped a light switch at the edge of the door frame. *Smart move, Sidney.* Turning on the bedroom lights should have been step number one.

With the overhead light on, she searched for something to wear. After fumbling around, she managed to get dressed in a flannel shirt, baggy sweatpants and moccasins that were a couple of sizes too big. Not exactly what she'd choose to confront the precisely groomed Agent Victoria Hawthorne, but this makeshift outfit would have to do.

She opened the bedroom door. To her left was a long hallway with rooms on one side and a carved, wooden balustrade on the other. Below her, on the first floor, was a vast, open room with a two-story moss rock fireplace. Standing at the banister, she looked down into a living room and a dining area where several people sat around a table.

Nick was there.

Her fingers tightened on the polished wood of the banister rail as she looked down at the back of his head. He still wore the trousers from his gray suit but had shed the jacket. His white shirt was rolled up to his elbows, displaying powerful forearms and wrists.

The muscular lieutenant from Marine Intelligence sat beside Nick. Across the table was Agent

Phillips. He sat with his elbows on the tabletop and his chin propped on his fist. The poor guy looked exhausted, barely able to keep his eyes open. Agent Hawthorne sat at the head of the table, of course.

From this angle, Sidney viewed Hawthorne in profile. Not a hair in her sleek brunette bun was out of place. On the table in front of her were folders and electronic equipment. Her tone was calm, and Sidney strained to hear what she was saying. It sounded like a recap of tonight's incidents.

At one point, Hawthorne reached over and patted Nick's arm. Her slender white fingers contrasted with his olive skin and the soft black hair on his forearm. The mere fact that another woman was touching him gave Sidney a pang of jealousy, and she was glad when he jerked away from her.

"In conclusion," Hawthorne said, "I assure you gentlemen that we will uncover the source of this information leak. I will need full cooperation from each of your services."

The marine officer shook his head. "Tell me what you want, and I'll take care of it."

"I prefer conducting my own interrogations."

"Not going to happen, ma'am. I have to protect the identities of my undercover operatives."

"We'll see," she said. "None of us like to think

we have a traitor, but how else would information about Nick be made available?"

"What's done is done," Nick said. "I'm more concerned about what happens next."

"We proceed as planned," Hawthorne said. "Three days from now, on Monday, we transfer you into the hotel where Hurtado and the others are staying. You will have private talks and interviews with the oil companies, politicians and investors. At the banquet, you will praise the little dictator. Then, you're done."

"Seems like a lot of fuss for public relations," he said with some bitterness. "Tell me again why this is useful."

Sidney wanted to know the answer to that question, too. It might be better for her to stay out of sight and listen while they talked. She ducked behind the carved, polished wooden spokes holding up the banister rail.

"How many times do I have to say this?" Hawthorne abruptly rose from her chair and pressed her hand across her forehead as though physically holding back a migraine. "It's in the best interest of the US to keep Hurtado in power, and the Tiquanna rebels are garnering sympathy. It's your job to make Tomas Hurtado look like a hero."

"So the oil development firms will choose to do business with him," Nick concluded her speech.

"It's no big deal," she snapped. "All you have

to do is put on your uniform, flash your charming smile and tell everyone about being rescued by Hurtado."

Those were stories Sidney wanted to hear. While Nick was gone, she'd imagined him suffering a horrible fate and then tried to convince herself that he was off at a picnic in the Tiquanna jungle. After he told her the real version, she might be able to let go of the tears she'd wept and the pain she'd imagined.

She sat cross-legged on the floor and peered down from the balcony. They wouldn't see her unless they were really looking, but she had a clear view of the table. Her simple surveillance was kind of ironic, considering they were spies.

"You're not telling me the whole story," Nick said.

"Of course, I am."

"If it's no big deal, why did the rebels come after me tonight with guns blazing? I deserve a real answer. My fiancée is lying in a bed upstairs with a gunshot wound."

When he gestured toward the balcony, their heads turned in her direction and she pulled back into the shadows.

Agent Hawthorne slapped her palms on the table and thrust her face toward him. In profile, her nose was as long and sharp as a ferret's. Her lips drew back from her teeth.

"I was going to ask you the same question," she said. "Is there something you haven't told us? Some bit of information you haven't seen fit to share?"

"My debriefings are complete. I gave you pages of intel on the rebel camps, on where they're getting their weapons and how their operation is run."

"How do you know it was the rebels who attacked tonight?"

Nick rose slowly from his chair and towered over her. "You tell me, Hawthorne. How did they know about Sidney?"

"A leak," she said.

"Could be something else," Phillips said. "They could have had Sidney under surveillance at the saloon."

Eager to get away from Nick's scrutiny, Hawthorne turned on him. "Why would they do that?"

"We haven't kept it a secret that Nick is here in town. He's part of the schedule for the Tiquanna meeting. The rebels might have figured that he'd contact his fiancée. And when she left work in the company of two official-looking guys, they'd draw the obvious conclusion."

Sidney nodded. Though she hated to think of being watched by rebel thugs, Phillips's explanation made logical sense. She wished that he was in charge of this operation instead of Hawthorne.

The thin female agent returned to her seat at the head of the table. "I knew it was a mistake to pick her up tonight."

"She would have found out that I was at the meetings with Hurtado," Nick said, "and there would have been hell to pay."

Phillips drawled, "Y'all wouldn't want to make Miss Sidney angry."

"Oh? Why not?" Hawthorne said.

Nick chuckled. Sidney couldn't see his face, but she knew he was grinning as he said, "My fiancée was planning a coup on the government of Tiquanna. You'd be wise not to underestimate my woman."

"Let's talk about another woman, shall we? I'd like to hear more about your relationship with Elena Hurtado."

Sidney vividly remembered Elena. An exotic, raven-haired beauty, she played the role of South American bombshell to perfection. Elena was a woman who deservedly inspired envy. If Nick had a relationship with her, Sidney wanted to know.

Not wanting to miss a word, she leaned forward. Her forehead bumped against the spokes holding up the railing. Just a quiet, little thump. But it was enough to draw the attention of the military guy and Phillips.

She was discovered. There was nothing she

could do but stand up. Trying to ignore the pain in her arm, she pasted a smile on her face and shuffled along the balcony toward the staircase in her oversize moccasins.

Chapter Five

Nick rushed to the staircase, where Sidney carefully descended, clinging to the banister and taking one step at a time. Less than half an hour ago, he'd been sitting on the edge of her bed watching her sleep soundly. Unable to keep his hands off her, he'd stroked her fevered forehead, brushing aside a gleaming hank of smooth blond hair. He'd longed to kiss her, to make love to her. Hell, he would have been happy just to hold her close.

But she needed her sleep. Her breathing had been steady and regular. The doc had given her enough painkillers to hold her until morning.

He climbed the staircase and slung an arm around her waist for support. "You shouldn't be up."

"I was hungry," she said.

"Let me bring something to the bedroom."

"I'd rather join the team."

When she raised her arm to wave to the others, he felt her sag against him. She barely had the strength to stand. Her complexion was pallid. Her beautiful blue eyes were bloodshot. But her determination was intact; she wasn't going back to bed unless he picked her up and carried her.

He made one more attempt to reason with her. "I'll come to bed with you."

She hobbled down another stair. "I'll be fine."

"I guess it's true what they say. You can't keep a good woman down."

"Please don't refer to me as your woman," she said. "We aren't Neanderthals."

Her body was weak, but there was nothing wrong with her razor wit. He returned, "Whatever you say, babycakes."

"Honey lamb," she muttered.

"Pookie pie."

At the foot of the staircase, Hawthorne confronted them with a cold, I-mean-business glare. "How are you feeling, Sidney?"

Nick felt a surge of strength go through her as she straightened her spine. No way would Sidney let Hawthorne know how much she was hurting.

"Don't worry about me," Sidney said. "Please continue with your debriefing. I believe you were talking about Elena Hurtado."

From Nick's point of view, Sidney's interruption had come at a good time. He wanted to avoid discussion of Elena until he had more information.

He continued down the staircase. "We're going to the kitchen, Hawthorne. Sidney's hungry."

They made their way across the spacious front room and dining room into the attached kitchen, where two armed agents dressed in cowboy gear were drinking mugs of coffee. This safe house outside Austin had once been a working cattle ranch with a barn, bunkhouse and outbuildings in addition to the two-story main house. The kitchen was big enough to cook for twenty or thirty hungry ranch hands.

After he got her seated at a round wood table, he grabbed a bottle of water from the fridge, placed it on the table beside her and sat. He noticed a tremble in her fingers as she screwed off the lid on the water bottle.

According to the doc, her injury and the resulting loss of blood weren't particularly serious, but Nick couldn't help worrying about her. "Are you in pain?"

"My arm hurts a little." She chugged the water. "Mostly, I'm dizzy. You know how I hate to take pills."

She didn't like being intoxicated and losing control. He'd never seen her drunk. "Do you remember getting stitched up?"

"Not very well. I had twelve stitches, right?"

"It's going to leave a scar."

She gave him a goofy grin. "Cool."

Most women would be upset, but not her. "Really? You think it's cool?"

"I like the drama. If somebody asks about my scar, I can tell them I was injured in a firefight with terrorists. Is that right? Were they terrorists or rebels?"

Nick thought of the man he'd recognized when he pulled off the mask. Rico Suarez was a cool, handsome businessman who worked with Hurtado and had connections with the oil companies. "It's hard to say who they were or what they were after."

"Don't you know?"

"There's a lot I don't know." And more that he couldn't talk about. He'd spent six months involved in a political dance where the partners seemed to change every day. "What do you want to eat?"

"Something easily digested. I haven't been nauseated, but I don't want to push my luck. Maybe crackers or a cookie?"

He asked the other two agents where to find food, and they pointed him in the direction of an earthenware cookie jar. He brought her a couple of homemade sugar cookies on a napkin.

She nodded. "Coffee?"

"That's a negative," he said. "You need your sleep."

She pushed back the sleeves of her plaid flannel shirt. "Do you like my outfit?"

"Very cute."

"I call it hobo chic." She picked up a cookie and took a ladylike nibble. A crumb fell onto her chin. He wanted to brush it off but didn't trust himself to touch her. One simple caress would lead too quickly to another, and before he knew what was happening he'd be kissing her, scooping her into his arms and carrying her up the staircase to the bedroom.

For the past six months, he dreamed about making love to her. Being so close and not being able to taste her mouth or run his hands through her straight blond hair was driving him crazy. He was desperate to feel her sweet, slender body pressed against his.

He had to be careful, had to hold back. Sidney was smart and perceptive. He wasn't ready for her to know the whole truth, not just yet.

Hawthorne came into the kitchen. Scowling, she announced, "It's almost three in the morning. We'll call it a night and start again tomorrow."

"Agreed," Nick said. He had considered talking to Lieutenant Butler about Rico. Butler was the closest he had to a confidant. But after tonight's attack, Nick wasn't sure he trusted the lieutenant. Butler had arrived at the scene quickly; he'd been in the backyard at the right time to shoot Rico.

Hawthorne pivoted and marched into the other room. The two other agents shouldered their weapons and went out the back door. Nick was alone with Sidney in the kitchen. Not that they were truly alone. This was a CIA safe house; he'd be wise to assume that every conversation was bugged.

Unable to resist her, he moved a little closer. "I missed you. I kept thinking about you and what you were doing every minute of the day. Rubbing lotion on your long legs. Combing your hair. Brushing your teeth while you hummed the *Jeopardy* theme song."

"That tune lasts a minute," she said. "It's important to spend at least a minute, twice a day, on oral care."

He closed his eyes and inhaled deeply, catching a hint of her special scent through all the other odors in the house.

"That routine pretty much covers what I was doing," she said. "My days were the same as always, except for when I fell into the panic-and-depression thing, which I don't intend to talk about. Oh, and I went to a psychic."

He was surprised. "You don't usually go for nonscientific explanations."

"When logic fails, I'll try other methods." She finished one cookie and started on the other. "This was a Navajo woman who mostly deals with herbal remedies. She told me we'd be together again."

Her lips pressed together, and he could tell she was holding something back. "What else?"

"She said something would come between us, but she wasn't specific or logical."

Turning her head, she stared at him with wide, curious eyes. Quickly, she averted her gaze. He had the sense that she didn't like what she'd seen.

Nick had secrets he'd kept from everyone. He'd passed through a battery of interviews from several intelligence agencies, talking to people who were trained to spot deception. As far as he knew, none of them suspected him. But Sidney knew him better than anyone else.

Her voice was soft and subtly persuasive. "Tell me what happened to you in Tiquanna."

"It's a long story. We should go upstairs to bed."

CLIMBING THE STAIRCASE to the second floor took effort, but Sidney managed. In the bedroom, she kicked off the moccasins and slipped out of the sweatpants, her back to Nick. Too tired to remove the flannel shirt, she crawled into bed and lay on her side with her injured arm facing the ceiling. She allowed herself a little smile. Her scar would be a badge of honor, totally impressive to all the tech guys at work.

Under the comforter, warmth wrapped around her like a gentle cocoon. Sleep beckoned. If she relaxed a tiny bit more, she'd be unconscious. But she wasn't ready to let go.

Her mind hopscotched from one point to another and back again. Nick was her fiancé, the man she wanted to spend the rest of her life with. She should be able to embrace him without reservation. The less analytical part of her brain told her to open her arms and accept him. *Forget the doubts. Take the kisses.* It would all work itself out. Or would it?

She'd never been a woman who would settle for less. Before Nick left for Tiquanna, their happiness had been as close to perfection as she could imagine. They'd bought a house. They were getting married. And now…he was different.

She hadn't gone through six months of hell, not knowing if he was dead or alive, to end up with a troubled relationship. Until she could look into his eyes and see the truth, she'd keep him at arm's length. No matter how much she wanted to succumb, she'd resist. No kissing. No touching. Definitely, no lovemaking.

Nick turned off the bedside lamp and unbuttoned his shirt. Her strong resolve crumbled when she saw the outline of his bare chest. Her heart beat faster. She had memorized those swirling patterns of hair and the ridges of hard muscle. Her fingers itched to touch him.

"No," she said aloud.

In the dim moonlight shining around the edge of the window, she saw him pause. "Did you say something?"

Though she wanted him with all the pent-up yearning of six long months, she said, "Don't you have your own bedroom? I figured Hawthorne would enforce a no-fraternization policy."

"There's another room. But the view isn't anywhere near as pretty."

"Maybe you should go there, anyway."

The mattress bounced as he sat on the bed beside her. Gently, he stroked the hair off her forehead. "Are you throwing me out?"

"I don't feel good." She squeezed her eyes shut, unable to bear looking at him. "Just for tonight, it's better if I sleep alone."

"I'll stay with you until you're asleep." His hand caressed her cheek. "It's been a hell of a day."

"It has." She couldn't help turning her head and lightly kissing his palm.

"I'm sorry about what happened at the house."

"I can't imagine what our neighbors think." Her memory pulled up a grim recollection of police vehicles and ambulances, flashing lights and gunfire. After that circus, she was pretty sure that nobody on their block would ask her to babysit. "We'll have to make it up to them. Maybe have a barbecue."

"Yeah, nothing says 'I'm sorry' like pulled pork."

His voice went still. A heavy silence invaded the bedroom. The distance between them spread like a fading echo.

Was she doing the right thing? The temptation was great to put aside her concerns and make love to him, but she had to make things right. She wanted their relationship to be the way it was before.

"As long as you're here," she said, "I want to know what happened in Tiquanna."

He leaned down and kissed her forehead. Then he stood and walked away. She opened her eyes and watched as he went to the window and pulled the curtain aside to look outside. Moonlight traced his profile. "It's a long story, and you're tired. Maybe tomorrow."

He was avoiding the topic. He didn't want to tell her, but she had to know. "We've got time."

"Okay," he said. "Remember what the country was like when you visited a couple of years ago? Tropical climate, lush and humid. Rain forests. Villages with thatched roof huts. Tourists in the capital city on the Atlantic coast. Abundant natural resources."

Her most vivid memories were the heat like a steam bath, the brilliant green of indigenous foliage and odd creatures like lizards and frogs and insects. Less charming was a filthy hospital, beggar children on the streets and a long line of women waiting by a supply truck for freshwater. "I remember."

"Your company didn't invest in oil exploration there," he said.

"Lack of infrastructure."

He nodded. "Like roads and plumbing."

Thinking of the children, she said, "More than that. It was a beautiful place but sad."

"It's gotten worse," he said. "Hurtado and his handpicked ministers siphon off all the aid money. Anybody who objects gets tossed in jail. The rebels claim to be representing the people, but they're nearly as corrupt as the dictator. The level of violence is brutal."

"Why were you sent there?" she said.

"The ambassador requested a squad of marines to protect the embassy, but we didn't stay there for long. Hurtado was hosting a bunch of companies that wanted to invest in Tiquanna. These top executives stayed with Hurtado. Pretty soon, that's where we were stationed. Our job was to add a layer of protection for American VIPs."

"What happened when you were taken?"

"An explosive device tore a hole in the wall surrounding the presidential compound."

"Presidential," she said. "Hurtado became president?"

"A couple of years ago. Sham elections."

Though she knew better than to get worked up about political fakery, she was disgusted. "Let me guess. He's president for life."

"The rebels are making noises about calling for a new election. Each time an opposing candidate steps forward, he's charged with a crime and ends up in prison."

She suppressed a shudder. "Let's get back to you. After they blew a hole in the wall, what happened?"

"A couple of my guys were injured. I went to help them. It was night. Smoke from the explosion streaked the air and stung my eyes. I put on my infrared goggles. In the street beyond the wall, I saw flashes of gunfire. I wanted to shoot back, but the rebels weren't alone."

"Who was there?"

"Civilians. I saw women and kids running from house to house, trying to get away. There was no way I could open fire."

Her heart ached for him. She'd always known his profession, had always been aware of the risks in the military and the hard decisions he had to make. And she had to believe that his sacrifices fulfilled an important purpose.

"After that," he said, "I don't know what happened. My mind went blank. When I woke up, I was in a thatched hut."

"Were you injured?"

"I've got a couple of scars I can show you." He stepped away from the window and went to the overstuffed chair, where he sat, leaning back with his long legs stretched out in front of him. "I was moved from place to place, sometimes in a house and other times in the forests."

"Was it the rebels?"

"I don't know." He hesitated for a long moment. "Who else would bomb Hurtado's palace?"

"You don't sound sure."

"Like I said, I don't remember. I was a hostage for six or seven weeks before I started making sense of things. There was an old man with a grizzled beard who gave me food and played chess with me. His name was Estaban. He told me that I got beat up pretty badly and almost died."

Her heart clenched. "Oh, Nick…"

"Stop," he said. "It's over. It's done, and I survived. Probably the worst thing that happened was a stomach infection, probably from drinking the water."

Peering across the unlit room, she tried to see his eyes. She wanted to hold him and comfort him, but she knew he'd reject anything that smacked of pity. "I noticed you have a small limp."

"I tried to escape, took off running through the forest. Do you remember those forests?"

"Incredible." Her mind traveled back to a hike through Tiquanna where she saw intensely green foliage at the edge of the rain forest. The reds and blues were so brilliant that they seemed to vibrate. The birds and animals were remarkable. "Did you see any of the poison dart frogs?"

"Some."

Those tiny jewel-toned creatures actually were toxic enough to kill. She had heard their venom was used in torture. "What happened in your escape attempt?"

"Long story short, I tripped over a tree root and got a sprained ankle. It's still not completely healed."

She heard detachment in his voice, as though he was reciting a story about some other hostage. It was going to take time for him to open up. "Nick, I want you to know—"

"It's okay." He sank back in the chair. "You need your sleep. We'll talk tomorrow."

Pulling away, he was pulling away from her. The space between them loomed as wide as the Grand Canyon. "Good night, Nick."

Chapter Six

The next morning, Sidney awoke with the certainty that Nick was keeping something from her. She didn't know what, didn't know why, didn't know how he'd gotten the notion that he could be less than honest with her. But today, she meant to find out.

Ignoring the stab of pain when she moved her arm, she threw off the comforter and hauled herself out of bed. Her movements were clumsy, her muscles felt kind of stiff and she had a nagging little headache. Though she'd never experienced anything like yesterday, she was reminded of the day after a car accident when she'd separated her shoulder. Her fault, she'd been driving too fast and had gone into a skid on an icy mountain road and ended up in a ditch. She remembered the hangover from painkillers. God, she hated taking pills.

On the floor beside the window, she found the big black suitcase that was usually stashed in the back of her closet. With a sense of dread and trepidation, she unzipped the back panel on the bag that looked exactly like thousands of other practical suitcases. But this piece of luggage was different. On the inside was a long, flat metal box with a keypad lock that she used as a safe. The men who had broken into their house weren't thieves, but she was still worried about these precious belongings and had requested that this specific suitcase be brought to her.

Inside the back panel, she keyed in the number to unlock the safe. The lid clicked open. She sorted through velvet bags containing a pair of diamond studs, a couple of antique brooches, a string of pearls and—most important—her engagement ring. Holding the diamond in her hand, she breathed a relieved prayer that it hadn't been taken. Last night, she'd left her ring in the safe, not wanting to wear it while she worked at the saloon.

She was a little surprised that Nick hadn't mentioned the ring. A ray of sunlight crept around the window curtain and lit up the glittering facets of the marquise cut stone. A beautiful piece of jewelry, it was meant for special occasions. She placed the ring back into the blue velvet box and returned it to the safe.

After zipping the back panel, she pawed through the rest of the clothing and shoes. The person who had packed for her seemed to have planned for several possible occasions. In addition to jeans, shirts and sweatshirts, the individual had included a nice black dress and a couple of skirts.

Eager to get a start on the day, she gathered up a handful of clothes. Two doors down from her bedroom was a huge bathroom. She locked the door. A shower would have been quicker, but she opted for a bath in the quaint claw-footed tub so she wouldn't get the dressing on her wound wet. The injury was problematic when she washed her hair. Raising her left arm above her head hurt, but she managed.

There was a knock on the door.

"Nick?"

"It's Agent Hawthorne. I trust you found the clothes we picked up from your house."

"I appreciate having my own things," Sidney said.

"Take your time getting ready. Other than a debriefing on the events of last night, we shouldn't have to bother you."

"I want to help."

"There's nothing you can do. Just relax and recuperate."

But Sidney wanted to be part of the investigation. "I might be able to share some insights on the resources in Tiquanna. My data is a couple of years old, but I doubt much has changed. Is Rafael still the minister of energy?" Her voice echoed hollowly in the tiled bathroom. "Hello? Agent Hawthorne?"

There was no answer. Apparently, Hawthorne had walked away and left her hanging. She'd been dismissed. Sidney glided the flat of her right hand across the surface of the hot water in the tub. She hadn't counted on being treated well by Agent Victoria Hawthorne, but the disrespect was still irritating.

It didn't matter what the CIA and the other intelligence people thought. Nick was her focus, and she was confident that she could make sense of him. Her training and her memory were geared toward problem solving. Starting with the assumption that he was keeping something from her, she worked deductively. Why wouldn't he tell her? He might be trying to protect her. If so, whom was he protecting her from?

Last night, the rebels had broken into her home. They might have taken her hostage and forced her to cough up information. Nick hadn't anticipated the attack at the house. He'd been acting as if she was in very little danger. Therefore, she reasoned, he wasn't withholding information to protect her.

More likely, he was keeping secrets as a part of his assignment—one of those "tell no one" things. And why would that secrecy extend to her? She wasn't part of the political scene. Her company had no interest in Tiquanna.

Was Nick protecting someone else? *Elena Hurtado.* A gorgeous woman like her would have dozens of men—possibly even Nick—leaping forward to take care of her. Not that she needed them. The dictator's wife was one of the strongest women Sidney had even met.

Once out of the tub, she got dressed, choosing jeans and a sleeveless shirt that would allow easy access to the bandage on her arm and pulling a light blue cardigan over it. After toweling her hair dry, she dragged a comb through it. The thoughtful suitcase packer hadn't tossed in a supply of cosmetics, so she used the lipstick in her purse and wished for mascara to darken her blond lashes.

If she asked Nick directly about what he was holding back, she wondered what kind of response she'd get. He knew her well enough not to play the "I'm doing this for your own good" card. Nick had never been dismissive with her, never.

The more she thought about it, the more she knew that all she needed to do was get him alone and have a direct conversation. *He'll tell me.* When he told her the truth, she'd see the doubt clear from his eyes. Then she could open her heart to him.

As she descended the staircase into the large front area, she had a new appreciation for the rugged charm of this former ranch house. Morning sunlight poured through pine-framed windows and splashed against sandy-colored walls. Rough-hewn wood furniture was arranged in a conversation area near the two-story fireplace. Earthy blues, greens and browns from woven rugs added warmth to the slate floors. It was a little too tidy and classy for a working ranch. This was more like a dude ranch where urban cowboys would kick up their boots and relax.

Agent Phillips, looking very comfortable and Texan in his jeans and boots, came into the dining room from the kitchen and gave her a weary wave. "Are you feeling like breakfast?"

"I could eat."

"Help yourself to chow in the kitchen. After that, I think the doc wants to take another look at your arm."

None of the other agents were in sight, and she had the feeling that Phillips had been left to "handle" her. Since he'd established a foundation of trust with her over the past several months, he was the logical choice. But she didn't want to be shuffled out of the way.

"Where's Nick?" she asked.

He set down his coffee mug beside a plate of scrambled eggs and bacon. "In a meeting with

Agent Hawthorne and some others. This smells like heaven."

She glanced down at his plate. "With all that bacon, I'd have to say it was hog heaven."

He grumbled, "A man deserves a little bacon now and again."

She sat beside him. "Does anyone ever call Agent Hawthorne Vicky?"

"Not if they value their ass."

"I'm guessing that she doesn't want me interrupting whatever big-deal meeting she has going on with Nick and the other agents. I think she considers me a loose cannon."

Phillips picked up a strip of bacon. "The loosest."

"I'm not going to let her railroad me." For six months, Sidney had followed the rules, and her cooperation had gotten her nowhere. "My house was shot to pieces. Men were killed on my patio. I've got a stake in this game."

Phillips finished his bacon and picked up his coffee mug. "What are you fixing to do?"

"I'm not sure. I need more information." The combined aromas of coffee and bacon were having an effect on her. Though it probably wouldn't hurt to grab a bite before she took on the CIA, she needed to keep her priorities straight. "Where are they meeting?"

He shrugged. "If you poke around in that back

hallway, you'll find them. This isn't that big a house."

"What are they talking about?"

"Stop your worrying, Sidney. There's nothing clandestine going on."

She had no reason to mistrust Phillips. He'd been more straightforward with her than anyone. If he hadn't pointed her in the right direction at the CIA office, she might not have found Nick. Leaning close, she gave him a hug with her good arm. "What did your twins wear for Halloween?"

He reared back in his chair. "How do you know about my kids?"

"One of the times I was in the office, you mentioned that it was their fourth birthday. Two boys. Ron and Eric." She tapped the side on her head, reminding him of her eidetic memory. "So? Were they Tweedledee and Tweedledum?"

"Ninja turtles," he said. "Thanks for asking."

In the kitchen, she met Delia, the cook and housekeeper, and a couple of guys who worked here at the ranch, taking care of the horses and such. Sidney wrapped a blueberry empanada in a napkin, filled a coffee mug and set out in search of the meeting.

The third door she opened was an office space with a long sofa, a couple of chairs and a big carved-oak desk. Nick rose to greet her and directed her to a chair near the coffee table.

Predictably, Hawthorne objected. "Sidney, there's no reason for you to be here."

"I'll be quiet," she said.

Hawthorne had shed her black suit in favor of jeans, a white turtleneck and a puffy vest that added a little bit of bulk to her skinny frame. "I have to be frank," she said. "You're in the way."

"She's staying," Nick said. "We can use Sidney's expertise when I'm talking to Gregory about the oil development."

He introduced her to another CIA agent—Jim Gregory—who had a stack of maps, grids and documents piled up on the floor beside him. He worked mostly with Underwood Oil Exploration, but he also knew a couple of men who worked for her firm, Texas Triton.

She shook his hand firmly. "We've met."

"I don't think so." He blinked behind his glasses.

"I didn't know your name," she said, "but I saw you at my house when the bullets were flying."

"That's correct. I was with the first response team."

Curiously, she eyed his research-and-development paperwork. "I'm surprised you brought so much material with you."

"We do our research," he said proudly.

She actually hadn't been wondering about the amount of information he had compiled. She questioned why he brought hard copies. Her team kept most of its data on computer and flash drives. Giving Gregory the benefit of the doubt, she decided he'd brought paper so he could have information at his fingertips and more easily explain to the other agents. "Are you an engineer?"

"I used to be an accountant."

He looked the part with his tortoiseshell glasses and khaki trousers. Gregory was probably the only person in the room, other than her, who wasn't armed. She gave him an encouraging grin. "I'd be happy to help with any information."

She wondered what had changed to make Tiquanna a more appealing site for oil investment. Three years ago, when she visited the country, she had concluded that there were significant oil reserves, similar to Venezuela, but they would need to invest far too much initial capital in pipelines, roads, refineries and housing.

"All right, Nick." Hawthorne snapped his name, compelling his attention. "We've covered the basics of what you need to say to the executives from Underwood Oil. Emphasize the brutality of the rebels, especially when talking about how they injured your leg. Don't forget to practice with that cane I got for you."

She waited for Nick to correct Hawthorne. Last night, he'd told her that his injured ankle was the result of an escape attempt, not due to mistreatment by the rebels. He didn't say anything. Instead, he nodded.

Had Sidney misunderstood last night? She didn't think so. He'd been specific about tripping on a tree branch. And he'd talked about poison dart frogs. Or was that something she'd been thinking? Last night, her brain had been fuzzy. And what difference did it make how he'd hurt his leg?

She sipped her coffee and studied his profile. Blaming his sprained ankle on the rebels made them seem more dangerous. When he talked about the old man who cooked for him, he hadn't been hostile or afraid.

A possibility occurred to her. He might be lying to Hawthorne. But that didn't make any sense. Why would he want to mislead the CIA?

To keep herself from blurting out something that would get her tossed from the meeting, she took a gooey bite of blueberry empanada. Nick sat on the sofa next to the muscle-bound Lieutenant Butler. Another CIA agent was at the desk with a laptop open in front of him. Hawthorne approached him. "As long as Sidney is here, I might as well show her the photos of the men who were killed last night."

The agent behind the desk scrambled to find an electronic tablet, which he passed to Hawthorne. She held the screen toward Sidney. "Take your time."

After brushing the sugar off her fingers, Sidney took the tablet. A glaring light illuminated the face of a dead man with red blood streaking through his thick black hair and down his forehead. His eyes were open. His jaw hung slack. A tattoo of a spider web crawled up his throat.

Sidney had never been squeamish. When she was a little girl, she helped her anthropologist mother sort and catalog human and animal bones from various dig sites. Still, it was disturbing to look into the flat, empty eyes of this man, who couldn't have been much older than twenty.

Carefully, she studied his features, trying to imagine what he looked like three years ago when she was in Tiquanna. "He's not familiar."

Hawthorne changed the picture on the screen. "How about this one?"

He'd been shot in the head. The left frontal bone of his cranium was shattered. He hadn't yet been cleaned and prepped for autopsy, and blood matted with his hair. In places, she saw the white of his skull and the ooze of brain matter. His left eye was gone.

She concentrated on his well-shaped lips and the side of his face that was still intact.

"Rico Suarez," she said.

Hawthorne glared at her. "You know him?"

She looked away from the grotesque photo. "He was a dashing, handsome man who dressed well and wore a lot of gold jewelry. I met him at the palace. He took the representatives from my company out for a night of mojitos and salsa dancing."

"You must be mistaken," Hawthorne said.

Agent Gregory took the screen from her. "She's right. It's Rico. How could I have missed this?"

In a voice that was too innocent to be believed, Nick said, "Sidney said she met him at the palace. Was he a friend of Hurtado?"

"He must be working with the rebels now," Hawthorne said as she dodged behind the desk. "This requires a change in strategy. Would you all please leave? We'll continue this meeting later."

Still clinging to her coffee mug, Sidney hustled out into the hallway, where Nick slipped an arm around her shoulders. "Nice job," he said. "We could have been stuck in there for hours."

"Can we go somewhere alone, just you and me?"

"Thought you'd never ask."

Chapter Seven

Without stopping or consulting with any of his handlers, Nick escorted Sidney through the kitchen and out the door, heading toward the barn behind. For reasons he couldn't explain to her right now, he needed to get away from the safe house and the multitude of surveillance that surrounded them.

"Nice day." He squinted up at the sun and inhaled a gulp of fresh air. The quiet rustle of wind through autumn leaves, the sounds of horses and occasional bird squawks replaced the dark hum of tension inside the house. "Warm enough that we won't need jackets to go for a ride."

"A horseback ride? I'd like that."

The bright note in her voice made him wish that they could simply be together and relax. Not yet. "We need to hurry."

"I'm right behind you."

Inside the wide-open double doors of the barn, he left her sitting on a hay bale to finish her coffee. He went to the corral behind the horse stalls and recruited one of the ranch hands to help him saddle up two horses, a pinto and a bay.

He brought the horses to where she was sitting. "How's your arm?" he asked. "Riding won't bother you, will it?"

"Not a bit."

"Would you tell me if it did?"

She downed the last of her coffee. "I don't mind a little 'owie' if it gets me closer to what I want. We need to talk."

"And we will." *But not yet. Not here.*

They needed to be alone, truly alone and away from the house. There was no one he could trust, not even this crusty old cowboy who didn't appear to have any connection with the CIA. Everyone was watching and listening. Nick was just as much a captive here in Texas as he had been in South America. Maybe even more so; the CIA surveillance was more subtle. He couldn't see all the hidden bugs and cameras that were keeping tabs on his every movement.

Last night, he'd made a big mistake when he started to talk to Sidney about Estaban and his time with the rebels. He was certain their conversation had been bugged when Special Agent Hawthorne presented him with a cane this morning and reminded him that his sprained ankle hadn't been due to a stumble. The CIA wanted his injury to look like torture.

Before they mounted up, Lieutenant Butler marched into the barn. "I wondered where you two went running off to."

Not a clean getaway. But Nick wasn't going to let Butler stop him. He took the coffee mug from Sidney's hand and set it down on the hay bale. "I wanted to grab some alone time with my fiancée."

"It's not safe. I should come with you."

The last thing Nick wanted was a chaperone. "Lieutenant, I'm armed. I paid attention to the briefing last night, and I know where the safe boundaries for this property lie."

"None of that protects you from a sniper." His short, military-style haircut was hidden under a cowboy hat. He tugged on the brim. "There's a leak. Someone could be watching."

"Sidney and I need some time, sir. She went six months without knowing whether I was dead or alive." He fixed the other marine with a steady gaze. "You know what it means to leave loved ones behind."

They were both military men. Both had faced the loneliness of battle and the struggle of coming home again. If anyone could understand the need for a moment of privacy, it had to be the lieutenant.

"Be back at eleven hundred hours," Butler said, "and don't go beyond the safe area."

"Okay."

Nick helped Sidney mount the pinto. As soon as she was in the saddle, Butler reached up and patted her on the knee. "You've got a good man there."

"I know," she said.

"Nice work in identifying Rico from the photo. Hawthorne looked like she'd been kicked in the gut by a mule. I guess she doesn't know everything, after all," Butler said.

"Guess not," she said.

Before the lieutenant could change his mind, Nick flicked his reins and rode out of the barn with Sidney following close behind. A swift breeze swept through his hair, and the morning sun warmed his face. The high prairie grass and sage had faded to a dull khaki, and the live oak and cedar forests in the distance mingled the gold and orange leaves of late autumn.

After they were beyond the bunkhouse, he slowed, and she trotted her pinto up beside him. The sunlight picked out strands of gold in her straight, maize-colored hair. Graceful and athletic, she sat comfortably in the saddle. For a moment, he was mesmerized by the sight of her. She was even more beautiful than he remembered.

"This is nice," he said, "just you and me."

"Nick, I have some questions."

He knew she was suspicious, and he wanted to put off the explanations for as long as possible. There wasn't much he was free to say. "There's something I've been thinking about," he said. "Something you and I do that no other couple does."

Her blond eyebrows shot up. "What are you talking about?"

"You know." If they'd had more time, he would have teased until she exploded. But she was already close to eruption, and he knew better than to poke the bear. "I want you to tell me one of your stories."

"Oh, Nick. Not now."

He liked playing this storytelling game using her eidetic memory. After he gave her a date, she'd tell him exactly what had happened. "March 14, 2013."

"Pi Day." She gave him an indulgent smile. "You didn't even know it was a special occasion until I explained that pi was three-point-fourteen, which makes me the biggest nerd girl on the planet."

"You're my nerd girl," he said.

"You flew into Lackland Air Force Base, borrowed a Hummer and got to my apartment at 10:48 in the morning. We hadn't seen each other for six days." A dreamy expression softened her features. "And we made up for lost time."

"Details," he said. "I want details."

"I made you an omelet with mango salsa and cheese."

"And what did we do before we ate?"

"I remember a kiss," she said, "a really long and passionate kiss. I knew you'd caught a late-night flight and it had taken a while for you to drive to my place from San Antonio because your stubble was growing out and your cheeks were already scratchy. I liked the way it felt when you kissed me here." She arched her neck and pointed to the hollow of her throat. "And here." She cupped her breast.

As she continued, her voice got husky, low and sexy. He wondered if she was reliving the sensations of their lovemaking as she described unbuttoning his camo uniform shirt and slipping out of her pink cotton nightgown. He was definitely feeling it, hanging on every word.

"And after we made love—"

"Hey," he interrupted. "You're leaving out the best part."

"I think not," she said archly. "The best was right before sunset at 7:39."

"There was a lot of time between ten and seven." And they had kept busy. He actually didn't need a lot of description of their lovemaking. The feel of her silky skin, her scent and her taste were indelible parts of his memory.

"7:39," she said firmly. "We were dressed to go out for dinner. You were wearing a black suit with a gray shirt and a burgundy necktie. And you went down on one knee."

"Even better, you said yes."

"And you gave me a pi diamond, 3.14 carats." She held up her bare left hand. "The ring is too beautiful to wear, really. I took it off before work last night and left it in the safe in my suitcase."

But she hadn't put it on. *Interesting.* She must really be mad at him, and he had the feeling that it was going to get worse when he revealed the real reason for bringing her out here.

"Whoa." She reined her horse to a sudden halt. "You've gotten me completely distracted. I have questions."

"You're wondering about that cane, right?"

"Well, yes. I've noticed you walking with a slight limp, but you definitely don't need a cane."

"A bit of theatrics to please Hawthorne," he said. "This is her show, and she has her own ideas of how it should play out."

"It's not just the cane," she said. "It's the story that goes with it."

Sitting tall in the saddle, he scanned the area and spotted surveillance equipment on a fence post. He needed to get outside camera range before he used his burner phone. The forested land would provide shelter from the watchers, but it was too far away to ride there and get back in time to meet Butler's deadline. The best way to send his secret text message was to use the horses and Sidney for cover. "Do you mind if we walk a bit?"

"Here's what I mind," she said. "You keep changing the subject. You're hiding something from me."

She was too smart and knew him too well. No way could he hope to deceive her, but he couldn't explain the intrigues that spun around him in a web of lies. Half of what he knew was guess-work. The other half was based on intuition. He didn't want to drag her deeper. She'd already been injured. Every time he thought of that scar on her arm, he cringed. It could have been worse. It never should have happened.

He directed his horse to a rutted dirt road, nothing more than a couple of tire tracks through the high grasses. He dismounted. The grasses were as high as his thigh.

When he went to help her down from her horse, she waved him off, kicked the stirrup out of the way and slid to the ground. Her cheeks flushed pink from the exertion of riding…and probably because she was getting angry. "Nick, you've got to tell me what's going on."

He stood with his back to the surveillance camera and spoke softly. "I need to send a text, and I couldn't do it from the house."

"Why not? Nobody can overhear a text message."

"Some other time I'll give you a lesson in spy technology and cell phones. For now, I need to get this message out. I can't tell you who I'm calling or why."

She looked down at the toe to her sneaker. When she lifted her chin, her blue eyes stabbed him like lasers. "Just do it."

He started to maneuver to hide his actions, and she grabbed the collar of his shirt and pulled him toward her. They stood together between the horses, hidden from observation. "Like this," she said, "it'll look like we're kissing and you won't be seen by the camera on the fence post."

"You noticed the surveillance."

"I'm not blind, Nick. Send your message."

He took a burner phone from his pocket, plugged in a battery and hit three call numbers. He typed in a name, a date and a time, sent it and went off grid again. "This isn't the way I wanted it to be when I saw you again."

"My fault. I showed up too early."

"Don't blame yourself." As soon as he arrived in Austin, he had considered the probability that she would become accidentally involved.

"I brought you to me. I wanted you to know I was alive, safe. And I thought I could take care of you."

"What are you saying?"

"You're in the oil business. And you're one of the few people in this city who is familiar with Tiquanna. I was afraid that you'd get wind of the meetings with Hurtado."

"When they brought me to the CIA office," she said, "you told Phillips to point me in your direction."

He nodded. "I didn't want you to show up at a bad time."

"A bad time?" She gave a quick, ironic laugh. "Something worse than having our house shot to pieces?"

"You tell me," he said. "You're the one who learned to shoot so you could launch a one-woman attack in Tiquanna to find me."

"How did they know, Nick? How did the rebels know about our house? Why set up the ambush?"

"If the rebels were behind that action…"

"Rico Suarez," she said. "Not a rebel, he was one of Hurtado's men."

It seemed unlikely that Rico was playing both sides against each other. His focus was profit, and the rebels had precious little in the way of monetary resources. If Rico hadn't been killed, what would he have said? Whom would he have implicated?

The death of Rico Suarez had been convenient. And it hadn't escaped Nick's attention that the kill shot could have come from Butler, Phillips or Hawthorne. They were all at the house. And so was Agent Gregory, the accountant. Sidney had seen him there.

Part of Nick wanted to confide in her. She was smart and perceptive. She could help him make sense of these intrigues. Spending time with her made him smarter, too. It was one of the things he liked best about their relationship. When he was with Sidney, he was better in so many ways. His IQ jumped ten points. He saw the world more clearly.

"I won't put you in danger." He was speaking as much to himself as to her. "There's nothing more I can say."

Her hands dropped to her sides, and she turned away from him. "You never kept secrets before. Or maybe you did, and I just didn't know. I really don't know what you do when you take off on your assignments."

He wanted to tell her. But where would he start? He couldn't reveal one detail without telling another and another. He'd been trained by the best in the world, the navy SEALs, and they would advise him to maintain his silence.

He checked his wristwatch. "We need to get back if we're going to make Butler's deadline."

She spun around to face him. "I'm suspicious of Special Agent Gregory. I'd like to take a look at his information on the oil resources and infrastructure in Tiquanna."

"Sidney, you've got to stop. You're not an investigator."

"Well, maybe I should be. I could probably do as well as Hawthorne."

"Mount up. We need to get back."

She placed her right hand on his shoulder. "Nick, I saw part of the text message you typed."

"What?"

"I'm not blind," she said for the second time.

"I shielded the screen."

"And I read the letters as you typed them. I didn't get the numbers, but you typed the word *Elena*."

Too damned smart for her own good.

Chapter Eight

Sidney watched as he mounted the bay. Nick's jaw clenched so tightly that he could have cracked walnuts. His brow furrowed. It didn't take a genius to see that he was angry.

And so was she. The dictator's wife was remarkably beautiful. More than the long, thick, black cascading hair and the glowing, unblemished skin, she radiated charisma. When Elena Hurtado walked into a room, all eyes went to her. And Nick had spent six months in her company.

He hadn't actually been with her the whole time, but he'd been close. And the text message he'd sent to covert ops showed there was still a connection between them.

In normal circumstances, Sidney didn't consider herself to be a jealous person. And she didn't want to believe that there was anything romantic going on between her fiancé and Elena, but Nick was only human. If he'd fallen in love with another woman, it would explain why his eyes didn't quite meet hers when they looked at each other. He was different. His kiss was different.

Infidelity was an ugly word. Nothing like this had ever happened to her before. Plenty of her girlfriends had confided in her about their cheating men, and she'd always told them to be sure of their facts. The same applied to her. Sidney had opened this Pandora's box, and she had to face whatever evil spilled out.

She mounted the pinto and rode up beside him. Their horses proceeded at a steady walk. "Tell me about Elena."

"I'm to meet her at the hotel in Austin. Then I take her to a specified location and turn her over to handlers. The text I just sent was to verify the time and date."

"Why couldn't she go to the embassy in Tiquanna?"

"Hurtado suspects something. He has her on a short leash, constantly surrounded by guards. If he finds out that she's going to betray him, he'll kill her."

She took a moment to digest this information. With Nick being held hostage, she'd kept up with news from Tiquanna. The Hurtado regime was more infamous for being greedy than brutal, but the country's prisons were full. "Where do you come in?"

"Hurtado's men know me. If I escort Elena away from the meetings, they won't stop us."

"Because you and Elena are…friends?"

He reined his horse to a stop. "There isn't time for a full explanation, but know this. Elena helped me escape. I owe her."

Every layer of this story got worse. Not only was Elena gorgeous, but she was brave and had saved Nick. How could he help falling in love with her? "Why does she want to be in the US?"

"She wants to end her marriage."

Sidney's breath caught in her throat. "Is she in love with someone else?"

"Yes," he said quickly, too quickly.

In a small voice, she asked, "Who?"

"The worst possible match you could think of."

No, no, no, not him, not Nick. "Say the name."

"Miguel Avilar, the leader of the rebels."

She exhaled in a whoosh. An international conspiracy that might topple a government and cost millions in oil investments felt insignificant compared with having Nick fall in love with the magnificent Elena.

Gazing up at him, she couldn't help admiring his broad shoulders and lean torso. He was such a handsome, masculine man. The collar of his shirt was open a few buttons, and she could see a curl of chest hair. "Is there anything else you need to tell me about Elena?"

"She's smarter than you'd think. She's tough, bordering on ruthless. And she's ambitious. I wouldn't be surprised if she tossed the men aside and took over the running of Tiquanna herself."

"And she's beautiful," Sidney said.

"Remember how Eva Perón became the most powerful person in Argentina? Elena Hurtado thinks of herself in that pattern."

Again, he was talking politics. The answers she wanted were personal. "How do you feel about her?"

"She's high maintenance, a little scary."

Sidney had never been subtle. She couldn't keep dancing around the issue. "Are you in love with her?"

"Hell, no."

He stared directly into her face. His light brown eyes shone with the warm, strong light she remembered. He was telling the truth.

Ignoring the pain from her injured left arm, she reached toward him. He caught her hand and pressed his lips into her palm. "There's room in my heart for only one woman. That's you."

Her Nick—the man she wanted to spend the rest of her life with—was back. "I've missed you so much."

"Being away from you was the hardest thing I've ever done. For a while, I was sick and I welcomed the fever because it helped me forget that we were apart…" His voice faded. "You shouldn't be here. It's not safe."

"There's only one place I want to be, and that's with you."

He gave her hand a final squeeze, and then sat up straight on his horse. His smile was so sweet and so tender that her heart fluttered. "I have a couple of rules."

"Okay."

"Try to stay out of the line of fire. Don't play Nancy Drew and start investigating. And here's the big one—trust no one."

She nodded. "I can do that."

"The safe house is one big spider's nest of surveillance. Assume that anything you say will be overheard. Anything you do will be watched."

"Even in the bathroom?"

"Spies have no shame."

He tapped his heels against the flank of his bay and took off at a gallop. She did the same.

BACK AT THE HOUSE, she and Nick were alone in the upstairs bathroom. Sidney perched on the edge of the claw-footed bathtub as he carefully removed the dressing on her battle wound. The slash across her upper arm still hurt, but not enough to take mind-numbing painkillers. She wanted to stay as alert as she could.

"How's my scar?" she asked. "Do I look like a biker chick?"

"Oh, yeah. A regular kick-ass." His fingers glided down her arm, and his thumb lightly caressed the sensitive skin inside her wrist. "You're unbelievable. An MIT-trained engineer who works part-time at a saloon and is healing from a gunshot wound."

"I try to keep it fresh."

Recalling what he'd told her about surveillance, she glanced around the bathroom. Was anyone watching? Even if they were, it wouldn't hurt for her and Nick to kiss. They were engaged, after all.

"There's no infection," he said, "but I'd still like to have a real doctor check out your wound when we get into town."

"And when will that be?"

"The meetings are scheduled for Tuesday. We'll probably move to the hotel in Austin on Monday night."

Today was Saturday. "So a couple of days. Since I'm going to miss work on Monday, I should call my office."

"Let Hawthorne take care of the phone calls," he said. "That way she won't worry that you've said the wrong thing to the wrong person."

"You mean like tipping off my bosses about the oil development in Tiquanna? I can assure

Hawthorne that my company isn't interested. We checked it out three years ago."

"The situation might have changed."

She wondered if those changes would make a difference to Texas Triton. As far as she knew, the company hadn't been invited to the meetings with Hurtado, which seemed strange since it'd shown an interest in Tiquanna earlier. These politics might be of interest to her and the people she worked with.

She couldn't ask Nick if there were other financial incentives being offered or other perks. Those topics would surely be off-limits if their conversation was being bugged.

With a gentle touch, he applied an antiseptic to the stitches and put on a smaller bandage. "All done."

She stood and faced him. Cameras be damned, she needed a kiss, needed it now. Her right hand glided up the front of his shirt and slipped behind his neck.

For a long moment, she simply stared into the facets of his deep-set brown eyes flecked with pure gold. His lashes were thick and as black as his hair, once again proving that Mother Nature was unfair. Men always got the great eyelashes. The depth of his gaze recalled their past. These were the eyes she'd known before. This was the man she'd fallen in love with.

When she joined her lips with his, an electric buzz went through her. It was a wake-up call to her senses. The inside of his mouth was hot and, for some unexplainable reason, tasted sweet as honey. The surface of her skin prickled with awareness. Her pulse jumped. She could almost feel the blood surging through her veins.

His arm wrapped around her waist and yanked her closer. He took charge of their kiss. His tongue plunged deep. He held her so tightly that she could barely draw breath. Who needed oxygen when she could breathe him?

Their earlier kiss was nothing compared with this. She'd spent six months waiting for Nick, and he was worth every second. How could she have doubted him? Gasping, she broke the kiss and looked up at him. "Nick, I trust you. I'm so—"

"Hush."

He laid a finger across her mouth to silence her. Others could be listening. She had to be careful. "There's so much I want to say."

"Show me," he murmured.

She leaned into his embrace, needing to be closer, to mold her body to his. Her legs twined with his, and she felt his erection pushing against the fabric of his jeans. When her hand slipped between them and she rubbed his hard sex, he stiffened.

His response sent a thrill straight to her core,

and she trembled. It had been way too long since she'd been with him. Memories of their lovemaking exploded behind her eyelids like fireworks.

And he pulled back. "We have to stop."

"No," she moaned. "No stopping."

"Somebody's at the door."

When she heard Hawthorne calling his name, Sidney imagined the skinny agent watching them on surveillance and choosing the worst moment to interrupt.

"Nick," Hawthorne repeated. "We're having a meeting downstairs."

"Be there in a minute," he responded.

"You need to hurry. It's important."

Sidney collapsed against his chest and murmured, "Can I kill her?"

"Probably not a good idea."

"I know how to handle a gun, and I'm pretty accurate."

His arms still enclosed her. He brushed his lips across her forehead. "But then you'd get arrested and I'd have to break you out of jail and we'd have to go on the run together."

"Like Bonnie and Clyde." As she accurately recalled, they'd died in a hail of 163 bullets. "Or you could just go to Hawthorne's very important meeting."

He ended the embrace. "Come with me."

"If you don't mind, I'd rather not listen to Hawthorne drone on."

A look of concern crossed his face. "What are you planning to do?"

"I promise not to get into any trouble. I'll stay in my room. Or maybe go down to the kitchen and see what's for lunch."

She understood the rules he'd laid down. And she had absolutely no intention of breaking them.

NICK DIDN'T TRUST her promise to avoid trouble. Not that Sidney would purposely set out to aggravate him. But she was inquisitive by nature, and he had opened the door to questions she'd want answered. When they parted at the top of the staircase in the safe house, he saw a preoccupied look in her bright blue eyes. She was already thinking, already figuring things out.

He wouldn't want her to be different. Her curiosity was one of the things he loved about her. As she explained, her need to know came from being raised by her scientist parents. As a kid, she'd ask why the sky was blue, and her mom or dad would hand her a reference book and make her question into a teachable moment. Someday, when they had kids, he hoped to follow the same pattern.

In the office, he joined the others, taking a seat on the sofa and making a big production of checking his wristwatch. "I hope this isn't going to run long. It's time for lunch."

Phillips, Gregory and Lieutenant Butler echoed his sentiment. Everybody was hungry, but nobody was going anywhere until Hawthorne had her say.

"Gentlemen," she started, "we have a problem. There have been a number of defections among Hurtado's loyal followers. Rico Suarez was the tip of the iceberg."

"And now poor Rico is on ice," Phillips joked.

"Not funny, Special Agent Phillips."

"Yes, ma'am."

"We can't allow a threat to the president of another country while he is in the US."

As she ran through various modifications in their basic plan, Nick listened with half an ear. His only concern was to find Elena and deliver her to his handlers in the covert operations branch of Marine Intelligence.

Facilitating Elena's defection wouldn't be easy. For weeks, he'd been passing information about her finances and possessions to the people in charge. Every divorce was difficult. But divorcing a dictator came with its own set of complex problems, the greatest of which would be avoiding a bloodbath when Hurtado realized he'd been betrayed.

He tuned in to Hawthorne's monologue. "What did you say?"

"Pay attention, Nick. Just because your girlfriend is here doesn't mean you aren't playing a part."

"My fiancée," he corrected.

"The best way around this threat," she said, "is to shake up the prior plan of organization. I've spoken to the regional director, and he agrees."

His patience was running thin. When Hawthorne was unsure of herself, she tended to overspeak, using ten sentences where a couple of words would do.

"You're talking about a change in plans," he said. "Fine. What do we do different?"

"I want Hurtado under our protection. Therefore, I'm changing the timetable. He and his entourage will arrive on Sunday instead of Monday."

"Tomorrow? They'll be here tomorrow?"

"And they'll come here to the safe house, where we can keep an eye on them."

His disabled cell phone was burning a hole in his pocket. He needed to send a text message about the change in schedule, immediately if not sooner.

Chapter Nine

Upstairs in her bedroom, Sidney stood at the window, watching a tall man in a cowboy hat and grungy down vest saunter across the dry, dusty grass toward a live oak with rust-colored autumn leaves. She didn't recognize the man. Everybody, agents and cowboys alike, was wearing jeans and casual clothes. A couple of trucks and an open-top Jeep were parked by the white corral fence beside the barn. The shiny CIA vehicles were not in plain sight, probably hidden inside a closed garage so they wouldn't attract attention.

From her vantage point, she couldn't see the two-lane asphalt road or the long driveway leading to the front door. To the casual observer, this place would look like a nicely tended ranch, nothing special, certainly not a safe house. Things weren't always the way they seemed. Layers of deception clouded her vision. Nick had warned her to trust no one.

She ran her thumb across her lower lip, still

tasting his lips against hers. It felt so right to be in his arms. A residual shiver of excitement slid down her spine. Her pulse rate still hadn't returned to normal. All she could think about was him, being closer to him, making love for the first time in six months. Right now, they should have been twined together on her bed like any other normal engaged couple.

To be certain, there were dozens of other things to worry about, but nothing else compared in importance. Her gaze flitted around the room, trying to spot the surveillance he'd told her to expect. Even now, at this very moment, some CIA-trained computer geek might be watching her. She hated the idea. And she intended to do something about it.

Though she'd promised Nick that she wouldn't play detective, she didn't think he'd mind if she figured out a way for them to grab some privacy. Her plans would have absolutely nothing to do with international intrigues or Elena or the oil reserves in Tiquanna. She just wanted to be with her man. He wouldn't object. And if he did, she'd change his mind. They weren't one of those couples who fought and bickered all the time. They seldom disagreed about anything.

The closest they'd come to a real argument was, ironically, March 14. When he gave her the pi diamond, she was happy, of course, to be engaged. But the ring dismayed her. That big beautiful diamond wasn't practical and was too expensive, and she'd rather have something less spectacular that she could wear all the time.

When she'd voiced those concerns, he was hurt. The light in his golden eyes dimmed, and his voice dropped to a deep, serious tone. He'd told her that he'd never expected to settle down. Marriage didn't fit with his work in the military. Too often, he had to be gone for extended periods of time. And there was the constant threat of danger.

She crossed the bedroom to the closet, pulled out her suitcase and opened the keypad lock. The blue velvet box felt warm in her hand. The 3.14-carat diamond sparkled with an ethereal light.

When Nick had talked about absence and danger, she hadn't really understood what he meant. Basking in the glow of being newly engaged, she'd been unable to imagine those negatives. That had been before Tiquanna. These past months had tested their relationship. She'd been furious and sad and terrified. Yes, she'd thought she might have made a mistake by getting engaged to him. But not once, not even for a moment, had she quit loving him.

On Pi Day, he'd said that being with her made him hope for the impossible. He wanted her to have a diamond so big it could be seen from outer space. That was how much he valued her, how much he valued their relationship. How could she argue with that kind of wild, romantic logic?

Newly resolved to make this work, she placed the ring on her finger. Her next move was to find a way they could be alone in the safe house.

The logical first step was to find out where the camera feeds were being observed. She imagined a dark room with floor-to-ceiling screens as she'd seen at the movies. And there would be a massive control panel with blinking lights, and the whole operation would be touch screen. It would take some expertise to set up this operation or a more modest version of it, which meant there had to be an expert.

At the meeting earlier this morning, an agent had been stationed behind the desk with a laptop and a couple of electronic screens. His name, she recalled, was Curtis. He had carrot-red hair and the kind of bloodshot eyes that came from playing video games until late into the night. He might very well be the tech guy who kept the surveillance equipment humming.

Leaving the bedroom, she went down the hall to the banister overlooking the front room and dining area. At the top of the staircase, she got her bearings. The two-story room with the fireplace seemed to be the hub of the safe house, with other rooms and corridors radiating from it. The dining area led to the huge, professional kitchen, which opened onto a covered outdoor patio and barbecue. The office where they'd met this morning was down a long corridor to the left of the front entrance. A short hallway stretched to the right and opened into a television room.

Either she could ask for directions or she could wander until she stumbled into the surveillance headquarters. The first alternative seemed the least suspicious. She followed her nose into the kitchen, where a vat of spicy, fragrant chili was simmering on the stove top. After politely offering to help and being turned down by the housekeeper, Sidney asked, "Do you know where I can find Curtis? I had a question about my cell phone."

"You're probably wondering where it is," Delia said as she pulled a tray of golden-brown corn bread from the oven. "Nobody gets to keep their phone while they're in the house. Not even me."

"Why is that?"

"Something about the GPS signals. This is supposed to be a safe house, you know."

"Are you an agent?"

"Me? No way." She set down the corn bread and straightened to her full height, which had to be nearly six feet. Delia was a robust woman with short, sandy brown hair and a ruddy complexion. "Somebody told me you're not an agent, either."

"Nope, I'm an engineer. I work for an oil company." She'd never make a good agent. Lying made her skin crawl. Even this tiny fib to Delia was uncomfortable. "I'm looking for my phone so I can call my office."

"Good luck with getting Curtis to share. He's protective of his gadgets. The only thing he lets us use is the television, and that's because if we didn't get our weekly dose of football, there'd be a mutiny."

Sidney noticed her maroon jersey. "You're for Texas A&M."

"Gig 'em, Aggies. The game starts at one. That's why I've got lunch ready to go. Who's your team?"

"I went to MIT, but I've lived in Austin for the past five years." She knew better than to mention the University of Texas Longhorns to a robust woman in a maroon jersey. "I'm an Aggie fan."

"Good answer." Delia leaned close and glanced to the left and the right. "You didn't hear this from me, but you can usually find Curtis and all his equipment in a room at the end of the back hallway behind the TV room."

"Thanks, Delia. The chili smells great."

"Be sure to sit down for lunch early. I've got a full house, and these guys can eat."

Sidney rushed past the dining table and down the short hall to the TV room, where half a dozen men in jeans were already watching a college game. She recognized the black-and-gold uniforms. "University of Colorado Buffs."

"That's right," one of the men drawled. "And the Oregon Ducks are kicking the Buffaloes' butts."

She couldn't have asked for a better distraction. For the duration of the football games, none of these agents or cowboys would pay the least bit of attention to her. If Special Agent Curtis happened to be a fan, the surveillance would be lax this afternoon.

The last door at the end of the hallway was closed, and she tapped on it before opening. "Special Agent Curtis?"

He sat behind a long desk console before a double row of six screens mounted on the wall. It wasn't the high-tech marvel she'd imagined, but it was fairly impressive all the same.

She'd caught him playing a video game. He turned the screen to blank and bolted to his feet. "You shouldn't be here."

"Nice setup." She closed the door behind her and moved toward the screens. Some of the images changed every thirty seconds. Others remained the same. "Are these feeds from rotating cameras?"

"Seriously," he said, "this area is restricted access."

"No need to worry about me. I'm just a civilian."

"You have to leave."

For a moment, she considered playing the part of a dumb blonde, the kind of babe he'd find in one of his online games. Then she decided that she wasn't a good enough actress to pull it off. It was better to find common ground and encourage him to open up to her.

"The only reason I'm at the safe house is to be with my fiancé." She pointed to the engagement ring as proof. "I'm not a threat, but I am an engineer and I've done a lot of geological mapping and triangulation. I'm interested in how you constructed your surveillance patterns."

"You didn't come looking for a lesson in remote cameras." Though Curtis was a grown man, there was enough of the insecure teenaged nerd in him to be confused by attention from a woman. He eyed her suspiciously. "What do you really want?"

"To use my cell phone to call my office," she said. "I've got a project due on Monday, and I should talk to my assistant."

"Hawthorne hasn't authorized the use of your phone." He rubbed at the corners of his eyes. "If she gives the okay, no problem. Otherwise, forget it."

She had edged close enough to the desk console to be impressed with his neatness and attention to detail. The screens were numbered. The masses of wires and cables were neatly organized. She pointed to a screen built into the console that showed the CIA logo of an eagle's head above a compass rose. "Is that where you access information from official databases?"

"Yes, and it requires a password to open."

She truly was fascinated by the equipment. "If you sent a photo to this computer, would you get an ID and other information?"

"Correct."

"Can you do me? Get a picture of my face and run it?"

"It's not a toy." He squinted and blinked.

"You look like a man with eye strain," she said. "I get the same thing when I spend the whole day at the computer. Why don't you sit down and let me give you a temple massage?"

"A what?"

She directed him into the swivel chair and took a position behind him. "Sit back and relax. First, I'm going to work out some of these knots on your neck. Then I'll massage your temples and forehead."

The touch of her fingertips on the nape of his neck relaxed him immediately. After years of working with people who hunched over precision equipment and computers with fierce concentration, she had learned how to alleviate the pressure on those knotted muscles and tendons.

"You should get a goldfish for your desk," she said in a soothing voice.

"Why?"

"For one thing, a fish is more fun than plants. For another, watching the random swimming movement is good therapy to relax eye strain. Once an hour, take a one-minute pause and check out the fish."

A lazy smile spread across his face. "Maybe I'll do that. What are other stress-relief techniques?"

"Sex." As soon as the word jumped out of her mouth, she bit her tongue. "Sorry, I didn't mean to be a jerk."

"It's okay. I happen to agree with you."

"Good." She continued her massage across his scalp. "You could also do yoga."

"Don't have the patience for it."

She completely understood. Though she tried to meditate, she found it nearly impossible to empty her mind of all thoughts. She looked up at the rows of screens ranged across the wall: six on top and six on the bottom. "I'm guessing you have your surveillance set up in six quadrants outdoors and six indoors. How many cameras are in each quadrant?"

"It depends on obstacles and sight lines," he said. "I took care not to be redundant so I don't have more than one view of any particular area.

The outdoor cameras are infrared so I can see in the dark."

"But not the indoor ones?"

"The ambient light is sufficient. Plus there are audio feeds. If an area looks suspicious, I can turn up the bug and hear what's going on."

"Nick told me that you had cameras in the bathrooms."

He turned in the chair to look at her. "I swear that I'm not spying on people doing their business. As soon as someone goes into the bathroom, I blank the screen."

"I appreciate that."

"I'm not a Peeping Tom."

But he didn't mind telling her about a breech in his surveillance security. She should have felt as if she was taking advantage of Curtis. She was using him. But her end goal was positive. Finding a way to be alone with Nick was worth a twinge of guilt.

Chapter Ten

Nick stabbed his spoon into a meaty bowl of chili and glared across the dining table at Special Agent Hawthorne. No wonder the woman was so scrawny; she'd loaded her plate with a wimpy green salad and taken only a spoonful of the great-smelling Texas chili. He hoped she'd choke on a crouton.

Her change in plans for the Hurtado meeting created massive complications for him. He was supposed to meet Elena *at the hotel*. He should have been able to stroll with her to a location where she'd easily be transferred into protective custody.

Not anymore.

The dictator and his wife and their entourage of three would arrive at the safe house ranch tomorrow afternoon and would stay until Monday afternoon. During that time, the only way Nick could separate Elena from her husband and his men would be to make a run for it—a dangerous alternative. And he'd need help from some-body inside, somebody who was already here at the ranch.

He shoveled the spoonful of chili into his mouth. The spicy heat came from the perfect combination of cayenne and chili peppers. His taste buds lit up. He groaned with pleasure and reached for a glass of sweetened iced tea to wash it down. "Damn, that's good."

The others murmured in agreement. Could he trust any of these three to work with him? But-ler, Phillips and Gregory all had agendas of their own. If they refused to play along with his plans or told Hawthorne what he was planning, Nick's assignment completely fell apart. He would have wasted a lot of time setting this in motion. Worse, he'd be putting Elena in danger.

"Y'all got to admit," Phillips said, "ain't noth-ing as good as real Texas chili."

"Amen to that," said the lieutenant.

Butler was the most logical person for Nick to approach. They were both marines, brothers. They shared much of the same training, knew many of the same people. But Butler was a spit-and-polish officer who looked like a recruiting poster with his close-cropped hair and his muscu-lar build. He wasn't somebody who bent the rules, much less broke them. More than once, he'd made comments about how Nick just couldn't stay out of hot water.

And Nick hadn't forgotten how quickly Butler had responded to the attack at the house. He had explained his presence by saying he'd followed their car because he wanted to talk to Nick in private about having Sidney stay with him. Butler had been in the right place to shoot Rico Suarez. A coincidence?

The easygoing Texan, Special Agent Phillips, was somebody Nick intuitively connected with. He had trusted Phillips to give a message to Sidney so she'd come looking for him at the CIA office. But Phillips was CIA. If he helped Nick, he'd be hurting his own career. That was too much to ask. Phillips might be okay with looking the other way if he caught Nick breaking the rules. But he couldn't participate in an unauthorized action with Elena.

Nick didn't waste much time considering Special Agent Jim Gregory. He was more of a numbers man, hiding behind his glasses and his stacks of information. Besides, Sidney was suspicious of Gregory.

The sound of her laughter preceded her into the room. She was walking beside Curtis the computer guy, who usually faded into the woodwork in spite of his flaming red hair. With Sidney at his side, Curtis stood a little taller, grinned a little broader and had a swagger in his step.

He stopped beside Nick's chair and patted him on the back. "A pi diamond," he said. "That's very cool, man."

Sidney flashed her engagement ring for them all to see.

"Thanks," Nick said to Curtis without taking his eyes off his lovely fiancée. She'd make a good accomplice on the inside. She was smart, quick-thinking and—according to her—knew how to handle a weapon. But he didn't dare put her at risk.

AFTER LUNCH, ALMOST everybody gathered in the TV room to watch the Aggies play football. Sidney snuggled next to Nick on a sofa against the back wall. Not the best vantage point, but she was far more interested in being close to him than in watching the game. She kicked off her sneakers, tucked her legs under her and rested her head against his shoulder.

The time she'd spent with Curtis hadn't been wasted. Not only did she find she had a lot in common with the computer guy, but she also had an idea of how to circumvent his surveillance. Figuring out the way through the cameras would take some serious math skills, but she was confident.

When she laced her fingers with Nick's, she

felt the tension in his grasp. She leaned close to his ear and whispered, "What's wrong?"

"I need to send another text."

There was a quick solution to his problem, but she hesitated to tell him. Curtis had trusted her, and she didn't want to betray him. On the other hand, the whole idea of being under the constant scrutiny of hidden cameras didn't seem right or fair.

Curtis had explained that the surveillance was there for their protection so they'd have advance warning of anyone trying to sneak up on the safe house. But it felt more as if they were the prisoners—rats in their cages, being watched so they didn't pull any kind of stunt or try to escape. Nope, she didn't like those cameras. Plus, she believed in Nick's cause. He was trying to save Elena, to rescue her from a dangerous marriage.

The Aggies made a touchdown, and the room erupted in cheers. They were all on their feet.

Using that noise as a cover, she whispered to Nick, "Go into the bathroom. Within a few minutes, Curtis will turn off the camera. Run the water for the shower to cover the sound."

Skeptical, he raised an eyebrow. "Why would he kill the camera feed?"

"He's not a Peeping Tom."

He slung an arm around her shoulder and gave

her a squeeze before they sat again. After ten minutes, he left the TV room.

She perched on the arm of the sofa so she'd have a better view of the huge screen mounted on the wall. Football wasn't her favorite sport. She preferred the symmetry and logic of baseball, but she kept her unwavering gaze pinned to the television so she wouldn't be sneaking peeks to see where Nick was. Based on her conversation with Curtis, her advice ought to work, but nothing was foolproof.

To her surprise, Special Agent Hawthorne sat on the sofa and patted the space beside her. "Sit with me, Sidney."

This felt like a trap. Sidney eased her butt onto the sofa and gave the agent a nervous smile. "How's it going?"

"As well as can be expected." She sipped from a coffee mug. Though the agents were technically on duty, most of them were drinking beer. Not Hawthorne. She was by the book.

"As you know," she said, "the defection and death of Rico Suarez caused some problems, but I've come up with a solution. Has Nick told you?"

Her gaze was cold, piercing and a little bit predatory. Every conversation with this woman felt as hostile as an interrogation. *No problem.* Sidney had nothing to hide. "Nick hasn't told me anything."

"This might interest you because you've been to Tiquanna and have met the president and his wife."

"He wasn't a president when I met him," Sidney said. "Just another dictator."

"Times have changed. He's now our ally, and it's our responsibility to protect our allies. Hurtado and his wife will be arriving tomorrow with their bodyguards, and they're coming here to the safe house."

"That's big." She understood why Nick had to send another text message. His plans had been totally disrupted.

"But very efficient. We will have complete control of his security."

Her narrow lips twisted in a self-satisfied smirk. If her hands hadn't been occupied holding the coffee mug, she would have been patting herself on the back.

"You like being in control," Sidney said.

"As a woman in an occupation that's dominated by men, I find it necessary to assert myself. Don't you?"

"I don't think about it much."

On the big screen, the Aggies fumbled. The guys let out a chorus of groans.

Hawthorne stared pointedly at her diamond. "I suppose your career isn't as important as your other concerns. When's the wedding?"

Sidney didn't like the implication that getting married meant she'd be quitting her job, but she wasn't going to rise to the bait. She didn't have anything to prove to Special Agent Hawthorne. "Why would you think I'd be interested in your plans for the Hurtados? I've met them, but we're certainly not friends. Our meetings were strictly business."

"But you've visited Tiquanna," she said. "It's such a beautiful country with the sultry air and the verdant foliage. When I was there, I fell in love with it."

Really? Was ice-cold Special Agent Hawthorne waxing poetic about Tiquanna? "Did you visit the rain forests?"

"The forests, the beaches, the little shops. Charming."

She sounded almost human, and Sidney wondered if she'd misjudged her. It might just be possible that Special Agent Victoria Hawthorne wasn't a completely soulless harpy who had purposely kept her apart from Nick.

Sidney looked toward the door and saw Nick. He motioned for her to join him. To Hawthorne, she said, "Excuse me. Enjoy the game."

She picked her way through the Aggie fans on her way toward her tall, dark and handsome fiancé. He would never ask her to give up her job for him, and she wasn't sure if she would. Her work wasn't as important to her as her dreams. There was a lot of world she wanted to explore. She'd given some thought to building her own one hundred percent green house. There were classes she wanted to take, studies she wanted to pursue. Nick had always encouraged her. He never set limits. With him, anything was possible.

As she moved closer to him, her heart beat faster and her stomach tightened in a knot. In his faded jeans and his plaid shirt, he could have been an advertisement for any number of rugged and manly products. She'd buy whatever he was selling. His black hair was spiky and wet. He must have actually used the shower in the bathroom.

He enveloped her in a hug. "It worked."

She'd almost forgotten the real reason he'd left the room. "I guess that's good."

They walked together in silence into the large front room with the moss rock fireplace. She heard someone messing around in the kitchen. Otherwise, no one was in sight. There was so much she wanted to say to him, but the audio surveillance was operational and it made her uncomfortable to know that Curtis was listening and recording their words.

Nick guided her toward the staircase. "I thought we might take a little nap."

"In bed? Together?" That was either the most

wonderful idea she'd ever heard or the most insane. With the way she was feeling, she didn't think she could lie beside him and not make love. "I don't know if I have that much willpower."

But she didn't hesitate to climb the stairs. Her arm suctioned around him like a barnacle on a rock. She didn't let go until they were in her bedroom.

He closed the door and scooped her off her feet. They fell together onto the bed, already entangled. His thigh separated her legs. One of her arms circled his shoulder while the other hand slipped around to his muscular back.

Their kiss was hungry and deep. His tongue plunged into her, and she savored the taste of him. So good, he was so good for her, with her. She wanted him inside her even though she knew they could only go so far, since they were being watched. Frenzied, she clawed at him. They pressed tightly against each other, separated only by their clothes, but she wanted him closer, wanted him to be an indivisible part of herself. Those desires didn't make sense, and she didn't care. No thought or logic intruded on her pure, physical need.

Rough and impatient, he tore her shirt free from the waistband of her jeans and ran his hand over her ribcage to her breast. His touch was familiar and exotic at the same time. Straddling his hips, she arched above him, baring her throat to a trail of fevered kisses that started at her jaw and ended at her breast. He pushed the silky fabric of her bra aside and teased her nipple into a tight peak, sending her to a higher level of excitement.

She was already trembling at the edge of an orgasm. It had been six months. There was a lot to make up for.

Waves of sensation crashed over her, and just when she thought she might drown from too much excitement, he flipped her onto her back. There was a sudden intense calm. She locked gazes with him. This was the moment when they should have been naked and making love. Their clothes should have melted away.

It wasn't going to happen. Not now, not while they were being recorded. "I guess I'm not cut out to be a porn star."

"Don't stop."

She knew there were people who got turned on when they thought they might get caught in the act. She wasn't one of them. "What about the cameras?"

He pulled up the blanket from the foot of the bed and covered them. Reaching inside, he unbuttoned the waist of her jeans. His hand slid down her belly.

Her frantic desire centered on his stroking

touch. She bucked and gasped, unable to control the shuddering, trembling sensations that ratcheted higher and higher until she exploded. Spasms of tension rocked her body. She was flying and falling at the same time, totally out of control.

With a fierce moan, she collapsed against him, breathing as hard as if she'd run a marathon. Would she quit her job for him? Oh, yeah. She'd follow him into a burning building. She'd do anything for him…almost anything.

Chapter Eleven

For the rest of the afternoon, Sidney focused on a project that reminded her of when she was a little girl. Her scientist parents had a love/hate relationship with computers. They appreciated the way the internet opened a wider scope of communication and research, but they didn't want her to solve every problem with the jiggle of a mouse. She needed to have a solid understanding of the basics. The end result was that Sidney spent a lot of time working out equations and logic problems the old-fashioned way, by hand.

Since Hawthorne had confiscated all the phones and wouldn't allow the use of computers without supervision, she sprawled on her stomach across her bed with a yellow legal pad and a pencil. Her notes were designed to calculate the range, rotation and visual scope of Curtis's cameras. Once she'd found the gaps in his system, she could plot a pathway to walk through the surveillance undetected.

In his explanation of the schematics, Curtis had inadvertently shown her a couple of areas that didn't have cameras. The loft in the front section of the barn would be their destination tonight. If she and Nick could get there unseen by cameras, they would have privacy.

And she could hardly wait. Their intimate moments together in the bedroom had been even better than she expected. But she hated that a camera had recorded them and couldn't help imagining Special Agent Hawthorne spying.

Being watched constantly was ridiculous. There should have been a way she and Nick could pull the curtain. Their private life was nobody's business but their own.

He joined her in the bedroom and stretched out beside her. The bed was too short for his long legs, so he turned on his side. He reached out and patted her bottom as he looked down at her legal pad.

"What's all this?" he asked.

"How much do you remember of your basic geometry and algebra?"

"There was something about the square of the hippopotamus."

"Hypotenuse," she corrected. "So…nothing?"

He shrugged. "I spent most of my time in math class counting the minutes until recess."

"These equations are kind of a game," she said, being mindful that someone was probably listening. "Something I learned as a kid."

On the legal pad, she wrote in tiny letters: *Making a map to show us how to get past the surveillance cameras.*

After he read the words, she scribbled over them with the tip of her pencil. When she was done, it might be wise to burn these pages. "What have you been doing?" she asked.

"Waiting for recess."

"As in school?"

"As in dead-boring meetings."

His hand slipped under her sweater and caressed the bare skin of her back. His touch was gentle and meant to be casual, but she still felt a little shiver of excitement down the length of her spine.

Being close to him was driving her absolutely crazy. They'd always been good in bed, but this kind of intimacy was different. She had nothing in her memory banks to compare with the heart-pounding lust she was feeling.

When she was separated from him and feared the worst, she'd kept busy and held her emotions in check. Now she was brimming with crazy desire. She looked down at the legal pad where she'd drawn a little heart. *Really?* Was this the way a twenty-eight-year-old engineer behaved?

As Nick spoke, she watched his lips, mesmerized.

"Super-Special Agent Victoria Hawthorne," he said, "is figuring out security to protect Hurtado and his party while they're here. Her primary game plan is to bring in more men. When we move to the hotel in Austin, we'll have an entire floor to ourselves."

He continued to lightly massage her back, apparently unaware of the thrilling effect on her. She forced herself to pay attention, noting the disgust in his voice. "Wait a minute. Why is Hawthorne talking about security? Isn't protection more up your alley than hers?"

"That's right," he growled. "If you want something kept safe, you send in the marines. If I was running this show, there wouldn't be cameras and bugs and fancy little devices. I wouldn't need a battalion of armed guards. All I'd need would be six trained men."

Six was the same number used by Curtis to divide the area into quadrants. "Why six?"

He explained exterior sight lines, directionality and triangulation. Much of the language he used echoed what Curtis had told her about covering the entire area. "You're a lot better at math than you think."

"But I'm not in charge, and Butler is content to sit back and listen to Hawthorne." He shrugged. "What do you think of Butler?"

She had plenty to say but wasn't sure she ought to speak up. On her legal pad she wrote: *Bugs?*

Nick took the pencil from her and scribbled: *Can I trust him?*

She framed her thoughts carefully before she spoke. "Lieutenant Butler is obviously disciplined. One look at his body tells you that he follows a daily routine with his exercising. He impresses me as being one hundred percent marine, which is a very good thing."

"Agreed."

"When he's given an order, he follows through. If he was under your command, he'd be totally trustworthy."

But someone else was giving Butler his orders. Next to Nick's question on the legal pad, she wrote: *No.*

He leaned close to her. When he whispered, his breath was hot on her neck. "Have you figured out how we can be alone tonight?"

"You bet I have."

If it required reformatting the pattern of stars in the night sky, she'd find a way.

He nipped her earlobe. "I can't wait."

FOLLOWING SIDNEY'S INSTRUCTIONS, Nick climbed out a downstairs bathroom window at twenty-three hundred hours that night. He had no worries about alarms because Sidney had already disabled the motion detector. His beautiful fiancée was a woman of many talents. Outsmarting any sort of electrical system was one of them.

He crouched below the window and waited for her. The November moon was on the wane. Last night, the night sky had been brighter. Tonight, hazy clouds obscured the moon and stars, and the shadows spread in a murky gloom across the yard between the house and the barn.

His position was hidden by a couple of prickly shrubs, and he was motionless, watching for the newly arrived security team that Hawthorne had enlisted to keep them safe. Part of the reason Nick wanted to follow Sidney's map was to check out the current precautions.

He spotted two armed men in dark windbreakers wearing baseball caps. By the odor he could tell one of them was smoking. If Hawthorne caught him, she'd have his butt on a platter. They meandered across the open front of the barn, walked the line of the corral fence and continued toward the multicar garage until they were almost out of sight. Then they returned on roughly the same route. He knew there was another guard posted on the wraparound front porch. And a sniper on the roof.

To his left, he heard the snap of a twig and the crackle of footsteps through dried leaves. Sidney stood at the corner of the house and motioned for him to join her. She'd tucked her straight blond hair up inside a baseball cap. With the brim pulled down, she looked like a tomboy, but her black turtleneck outlined curves that were one hundred percent female.

She'd already told him to follow her moves exactly. His job was timing, making sure they avoided being seen by the guards. He gave her the go-ahead.

At the ninety-degree corner of the house, she set out in a transverse angle, walking in a straight line to the live oak in the backyard. Her path was so direct and so bold; he couldn't believe she wasn't being picked up by a surveillance camera, even though she'd explained how the range of the different cameras left gaps. He followed her.

At the tree, she zigzagged to a fence post where she paused and waited for him. When he joined her, she whispered, "Here's the only part that will show up on tape. Stay low and keep to the shadows."

He had spent enough time in stakeouts watching flat screens to know how boring surveillance could be. The system Curtis used alternated views from several cameras on each screen, so the odds against having him spot them were good. Still, Nick felt the prickle of unseen eyes on the back of his neck as he moved to a point farther down the fence.

After checking to see that the bodyguards were down by the garage, he motioned her forward. They crossed the open yard to the east side of the barn. Beside a closed door, she leaned against the weathered wood and gave him a huge smile.

"We made it," she said quietly.

Nick wasn't so sure. The smell of cigarette smoke hung in the air, but the guard who'd been smoking was a hundred yards away. Even if Hawthorne's guards did their job and found them, Nick and Sidney weren't in any real danger. They could make an excuse about trying to get privacy and would get off with nothing more than a slap on the wrist.

But he sensed a change in the atmosphere. They were under observation. Hostile eyes tracked their movements.

He drew his Glock from the holster on his hip and opened his senses to the night. He scanned the flat side of the barn. Ten feet from them was a waist-high storage bin. A stack of metal fencing for a movable corral leaned against the wall. According to Sidney, this side of the barn was not within range of any camera. Had someone else discovered the anomaly?

Nick gestured for her to get down while he made sure they weren't walking into a situation. A tall man with a cowboy hat hiding his features stepped out of the shadows from the storage container. "Hello, Nick."

The deep voice, lightly accented, needed no other introduction. "Miguel Avilar."

The leader of the Tiquanna rebel movement stood before him with his hands raised in the air. Nick didn't lower his gun. He was ambivalent about Avilar, didn't know if he was friend or foe, even though Elena had vouched for him and his cause.

Nick believed he'd been taken hostage by Avilar's men. Though he couldn't recall details, he hadn't forgotten the pain. He'd been stripped, beaten and starved. He knew Americans were involved. He'd heard their accented Spanish. But he had thought Avilar was in charge. And he couldn't forgive the way the rebels had captured him. Two other marines had been seriously injured.

In a voice pitched as low as a whisper, Nick asked, "Did your boys shoot up my house in Austin?"

"You know better. I would never work with Rico Suarez."

Sidney peeked around his arm. "How did you get past the security cameras?"

Avilar swept the cowboy hat off his head, took a step closer and gazed into her eyes. "You must be Sidney Parker. I have heard much about you."

The rebel leader was a good-looking man and charismatic enough to have captured the heart of Elena Hurtado. But Sidney seemed unimpressed. "Yeah, I've heard about you, too. And I didn't think you were clever enough to get past the safe house surveillance."

"You were wrong."

"Did you hack into the computer system? Dummy up the camera feeds for this quadrant?"

"Let it go," he said.

"I don't like you, Avilar. Because of you, Nick was held hostage. I thought he was dead. Because of you, my heart nearly shattered." Her accusations were more dramatic because she spoke in a quiet, matter-of-fact tone. "Give me one good reason why I shouldn't scream for the guards and have you taken into custody."

Disbelief flickered behind his eyes. He hadn't expected to encounter an angry woman with a grudge. His right hand moved toward the back of his belt, reaching for a weapon.

Nick raised his gun. "Don't even think about it."

Avilar donned his hat and straightened the

brim. "Here's your reason, Sidney. We're on the same side. We want the same thing. To keep Elena safe."

Nick wasn't sure how much Sidney cared about Elena, but he tentatively decided to accept Avilar as an ally. "Why are you here?"

"Elena will be brought to this safe house tomorrow. I will rescue her and take her away with me."

Not according to Nick's orders. "That's not the plan."

He heard the clumsy approach of the two guards who were patrolling this area. If he was found with Avilar, he'd never be able to complete his assignment. All this planning would have been for nothing.

He nodded toward the storage bin where Avilar had been hiding. As they ducked into the shadows, he knew it wasn't sufficient cover for all three of them. If the guards came closer to investigate, there would be no escape.

To Sidney, he whispered, "Take us to the loft."

Stealthy as a cat, she glided to the end of the east wall. At the corner, a corral fence with four wood slats attached to the barn. She climbed quickly and dropped into the hay on the opposite side. He followed. Avilar came after him.

They waited in silence, measuring each breath. The guards rounded the opposite corner of the barn where they had been standing a moment ago. They exchanged quiet comments. Nick heard them coming closer.

The stalls were just inside. Moving past the horses was risky, but there didn't seem to be an alternative.

Sidney darted across the corral enclosure and slipped through the open door. As far as he knew, the only time she'd been in the barn was this morning, and she might have observed the layout on the camera surveillance. Still, she moved with the confidence of someone who had been in and out of the barn dozens of times before.

He knew that she was visualizing the interior of the barn in her remarkable memory. Without a single misstep, she led them to a wood ladder built into the wall and climbed.

When they were all three in the loft, they lay flat on the wood floor. Below them, the guards made their search. They rattled the door on one of the stalls, and the horse inside whinnied and stamped his feet.

"Now look what you've done," one of the guards said. "You got the animals all riled up."

"I'm telling you that I heard something. And I smelled cigarettes."

"That was me, you idiot. I smoke. Deal with it."

The guards left the barn, and Sidney sat up. She pulled off her baseball cap and shook her head. Her straight blond hair fell to her shoulders. She gave him a baleful glance. "So much for our privacy."

"Just for tonight," he said.

Avilar sat up to face them. His swagger had toned down a few notches. "I'm glad I ran into you tonight."

"Sheer luck," Nick said. Their meeting couldn't have been planned because he hadn't even been sure when they'd leave the house. "Now I'm going to give you advice that will save your life. There's no way you and your men can take Elena by force. Not without getting her killed in the process."

"I got through the surveillance cameras easily," he said. "Using our computer signals, we can jam all transmissions."

"Listen to me," Nick said. "You don't want this to turn into a shootout. Hurtado would rather see Elena dead than to have her go with you."

"I have no choice." Though Avilar was whispering, Nick heard real emotion in his voice. "If I don't get her away from him, he'll kill her tomorrow night. All along, this has been his plan. He had to get Elena away from our native country, where she is much beloved. If she was killed in Tiquanna, there would be riots in the streets."

Nick doubted the reaction would rise to the

level of rioting, but he was aware of Elena's many supporters. "Go on."

"He will assassinate her here, and blame her death on the rebels. That was why you were attacked at your house, to establish the supposed presence of the Tiquanna rebels in your country."

His narrative made sense, except for one piece. "Who informed you that I would be returning home with Sidney? How did you know where I live?"

"I didn't know," Avilar said. "Hurtado's men arranged the attack. They had the information."

Their CIA team was in contact with Hurtado and his energy minister and the head of his security. Hawthorne probably communicated with Tiquanna once or twice a day. This was more than a leak. It was a sieve.

Chapter Twelve

Sidney strained to hear as Nick and Miguel Avilar spoke in hushed tones. The rebel leader confused her. She'd taken an immediate dislike to his arrogance, an attitude so typical of men in power. But he seemed sincere in his love of Elena and his concern for her safety. If his forces had the technical skills to hack into the CIA's surveillance equipment, she had seriously underestimated them. What else were they capable of?

Was Avilar an enemy or a friend?

"Not here," Nick said. "Don't try to take her from the safe house. Wait until we're at the hotel."

"You can't guarantee Elena's safety," Avilar said. "What's to stop Hurtado from shooting her and blaming her death on my rebels?"

"I won't let that happen."

"I trust your intention, my friend. But there are forces beyond your control."

Avilar's light accent reminded her of Tiquanna. She appreciated the tropical beauty of the country and understood how the oppressed population needed better leadership. But did the rebels have the right answers? Hurtado had been in charge for years. He'd made the transition from dictatorship to elections, even though he would undoubtedly be president for life. And he was bringing new money and business from developing the oil resources. At the very least, Hurtado represented stability for his people.

As Avilar prepared to leave them, he turned to her and said, "Remember me, Sidney."

"I couldn't forget you if I tried."

Avilar disappeared through the hatchway and down the wooden stairs into the barn.

As soon as he was gone, she inched across the slatted wood floor to be closer to Nick. Her movements kicked up a layer of dust sprinkled with dry hay stalks. She lay on her side next to him. Her plan for tonight had been to find a private place, but her need to make love was eclipsed by her hunger for information. If she didn't grab this chance to talk, she might never get answers.

"I need to know," she said. "Who are the good guys and who are the bad guys?"

"It's not that simple."

"The CIA is backing Hurtado. Hawthorne and her pals are doing everything they can to help him set up a business relationship with Underwood Oil."

He took her hand, brushed a light kiss across her knuckles. "I don't work for the CIA."

"Your orders come from somewhere else. Where? Who are you sending your text messages to?"

"It's complicated."

Though ready to scream with frustration, she kept her voice low. "I understand that there are other forces at work. I need to know who and why."

Even in the dim light, she saw his gaze turn secretive. He was holding something back from her. She wanted to trust him, needed to believe in him.

The deep, quiet tone of his voice soothed her. "My assignment is to keep Elena Hurtado safe."

How could that be bad? Saving the life of an abused wife ranked high on Sidney's list of noble actions. But the CIA wasn't on Nick's side. And he was friendly with Avilar, the leader of the rebels. She hated the dark thoughts that bubbled up from the back of her mind.

Sidney had never been much interested in politics. Her work dealt in numbers, facts and absolutes. She liked things to be black-and-white. "I have to ask this question, Nick."

"Go ahead. Clear the air."

She inhaled a deep breath. "Are you on the right side?"

"I'm not a traitor, Sidney."

"Of course not, I'm just—"

"I've spent my life in service to the US Marines. I'd die before I'd betray my country."

How could she doubt him, even for a moment? He was a good man, a good person. And yet… "Help me understand. I believe you're loyal. But what does that make Hawthorne and the CIA?"

"Misguided."

"Why can't you explain to them?"

"If I could, I would. But I'm not a philosopher or a statesman. I don't make speeches. I deal with actions, not words. And I have to do what I believe is right."

"Didn't you tell me that Avilar was responsible for your kidnapping?"

"I told you the palace was attacked, and it made sense that the rebels would be responsible."

"But you don't blame Avilar."

"I never saw him." He shook his head and looked away from her. "We already talked about this stuff, Sidney. Do we have to go over it again?"

"Someone grabbed you and took you away from me for six months. I need to know who it was, full disclosure. I deserve an answer."

"What if I don't have one?"

"We'll figure it out together," she said. "Tell

me what happened when you were taken hostage. Don't leave anything out."

"They hit me with a stun gun. I was hooded. Everything went black. When I woke up, I was on the ground. My ankles and knees were tied with heavy rope. My wrists were tied in front of me. I tore off the hood."

"Did you see your captors?"

"My vision was hazy. For a while, I thought I was going blind. Then my eyes accustomed to the night. I was in a hut with a thatched roof. Two men were watching me, both armed.

"I wanted to escape, to get up and run. But I could barely move. My muscles wouldn't respond. It took all the strength I had to sit up."

His voice faded to silence, and she waited for him to continue. Talking about his ordeal was hard for him. Hard for her, too. She hated to think of what he had suffered, but it was better to know, always better to talk about the pain than to keep it bottled up inside.

Earlier when he'd told her about his time in captivity, he made it sound like a bad camping trip. This was different. This time, she heard the pain and the rage in his voice.

"They'd taken my clothes and my boots," he said. "I was stripped down to my skivvies and my dog tags.

"The inside of my mouth was dry. My tongue

was swollen. I couldn't summon up enough spit to lick my lips. I tried to ask for water, but the only sound I could make was a croak. One of the men took pity. He kicked a plastic water bottle toward me. I used my teeth to get the top off, and I drank. I've never tasted anything so damn good. That was the last bit of kindness they showed me for a long time."

Hot, angry tears gathered behind her eyelids, and she dashed them away. He'd been tortured. "How can you stand to look at Avilar?"

"I never knew if it was him. I didn't know if I'd been taken by the rebels or by someone else, someone working for Hurtado. They wanted information from me. They beat me up pretty good. The doctors tell me my shoulder was separated, twice. I was sore all over, filthy and hungry. Then they let up, and things got better."

"You were with the old man, Estaban," she said.

"I was in a camp, wearing the same rags they wore, eating the same food. There were other hostages with me, people from the town. They kept us together. That's when I met Avilar."

"Is he the leader of all the rebels?"

"There are several factions. His group is the largest, the best equipped and the most powerful. Miguel Avilar is college educated and comes from a wealthy family, all of whom have left

Tiquanna. When he met me, he apologized for the way I'd been treated. And he said he wasn't responsible."

"And you believed him."

"Not at first," Nick said. "I thought this was just another tactic to get information from me."

"What changed your mind?"

"Elena was with him. She pretty much took charge and arranged for me to be returned to the presidential compound. As far as I know, she's never lied to me."

Sidney regretted every nasty thought she'd ever had about Elena. "She saved your life."

"Not because she's Saint Elena. The supposed rescue of an American citizen made Hurtado look like a hero. And Elena gained leverage. As long as I was there as a witness, her husband had to treat her right."

"If Elena and Avilar are allies," she said, "Hurtado is their enemy."

"He's greedy and he's cruel. A dictator. But he's not going forward with this multimillion-dollar development by himself. Somebody else is pulling the strings."

"Oh, my God, Nick. You don't think the CIA was behind your kidnapping, do you? What would they have to gain?"

"I don't know."

"I hope you aren't suggesting it's an evil oil

development company," she said. "Those are the people I work for. Texas Triton tries really hard to be ecologically and socially responsible."

"Can you say the same about your competitors?"

"Them? Oh, well, they're the scum of the earth." She grinned. "Not really."

"And that takes us right back to the beginning," he said. "It's complicated."

Though they hadn't resolved a thing, she felt better. At least he was talking to her. "Go ahead, Nick, say it."

"Say what?"

"I told you so."

His large hand grasped the small of her waist and yanked her toward him until her body aligned with his. His natural heat permeated her clothes and warmed her skin. Unable to resist, she snuggled against him. With her ear to his chest, she listened to the strong, steady thump of his heartbeat. Her pulse synchronized with his.

There were no cameras here. If there had been surveillance, the guards would have known Avilar was here. They would have been found out. Though she was satisfied that they weren't under observation, she hesitated. "This doesn't feel private."

He squeezed her closer. "Not real sexy."

"It's like that creepy feeling on the back of your neck when someone's watching."

He lightly kissed her lips, and then pulled her up so they were both sitting. "No more sneaking around. When we make love again, it'll be perfect."

She patted the wood floor. "At least, we should have a bed."

"Silk sheets and champagne," he said. "When this is over, we'll take a trip to a mountain cabin in Colorado. Just you and me, we'll be completely alone. At night, we'll build a fire. And we'll make love until dawn."

For a long moment, she stared at him through the darkness. There was no equation for how to deal with his absence or his return to her. Somehow, she had to trust that they'd find their way back to normalcy.

THE NEXT DAY, Special Agent Hawthorne was in a frenzy of organization. She reshuffled several of the rooms to make sure Hurtado and his wife had the master suite with the attached bathroom. The dictator would be accompanied by two bodyguards who would share a room on one side of his suite. Hawthorne posted CIA guards directly outside the room and had beefed up security in general, which Sidney found a little sad since Avilar had so easily slipped inside last night.

Not that she was an expert on how to keep a safe house safe. Sidney didn't have much to add to any of the bustling around, which suited her just fine. The only directive she received from Hawthorne was to address the dictator as "President Hurtado."

In the morning, she took one of the horses out for a run. A light rain was falling, but her ride was refreshing. With the ongoing drought conditions in Texas, nobody complained about the moisture.

After lunch, she milled around, wishing she had access to a computer so she could hook into work and get something done. She offered to help out in the kitchen, but Delia had the roast beef and scalloped potatoes under control. Sidney tried to nap but wasn't tired. Finally, late in the afternoon, she grabbed a few minutes with Nick. They sat on the porch swing, looking for rainbows behind the barn.

"You've had lots of meetings," she said.

He slung an arm around her shoulder. "Your buddy Curtis is keeping busy. Hawthorne treats him like her personal assistant, making her phone calls and setting up reminders."

It was a shame to waste the tech skills of somebody like Curtis. He was smart and funny and insightful, but he lacked the ambition and aggression to shove his career into high gear. People like Hawthorne would always try to use him.

"What about you?" she asked. "How does Hawthorne treat you?"

"She's wary, doesn't know what to expect. She's afraid I might do something that will cause her trouble."

And she was correct in that assumption. When Nick got Elena away from Hurtado, the dictator was going to go ballistic. Or maybe not. Maybe he'd be glad to get rid of a troublesome woman. "How long before the big arrival?"

"Any minute now." He checked his wristwatch. "Hawthorne expects them to arrive around four o'clock, which gives them a chance to see their room and get changed before dinner. I guess we'll be having cocktails before we eat."

"Am I supposed to get dressed up?" She remembered the little black dress that had thoughtfully been packed in her suitcase.

He shrugged. "You look beautiful just the way you are."

She didn't expect him to understand. Being in the same room with the gorgeous Elena Hurtado was enough to make any normal woman feel insecure. Sidney decided it wouldn't hurt to spend a few extra minutes on her grooming.

He pulled her close and whispered in her ear, "Tell me a story. Fourth of July, last year."

"That's a totally indelible memory." When she thought of that day, she couldn't help smiling. "We were in Aspen. There were fireworks in the sky and in the hotel bedroom."

"Give me the details."

It was the first time they'd made love, and she remembered shedding their clothes, seeing him naked for the first time, tasting his honey mouth. The memory made her feel warm and gooey inside. "Not appropriate. I have to act like a proper person, and I'll get all excited if I give you a blow-by-blow description."

"Blow-by-blow," he said with a grin. "That's what I want."

"Not going to happen."

A black SUV pulled up in front of the porch, and Special Agent Gregory got out. As usual, he was carrying a satchel full of written information and looking self-important. Maybe she could talk to him later, assess his trustworthiness. If he really was an expert on oil exploration, they might have something in common to discuss. Or he might have something to hide.

She heard the thwhump-thwhump of the chopper blades before she saw the running lights. The black helicopter dipped through gray clouds and prepared to land in the open area between the house and the road.

She couldn't help but whisper under her breath, "Showtime."

Chapter Thirteen

With all of Special Agent Hawthorne's fussing about preparations, Sidney felt as if the helicopter should have arrived with more fanfare, maybe a brass band or a heavenly choir.

"Nice transportation," she said.

"Butler set it up. They were flown into Lackland Air Force Base."

"That doesn't look like a military chopper."

"I'm guessing it's a little something from the CIA."

Hawthorne appeared on the porch wearing one of her trademark black suits, but her blouse was teal silk and her dark brown hair hung in loose curls to her shoulders. Her cheeks flushed pink, and her lips were glossed to a high sheen. She looked like a robot trying to transform into a Kewpie doll.

She motioned to Curtis, who popped open an umbrella and followed her to the chopper.

Hurtado, make that President Hurtado, emerged

first. He wore the same kind of uniform as when Sidney met him three years ago: a khaki-colored jacket with a matching belt and a blue ascot. There appeared to be even more medals on his chest.

A tall man in his late forties, he wasn't bad-looking with his high forehead and narrow, patrician nose. He had a great tan, and his fingernails were manicured and buffed. This was a guy who knew how to take care of himself.

All the buffing and fluffing in the world couldn't draw the attention to him when Elena stepped out of the helicopter. Her long black hair cascaded past her shoulders. Dramatic eyes stared out from a flawless complexion. Her royal blue designer dress hugged her curves, and a patterned shawl added an aura of feminine mystery.

Sidney heaved a sigh. "She's as beautiful as I remember."

"Not my type," Nick said.

"Oh, pul-eeze, she's every man's type."

"Not for me," he repeated. "I like straight blond hair, long legs and attitude."

"And here I am. What a coincidence!"

The two bodyguards wore beige uniforms and blue berets. They carried automatic repeating rifles.

As she watched them approach, she was hit with a memory. Still mindful of the bugs, she whispered to Nick, "Three years ago. I was in

Tiquanna. We were out on Hurtado's yacht. Rico Suarez was with us. He was trying to get my boss to invest a half million dollars in a resort hotel that could turn the beachfront into a tourist's dream location. He mentioned Underwood Oil."

"What did he say?"

"Underwood Oil was making investments in their country, providing for their needs. I asked if he was referring to building schools or providing medical aid, but that wasn't it. Then I lost my train of thought." She chuckled. "Hurtado was wearing a Speedo."

"And you got distracted."

"But not in a good way."

"That's actually a helpful memory. I can check records and see what they were investing in."

Nick had pasted a smile on his face as they waited for the group from Tiquanna to approach. When Sidney looked up at him, she saw an example of perfect diplomacy. But she felt tension in his arm. Anger glimmered in his golden eyes. It was obvious to her that Nick viewed Hurtado as the enemy.

Had the dictator arranged for Nick's abduction? It didn't make sense for him to blow a hole in his own palace compound. And what could he hope to gain? She realized that the whole episode had worked out well for Hurtado. By pretending to rescue Nick, he became something of a hero. But he couldn't have expected that outcome.

He approached her with arms outstretched for a hug. "Miss Sidney Parker, you're the girl who remembers everything."

When his arms enclosed her, she was overwhelmed by the heavy leather scent of his cologne. "Nice to see you again, Mr. President."

"When Vicky told me you were here, I couldn't believe it."

Vicky? As in Victoria Hawthorne? Finally, Sidney had her answer. If you were the head of a nation, you got to call Special Agent Hawthorne by a nickname.

Elena had gone directly to Nick, who politely kissed her hand and said, "I hope you'll enjoy your stay in our country."

She scanned the rain-soaked horizon. "I'm not as much interested in ranches and cowboys as I am in shopping. Perhaps Sidney can show me around."

Hawthorne stepped up. "We'll arrange a day for you at Neiman Marcus."

"Lovely." She faced Sidney and took her hand. Her violet eyes were serious. "I thought of you so many times. It must have been terrible to have your fiancé missing."

Sidney hadn't expected empathy. Elena was either a thoughtful and trusted ally as Nick believed or she was cleverly perceptive in knowing what to say. "Thank you."

Hawthorne herded them toward the front door. "We'll get you settled inside, and then we can talk about dinner."

Upstairs in her bedroom, Sidney quickly changed into her little black dress. Since it was sleeveless, she covered up with a dark rose cashmere cardigan. Her shoes were comfortable black flats. If she'd been at home, she would have added jewelry, but the person who packed her suitcase had skimped on accessories. Her spectacular engagement ring would have to be enough.

In the hallway, she met Nick, who was wearing his dress blue uniform with gold buttons down the front and real medals on his chest. He was so handsome that he took her breath away. What was it about a man in uniform? When she placed her hand on his arm, she was trembling.

"You look great," he said.

"Not me. You."

In his formal attire, he was ready to escort her to somewhere wonderful. She was already rethinking the sleeping arrangements for tonight, trying to figure out a way she could get him into her bed without camera surveillance or bugs. Being this close and not making love was driving her crazy.

Downstairs, the rest of the crew had gathered.

In addition to Phillips, Gregory and Curtis, there were three other CIA types in suits and the chopper pilot.

Nick went directly to the pilot. "Are you headed back to Lackland tonight?"

"No, sir. I'll be transporting a group to the hotel tomorrow morning."

Lieutenant Butler, in his own resplendent uniform, joined them. "Looks like Hawthorne has everything under control."

Sidney wasn't sure what that meant. As far as she knew, the major change in plan was the date. "Are you expecting trouble?"

"Nothing to worry about." He looked down into a crystal tumbler of amber liquid. "We've picked up some chatter on the internet. According to our sources, the rebels are in Austin. Avilar might be with them."

Beside her, Nick stiffened. "Why wasn't I informed about the chatter?"

"Not your purview. You're here for the show. You'll meet with the people from Underwood Oil, tell them what a swell guy Hurtado is, and then you're free to get out of here."

She could tell that Nick wanted more. He'd invested his time, his energy and his blood in the struggle between the rebels and Hurtado. He had more experience with their politics than anyone else. As far as she was concerned, he should be in charge.

Butler leaned close enough that she could smell the whiskey on his breath. "I don't mind saying that I wish I could leave with you."

"Why is that?" Nick asked.

"I've got no problem with taking orders from a female. My CO is a woman. But Hawthorne won't listen to a damn word I say. She acts like it's a sign of weakness to seek other opinions."

"Like the way she set up guard duty," Nick said.

"Hell, yes." Butler grumbled into his drink. "I could have handled that responsibility with half the men and twice the effectiveness."

As the two military men fell into a discussion of surveillance strategy, Sidney's gaze shifted toward Special Agent Phillips, who was doing a great job of fading into the woodwork in his brown suit. He gave her a wink. When it came right down to it, she trusted Phillips more than anybody else. He was a kindhearted man. He had a family. She didn't want to think that he was working for the bad guys.

Gregory was another story. There were lots of secrets behind his horn-rimmed glasses. If she ever got a chance to be alone with him, she'd make a point of talking to him about their common interests to see what he might reveal.

A hush dropped over the room as the dictator/president and his wife descended the staircase in a practiced manner. These two were accustomed to making an entrance. He was dignified, and Elena was stunning. Her designer dress in coral and cream managed to look formal without being too fancy.

Though Sidney could imagine Elena running off with Avilar, she didn't think this pampered princess would be happy living in a rebel camp. She probably looked great in camouflage fatigues, but Sidney didn't think the lady had ever shopped at an army surplus store.

Agent Hawthorne—Vicky—trailed behind them, looking very much like a disgruntled lady-in-waiting. She'd taken off the black jacket to her suit to show off the attractive draping of her silk blouse, but she was still a long way from glamorous.

A burst of gunfire shattered the genteel mood. From outside, Sidney heard guards yelling. More shots were fired.

Hurtado's guards leaped in front of him and Elena with their weapons held at the ready. The agents in suits dropped their drinks, pulled their guns and sought cover.

In those first seconds, she was too shocked to be scared. Was this really happening? Why were they being shot at?

Nick shoved her down behind the dining room table away from the windows. He hadn't been wearing a sword with his dress uniform, but he had a Glock in his hand.

"Stay down," he said.

"Do you have another gun in an ankle holster?" She really had practiced shooting, not so much because she intended to take on the world but because it seemed smart to be able to protect herself. The extra bonus was that she liked it—the noise and the feeling of power when she squeezed the trigger.

He gave her a worried look but didn't argue. As he placed his second Glock in her hand, he said, "Don't get shot again."

"One scar is cool. Two are excessive."

The weight of the gun in her grasp brought her back to reality. They were in a serious, dangerous situation. Adrenaline rushed through her, and her pulse jumped into high gear as the battle outside grew louder. The booming rattle from repeating rifles mingled with single shots. And there were a lot of indecipherable shouts. One of the large windows that opened onto the patio shattered, spewing glass across the floor.

Butler appeared next to Nick. "Sounds like chaos out there."

Nick looked over his shoulder, and she followed his gaze. The Tiquanna guards were hustling Hurtado and Elena from the room. She wondered why Hawthorne wasn't with them. Having the leader of a foreign nation attacked on American soil had to be the special agent's worst nightmare.

Nick asked Butler, "Where are they going?"

"Didn't you pay attention in the meetings? The safe room is the wine cellar under the kitchen."

"I'll accompany them."

He gave her a quick kiss and took off. Sidney understood his reasoning. If Avilar was correct, Hurtado wanted to have Elena assassinated and blame the rebels. This was a perfect opportunity for that scenario.

She looked to Butler. "What can I do to help?"

"You stay here. I'm going to organize this crew."

She ducked down and pushed aside the white linen tablecloth so she could watch Butler take charge. His military training served him well. Nobody—not even Hawthorne—objected when he ordered the various agents into teams and sent them to various locations with specific assignments.

Sidney's job was to stay out of harm's way. As the front room emptied, she moved into the kitchen, where Delia had armed herself with a hunting rifle. Down on one knee, she braced the rifle on the window ledge and peered out toward the barn.

"What do you see?" Sidney asked.

"It's a dark night. Rainy." She adjusted the night scope and squinted into it. "I can't tell what's going on. There's a bunch of guys running around. Looks like they're headed toward the barn. That's bad."

"Why?"

"They're going to scare the horses."

Thinking of Nick, she asked, "How do I get to the wine cellar?"

"There are stairs to the basement behind the mudroom. Once you're down there, you'll see a heavy wooden door. It locks on the inside and the outside. If you get in there, you're safe. Unless the house falls down on your head."

The wine cellar sounded like a clandestine place. Anything might happen there. She decided to join Nick, to be another witness in case Hurtado tried to hurt Elena. First, she asked Delia, "Is there any way I can help you?"

"I don't think so. Nobody is headed our way."

A gigantic explosion rocked the house. A fierce orange light burst through the windows toward the front. Sidney's heart thumped hard against her ribcage, and she inhaled a deep breath to fight her rising panic. It felt as if the whole world had exploded, leaving her disoriented with the inside of her head ringing.

With Delia, she darted along the hallway toward the front of the house. Both women held their guns at the ready.

Another huge boom erupted. The noise was so loud, it hurt her ears.

Peeking around the corner of the hall into the front room, she saw the metal skeleton of the helicopter going up in flames.

Chapter Fourteen

Nick stayed close to Elena in the wine cellar. Hurtado might not have qualms about shooting his wife and blaming the rebels, but he couldn't get away with killing both Elena and Nick, a decorated marine with friends in high places, without many questions being asked. Still, Nick didn't make the mistake of counting too much on his citizenship or his reputation. Those factors hadn't saved him from being abducted and beaten in Tiquanna.

This time, he was armed. As soon as they entered the wine cellar, he imagined several possible actions where he took out the guards and Hurtado. Riding his current wave of anger and frustration, he figured he could handle three men with no sweat. He almost hoped for a confrontation.

The dull light from a few bare bulbs did nothing to lift the chill of the climate-controlled temperature and humidity. Rows of bottles were stored on their sides on specially made racks. This underground room was solid. Down here, the sound of gunfire from outside sounded as harmless as popcorn in the microwave.

Nick set up a table and chairs behind the racks, giving them cover if attackers came through the heavy wooden door, which was locked on the inside. He had only one complaint about this "safe room." There was only one way in and out. They were trapped.

Then they heard the explosion.

"What the hell was that?" Hurtado demanded.

"The chopper," Nick said. He was honestly surprised. "How would the rebels get their hands on that kind of firepower?"

"Simple," Hurtado said. "A stick of dynamite."

"But they'd have to come close to throw it."

Avilar wasn't a fool. He wouldn't risk his men by trying to penetrate so deeply past the heavily armed perimeter surrounding the safe house. And that brought up the obvious question: Why had he staged this attack?

Nick guessed that the purpose was to force Hurtado to move to the hotel. Blowing up the chopper would send that message. Going to Austin suited Nick just fine. The sooner he could turn Elena over to his handlers, the sooner she'd be safe. And he could go home.

Hurtado straightened his shoulders and puffed

out his chest, preparing to make an announcement. "I warn you, Captain Corelli, these rebels cannot be underestimated. They have made secret alliances."

"Are you sure this is the action of the rebels?"

"Who else?"

"I have to point this out, sir. You have other enemies."

"That's true," Elena said quietly. "Your own cousin is putting together an army."

"He's organizing a few men for his own protection," Hurtado said. "My cousin, the fool, is a frightened little toad. He finally understands that he must use force against Avilar."

While he was recovering, Nick spent nearly a month in the presidential compound, where he could observe Hurtado in action. His regime was rife with deceptions and intrigues. It was nearly impossible to locate a single grain of truth amid all the lies.

Nick wasn't a card-carrying member of the Miguel Avilar fan club, but he much preferred the rebel to the dictator. And he wasn't above getting in his digs at Hurtado. "The rebels must be growing stronger. Financing this attack in the US had to cost a lot of money."

Hurtado scowled. "Not so much as you might think. I could have financed such an attack."

"I suppose you could." And possibly did. He

wouldn't put it past Hurtado to arrange his own attack so the rebels would look bad. Avilar had suggested that the shoot-out at Nick's house was the work of Hurtado's men, and the proof was Rico Suarez.

"They must be stopped," Hurtado said. "Your government must help me stop them."

Nick cringed. Words of war. He hated them and hated the men like Hurtado who saw force as the only option. "You might want to think about this," he said. "How did Avilar locate the safe house? Does he have a contact on the inside?"

"A traitor to my cause?"

Hurtado's gaze went to Elena, which wasn't the direction Nick wanted him to pursue. His job was to keep her safe. There were plenty of other people to throw under the bus. "Special Agent Hawthorne thinks there's a leak in the CIA."

"Does she?"

"That's why she wanted to bring you here," Nick said. "A spectacular failure."

In her flimsy dress, Elena shivered. Nick unbuttoned his uniform jacket and draped it over her slender shoulders. She was a lovely woman, but he hadn't lied when he said Elena wasn't his type. She was super high maintenance. The man who hooked up with this beauty would be dedicating his entire life to her whims.

Sidney was a partner who gave as good as she got. Living with her would never be boring.

He heard a voice from outside the wine cellar. "It's Hawthorne. Unlock the door."

One of the guards unfastened the latch while the other held his weapon at the ready. Hawthorne rushed inside and yanked the door closed. "It's over," she said. "Are you all right?"

Hurtado answered for all of them. "No injuries to report. Vicky, how could this happen?"

"I'll have a full report later, sir."

"This was the action of the Tiquanna rebels," he said. "Captain Corelli agrees with me."

Nick didn't recall any such agreement. "I'm not so sure."

"Who else could it be?" Hurtado made a fist and punched it into his other hand. "We must hunt them down like dogs. They can't get away with this. Not on American soil."

Nick wasn't in the mood for the dictator's pontificating. There was nothing Hurtado could say that would impress him. He approached Hawthorne. "Casualties?"

"Nothing serious." A puzzled frown creased her forehead. "It sounded like a battlefield with bullets flying, but we had only a few minor hits. Either these guys are really bad marksmen or they were shooting into the air."

"Drawing everyone toward the barn," Nick said.

She nodded. "Then the chopper blew."

The helicopter had been the mark from the first. All that other firepower was meant as a distraction. Nick appreciated the strategy. "If this was Avilar, he was making a statement. Nobody has to get killed."

"No," Hurtado said emphatically. "These dogs can't be permitted to live."

Hawthorne placed a consoling hand on his arm. "Please accept my deepest apologies, sir."

He shook her hand off. "I will never align the interests of my country with cowards."

Head held high, he stalked toward the door, threw it open and marched out. His guards rushed to follow, and Hawthorne brought up the rear.

Nick was left alone with Elena. He shrugged. "That went well."

"You have no idea."

Her smile was cool and secretive. He suspected that she knew all about this attack, had maybe even planned it with Avilar, but he didn't bother asking. She'd tell him when she was ready and not a moment before.

SIDNEY SUMMED UP the helicopter explosion as good news versus bad news. The bad part was, of course, the destruction of an expensive piece of machinery. The good news was the rain. If the fields had been dry, flames from the explosion would have spread across acres and acres of prairie grass. The safe house—which she'd come to think of as the "unsafe" house—might have burned.

She and Delia helped where they could, hauling buckets of drinking water for the ranch hands and guards who were fighting the fire. She ran back and forth to the barn, fetching various tools and implements. Her little black dress was ruined after the second trip, carrying hoes and shovels in a wheelbarrow, but she didn't care. At least she was useful.

Thick, metallic, black smoke billowed straight into the air in an angry plume against the dark night sky. The sparks below sizzled and hissed. People from neighboring ranches showed up and got busy. When the local fire brigade arrived, every hope for CIA secrecy was gone.

Sidney had wondered how the former ranch was explained to the people in the area without telling anybody it was a government safe house. Lodge or dude ranch were the most common explanations.

As Hawthorne mobilized their group to evacuate, Sidney had to fight for her place in one of the SUVs that would form a convoy to the hotel in Austin. Sidney wasn't considered to be a number one important person at these meetings. But Nick was. And he insisted on having her with him. After she wiped the smudges of smoke off her face, she changed into jeans and a sweat-shirt, packed her suitcase and lugged it down-stairs, where she found her place in the second vehicle with Nick, Gregory, Phillips and Lieu-tenant Butler.

They drove away immediately, following the vehicle carrying the Hurtados and Special Agent Hawthorne. Another SUV fell into line behind them.

She and Nick sat in the farthest backseat. They weren't alone, but it felt private. She snuggled against him.

"Don't take this personally," he said, "but you stink."

"That smoke was awful."

"I might be the smelly one," Phillips said. "Have y'all ever seen anything like that explosion? I wish I'd recorded it on my phone to show the kids. They don't think their daddy has an exciting job."

"What do you tell your twins about your job?" she asked.

"I just tell them that I'm an analyst for the government. They don't care. They're only four." He glanced over his shoulder and made eye contact with her. "When my boys are older, I could have a problem not telling the whole truth. But I can't very well say that I'm a secret agent. If I did, it wouldn't be a secret."

"What about your wife?"

"Y'all ask a lot of questions, Sidney."

"I can't help being curious."

"That's true," Nick said. "She wants to know everything."

"Me and my wife don't talk about my job." He frowned. "If something comes up, like this fire, I change the subject. Here's what I'd say. That fire could have been a real disaster, but those ranch hands really know what they're doing."

"All true," she said. But he avoided any detail that would have been a breech in secrecy. It must be exhausting to live like that, hiding your real work.

"I'll tell you this," Butler grumbled from the front seat. "Those cowboys were a hell of a lot more efficient than the CIA. The bodyguards were running around like chickens with their heads cut off. No leadership whatsoever."

"Could have been worse," Phillips said. "Nobody got shot."

Butler turned in his seat to glare at all of them. "The enemy achieved their objective, which was, obviously, to torch the chopper. They distracted the security force with gunfire at the rear of the house while they did whatever they wanted at the front."

"Do you have any idea what caused the explosion?" Nick asked. "Any chance it was long-range weaponry?"

"I doubt they needed anything that sophisticated," Butler said. "If we've learned anything from Iraq and Afghanistan, it's that it doesn't take a lot of expertise to put together a bomb."

"What happens when we get to the hotel?" Gregory asked. "I don't think we have reservations for tonight."

"Hawthorne has it under control," Phillips said. "I think we have an entire floor booked for a week, including some fancy suite for the president and his wife."

"I'm aware of that," Gregory snapped. "I'm handling the meeting preparations for Underwood Oil, so I've been talking to the hotel. I just want to know about tonight."

She nudged Nick in the ribs. "Maybe they won't have a room for us, and we'll have to fend for ourselves."

"All by ourselves. That wouldn't be so bad."

"Not for you," Gregory muttered. "I've been working on this for years. Finally, it looks like everybody is on board. Finally, I can get some solid agreement."

"About what?" she asked. The negotiation of drilling rights shouldn't be so complicated. When her company checked out Tiquanna, their main concern had been lack of infrastructure. "How much is Underwood Oil willing to finance in building roads, providing housing and clean water? Are they going to deal with the lack of schools? What about medical conditions?"

"Humanitarian aid is *not* my problem." He pushed his glasses up on his nose. "And it's none of your business."

She was about to protest. The mistreatment of these people should be everybody's problem. Clearly, the rebels saw a problem in the way their country was being developed. She remembered the squalid conditions in the slums of the capital city.

Before Underwood Oil turned on the tap and sent a gush of money flowing into Tiquanna, there needed to be considerations for the people who lived there.

If the only purpose for these meetings was to ensure Hurtado's wealth and fortune, she wanted to make it her business. But it wouldn't do much good to poke at Gregory. He had his strategy mapped and wasn't going to change his mind.

No matter who got hurt.

Chapter Fifteen

Sidney waltzed through the door to their hotel room on the fifth floor. It was a typical room with a queen-size bed, a dresser, a television, a desk and a bathroom. The walls were painted a soft gold. A floor-to-ceiling window was covered with a nubby curtain. The carpet was beige. Nothing spectacular, but she thought it was the most fantastic room she'd ever seen. This space—this wonderful space—belonged to her and Nick alone.

There hadn't been a room available for them on the floor that the CIA had rented, so they got their own random vacant room at the hotel. No surveillance cameras. No bugs. Finally, they had privacy. And that was a thing of beauty.

While Nick tipped the bellman, she flopped across the bed and stared up at the ceiling. "I love this place."

"You're easy to please."

"Seriously, Nick. If I want to talk in a normal

voice about why Hurtado is an evil dictator, it's not a problem. Nobody is listening to us. Nobody is watching."

He sat on the bed beside her. "We can get into all kinds of trouble."

It felt as if they should do something outrageous to celebrate. Her arm slithered toward him, free to touch wherever she wanted. "Do you want to talk dirty?"

"Do you?"

"Well, it's never really been my thing. But if I wanted to sleaze it up, I could."

"Knock yourself out."

"Oh, baby, I want you. I want your…" She grabbed his leather jacket and yanked him toward her. "You know what I want."

He gathered her in his arms and kissed her without holding anything back. Though she wanted to record every second, she couldn't keep track as his hands coasted over her body, exploring and teasing. His rough caresses demanded a response, and her instincts took over. She hadn't been aware of how restricted she'd been when she thought they were being watched. Now she was free and loving every touch, every twitch, every gasp.

What she didn't love was the stink. She drew back. Her nose wrinkled. "I smell like smoke."

"We need a shower."

"Yes, please."

The simple, white-tiled hotel bathroom seemed like a garden of earthly delights when she turned on the hot water and steam rolled out from behind the curtain. For the past few days, she'd been dying to get her hands on his body. Though a sexy striptease would have been a treat, she was too eager to waste time with game playing. They tore off their clothes in a matter of seconds. She stared. His broad-shouldered body was even better than she remembered, too good to be true.

The yearning that had tortured her for months transformed into pure desire. Nothing in the world existed beyond him, her fiancé, her lover, her man. Naked, they stepped under the hot shower.

He leaned down and kissed her upper arm. "Your battle wound looks good."

"I almost forgot about it."

"It's going to be a sexy scar."

She tilted her head back and let the water sluice through her hair, rinsing out the stench from the fire.

"Look at you," he murmured as he peeled the wrapper off a bar of soap. "You're the prettiest thing I've ever seen. You're perfect."

"Now who's easy to please?"

He worked up the lather in his hands. "Come here, dirty girl."

He rubbed the soapsuds over her breasts and waist. Then he turned her around and washed her shoulders. His fingers traced her spine and cupped her bottom as she stood facing the spray of hot water. She knew his strength; he was a big, muscular man. But his touch was infinitely gentle.

He opened the shampoo and washed her hair. The sandalwood fragrance of the soap gradually erased the ugly stench of smoke. Though she could have stood there for hours, enjoying the purely sensual massage, her needs were more demanding. She'd been dreaming about him for six months. It was time.

They traded places. He was so tall that he had to duck to get the shower spray on his head. The water slicked his shining black hair and coursed in rivulets down his body. She treated herself to a slow study of his long, lean torso.

There were new scars. She touched a poorly stitched line on his upper chest. "Whoever did this to you deserves to die."

"Let's not talk about it now. This time is for us."

With an effort, she pushed back her anger. She wanted justice for him. She wanted retribution. But he was right. They had earned their moments of privacy.

She soaped every part of him, and when she

was done, she leaned her cheek against his broad chest. The cascading sound of the shower played a natural harmony that synchronized with the throbbing of her pulse. Their bodies suctioned together and pulled apart.

They'd made love in the shower before. The first time was on November 15th, almost a year ago. She had that memory preserved in her mind. But this felt like the first time. She marveled at his taut muscles, and she laughed when she stroked his side and he flinched in a tickle response. His kisses were deeper. His touch was more demanding. She spread her legs and rubbed against him.

"I'm still taking my birth control pills," she said.

"Good."

When he'd been gone three months, and she didn't know if he was alive or dead, she had considered dumping the pills. That had been a low point for her, when she'd almost given up hope that she'd ever see him again. If she lost Nick, she never wanted to make love with another man. No one could ever come close to taking his place in her heart.

Staying on the pill became an important part of her schedule, a daily affirmation. She needed to be prepared for the moment when he returned to her.

She looked up at his face. Her gaze locked on his golden eyes, and a rush of adrenaline coursed through her veins. "I knew you'd come back to me."

He traced her lips with a fingertip. "I'll never leave, never again."

Still standing, he lifted her thigh, adjusted his position and entered her. The shock of finally joining together thrilled her. Her moans of pleasure echoed in the shower as her greedy hands pulled him closer.

He filled her completely. His thrusts were slow at first, driving her wild. Her back arched. In a desperate frenzy, she writhed against him, wanting more and more, deeper and deeper. He plunged harder, drove her to the edge. She couldn't stop if she'd wanted to. A bolt of excitement shattered her. She came completely undone.

Trembling, gasping and falling, she clung to him, unable to stand on her own two legs. He had taken her beyond her imagination and her memories. He was her everything.

NICK TOWELED HER DRY, carried her to the bed and tucked her under the covers. Making love to her was more than sex. Not that the sex was anything to be disregarded. But this was pure love, blooming all around him, sweeter than the fragrance of gardenias and softer than the touch of morning sun. He knew what had to be done for him to live with Sidney, and he was ready to finish this assignment and get on with their future.

There would be changes for him. Less excitement and more desk work. But she was worth it. "Tell me about your plans for the house."

"Everything gets painted, like I said before. No more dark turquoise. Definitely, no more orange. Whenever I walk into that room behind the kitchen, I feel like I'm inside a juicer about to get pulped."

"What do you want to do with that room?"

"It'd make a nice guest bedroom, but it's kind of far from the bathroom. I'm thinking of a home office. It's big enough that we both could use it."

"Do you think we could share an office?"

Her full lips twisted in an adorable scowl. "I suppose we could. I've been working at a bar, and I kind of like that cheesy country music you always play."

"And my guitar."

She groaned. "Why would you play your guitar in the office?"

She was cute when she got irked with him. It made him want to tease her more. "The twelve-string helps me think."

"Or maybe we don't share an office," she said. "It could be an exercise room. Or a plant room in case I get into gardening."

"Or a nursery."

Her blue eyes widened. They hadn't talked much about having kids. Of course, they both wanted children. And their little brick house with the big backyard would be a good place to start a family.

"Someday," she said.

There were a lot of other things that had to happen first. "Can we get a border collie?"

"Only if we get it from the pound," she said.

If he slipped under the covers beside her and felt the silky texture of her skin, he wouldn't be able to resist making love again. Not a problem. He was already halfway aroused again and ready for a full night of passion.

A glance at the digital clock on the bedside table showed it was after ten o'clock. He wondered how late room service was available. "Hungry?"

"You bet I am. All afternoon I could smell the pot roast Delia was making for dinner."

He put on a terry cloth bathrobe provided by the hotel, grabbed the phone and placed their order: a hamburger for him, roast beef for her and a bottle of the house red wine. Going out to dinner would have been great, but he'd promised Hawthorne that he wouldn't leave the hotel.

With all the other distractions, he wasn't worried about using his secret cell phone to send a message. The response to his text was immediate. Tomorrow at one-thirty, he should bring Elena to the roof of the building.

Why the roof? As he removed the battery from the phone so it couldn't be traced, he decided that before that meeting, he would check out the roof. He needed to be aware of escape options if something went wrong.

Sidney had opened her suitcase and found her own pastel blue robe decorated with snowflakes. She perched on the edge of the bed and dragged a comb through her straight blond hair. "I want to take you to the Silver Star Saloon, where I was working. They have incredible beers."

"This could be over tomorrow," he said. "And we're going on a real retreat, someplace in the mountains where nobody knows us and nobody wants anything from us."

"How do you think this is going to turn out? What happens after Elena disappears?"

"It's not my problem, but I'd say that's the beginning of the end for Hurtado."

"Good. I've decided that he's the bad guy."

"Even though it's likely that Avilar blew up the chopper?"

"I've been thinking about that," she said. "I don't think it was accidental that no one was seriously injured. Avilar wanted to make a statement. He wanted to get Elena away from the safe house early, and he accomplished that without casualties. Kind of impressive."

He agreed. A dead helicopter bothered him less than the loss of human life. "If Avilar is behind this, he's put together a significant force inside the US. How is he being financed?"

"You mentioned that his family has money."

Nick was well aware of the resources available to the rebels. In some ways, they looked like a ragtag army, poorly funded and struggling. But their weaponry and access to computer technology were first-class.

Finding their financial backer was one of the reasons he'd been stationed in Tiquanna. At first, he thought they were being armed by Underwood Oil. Earlier today when Sidney mentioned an investment from the oil company, he was reminded of the many times he had tried to follow the money trail. Somehow, Underwood Oil money always led back to Hurtado and his friends.

When room service came, he scarfed down half his hamburger without taking a breath. He sipped the wine, savoring the tang. "It's good."

"Delicious," she said, finishing her roast beef. "I'll bet Delia's beef is better. She's a really good cook. Is she part of the CIA? How does the safe house work with the locals?"

"Delia and a couple of the ranch hands are live-ins. I expect they have some kind of security clearance, but they aren't officially CIA or FBI. They know the ranch is owned by the government and if they want to keep their jobs, they don't talk about the people staying there."

"With all the cameras and such, that seems a bit lax."

"It's the other way around," he said. "If they were overheard talking about anything suspicious, they'd be in trouble."

"I'd hate to live like that. I've never been good at keeping secrets."

He heard a tap on the door and went to answer. Holding his gun, he peeked through the fish-eye and saw Special Agent Curtis standing in the hallway, shifting his weight from one foot to the other.

Hoping that Curtis wasn't bringing news of a new disaster, Nick opened the door. "What is it?"

"Is Sidney here?"

As soon as she heard Curtis's voice, she left her chair and bounced up to greet him. "What can I do for you?"

He gave her a shy smile. His cheeks were almost as red as his hair. "Actually, I have something for you. Your cell phone."

She took it from him. "Is it okay for me to call my office?"

"Hawthorne asked that you not give your location or make plans to meet with anybody until the Tiquanna meetings are over. But information about Hurtado and Elena being at the hotel is common knowledge. Tomorrow, they'll be talking to the press."

"I appreciate this," she said.

"Have a nice night."

Nick closed the door and watched as Curtis went back down the hall to the elevator. "How did he know which room we were in? I didn't tell anybody."

"He's CIA," she said. "They know everything."

"You like him, don't you?"

She shrugged. "He's sweet. Within a few minutes of meeting him, he let me give him a neck massage."

Nick wasn't surprised. "You can be very persuasive."

"Stop being a guy for a minute," she said. "It wasn't a sexy massage."

"Uh-huh." As if he believed that.

"Curtis and I bonded on a nerd level." She sipped her wine. "He understands me."

"How do you figure?"

"I was asking him tons of questions about degrees of angles and camera rotations. He probably knew that I'd try to circumvent his surveillance. But he also knew that I'm not a dangerous person."

He took the cell phone from her. "Do you have the information on your cell backed up?"

"Yes, it links up with my computer."

"Good."

In the bathroom, he removed the battery. Using the heel of his boot, he smashed the phone and tossed the pieces in a water glass.

"You killed it," she said.

"We don't need any more cameras or bugs." He was pretty sure that picking up surveillance on them had motivated the supposedly nice gesture of returning her phone. "Your pal Curtis might be a nice guy. But he still works for Hawthorne."

Nick still needed to be cautious. The game wasn't over. Not by a long shot.

Chapter Sixteen

After a night of passion that took up rows and rows of space in her memory banks, Sidney might have been content to roll over and sleep until noon. With any luck, she'd miss any more fireworks, Nick could fulfill his orders with Elena, and they could leave this chaos behind them in the rearview mirror.

Whatever happened in Tiquanna wasn't her problem. She was just one little person who had gotten swept up in an international intrigue. Not. Her. Problem.

Unfortunately, whether she liked it or not, Nick played a role in this battle. He'd been kidnapped and tortured, rescued and recruited to help Elena. He had a stake in the outcome. Tiquanna was important to him. Therefore, she was involved.

At eight o'clock in the morning, she was dressed and ready to go. Her little black dress was destroyed after last night, but she had a light wool plaid skirt that she wore with a blazer. She chose flats instead of heels in case she needed to move fast.

Nick came out of the bathroom wearing the heather-gray sweater she'd bought for him on his last birthday, March 22. He looked preppy and cool as he slipped on a sports jacket to cover the gun at the small of his back.

He glanced at her outfit. "You don't have to come with me."

"I want to."

"There's nothing to worry about," he said. "Nothing dangerous about today."

"You've been wrong about that before," she pointed out. "Bad guys shot up our house. We bumped into a rebel leader in the barn. And there was that exploding chopper..."

"Okay, I get it."

She took a sip of the instant coffee she'd made using the machine in the bathroom. The taste was gross, but caffeine was caffeine. "What's our plan?"

"We go to the ninth floor, where Hawthorne has the whole operation set up. We hang around there until it's time for me to take Elena to the drop-off point."

"And what time is that going to happen?"

"I'd rather not tell you when."

Too bad for him. She refused to be left in the

dark. "I'm not insisting on coming along, but I want to know."

"Last night, you admitted that you aren't good at keeping secrets."

"Yes, I did say that. And yes, it's true." If he told her the time, she'd be checking her wrist-watch and doing mental countdowns. "Can you tell me where?"

He thought for a moment, and she imagined his mental process. The location where he would hand over Elena seemed to be bothering him. He'd like to have her input. But he wanted to keep her at a distance.

His common sense won out. "Okay, I'll tell you."

"Where?"

"According to my instructions, I'm supposed to take Elena to the roof. I want to go up there this morning and check for obstacles."

"Makes sense to go to the roof," Sidney said. "They'll pick her up with a chopper."

It was his turn to look surprised. "You figured that out pretty fast."

She shrugged. "Their problem is to get Elena out of the building without being harmed. If the exits are watched by armed men, she's an easy target for a sniper. Or she could be followed on the street."

"True."

She continued, "It's already been established that the rebels are willing to use force. They'd be blamed if Elena was attacked. Hurtado could pretend to be a grieving widower, and he'd be excused for using force on his enemies."

"You have a knack for this," he said.

"Thank you."

In the hallway outside their fifth-floor room, she was fairly sure they'd be picked up on hotel surveillance and probably CIA, as well. With all these cameras, she ought to feel like a movie star. Instead, she was annoyed.

She glanced at the green exit sign above the door to a stairwell. "I'm guessing all the doors to the stairwell open on this side and lock when they're closed."

"Good guess," he said. "But I know a way around the locks."

"You've done this kind of thing before."

He had a lot of interesting skills that she knew nothing about. His abilities went far beyond basic training for a captain in the marines. She followed him into the stairwell.

Whitewashed concrete walls closed around them. Their steps on the staircase echoed as they climbed past the ninth floor to the roof on the fifteenth.

Sidney was in pretty good shape, but hiking up ten flights left her huffing and puffing. She leaned her back against the wall and caught her breath while Nick took a metallic tool from his pocket and fiddled with the lock on the door labeled Roof. There was a soft popping noise and the smell of gunpowder. He pushed open the door.

Outside, the rain had faded to a gray drizzle that obscured what would have been a beautiful view on a clear day. She looked down at the wide Colorado River as it cut through town. The capitol building wasn't in her sightline. Nor was the Silver Star Saloon. For a moment she wondered what had happened to her car, which she'd left parked behind the saloon.

Nick walked across the gravel-topped roof to the center of a concrete circle. "Heliport."

"We were right," she said.

"Not much cover up here." He turned three hundred and sixty degrees, and then he hiked to the edge of the roof, where a beige brick parapet rose two feet high.

She joined him and looked down a wall made of alternating brick and glass. A sense of vertigo caused her vision to telescope, and she took a step back.

"Careful." He reached out and braced her.

"That's steep."

"I wanted to see if there was some alternate way down from here. There's supposed to be a restaurant or something."

As in climbing down fifteen stories? Was he crazy? "Nothing here. You're out of luck."

He led her to the corner of the building and pointed down to a terraced area, lavishly decorated with potted plants. The glass-top dining tables surrounded a circular pool. "Here's the escape."

"That's a thirty-foot drop onto concrete, otherwise known as a suicide mission."

"It's not so bad. There's an overhang above the door. That's only about fifteen feet. And it's possible to jump all the way to the pool."

There was no way she'd allow him to come up here with Elena by himself. Whether or not he wanted her company, he needed backup.

ON THE NINTH FLOOR, Sidney and Nick were met at the elevator by an agent she didn't recognize who provided them with prepared name tags to hang around their necks. This was usually a concierge level with an open reception area. At both ends, there were high ceilings and lots of windows that gave an open feeling to conversational groupings of sofas and chairs. Behind a Plexiglas wall, there was a meeting in progress. As Sidney watched the various agents seated around a long table, she was reminded of a fishbowl.

Though there were armed guards posted at intervals, Special Agent Hawthorne had done her best to create an upbeat, relaxed atmosphere for the meetings involving Hurtado, various politicians and Underwood Oil. When Lieutenant Butler swooped down on them and pulled Nick aside, she made a beeline for the silver coffee urn.

Not knowing when she'd get another chance to eat, she grabbed two muffins and packets of cream cheese before she sat at the end of a sofa. Two women in business suits sipped coffee at the other end of the sofa. Their ID badges showed they were with the governor's office, and Sidney wondered if she'd ever served them at the Silver Star Saloon.

"Excuse me," one of the women said. "Have you met her?"

"Her?"

"Elena Hurtado." Her voice quavered with excitement. "I've been told that her photographs don't do her justice."

"She's very beautiful," Sidney said with sincerity. "Always wears designer clothes."

"I've had private correspondence with her about early schooling and vaccination programs in Tiquanna. In spite of her husband's policies, she might really be able to help the poor people of her country."

Don't get your hopes up. Sidney nodded.

From a room with double doors at the far end of the hallway, she watched as President Hurtado emerged in his impressive uniform. Special Agent Hawthorne marched beside him, and his two bodyguards fell into place behind him.

Halfway down the hall, their procession halted.

"May I have your attention?" Hawthorne said. "Ladies and gentlemen, thank you for attending this impromptu breakfast. The president will be available for the next half hour to take questions."

"What about Elena?" someone called out.

"His wife isn't feeling well," Hawthorne said. "I'm sure she'll be here for lunch."

Sidney glanced over at Nick. A simple way to foil Elena's defection would be to keep her locked up. After excusing herself to the ladies from the governor's office, Sidney joined her fiancé. "What do you think?"

"I'd like to see Elena join the group."

"I can handle this." Being a woman would come in handy. "I'll have her mingling in no time."

Sidney quickly made her way to the end of the hallway, where she informed the uniformed guard that she was a friend of Elena's and needed to be with her.

"Sorry, ma'am. My orders state that no one but her husband is allowed to see her."

Sidney tried another tactic. "Vicky Hawthorne said I could go inside." The guard didn't budge.

She tried one more direction. "My fiancé would

want me to check on Elena and make sure she was all right. My fiancé, Captain Nick Corelli."

"Yes, ma'am." He snapped to attention and opened the door.

The interior of the opulent suite glowed, even though the rain-filled light through the tall windows was gray and flat. Elena rushed toward her in a swirl of ostrich feathers and coral chiffon from her peignoir. She was a vision of energy, vivacious and very much alive. She grasped both of Sidney's hands. Her violet eyes were electric. "I have to get out of here."

Sidney was a little overwhelmed by the direct attention. "Your husband said you're sick."

"Sick of him," she muttered as she turned away and stalked across the room, trailing bits of feather.

Some of her big personality was purely for dramatic effect. This was a woman who liked constantly being on camera, and Sidney was one hundred percent certain that they were currently under surveillance. She had to wonder what was underneath the flourishes and pirouettes. Did Elena truly believe that her husband wanted her dead?

Sidney cleared her throat. "I spoke to a woman outside who came here specifically to see you. She wants to talk about schools for the children of Tiquanna. It'd be a shame for you to stay in this room."

"Vicky Hawthorne says I must not risk going out. She looks at Tomas as though he's a god. I would be happy for her to take my husband far away from me."

Sidney went to the silver coffee service on a glass-topped table in the center of the suite and poured a cup. She'd had tastes of the instant and the stuff in the outer lobby, but her need for more caffeine was still present. Her thoughts weren't clear. She couldn't tell if Elena was afraid of the rebel threat or of her husband. "Do you mind if I ask a personal question?"

She arched a beautifully shaped eyebrow. "Of course not."

"Why don't you just divorce him?"

Elena threw her head back and laughed. Again, this was big drama, the kind of gesture you'd expect to see onstage. Somehow, she pulled off the diva routine without looking crazy.

"Divorce is not possible for the machismo man, such as Tomas," she said. "The woman doesn't make such decisions. We are married, and that's final, *finito*."

"An Italian word," Sidney said.

"I was born in Milan."

Sidney hadn't known that. She was hazy on

Elena's biography. "I thought you grew up in Tiquanna."

"With my parents, I traveled Europe until I was fourteen. My father was killed in an accident. We lost our fortune, and my mother was forced to bring me to Tiquanna to live with her family." Her full lips parted in a toothy smile. "I fell in love with Tomas. I was ready to marry him, but he insisted that I get an education in America."

"Because you were only fourteen at the time." Even in Tiquanna, the dictator couldn't justify marrying such a young girl.

"With my mother as chaperone, I went to school in California. I studied international business and politics. I speak six languages, four of them fluently. When I returned to Tiquanna, I was prepared to marry Tomas and become first lady of my country."

Her story was unbelievable and fascinating. Sidney imagined the dramatic rooftop escape in a helicopter to be just another chapter in Elena's operatic life. It was time to move forward with that plan.

She took Elena's hand and made direct eye contact. "My fiancé appreciates everything you've done for him."

"Nick is a good man. He loves you very much."

It did Sidney a world of good to hear those words from Elena. "I'm certain that he would want you to leave your suite and meet with the people who have gathered here."

"My husband wishes for me to stay."

Sidney noticed a glimmer of fear behind the big personality. She suspected that Tomas hadn't been gentle in teaching life's lessons to Elena. If there hadn't been surveillance, she could have told the woman that the time for her escape was near. It would be only a few more hours.

"You can't disappoint the people who have come to see you," Sidney said. "Get dressed, Elena."

She darted into the bedroom.

Within two minutes, the door to the suite swung open and slammed hard. Special Agent Hawthorne stood there with her fists braced on her skinny hips.

"What the hell are you doing, Sidney?"

Chapter Seventeen

Sidney felt absolutely no need to justify her actions to Special Agent Hawthorne. Her grudge against this woman was long-standing. During the months Nick had been held hostage, he'd told her Hawthorne had gathered detailed information about his condition that she hadn't seen fit to pass along. She could have arranged phone calls or online visits between Sidney and Nick. Instead, she'd kept them separate.

Hawthorne had called it "keeping control" of the situation. Sidney called it "payback time." This situation was about to get very, very messy.

"It's a miracle," Sidney said. "Elena is feeling better. She's going to get dressed, and we'll join the others."

"This isn't about her health. I want her in this room. It's the only way I can be sure she's safe from the rebels."

"You can't seriously believe the rebels would

attempt an attack at the hotel. Not with all the law enforcement present."

"I'm doing my best to avoid a confrontation." Hawthorne pursed her narrow lips. "I don't have to explain to you."

"If there's a real danger," Sidney said, "why is Hurtado parading around in the hallway? Wouldn't the greater threat be directed toward him?"

She couldn't argue with that logic, and Sidney pressed her advantage. "The real reason you want Elena to stay in her room is because her husband wants it that way. For some reason, Tomas is keeping Elena locked away. And you're helping him."

"It's my job to make sure he stays happy with us. We need for him to be on our side."

"What about Elena?" Sidney took an educated guess. "There are people in government who trust her opinion more than his."

Apparently, she'd struck a chord. A muscle at the corner of Hawthorne's eye twitched. "I forbid you to get involved."

"You forbid me?" Who did she think she was? The Wicked Witch of the West? "I'm delighted to be the one to inform you that you're not calling the shots anymore."

"And who is?"

The door to the bedroom flung wide, and Sidney gestured. "She is. The first lady of Tiquanna."

Elena sailed through in full diva mode. Her green-and-white-patterned dress clung to her slender waist like a designer's caress. The deep V of the neckline showed off a platinum and emerald necklace. Her black hair billowed around her shoulders.

"Come," she said to Sidney, "I have people to meet."

Hawthorne blocked the doorway like a pugnacious bulldog. "I'm sorry, Mrs. Hurtado. I must insist that you stay in your room today."

"I am not a coward," Elena said with her head held high. "It is my duty to represent my country and my people. This is my responsibility."

Sidney pushed past Hawthorne and opened the door. "Right this way, Elena."

"Thank you."

As soon as Elena the Diva entered the hallway, the atmosphere changed from political discussion to party, party, party. The women were fascinated by her sense of style. And the men were drawn to her beauty.

When Sidney stepped aside to let Elena shine at full voltage, Nick joined her. "Good job getting her out here."

"All I had to do was remind her that she's a superstar."

"She's impressive."

Sidney hadn't realized how truly impressive Elena was. She had prepared herself to take a position of power, and her husband was right to be worried about her sphere of influence. If Elena and the handsome rebel leader hooked up, they might take over the world.

IF SIDNEY HADN'T been with him, Nick would have been knee-deep in a swamp of negativity. How the hell did he expect this to work? A helicopter escape off a hotel building? It wasn't exactly subtle. Even though the plan started as a secret, the truth would be out in a matter of minutes. The media would be alerted. Talent agents would be casting the miniseries.

Just because Elena's defection could turn into a publicity circus, it didn't negate the danger, especially for him. Elena would be flying away, but how was Nick going to get out of the building without being arrested by Hawthorne and her gang? He'd be lucky not to end up in a CIA prison.

As he chatted with people in the meeting area, it didn't help that most of his conversations tracked back to his time as a hostage and how heroic he was to have endured. Playing the role of a war hero made him uncomfortable. He was a soldier, a marine, and he didn't do his job for medals or pats on the back. It was his job to serve his country. His satisfaction came when a mission was accomplished.

As he watched Sidney interact with many of the women present, he decided that her engagement ring had paid off in clarifying their relationship. When other women checked out the pi diamond, they oohed and aahed and crossed him off the list of eligible men. The only one who wasn't impressed by its size was Sidney, who wanted something smaller and more efficient.

She sidled up beside him and went up on tiptoe to whisper in his ear, "Now?"

"Not yet."

It had been a smart move on his part to keep the departure time a secret from Sidney. She was anxious enough without knowing the details.

At twelve-thirty, with less than an hour to go before the meet, everyone had settled at five-person tables for a casual lunch of beet salad and some kind of chicken breast with a sauce. He noticed that Sidney had rescued Elena from her expected position at her husband's side and seated her with a group of women. They were talking about food.

"A typical dinner in Tiquanna," Sidney said, "might include a fish stew, lentils, plantains and fried corn bread. The seasonings tend to be a combination of Caribbean and Mexican."

"And the drinks are rum," Elena added. "My country has a lighthearted side. And we love music, as you do in Austin. If there were more development in our country, tourists would flock to Tiquanna."

"Not enough development. That's your real problem," said a woman in a red suit with an ID badge from the governor's office. "Lack of infrastructure. When you get the oil business up and running, there will be plenty of people willing to invest in hotels and such."

"Before the hotels," said a nervous little blonde, "you need schools and hospitals. Otherwise, they'll never get built."

Nick motioned to Sidney, and she excused herself from the discussion that was rapidly evolving into a cultural exchange program with Austin and Tiquanna. She bounced over to him, smiling broadly.

"And that," she said, "is how the world's problems get solved. Five or six women sitting around a table will come up with a plan to make everything right."

"I believe it," he said, "as long as Hawthorne isn't at the table."

"Yeah, she's a pill."

His deadline was approaching. The time had ticked down to twenty-eight minutes before he needed to be on the roof with Elena, which meant he had to make his move in twenty minutes, give or take. "I'm going to need help separating Elena from her adoring fans."

"Right now?"

Excitement brightened her eyes, and he was reminded of his early days when he was less cynical and war-weary. There had been a time, long ago, when he didn't look at the downside. "In a few minutes."

She whispered, "Does Elena know what's going on?"

"Yes."

She didn't have the details, but she was aware of the arrangements being made for her defection. And she knew that Nick was the only person she could trust. If only he'd had a backup, he would have felt more confident.

Sidney gave him a wink. "I've got an idea."

"Oh, good."

"We've been talking about weddings. There's something I wanted to ask Elena."

He wasn't sure where she was going with this, but he played along. "Okay, sure."

Agents Gregory and Curtis stepped up to join them, and Sidney turned to them. "I'm going to ask Elena to be the matron of honor at our wedding. What do you think?"

The two men exchanged a glance and a shrug. Curtis asked, "What if she's in Tiquanna?"

"Well, I have to work out the schedule." She looked up at Nick and batted her eyelashes. "Will you ask her with me? It would mean so much."

He understood what she was doing. Sidney's ruse provided him with an excuse to get Elena away from these people. He had to admit that she was clever. What could be more innocent than a wedding? "Just give me a wave when you're ready."

"Maybe we can slip into one of the meeting rooms." She beamed a smile at the other two men and dashed back to the table. "Hope you guys are having fun."

Curtis looked at Nick. "She's something else."

"I'm a lucky man."

"You'd better get your woman in line," Gregory said. "She's got the engineers from Underwood Oil all worried about their survey figures."

"As if I could control her," Nick said.

In twelve minutes, he'd escort Elena from this room into an elevator. Then, he'd take the elevator to the top floor. He'd already prepped the door to the roof. They'd step outside. The chopper would be waiting. And she'd lift off.

As quickly as possible, he'd come back for Sidney. Then, they were out of there. They'd take a cab directly to the airport.

"Does she really remember everything?" Gregory asked.

"Oh, yeah."

"After you're married, it'll be hard to put anything over on her."

"Why would I want to?"

His life with Sidney would be completely free and open, based on trust. There would be no secrets. No surveillance. Their whole life would be like last night, when they were free with each other.

Six minutes to go.

Curtis was looking at him as if he'd asked a question and wanted a response.

"Sorry," Nick said, "I didn't hear you."

"How long will you be stationed in Austin?"

"For a while. That's why we bought a house here."

"Does that mean you won't be traveling as much?" Curtis asked.

Why did he care? Nick wondered if Curtis was trying to strike up a friendship. "Are you stationed in this area?"

"I live in Dallas," he said.

The time for conversation was over. Nick had to put his plan into effect. He looked across the room to where Sidney sat beside Elena, waiting for his signal. He gave her a nod.

"I'll see you guys later," he said. "I need to go talk about weddings."

Though he strolled casually through the tables,

he felt people watching him. Hawthorne's gaze had been disapproving from the moment she saw him without the cane she had provided for him. Hurtado glared with distaste. Nick glanced to the left and, for an instant, made eye contact with Lieutenant Butler, who quickly looked away. There was only one relatively friendly face, and that was Special Agent Sean Phillips, who didn't seem to be in the room.

Nick paused beside Sidney and Elena. "Ladies."

Sidney did the talking. "Elena, we have something to ask you. In private."

"Very well." She patted her lips with her napkin and rose. "I'll be back in a moment."

He escorted Sidney and Elena toward the elevators. A single uniformed marine, one of Butler's men, stood guard. The most direct escape would have been to hop on the elevator and ride to the top, but he knew better than to attempt a bypass on a marine with clear orders.

He brought the ladies down the hall, where they turned into a kitchen. This route—that Nick had found earlier—would add four minutes to their timing. "We need to hurry."

Sidney looked down at Elena's high-heeled platform shoes. "Can you move fast in those?"

"I've been running in heels since I was fourteen."

From the kitchen, they took an elevator all the

way to the basement of the hotel, then down a concrete corridor past a laundry, then back to the central elevators. They rode all the way to the fourteenth floor, one down from the roof.

In the hallway outside the elevator, Nick shepherded Elena into the stairwell. He turned to Sidney. "Stay here."

She nodded. "Be careful."

The doors to the second elevator swooshed open. Special Agent Curtis jumped out. He braced a Glock 17 in both hands. Before he could shoot, Nick pulled Sidney into the stairwell.

"What is it?" Elena demanded.

"We've been found out," Nick said.

"How?"

"Curtis must have planted a trace on one of us."

"Now what?"

"Up to the roof," he said as he drew his weapon from the holster at the small of his back. He pulled his second gun from his ankle and gave it to Sidney. "The door's open."

While the women climbed, he prepared to return fire. Curtis had the advantage. He had a door to hide behind. All Nick had going for him was a fierce will to live and pinpoint accuracy as a marksman. He liked his chances.

Chapter Eighteen

Sidney pushed open the door leading to the roof of the hotel. A burst of damp air slapped her in the face. The rain had stopped, but the gravelly surface beneath their feet glistened with moisture and the clouds hung low.

There was no helicopter.

This can't be right. Frantic, she scanned the skies and the roof. *No chopper.* They were trapped up here with no place to go and Curtis closing in.

Sweet, carrot-top Curtis was the traitor. It made sense. He had access to all communication and could easily alert anyone to where they were and what plans had been made. Had he intercepted the texts from Nick's cell phone? Had he led them to this place?

"Sidney, where do we go?"

She didn't know what to tell Elena. Sidney wasn't supposed to be here. She wasn't part of the plan.

From the stairwell, she heard the ricochet of gunfire.

She stared at the Glock in her hand.

In her shooting lessons, she learned that she didn't have to release the safety on this model. All it took was a squeeze of the trigger. Though her hands were trembling, she was careful to hold the weapon so it wouldn't accidentally discharge.

Should she return to the staircase? Could she help Nick? *Too many questions.* There wasn't time for her to examine the situation from every angle and come up with a rational conclusion. She needed to go with her instincts.

But she had no instinct when it came to battle. She imagined what Nick would tell her to do. He'd want her to fulfill the mission. Sidney shook off her panic. "This way, Elena."

Sure-footed in her high heels, Elena dashed onto the rooftop. "Where?"

"Over here." She pointed toward a metal vent that opened onto the roof. It was closer to the concrete circle for the heliport. "We'll hide behind this."

"Do you have another weapon?"

"No." Sidney was carrying her purse but was armed with nothing more lethal than a fingernail file. She didn't even have another ammunition clip for the gun. That meant she had only fourteen or fifteen rounds. Every bullet needed to count.

The door to the roof opened, and Nick dived through. He went to the left, found a ledge to hide behind and prepared to return fire. Sidney did the same, bracing her wrist and staring down the barrel. Her vision blurred. She shook her head and squinted hard. She wasn't much good at this, but Nick was a sharpshooter. All marines had high rankings in marksmanship, but he was better than most. He had an award for accuracy.

She hoped that would make a difference. Not that gunning down Curtis would get them home free. He had to be working with somebody else. There would be others with guns. They might be gathering right now, behind that door, waiting to swarm onto the rooftop.

A cold wind blew against her cheeks, causing her eyes to water. Sidney was trying her best to hold steady, but her fears multiplied by the second. Then she heard the most beautiful sound, the *thwhump-thwhump* of the helicopter blades.

"It's coming," Elena cried out. "The chopper."

The door from the hotel opened, and Curtis charged through. Two other armed men followed him. They were all bundled up in Kevlar vests while she and Elena wore flimsy skirts and dresses. Almost without aiming, Sidney fired a shot to let them know she meant business.

Nick fired twice. One of the men with Curtis went down, clutching his leg. The other two spread out. Curtis was closest to her.

He'd probably chosen his position strategically, knowing that she was inexperienced with weapons. She hated that he knew her well enough to make that judgment. During the time when they'd been talking in the surveillance room, she'd thought they were bonding and had so much in common. If she'd known his true character, she would have strangled him instead of giving him a neck massage.

The chopper was coming closer.

To Elena, she said, "As soon as the door opens, make a run for it."

"I don't want to leave you," she said. "Come with me."

"I will."

Jumping into the chopper seemed like the best way to get off the roof. Sidney didn't like the odds of surviving in a shootout, and she wasn't going to risk leaping off the roof onto the terrace swimming pool they'd seen two stories below.

The helicopter touched down with blades still circling. The side door swung open. Gunfire erupted from inside. A heavily armed man leaped out and rushed toward them.

Nick dodged across the roof, shooting as he came closer.

The man from the chopper grabbed Elena. Shielding her with his body, he carried her to safety. She was inside the helicopter.

Sidney tried to aim her weapon for one last shot before she ran to join Elena. But she couldn't see Curtis. She leaned out from behind the vent.

The gun was slapped from her hand. An arm circled her waist, pinning her arm to her side. She felt the bite of cold steel against the side of her neck. Curtis had her. She'd been caught.

"Don't move," he growled.

"No." She wouldn't go quietly. This was Curtis. He wasn't a big man. She could fight him.

Her free arm lashed out, and she hit his vest. She twisted in his grasp, struggling to free herself.

A blinding pain exploded on the right side of her face. Her head jerked back. For an instant, the world turned black. But she didn't pass out. Being unconscious would have been preferable to the throbbing hurt. My God, had he broken her jaw? She reached up and touched her face. Her fingers came back wet with blood. He'd hit her with his gun, hit her with force.

He yanked her upright. "Do what I say, and I won't kill you."

She wished she could have made a brave or clever response, but it was all she could do to stand without having her knees buckle. She'd never been hit by another person. There were injuries. Bumps and bruises from car accidents. Sports injuries. But never an assault. This was a new experience for her memory. She hoped it wasn't the last thing her brain recorded.

She looked across the roof at Nick. He stood facing them with his gun aimed at Curtis.

"Don't make me shoot her," Curtis yelled over the noise of the helicopter. For emphasis, he poked his gun into her neck.

"Let her go."

"If you get Elena back down here, I'll let Sidney go."

"Not going to happen." Shoulder hunched, Nick kept moving. "Put down your gun, and I won't kill you."

"You won't take a chance," Curtis said. "You might hit Sidney."

"That was your last warning," Nick growled.

Curtis dragged her behind the vent. He exhaled a wheezing noise, almost as though he was crying. "Sorry, Sidney. This isn't personal."

"It feels real damn personal." The chopper lifted a few feet off the roof. She saw her chance for escape floating away. "Why are you doing this?"

"Money. I'm getting paid a lot."

"Who's paying you?"

"Unbelievable." He tapped the gun against her

skull and scoffed. "You're trying to interrogate me. Don't you get it, Sidney? Game over. You lose."

"Whatever you're getting paid isn't worth it," she said. "Put down the gun."

"And spend the rest of my life in prison? That's not for me."

"You could get a deal." Was she actually trying to reason with a man who held a gun to her throat? "Please, Curtis. This isn't like one of your video games. When you die, you won't get a new set of bullets and a fresh start."

She looked down and saw red spatters of her blood smearing his sleeve. Each thud of her pulse drove home the pain. She wasn't crying, but her eyes watered.

Curtis leaned close. His breath was hot on her ear. "Do you really think Nick will kill me?"

"He's a marksman. You know that."

"I've heard. He's the kind of guy who can shoot the wings off a fly at fifty yards."

"Something like that," she said. "He trained with the SEALs."

Just then a shot whizzed by Curtis's head. A warning shot from Nick. The next one wouldn't miss.

"I'm sorry." Curtis, obviously realizing he had no choice, placed his gun on the rooftop. He raised his hands above his head and stood.

As soon as she was free, Sidney ran toward Nick. The pain was so intense that she felt nothing else. All she knew was that her legs were moving.

A spray of bullets exploded. She looked over her shoulder.

Curtis had been shot, not by Nick but by his own man. She heard herself cry out. She wanted to help him, to save him. But it was too late.

Nick grasped her arm and propelled her toward the chopper that had been circling. *Thwhump-thwhump*, the noise was overwhelming. She could see Elena through the door, beckoning her forward. The men in the chopper reached for them. Nick pushed her forward and someone caught her arm. They were pulled inside.

As the helicopter ascended, she looked down at the rooftop, where Curtis lay sprawled on his back. Dark blood circled his head. He shouldn't have had to die.

A DAY LATER, Sidney was still disoriented, maybe even more so. She and Nick had left the drab, rainy weather in Texas. They were on their way to their mountain retreat, the pot of gold at the end of the rainbow.

Bundled up in a brand-new parka and jeans, she leaned back in the passenger seat of an incredibly comfortable SUV and stared through the windshield at a clear, blue Colorado sky above glistening, snowcapped peaks. Her jaw wasn't broken but the entire right side of her face was swollen and bruised, which meant that—once again—she was taking painkillers that didn't help with her mental clarity.

She glanced over at Nick, who seemed to know exactly where he was going and what he was doing. Smiling for no reason, he hummed along with a twangy tune from his never-ending country-and-western playlist. She surprised him by singing along on the chorus.

"Whoa," he said. "How did you learn that?"

"I worked as a barmaid at a saloon. I probably know more of these songs than you do."

"But do you love them?" he asked.

She was more drawn to the almost mathematical precision of classical music, but she had to admit that she loved the outright emotional sentiment of country-and-western songs.

Changing the subject, she said, "How'd you hear about this cabin?"

"I told you before."

"Yeah, well, my brain isn't really working at tip-top condition."

"No prob. All you have to do is sit there and look pretty."

She touched her bruise. "Like the bride of Frankenstein."

"The cabin belongs to a friend of a friend. It's a little two-bedroom on the edge of a national forest with good trails for cross-country skiing or snowmobiling. I brought enough food and wine to last us for a week."

"I don't care about food," she muttered. No way would she attempt chewing with her sore face. This time, the stitches were below her jawline. "Not unless it's ice cream or soup."

"You're lucky they didn't wire your mouth shut."

"Real lucky."

Though tired, she kept her eyes open. Whenever she dozed, her memory replayed on an endless loop. She saw Curtis dying on the rooftop over and over and over again. Nothing she could do to stop it. No way she could change fate.

"You're thinking about him," Nick said.

"He said he'd gotten a lot of money. I wish I knew who was paying him off."

"It's not our problem. I fulfilled my orders, which were to deliver Elena to the people who will protect her."

She cast a suspicious eye in his direction. "And who are those people?"

"The good guys," he said, purposely evasive.

"What's going to happen to her?"

"Again, it's not my problem. Elena needed to get out from under her husband's control, and we provided an escape. What happens now is up to her."

"But wouldn't you like to have all the details tied up in a neat little package with a bow on top?"

He shrugged. "Life isn't so tidy. We made a small step forward for the people of Tiquanna by rescuing their first lady. Though I'm not so sure they'll see it that way. But it's enough for me."

Something about his involvement in this whole situation bothered her, but she couldn't exactly figure out why. Maybe later. Or maybe not. They had a week for themselves, plenty of time to get their lives as an engaged couple back on track.

Nick followed GPS directions, turning off the highway into an old-growth forest where the road narrowed to a two-lane that climbed in hairpin turns. They crested the summit above the timberline for a panoramic view. The pinkish tinge of sunset colored the cumulus clouds above the mountaintops.

She sighed at the sheer beauty of the landscape. Colorado was the place they would come to heal. What else could possibly go wrong?

Chapter Nineteen

After Nick got her settled on a plaid, overstuffed sofa and built a cheery fire, he unloaded their luggage and food. Their escape off the rooftop in the chopper meant they had to leave all their belongings behind. Sooner or later, those things might be returned to them after the CIA had the chance to study each garment and toothbrush. He didn't really care. Except for the engagement ring, which she'd been wearing, the rest of it was just stuff.

He wasn't sure what part all the different people had played in Elena's rescue but was informed that his future liaison would be Special Agent Sean Phillips, who was acceptable to both the CIA and the elite Marine Corps Undercover Intelligence Agency, MCUIA, that had initially sent Nick to South America. His highly classified group trained with the SEALs and was deployed on special missions with wide-ranging responsibilities. They had no office, no meetings and no real chain of command.

When Nick first started working for MCUIA, he thought of himself as a spy among spies. His missions were clandestine, and he reported to no one. If he was found out, he was on his own without backup, and he liked the loner aspect.

Not anymore.

As he tiptoed across the front room of the cabin to the kitchen, he looked down at Sidney. Her eyes were closed, but he doubted she was sleeping. The brutal death of Curtis affected her deeply. She wasn't the kind of person who bounced back and returned to battle in the blink of an eye.

He regretted her involvement. Her poor face was badly bruised, and she'd been shot. If he could have taken the pain for her, he would have. Her injuries were his fault. The danger of his life had boiled over, and she'd gotten burned. This wasn't the way he wanted to live.

Not anymore.

She deserved better, and so did he. They ought to be able to build a satisfying life, to have kids and a garden and a collie dog named Rex. He was done with spying, being surrounded by people he couldn't trust, holding on to secrets that didn't matter to him.

As soon as Sidney was feeling better, he'd tell

her about his real job. She wasn't going to like the fact that he'd kept things from her. She was all about truth and trust.

After he put away their clothing, he turned up the propane heater in the bedroom and made the bed with extra blankets to ward off the night chill. His cell phone buzzed.

He answered, "I didn't think I'd get reception here."

"Sorry about that," said Special Agent Phillips in his Texan drawl. "How are you and Sidney doing?"

Phillips was a friendly guy, but he hadn't called to check on the state of their health, and Nick didn't have the patience to chat. "What do you need?"

"Elena and Avilar want to meet with y'all."

Nick glared at the phone. He truly cared for Elena Hurtado and believed that her intervention had probably saved his life when he was a hostage. But this had to end. "When?"

"Tomorrow at noon. They'll come to you."

"Not here," Nick said. "I want our cabin to be private."

"And were you thinking that your little hideaway is secret and untraceable?"

In a world filled with GPS satellites, surveillance cameras, drones and liars on every corner, Nick had no illusions about disappearing. If someone wanted to find him, they could. "Hell, you're right. Send them here."

"And there's one more thing you should know." Phillips cleared his throat. "Hawthorne's gone off the grid."

"Not working for the CIA anymore?"

"She hightailed it out of Austin when Curtis was shot. We don't have all the pieces put together, but I'm going to go ahead and assume that the two of them were working together."

"Who was paying them?"

"That part, I don't know."

"What a shame that she's gone, flown off on her broom." Nick grinned. "Are you going to miss her?"

"Like a bad case of the flu."

"What about Hurtado?"

"The president is still in Austin, still chatting up the executives from Underwood Oil. The politicians are putting distance between themselves and the current government of Tiquanna, but the money people have already made some commitments."

Diplomacy and deal making were two parts of the job that Nick could do very well without. "Good luck with all the crazy people."

"I'm going to need it."

In the front room of the cabin, Nick considered what Phillips had said about the lack of privacy.

A certain amount of danger came in the aftermath of his assignments. He needed to make sure that he and Sidney would be safe. Tomorrow morning, he'd set up some basic protections.

Firelight shone on Sidney's face as she opened her eyes and looked up at him. "Who were you talking to?"

"Phillips." He sat on the coffee table next to the sofa and took her slender hands in his. "How are you feeling?"

"My stomach is growling, but I don't think I can chew anything without busting into tears."

He smoothed her straight blond hair and kissed her forehead. "I'll heat up soup. Chowder or tomato?"

"Tomato with crackers broken up in it."

Taking care of her made him feel warm inside. It was a different kind of heat from the sensual fire when they kissed or when his hands slid over her sweet, soft skin. This gentle glow felt innocent, almost pure. This was the kind of warmth that lasted.

She tried to smile. Instead, she winced and put her hand to her cheek. "What did Phillips have to say?"

"We're going to have visitors tomorrow. Elena and Miguel Avilar."

"How does this work with the CIA? How can

they be friendly with both Hurtado and Avilar when they're on opposite sides?"

She was still trying to figure out who were the good guys and who were the bad. In politics and in spycraft, those answers changed without logic or reason. Truth was ephemeral. Loyalty was nearly nonexistent. "Don't try to figure it out in your condition. It'll just make your head hurt."

"Elena and Miguel seem like a, um, nice couple."

"Sure they are," he said, "if you ignore the fact that he sometimes blows up helicopters and she has ambitions to rule the world."

She exhaled a sigh. "I'm glad we're not them. We don't have secrets."

He was going to have to tell her. All he could do was hope that she'd forgive him.

THE NEXT MORNING, Sidney took her time waking up. She'd cut back on her pain meds enough that she could distinguish three separate centers of hurt. The one on her jaw where Curtis hit her with the butt of his gun was the worst, and the bruising looked like hell. No amount of makeup would cover the purple fading to a sickly yellowish color. The stitches also hurt. And there was the continual light drumming of a headache.

At least her hunger pangs had faded. She'd lost some weight, not that she could tell from the fit of her new clothes. All she'd worn since they left Austin were shapeless sweatpants and turtlenecks. And today she'd be seeing the perfect Elena. That should be enough to slash her self-confidence to ribbons. Sidney decided that her big project for the day would be to get out of bed and get dressed.

Step one: out of bed. She flung her legs over the edge, took a moment to stabilize when she was standing and went to the window. Last night, it had snowed, and the surrounding hillsides were crusted with glistening white. Such a beautiful setting. Being here was exactly what she needed.

Nick came into the bedroom with a tray of oatmeal. "Morning, sunshine."

She pointed to her mouth. "Imagine that I'm giving you a great big smile."

"There are a couple of other things I'd like to imagine your mouth doing."

"Don't make me laugh."

"Where do you want your oatmeal?"

"The kitchen?"

"There's a little something I want to try in the bedroom first." He set down the tray on top of the dresser and guided her toward the bed. "I can't keep my hands off you."

"No kissing," she said.

"None for you," he murmured. "There's nothing wrong with my jaw."

Not with his jaw or his lips or his tongue. He lowered her onto her back on the bed and kissed the hollow below her chin. While she was distracted by the ripples of sensation that spread from each kiss, he unbuttoned the top of her pajamas to bare her breasts.

As gentle as rain, he kissed her tender flesh. His caresses were pure tenderness. Her response was all out of proportion. Her heart pumped too fast. She gasped. Her face throbbed.

"I don't want you to stop." She moaned. "But you have to stop. I could have a heart attack."

He rose quickly from the bed, and she missed him.

"As soon as you're ready," he said.

"I am," she said miserably. "But I'm not."

"Oatmeal first."

She followed him down the hallway and past the front room, where a fire flickered on the hearth. He placed the tray on the kitchen table and sat. "Is it better for you to move around or stay in bed?"

"I'm not sure." She was one of those people who never got sick. It had been only a couple of days, but she felt as if she'd been wiped out forever. She settled herself at the kitchen table and scowled. "I hate being an invalid."

"I like taking care of you, watching you while you're sleeping. It feels peaceful."

She dug her spoon into the oatmeal, took a bite and turned her gaze on him. "I'm just beginning to figure out that you haven't had much peace in your life. Right after college, you enlisted. Since then, you've been a soldier."

"That wasn't long after nine-eleven," he said. "Being a marine seemed like the right thing to do. No regrets."

There were few things in her life that she'd felt so certain about. She envied his decisive nature. "Today, I'm going to get dressed. Maybe even take a walk."

"No rush. I talked to your office before we left Austin, and your boss said you should take all the time you need."

"You talked to my boss?" She dipped her spoon into the oatmeal. "What did you tell him?"

"Just a quick recap. You'd been shot by terrorists, stayed in a CIA safe house and escaped off the roof of a hotel in a chopper."

She imagined the head of engineering at Texas Triton going into shock. "Did he believe you?"

"I actually told him you'd been injured and needed a little time to recuperate. I thought you should entertain the gang at the office with the tales of Sidney Parker."

"That'll be fun. Anything I can't say, you know, because of national security?"

"Don't use real names," he advised.

"But how can I talk about Hurtado and Elena without saying who they are?"

"It gets complicated, doesn't it?"

She finished her breakfast, took a leisurely bath and got dressed in a pair of black jeans, hiking boots and a sweater. By the time she and Nick took a short walk along the road outside the cabin, it was approaching the time when Elena and Miguel would arrive.

Sidney was content to sit at the kitchen table and watch while Nick put together a plate of sliced cheese and sausage and crackers. She reached for a cracker. "What else have you got for me?"

"Yogurt with blueberries."

"Yum."

With his sweater pushed up to his elbows, she could see the interplay of muscles in his forearms and the efficient movements of his large masculine hands. She remembered the skill and creativity in those hands when he made love to her. Oh yeah, she was definitely on the road to recovery. Maybe tonight…

The former first lady of Tiquanna and her companion arrived with zero fanfare in a black SUV. With her luxurious black hair pulled up in a simple ponytail, Elena looked almost like a regular person, except that her knee-high black leather boots were high-heeled, and her parka was lined with faux fur that was as thick and shiny as mink.

Avilar trailed behind her. He carried a briefcase and a laptop, which he placed on the kitchen table in front of Sidney. Apparently, they weren't going to waste any time on niceties. Elena was a woman with a purpose. When she sat at the table, Sidney felt energy and ambition radiating from her.

"This isn't a social visit," Sidney said.

"So much has happened so quickly." Elena glanced up at Nick. "There was a question you asked dozens of times, a question that didn't seem to have an answer."

He gave a curt nod. "Where did the rebels get their money and their weapons?"

She looked to Avilar. "Tell him."

"My family," he said. "When my father left Tiquanna, he had amassed a fortune. The same was true for my uncles and my cousins."

"Money that you failed to report," Nick said.

"Yes." His jaw tightened. "With offshore accounts and other investments, my family's wealth is nearly untraceable. We needed it all, every peso, to finance the rebellion and take our country back from Hurtado."

"Why keep it secret?" Sidney asked.

"Two reasons," Nick explained. "The first has to do with taxes and international monetary policies that are far too complex for me to comprehend or explain. The second, and more important reason, is perception. The rebels of Tiquanna wouldn't want to be recruited into another rich man's army. Avilar wanted to appear as one of them."

"They believed in me," he said. "And I didn't fail them. With Elena at my side, we can still take back our country."

Sidney could tell that Nick was angry. He had expected more transparency from Avilar.

"There is another source of money," Elena said. "I believe Sidney can tell us where it comes from."

They turned expectantly toward her, but she wasn't sure she wanted to play this game. If she helped them, where would it lead? When would it end?

Chapter Twenty

Nick saw Sidney's hesitation. He wanted to get out of the espionage business, not to be drawn deeper in. "Stop right there, Elena."

"Why?" She spread her hands wide in appeal. "Surely you want to help us."

"I expect you'll be a better leader than Hurtado," Nick said. After the time he'd spent with Elena in Tiquanna, he knew she wanted schools and roads, clean water and medical facilities for her people. Her heart was in the right place, but she wasn't a saint. She also wanted wealth and power. "I don't want to be part of setting off a civil war. Your country is a powder keg about to explode. People will be hurt."

"People already have been hurt," Sidney said. "Curtis is dead. He was prepared to surrender, and he was shot."

"All I ask," Elena said, "is for Sidney to use her expertise."

One little favor. That was how it started. Nick

knew better than to get Sidney involved. "Find another way."

"Wait a minute." Sidney gestured to the documents and the laptop that Avilar had set on the table. "If all I have to do is interpret some statistics, I can handle that."

"So can dozens of other people," Nick said. "Elena needs to start building her own connections in the field of oil exploration. If she needs to use you, she should go through your company."

"There isn't time. Please," Elena pleaded. "My husband is already in bed with Underwood Oil. The meetings in Austin are continuing. By the time he returns to Tiquanna, there may be final agreements."

"How can you stop them?" Nick asked.

"By showing the prior surveys and projections are invalid," Sidney said. "From the very start, I wondered about Underwood's enthusiasm. When Texas Triton checked out Tiquanna, we decided it wouldn't be profitable without significant investment from Hurtado on the infrastructure."

"Please, Sidney. You're the only one who can help," Elena said. "Do you remember those original figures?"

"I remember everything."

Sidney sat up straighter in her chair. Her injuries had weakened her, but she was still ready to respond to a challenge. Nick hoped she wasn't opening a can of worms.

She took a folder from the briefcase. "Give me some time and space to go through this stuff."

Nick shepherded Elena and Miguel outside onto the porch of the cabin. The skies were clear and the temperature rising. It was one of those brilliant Colorado days that hid the potential for danger. Snowfall had been heavy for this early in the winter season, and there was a solid base under eighteen to twenty-four inches of new snow at the top.

Earlier, he'd surveyed the area, determining how best to protect their cabin. Though sheltered by forest, the little one-story house faced a steep, open slope. A blast of gunfire into the air might trigger an avalanche. He hoped he wouldn't need to resort to that tactic.

On the porch, Elena confronted him. "Why do you oppose me?"

"You're my friend. I want the best for you." He glanced at Avilar. "I'm not so sure of you, but if she trusts you, I'm willing to forget our differences in the past."

She braced her fists on her hips and tossed her head. The woman just couldn't help posturing. Sidney referred to Elena as a diva, and that description was accurate.

Elena snapped, "You tried to get Sidney to say no."

"I'm getting out of the political game," he said. "I don't want anything more to do with it. I'm neutral. Call me Switzerland."

She lowered her voice. "You will no longer be a spy."

"No more." He owed Sidney that much.

"We suspect Special Agent Gregory of being involved with Underwood Oil. He has disappeared. I wouldn't be surprised if he's already in Tiquanna."

That made two on the run: Gregory and Hawthorne. Gregory didn't worry Nick much. The guy was a pencil pusher, looking for a safe place to hide. But Hawthorne was unpredictable. She'd lost status, control and position. At this point, she had to be desperate.

"Will you two return to Tiquanna?" he asked.

"Not until it's safe," she said. "Miguel's family has offered to protect me, and I have many contacts in the US."

She would build her power base here, a smart move. He had no doubt that Elena would land on her feet. In a few years, she might be running the show in Tiquanna.

"And you?" she asked. "What are your plans?"

"First thing," he said, "a border collie named Rex."

SIDNEY PICKED OUT enough data from the surveys and charts they'd brought to indicate areas where further study might be needed. Some of the issues were highly technical and would require the type of thorough research done in development. Others were obvious mistakes.

"Mileage," she said as she pointed to a map. "The distance between the drilling field and the processing facility is twice what's indicated, which means that the cost will be double the estimate. It wouldn't hurt to check all the roads. And estimate the need for freshwater."

"Infrastructure," Elena said.

"Exactly." Sidney refolded documents. "Tiquanna is a beautiful country rich in resources, but it is largely undeveloped. Not to mention there are many restrictions about maintaining the natural rain forest."

"Hurtado has done a poor job," Avilar said.

"And you have a chance to do it right." Sidney met his dark-eyed gaze. "I'd advise you to seek the opinions of experts in the US and around the world. When I was in Tiquanna, I noticed that the main requirement for being appointed to a political position was being loyal to the dictator."

"It's true," Elena said. "We need educated advisers. Instead of rushing into expensive mistakes, we need to be wise."

"You're already a step ahead," Nick said. "You know people who can be trusted."

The diva pulled an exaggerated frown. "I wish the two of you would join us."

"Only as tourists," he said.

After Elena and Miguel drove away in their SUV, Sidney sat on the porch with a mug of steaming coffee in her hands. The afternoon sun reflected off the snowy slope and warmed her injured face. In her puffy green parka, she felt comfy and cozy. But not contented.

Too many issues had arisen during the past few days. Just as Elena and Miguel needed answers, Sidney had persistent questions. And Nick was the only one who could answer them.

He joined her on the porch. On the wood table between their two rocking chairs, he set down the plate of cheese and crackers. She picked up a flavorful sesame cracker and let it dissolve in her mouth.

"By tomorrow," she said, "I should graduate to soft food."

"Mashed peas and pudding?"

"Disgusting," she grumbled.

"Warm enough?"

"I'm fine. I like being out here." She didn't want to be angry at Nick, but she couldn't keep ignoring these questions, these voices in her head. "I think I did the right thing by giving that information to Elena. All I really did was point out the truth."

"But now it's over," he said. "I don't want her or Avilar to get the idea that you're working for them."

She nodded. "You're right. They need their own experts and advisers. Not me. And not you, either."

"Nope."

"When you told Elena she already knew people she could trust, were you talking about your handlers?"

"Yes." He was terse.

Technically, she'd met his superiors. When she was scooped off the rooftop in the chopper, Sidney had entered Nick's world. There were men dressed like SWAT officers, people shouting orders into headsets and a medical person. She wished she'd been more alert. Everything was a frantic blur of action, pain and the constant *thwhump-thwhump* of the blades. The painkillers had pretty much knocked her unconscious. "Who were they?"

"Is this one of those good-guy-or-bad-guy questions?"

"No, I'm sure they were good guys. They helped us. And they didn't fire the bullet that killed Curtis." That was important to her. She hated that he'd been gunned down before he had a chance to change his mind. "There were a lot of them."

"Mostly marines," he said.

"Would it help me understand if I knew their names or job titles?"

"Probably not."

He was dancing around the issue, trying to keep from telling her anything, but this time she wouldn't be easily assuaged. This time, she would pin him down.

She paused for a moment, organizing her thoughts.

"Here's the thing, Nick. I really don't understand what you do. I know you're an ace marksman. And I know that you're given orders that must be followed. But I don't know who you're working for."

"I could say the same about you and your work."

"What?" She turned her head so quickly that her jaw hurt. "There's nothing mysterious about my job."

"You seldom talk about it."

"My projects are detail-oriented and, if you aren't familiar with the technology, you'd be bored to death with an explanation. Nobody wants to hear the various processes that make the engine in their car work. They just want to turn the key and have the ignition start."

"I could say the same."

"And I wouldn't believe you." She stared down into her coffee. "There's a reason you aren't telling me. You're keeping secrets. I saw it in your eyes when we met at CIA headquarters. You don't trust me."

"Oh, hell, no. That's not even close."

"Why else would you lie to me?"

She could feel their relationship coming apart. Huge chunks broke off and floated away. Had he lied when they first met? Were any of his assignments the truth?

"Not lies," he said.

"Were you in Afghanistan when you told me you were?"

"Most of the time."

But not always. "Were you assigned to an embassy in Paris?"

"No."

"What about Cuba?" she demanded. "Did you go to Cuba?"

"Yes."

"I don't want to sort through our life, picking out what's true and what's not." She surged to her feet. "Tell me your job, Nick. What the hell do you do?"

He stood to face her. "I'm a field officer in the Marine Corps Undercover Intelligence, trained with the navy SEALs. My assignments are highly classified, covert and undercover. I have only one handler. Other than that person, I work alone."

"So…a spy."

"I think of my work as research, gathering intel."

"Why were you really in Tiquanna?"

"I knew I'd be taken hostage, but I didn't expect to be gone for more than a month."

Rage flared inside her. "You knew and you didn't tell me? You put me through hell."

"I wouldn't do that to you." His voice was sincere but his intentions meant nothing. "There have been other times when I didn't contact you for as much as a week."

"So what?"

"You weren't supposed to hear about the hostage situation. I was supposed to get in and get out. I needed to infiltrate the rebels and find out where they were getting their weapons. Something went wrong. Instead of hanging around with Avilar's crew, Hurtado's men took over. The hostage situation and the beatings turned real. I had no escape."

The level of danger in his work was extreme. If she'd known, she would have worried about him night and day. "So, everybody lied."

He reached toward her. "I didn't want you to be upset."

She slapped his hand away. "Why would you take such a risk?"

"I'm careful. I know how to interrogate and negotiate. I have all the skills."

"And you love the work," she said.

In a horrible way, she understood why a man like Nick would thrive on this kind of challenge. If they were walking down the street and he saw a house on fire, he'd run *toward* the flames and try to rescue the people inside. He was smart and strong and brave. He'd been trained to penetrate behind enemy lines.

She turned her back on him. Suddenly cold, she returned to the house and stood in front of the dying embers of the fire. Nick was the sort of man she admired. He was everything a woman could dream about...a real-life hero.

And she couldn't marry him. She couldn't live with that kind of fear, knowing that he was putting his life on the line. Was it really so different from being a soldier? Yes, it was. In Nick's line of work, he had no backup, no one else he could turn to. And the threat was constant. If he was found out, he'd be killed as quickly as Curtis was shot down on the rooftop.

She couldn't endure the ever-present danger.

She knew what she must do.

"I shouldn't have told you," he said from behind her.

"By all means, keep lying to me." She huffed. "You know how I love that."

"It's over, Sidney." He stepped up close behind her. "Tiquanna was my last field assignment. I won't be going undercover anymore. My focus will be research."

She whipped around to face him. "Desk work?"

He gave a quick, curt nod. "I'm ready to settle down."

"Are you making this change because of me? Because we're getting married?" She took a few angry steps away from him and then back again. "I won't have it. I won't have you blaming me for quitting the work you love."

"It's my decision," he said. "I can't do this anymore."

Nor could she. Sidney was done with his elaborate deceptions. She knew he could never change. And she wouldn't force him to. But there would be no desk job in his future and she couldn't live like that. She tore the pi diamond off her finger and slapped it into his hand.

"Goodbye, Nick."

Chapter Twenty-One

Sidney adjusted the seat in the SUV, fastened her seat belt and drove away from the cabin. She hadn't packed her suitcase and didn't have any idea of her destination. She knew only that she had to put miles between herself and Captain Nick Corelli or else she would shatter into a million pieces that could never be put together again.

She didn't want to hear his rumbling baritone voice, speaking excuses that she would never believe. It was all lies, every word he spoke. She could never trust him again.

She couldn't bear to see his thick black hair or to look into his golden eyes or to bask in the heat of his smile. Touching him was out of the question.

Her fingers drew into a fist, and she hammered on the dashboard. "You can't change who you are." He would always be a hero. And she would always miss him.

It was over, well and truly over. The past six

months had taught her what it was to live without him. She'd survive. She'd be miserable and lonely and painfully depressed. She'd want to curl up and die, but it wouldn't happen.

She drove along the twisting two-lane road into the forest and cut the engine. She was about two miles from the cabin, far enough that he couldn't see her. *Where am I going? What am I doing?* She was still taking painkillers, shouldn't be operating a vehicle. As if that was a big risk? Nick routinely lived with more danger before breakfast than she experienced in a year.

She threw back her head and screamed as loudly as she could. The local wildlife would cover their ears and run away. Birds would drop from the trees. She screamed again.

Her throat vibrated. Her gut clenched.

Before leaving, she hadn't made any kind of plan with Nick, hadn't said she was going for a little drive and would be right back. Maybe she wouldn't return. She had her purse, her credit cards and her brand-new cell phone. Maybe she should point the SUV due west and keep driving until she hit the Pacific Ocean. Hawaii would be pleasant at this time of year.

She started the SUV and drove again, swooping above the timberline and then descending on the hairpin turns. It was darker on the shadowed side of the mountain, but there were a couple of hours to go before dusk.

At the edge of the forest, she hit the brake. Another SUV had pulled off on the side of the road. Elena and Miguel's car? Their front wheel was in a ditch. Had there been an accident?

Parked behind them, she climbed out of her car and gingerly approached. "Elena? Are you all right?"

The back window was shattered. Bullet holes pierced the rear fender. Both back tires were flat. The air bags had deployed in the front seats.

Sidney darted back to her car and dived behind the wheel. This was no accident. Elena and Miguel had been attacked. She yanked her cell phone from her purse. Call 9-1-1. That was the sane, sensible thing to do. Alert the police and get a search under way.

Her fingers hesitated above the phone. They had a better chance of survival if she called Nick. She hated what he did, but she'd be a fool to deny it.

His cell number was the only one on speed dial, and she tapped the number. Nick would know how to locate Elena and Miguel. He'd make sure they were all right.

She felt the impact of the first bullet hitting the back of the SUV at the same time she heard gunfire. She didn't think twice before throwing her SUV into gear, whipping a U-turn and heading back toward the cabin. Her only option was to run.

"Sidney?" His voice came over the phone. "Sidney, what's going on?"

She barked at the phone. "Elena and Miguel's SUV is in a ditch and all shot up. Somebody's chasing me."

"Where are you?"

"Not far. About six miles from the cabin at the twisty part of the road."

The back window exploded inward. She let out a scream.

"Sidney." His voice was harsh. "Sidney, concentrate."

She dropped the phone on the passenger-side seat. "I didn't fasten my seat belt."

"Don't worry about that now. Drive as fast as you can. Don't stop for anything."

Her foot tromped the accelerator. The SUV fishtailed around a curve but stayed on the road. Another bullet clanged against the side of the car.

Her hands gripped the steering wheel. Every muscle in her body was tense. "I'm scared, Nick."

"Keep driving. Don't stop for anything."

Finally, she hit an open stretch of road where she might be able to put distance between her SUV and the pursuers. She glanced in her rearview mirror. It was a blue truck behind her.

Someone leaned out of the passenger-side window brandishing a rifle.

More bullets smacked against the back of her vehicle. If she got to the summit of this hill, there was only a stretch of forest and then she'd be in the open field beside the cabin. She wasn't far, really. She might make it.

Her back tire was hit. The SUV wobbled, nearly out of control. She fought to keep it on the road. "Nick, they're shooting the tires."

"Keep going. You can make it."

In the thickly forested part of the route, she struggled to stay on the road. Her other tire was gone. She yanked the steering wheel.

The air bag deployed with a loud pop. The ignition died. These damn safety devices were killing her.

She fought her way free from the white powdery explosion, crawled across to the passenger side and shoved open the door. She grabbed the phone. "Nick, I'm on foot. In the forest."

She shoved the phone into the pocket of her parka. If he needed to track her later, he could use the GPS signal. *Why do I know that? Why do I have that knowledge at my fingertip?* Because I'm engaged to a spy. Not anymore, she corrected herself. That relationship was over. Or not…it might be best to postpone the breakup until after she'd escaped from whatever international criminals were trying to kill her.

She dashed into the forest. Her boots left clear tracks in the snow. It wouldn't be hard to find her or hunt her down like an animal.

"Give up, Sidney. You must be exhausted."

Hawthorne! She should have known that she wasn't through with that woman.

"Let's not waste time chasing each other. Especially since I know Nick isn't with you. You really don't have a chance."

Why wasn't she in pursuit? Probably because she didn't know if Sidney had a gun. It wouldn't hurt to bluff. She yelled back, "Don't come any closer. I'll shoot."

"You've never actually shot another human being, have you?"

"You'd be my first, Hawthorne."

Sidney charged deeper into the forest but kept the road in sight. If she somehow managed to escape, she didn't want to be lost in the vast lands of the national forest.

When she looked over her shoulder, she saw the shadowy silhouette of a tall man coming after her. "Stop," she yelled at him. "I'll shoot."

He kept coming. She had nothing to protect herself, and there seemed to be no point in resisting. In a matter of minutes, he had yanked her hands behind her back and fastened her wrists with a zip tie.

She looked into his face. "You're one of Hurtado's guards. How could you leave him unprotected?"

"The president is safe," he said.

Hawthorne stepped forward. "And I needed the assistance of his guard."

Her hair was tucked up inside a black knit cap. She wore a black parka and matching pants with no discernible style. She gave the guard a friendly smile. Apparently, her style of leadership was different with the men of Tiquanna. Sidney didn't think she'd ever seen Special Agent Victoria Hawthorne grin at her CIA cohorts.

This was Vicky. Not Victoria. "You're different."

"How clever of you to notice! This is where I was meant to be, living my passion. I was always stifled in the CIA, dealing with all those petty bureaucrats. In Tiquanna, I'll flourish."

If she believed that, she was seriously delusional. Sidney figured there were lots of agencies waiting to press charges against Hawthorne for all kinds of treason and espionage. "You always looked happier when you talked about Tiquanna."

"Of course, I did." She beamed. "Tomas Hurtado is my lover."

Sidney wasn't sure what that meant for her,

and especially for Elena. But she assumed Hawthorne's new relationship with the dictator wasn't good news.

THAT MORNING, NICK had taken the time to explore the cabin and prepare for danger in case he needed to protect Sidney. Though he planned to quit his undercover work, old habits die hard. And his preparations were turning out to be necessary.

On the snowmobile he'd found in the shed behind the cabin, he sped across the open field toward the forest. Hoping against the odds, he desperately wished that he'd see Sidney and the SUV emerge onto the main road. No such luck.

He couldn't take the snowmobile much farther. It made too much noise. He'd alert whoever had grabbed her and attacked Miguel and Elena. His first guess was that Hawthorne was behind this attack. He didn't know why, but he figured she was playing out some twisted agenda to get herself back into power.

At the forest's edge, he abandoned the snowmobile and grabbed a set of snowshoes. Using these, he could quickly and silently move through the trees. In addition to the long-range rifle slung over his shoulder, he carried two handguns.

As soon as he heard voices, he dumped the snowshoes. His primary objective now was to move silently. He came into sight of Hawthorne, a bodyguard and Sidney with her wrists fastened behind her back.

Hidden in the trees, he was in control of this situation. With two quick gunshots, he could take out Hawthorne and her man. But if he shot them down in cold blood, Sidney would never forgive him. And it wasn't the way he wanted to operate.

Nick wasn't a killer. There were other undercover guys who were assassins, pure and simple. That had never been his thing. He was more of an analyst. His goal in this situation would be to protect Sidney and take the other two into custody.

Hawthorne was talking in a strangely animated voice. "At first, when I'm in the presidential compound, my presence will be clandestine and secret. Tomas and I will share the sultry tropical nights and the brilliant sunlight."

"Has this affair been going on for a long time?" Sidney asked.

"Over a year." Hawthorne chuckled. "Right under Elena's nose. Her husband preferred me to her with all her fancy designer clothes and costly jewelry. He wanted a real woman."

"You've got it all figured out," Sidney said.

"It might take a while to get right with the CIA, but I'll get all my pardons in order. And the oil will be flowing from Tiquanna. And Tomas will be the leader of one of the richest and more powerful nations in South America."

Nick had heard enough. Clearly, Hawthorne was whacked-out. No way would Hurtado protect her. Once he'd gotten the oil contracts he needed, Hawthorne would be tossed aside like last week's old news.

Anticipating her moves, Nick got into position. Somehow, he needed to make sure Sidney was out of the line of fire, deal with the hulking bodyguard and disarm the crazy lady. And if that failed, he could always shoot Hawthorne.

He dodged through the trees until he was standing closest to the driver's-side door. The bodyguard reached for the door handle. Nick waited. Timing was everything.

Then he stepped back into the forest. Someone else was approaching. He heard the vehicle. A beat-up sedan parked behind the truck. The three men who got out were dressed in camouflage and looked like hunters. They reported to Hawthorne.

Nick should have known that Special Agent Hawthorne would need an army at her command. She wasn't the kind of person to handle a single-person operation. Her backup would have backup.

A young blond man said, "No luck. We still can't find the woman."

"She didn't disappear into thin air," Hawthorne snapped. "Didn't you see those high-heeled boots she was wearing? How could she get away from you?"

"Her boyfriend was laying down some pretty serious gunfire. We couldn't get too close."

"Elena is the one I really want," Hawthorne said. "The rest of them are collateral damage."

Nick wished he'd taken the shot at her when he had the chance. Now he had to deal with more armed men and a widespread operation.

Chapter Twenty-Two

Sidney jostled along in the backseat of the sedan with one guard keeping a casual watch over her. With her wrists zip-tied behind her back, she felt vulnerable, but it was clear that she wasn't important as a hostage, nothing but collateral damage, as Hawthorne had said, in her crazy vendetta against Elena.

Vicky Hawthorne hadn't ever been a warm, thoughtful, kind person. The only glimmer of humanity came when she spoke of Tomas Hurtado, her dictator lover. Now she was completely ruled by her desire for vengeance.

Elena had caused her trouble. It wasn't difficult to be jealous of that gorgeous woman, but Elena's affront to Hawthorne was personal. Hurtado had loved Elena and married her. She would always have a place in his heart, no matter how hard Hawthorne tried to erase her.

Sidney wondered if her memory would haunt Nick's life. Would the women who came after her be curious? Sidney had wanted to know about his other women. In the interest of full disclosure, they'd talked about former lovers. Had he been telling her the truth?

She wanted to ask him. Their relationship couldn't really be over. There were too many loose ends. All she'd done was storm off in a huff. She wanted another chance.

The three men in the car with her were talking about dinner and how much they were getting paid for this job. It sounded as if they'd been recruited from the local population. This was a quick way to make extra bucks.

Their job was to return to the crash site for Elena's SUV and start searching again.

The young man beside her nudged her shoulder. "What happened to your face?"

"It ran into the butt of somebody's gun."

He gave an appreciative snort. In spite of his beard, he looked young. "Are you a spy like Vicky?"

"I'm an engineer. I work for an oil company."

Apparently, her job wasn't exciting enough for him to pay attention because he turned away. Fine with her. She wished she could make herself small enough and insignificant enough that they'd forget she was here.

When they parked behind the SUV with exploded air bags, she thought that was exactly what would happen. All the guys got out of the car and started talking about which way they should go to search. She ducked down in the seat and prayed that they'd forget she was here.

The bearded guy who had been sitting beside her poked his head into the backseat. "We didn't forget about you."

He picked her up, carried her around the car and dumped her in the trunk. There was nothing pleasant about riding in a trunk, especially since this one stank of oily rags and junk that had been tossed and forgotten. Like her. Tossed and forgotten.

She wriggled around, trying to find something she could use to cut the zip tie. There was a crowbar. No sharp edges on that tool. A Phillips screwdriver might work.

From outside the trunk, she heard Hawthorne giving orders on how to search in quadrants. The door to her truck slammed. Sidney heard it drive away. The voices of the young men faded as they set out on their search.

The stale air in the trunk settled around her. It was quiet. And cold, her hands were cold. The swollen bruise on her face hurt.

Then she heard someone fiddling with the lock on the trunk. Had the young men come back? Had they already found Elena? Her muscles tensed.

"Sidney, it's me. Don't say anything."

"Nick?" This was a miracle. "How did you…"

"Quiet," he said.

The trunk lid popped open. He reached inside, lifted her out and sat her on the snowy road behind the car. He closed the trunk and ducked down beside her. "Stay down so they won't see us."

"Get this zip tie off me."

He pulled a fierce-looking knife, serrated on one side, from a sheath and cut the tie. Her arms wrapped around him. She never wanted to let go. "How did you find me?"

"I hitched a ride in the back of Hawthorne's truck." He held her close. His lips nuzzled behind her ear. "We need to get out of here."

"How?"

"We've got a perfectly good car right here."

"Do you know how to hot-wire a car?"

"Yeah, I do. But it's hard with newer models, almost impossible. And not necessary." He dangled the keys in front of her. "Our boys aren't any too bright. They left the keys in the ignition. That's how I got you out of the trunk."

She dashed around to the passenger side and climbed in. As they drove away, she saw one of the young men in camo running after the car. "What do we do now?"

"This isn't the kind of single-person op I usually handle. There's nothing wrong with calling in backup." He passed her his cell phone. "Special Agent Phillips is number two on speed dial. Call him and bring him up to speed."

"And where are we going?"

"We could keep driving all the way to Denver and wait for this to blow over. Or we could get a room in Vail. Or we can do a little reconnaissance and see if we can find Hawthorne's hideout."

"I want to look for Hawthorne."

"You're sure?"

She couldn't bear the thought of Hawthorne hurting Elena and Miguel if she could help. "Don't get me wrong. I'm not a secret agent, but I'm loyal to my friends. If I can help Elena, I want to try."

"That's how you get hooked in," he said. "You make one attempt to help. Then another. Then you're stationed in Tiquanna pretending to be a hostage."

Helping Elena was pretty much the opposite of the stance Sidney had taken when she broke the engagement and ran away. Didn't she accuse him of being a liar in a nest of liars? Didn't she say she couldn't live with that sort of constant deception?

She exhaled a sigh. There would be time enough for apologies later.

NICK HEADED IN the direction he'd seen the blue truck going. Tracking through unmarked roads in the national forest was like following a maze. Some routes led to developments. Others circled around and were dead ends.

After Sidney got off the phone with Phillips, he said, "Look for roads with recent tracks through the snow. And see if you can spot the truck."

She glanced out the window. "We don't have a lot of daylight left. What makes you think she's got a hideout?"

"She left Miguel somewhere. He wasn't with the guys in this car and wasn't in the truck."

"So she must have more men and a place where she's holding him."

"Don't underestimate her. The woman is an evil genius."

He'd spent enough time with Hawthorne over the past several days to know that she planned each detail, and then planned it again. She'd make sure she had plenty of men, guns and vehicles.

"She might have already dumped the truck."

"What did Phillips say?" he asked.

"I really like him, you know. He's a good person and he actually has a sense of humor. If it turns out that he's double-crossing us, would you please not tell me?"

"You want to preserve the myth that there's at least one decent man on earth."

"It's not a myth."

When he looked at her, his cynical heart swelled and he wished that he could take a ride on her rainbow. He wanted to believe that they were going to get married and everything would be all right. He wanted it. But that didn't make it true.

"Anyway," she said, "Phillips is coordinating with local law enforcement, and he'll get back to us with names. He was going to try to get a search chopper in the air before nightfall. And he said that the next time we take a vacation, we might try for someplace less dangerous, like an active war zone."

Nick guided the sedan along a narrow road where heavy ruts were forming in the melting snow. The cabin at the end of the road was dark with no tracks leading to it. They could circle around here for a long time without finding Hawthorne.

And he didn't think the car would hold out that long. They were down to a quarter of a tank of gas, and the engine light showed it was running hot.

"New plan," he said. "Let's go back to the cabin and pack up our stuff. When Phillips calls, we'll get ahold of the people in charge and offer to help."

"Very sensible."

He drove away from the snarled back routes toward the main road. The drive to the cabin would take a solid twenty to thirty minutes, and he didn't think they could maintain silence that long.

They had touched on her rage. And she'd been the one to suggest going after Elena. But there was still the matter of the engagement ring that was burning a hole in his pocket.

"Sidney, is there something you want to say?"

"It's about the lies."

"I know."

"I won't have you lying to me. Never again. Even if you think I'm going to be mad, you've got to tell me the whole truth."

"Works both ways," he said.

"Truth, this had better be the truth." She leaned forward so she could make direct eye contact. "Will you miss being an undercover intelligence agent?"

Without a moment's hesitation, he nodded. "Hell, yes."

"I thought so."

"Most of the time, I'm just standing at attention in my uniform trying not to look bored. But there are moments…" His voice faded, unable to express the feeling. "…moments of sheer excitement. And there are exotic locations. And I'm using a specialized skill set."

"Why would you quit?"

"That's a whole different question." He paused, wanting to express himself clearly. "I know I'm jaded. I've seen too much on the dark side. But I also know that I'm a lucky man, been lucky all my life. I had a good family and good friends. I'm pretty good at most things. And I found you—the woman I love with all my heart."

"It's not just luck," she said.

"But luck plays a part. I've gotten out of more than my fair share of dangerous scrapes, and I figure that I've just about used up my share of luck. Someday, I'll leap off a burning building and my parachute won't open."

"Mathematically," she said, "the odds don't work that way."

"There's a reason I don't want to push my luck," he said. "Until now, until I had a future with you, I didn't care. Win, lose or draw, I could handle anything. But I can't stand the thought of losing you. No job is worth taking that risk."

She unfastened her seat belt so she could climb over the center console and kiss him. Her lips pressed against his cheek, and immediately she reacted. "Ouch."

"Your jaw isn't healed enough for kissing."

"Let me try again." Another tiny kiss. "Ouch. Ouch."

"Stop it, Sidney. There's a lot we can do besides kiss."

"But I can't wait to use my mouth again. For talking and laughing and eating, especially for eating." She hugged him. "I love you, Nick."

"And I love you, too."

A sense of peace wrapped around him in a warm embrace as he drove across the wide field. The long shadows of dusk slid down from the peaks and reached toward them. The bright blue of the sky faded to a softer, gentler color.

When he pulled up to the porch, Nick was tempted to settle in for the night and pretend that he and Sidney were living in a soft little world of their own. But he thought of safety first. He scoped out the area as well as he could.

"Let's get packed," he said. "Ten-minute drill."

"Aye, aye, Captain Corelli." She pulled open the front door and sauntered inside.

What was wrong with this picture? He was certain that he'd locked the front door before he left. He drew his gun from the holster at the small of his back as he entered.

Hawthorne leaned against the counter that

separated the kitchen from the front room. In her right hand, she held a small device.

"This," she said, "is a dead man's switch. In this case, a dead woman's switch. If I release this lever, the package of C-4 explosive sitting on the kitchen table will detonate."

Chapter Twenty-Three

Nick had to seize control of the moment. This wasn't about luck. It was training. He had to find the trigger, to figure out what made Hawthorne tick and what would make her back down.

The fading light through the windows emphasized the hollows on her face. She was so thin, skeletal. When she bared her teeth in a smile, the effect was gruesome. "I'm sure you're familiar with the concept of the dead man's switch, Nick."

"Every soldier in Afghanistan knows about the dead man's switch and IEDs."

"If you shoot me or startle me or cause me to let go of the lever, the immediate explosion will kill us all."

Keeping his distance from her so she wouldn't feel threatened, he sank into a chair near the door. He had been trained for situations exactly like this one. He knew what to do. "What do you want from us?"

"We're going to wait right here until Elena comes back."

Nick started with logic. "What makes you think she's coming back here?"

"She doesn't have anywhere else to go. The cars are destroyed. My men are patrolling, and it's getting cold. She won't spend the night outside. This cabin is her only sanctuary."

She'd given too much explanation, a sign that she was nervous about her decision, trying to justify it to herself. He needed to decide which buttons to push with Hawthorne.

"I should warn you," he said, "I've already put in a call to the special agent who replaced you on the task force. He'll be arranging the search."

"Who's replacing me?"

She sounded affronted, as though she was doing a good job and the CIA should be giving her a bonus. Nick figured that she was vulnerable to an attack of her professional pride. "Special Agent Sean Phillips got the job. Everybody thinks he'll do great."

"That dumb Texan? He can't handle this type of widespread operation. They'll be sorry that they didn't treat me better."

"You failed, Hawthorne. You got yourself kicked out of the CIA. If you die pulling off this stunt…and it's likely you will…you won't earn a star on the Memorial Wall. Special Agent Victoria

Hawthorne will be referred to as a cautionary tale about a woman who traded her career for love."

Her cheeks flushed a feverish red. Her eyes narrowed to angry slits. Nick had been going for an emotional response, and that was what he'd gotten. She whined, "Why would you say that to me? Do you have a death wish?"

"You're not going to let go of that lever," he said. He'd found her trigger. "Not until you get your revenge on Elena. She's the one who screwed up your plans."

"Damn right, she did. When Tomas and I met, it was love at first sight."

Nick played along with her. "Seeing Elena suffer is the only thing that matters. You don't want to die until you know she's dead, too."

"Don't push me, Nick."

"I get you. We're a lot alike." They were nothing alike, not in the least, but he needed for her to identify with him. He was her last, best friend. "You deserve your revenge."

"I do," she said.

Nick turned to Sidney. "I want you to turn around and walk out the door. Get some distance between yourself and the cabin."

Sidney's gaze flickered. He could tell that she didn't want to leave him.

"Don't you dare move another step," Hawthorne said.

"If you release the lever," Nick said, "you'll kill yourself and Elena will get off scot-free. Maybe she'll even go back to her husband."

"He'll never take her back." Spittle gathered in the corners of Hawthorne's mouth. "Go ahead, Sidney, get out of here. I never wanted to hurt you."

Sidney walked backward to the door. Her movements were slow and deliberate, nonthreatening. She was outside. She was safe.

Now it was Nick's turn.

He met Hawthorne's gaze. "You're going to let me go, too."

"Without you, I don't have a hostage. I have no leverage."

"The search helicopter is going to be here soon. They'll find Elena before you will. All she has to do is signal them."

A sob caught in Hawthorne's throat. "It's not right."

"It wasn't right when you tricked Curtis into helping you and then had him shot."

"I didn't have a choice," she said.

"What about Special Agent Gregory? He falsified documents. His career is destroyed."

"He did that on his own, thought he was being clever."

"You could have stopped him," Nick said. "Over

the past few days, there's been way too much talk about what's right or wrong, good or bad."

"Elena is bad. She might have you fooled right now, but she will destroy you all."

She took a step toward him, and he uncoiled from the chair, ready to make a dash through the open front door. "Leave the bomb here. Let's go. Both of us. Nobody has to die."

From outside, he heard a shout. He went through the door to the porch. Hawthorne was right beside him.

Elena was hiking through the snow, coming up the hill toward the cabin. Sidney ran to meet her, to stop her from taking another step.

"I figured it right," Hawthorne said. "I knew she'd come back here. And now, I'll watch her die."

What the hell was she talking about? Elena was out of range for an explosion from the cabin. Nick stepped off the porch. He felt the snow move under his feet. The earth trembled.

He looked up at the ridge of snow that perched on the mountains above the steep field. It was moving. He started running toward Sidney.

Hawthorne dashed into the trees. She threw the dead man's switch. The cabin burst into a ball of flame. The massive noise from the explosion rumbled through the hills and canyons. The snow erupted. Avalanche.

Sidney and Elena were in the path of the churning white wall of snow and ice as it roared down the steep slope. Like a tidal wave, it uprooted trees, lifted boulders. It changed the very shape of the landscape.

Nick wouldn't lose her like this. His thighs burned as he charged through the snow that was getting deeper with every passing second. He fought with both arms, struggling to stay atop the sliding snow. He reached the two women as the snow crested over them in a heavy, concrete curtain. He couldn't breathe. Everything went black.

SIDNEY HAD NEVER been so cold. Buried in snow, every part of her body was frozen. She forced her eyelids to open, and she could see the light of the afternoon sun. She knew which way to dig.

One arm was pressed against her chest, and she wiggled her bare hand higher until she reached her mouth. She hollowed out a little place where she could inhale tiny gasps of air. Then, she punched upward with her arm. At first, she barely made a dent in the snow. The next hit was harder. Again and again.

Her other arm was pinned helplessly behind her back. But she could wiggle her feet. She kicked and she slipped to a new depth.

Her toe poked a step in the ice, then another. And she kept punching like a boxer on his last legs. Her fist broke through. She saw the sky, a dismal gray haze.

She heard Elena's voice.

Where was Nick? She'd seen him running toward her. He'd touched her hand, and then the snow crashed over them. She had to find Nick. It didn't take long to suffocate in an avalanche.

With Elena helping, Sidney dragged herself out of the snow. Gasping, she lay on the rugged sheets of ice. "Nick, where are you?"

"We'll find him," Elena promised. "He was close to us. We'll keep digging. We'll keep looking."

She heard a loud, guttural yell and looked toward the cabin, which was a ball of orange flame. She saw Hawthorne pacing at the edge of the snowy scree. "Why won't you die?"

Elena ducked down. "Hurtado is yours. My pig of a husband doesn't want me."

"You hurt him."

There was no point in trying to reason with Hawthorne. In her world, Elena was a she-devil who had to die even if it meant blowing up a cabin or triggering an avalanche.

Hawthorne pulled her Glock from a shoulder holster. She braced it in both hands as she took aim at Elena. Before she squeezed the trigger, another shot rang out. She went down.

Sidney turned and saw Nick behind her, holding his weapon. "I tried not to kill her." He spat out a mouthful of snow. "But I don't really care if she's dead."

She stumbled across the snow, flopped down beside him and kissed him on the lips. "Ouch."

THREE DAYS LATER, Sidney and Nick were staying in a luxury suite in a Vail hotel, paid for by Avilar's wealthy family, who were grateful for his rescue and release from the men hired by Hawthorne. She had survived, and Sidney was glad she wouldn't have to waste one instant feeling guilty about Vicky/Victoria's demise.

Draped in a silky white robe for dinner, she paused beside the hot tub. She and Nick really needed to install one of these at their house in Austin. Finding a place to put it wasn't a problem. Privacy was. They lived in a family-oriented neighborhood. And what good was a steamy, sexy hot tub if you couldn't bob around naked?

In the outer room of their fabulous suite, she joined him. Her jaw was recovered enough for light kissing and, more important, for eating medium-chewy foods like hamburger. They sat at a room service dinner for two with microbrew beer, burgers and fries. Sidney savored the first juicy bite.

"That's almost as good as sex."

"Should I be insulted?"

"I said *almost*."

The gold flecks in his eyes seemed to sparkle in the soft light of their suite overlooking the village. These past three days had been all about recuperation and making love. They'd both been hurt and were on their way toward healing.

"I have something for you." He placed a small velvet box on the tabletop. "It's not a replacement."

She opened the ring box and took out a white-gold band with a simple, reasonably sized diamond. "This is perfect. I love my pi diamond, I really do, but…"

"It's not practical," he said.

She slipped the ring onto her finger. "If not a replacement, what is it?"

"Backup," he said. "Everybody needs backup."

"No more single-person ops?"

"Never again." He raised his hand as though swearing an oath. "I will never again undertake a mission that I can't tell you about."

She bounced from her chair, rounded the table and sat on his lap. She placed a light kiss on his delectable mouth.

"Aren't you going to read the inscription?" he asked.

She took off the ring, held the band and read inside: True Love.

For them, that said it all.

* * * * *

LARGER-PRINT BOOKS!

HARLEQUIN *Presents*

PASSION
GUARANTEED
SEDUCTION

GET 2 FREE LARGER-PRINT NOVELS PLUS 2 FREE GIFTS!

YES! Please send me 2 FREE LARGER-PRINT Harlequin Presents® novels and my 2 FREE gifts (gifts are worth about $10). After receiving them, if I don't wish to receive any more books, I can return the shipping statement marked "cancel." If I don't cancel, I will receive 6 brand-new novels every month and be billed just $5.05 per book in the U.S. or $5.49 per book in Canada. That's a saving of at least 16% off the cover price! It's quite a bargain! Shipping and handling is just 50¢ per book in the U.S. and 75¢ per book in Canada.* I understand that accepting the 2 free books and gifts places me under no obligation to buy anything. I can always return a shipment and cancel at any time. Even if I never buy another book, the two free books and gifts are mine to keep forever.

176/376 HDN F43N

Name	(PLEASE PRINT)	
Address		Apt. #
City	State/Prov.	Zip/Postal Code

Signature (if under 18, a parent or guardian must sign)

Mail to the **Harlequin® Reader Service:**
IN U.S.A.: P.O. Box 1867, Buffalo, NY 14240-1867
IN CANADA: P.O. Box 609, Fort Erie, Ontario L2A 5X3

**Are you a subscriber to Harlequin Presents books
and want to receive the larger-print edition?
Call 1-800-873-8635 today or visit us at www.ReaderService.com.**

* Terms and prices subject to change without notice. Prices do not include applicable taxes. Sales tax applicable in N.Y. Canadian residents will be charged applicable taxes. Offer not valid in Quebec. This offer is limited to one order per household. Not valid for current subscribers to Harlequin Presents Larger-Print books. All orders subject to credit approval. Credit or debit balances in a customer's account(s) may be offset by any other outstanding balance owed by or to the customer. Please allow 4 to 6 weeks for delivery. Offer available while quantities last.

Your Privacy—The Harlequin® Reader Service is committed to protecting your privacy. Our Privacy Policy is available online at www.ReaderService.com or upon request from the Harlequin Reader Service.

We make a portion of our mailing list available to reputable third parties that offer products we believe may interest you. If you prefer that we not exchange your name with third parties, or if you wish to clarify or modify your communication preferences, please visit us at www.ReaderService.com/consumerschoice or write to us at Harlequin Reader Service Preference Service, P.O. Box 9062, Buffalo, NY 14269. Include your complete name and address.

HPLP13R

LARGER-PRINT BOOKS!
GET 2 FREE LARGER-PRINT NOVELS PLUS
2 FREE GIFTS!

♦ HARLEQUIN®

Romance

From the Heart, For the Heart

YES! Please send me 2 FREE LARGER-PRINT Harlequin® Romance novels and my 2 FREE gifts (gifts are worth about $10). After receiving them, if I don't wish to receive any more books, I can return the shipping statement marked "cancel." If I don't cancel, I will receive 4 brand-new novels every month and be billed just $4.84 per book in the U.S. or $5.24 per book in Canada. That's a savings of at least 19% off the cover price! It's quite a bargain! Shipping and handling is just 50¢ per book in the U.S. and 75¢ per book in Canada.* I understand that accepting the 2 free books and gifts places me under no obligation to buy anything. I can always return a shipment and cancel at any time. Even if I never buy another book, the two free books and gifts are mine to keep forever.

119/319 HDN F43Y

Name	(PLEASE PRINT)	

Address		Apt. #

City	State/Prov.	Zip/Postal Code

Signature (if under 18, a parent or guardian must sign)

Mail to the Harlequin® Reader Service:
IN U.S.A.: P.O. Box 1867, Buffalo, NY 14240-1867
IN CANADA: P.O. Box 609, Fort Erie, Ontario L2A 5X3
Want to try two free books from another line?
Call 1-800-873-8635 or visit www.ReaderService.com.

* Terms and prices subject to change without notice. Prices do not include applicable taxes. Sales tax applicable in N.Y. Canadian residents will be charged applicable taxes. Offer not valid in Quebec. This offer is limited to one order per household. Not valid for current subscribers to Harlequin Romance Larger-Print books. All orders subject to credit approval. Credit or debit balances in a customer's account(s) may be offset by any other outstanding balance owed by or to the customer. Please allow 4 to 6 weeks for delivery. Offer available while quantities last.

Your Privacy—The Harlequin® Reader Service is committed to protecting your privacy. Our Privacy Policy is available online at www.ReaderService.com or upon request from the Harlequin Reader Service.

We make a portion of our mailing list available to reputable third parties that offer products we believe may interest you. If you prefer that we not exchange your name with third parties, or if you wish to clarify or modify your communication preferences, please visit us at www.ReaderService.com/consumerchoice or write to us at Harlequin Reader Service Preference Service, P.O. Box 9062, Buffalo, NY 14269. Include your complete name and address.

HRLP13R

LARGER-PRINT BOOKS!
GET 2 FREE LARGER-PRINT NOVELS PLUS
2 FREE GIFTS!

HARLEQUIN

super romance®

More Story...More Romance

JAPANESE
PHRASEBOOK

Yoshi Abe

hrasebook
dition

ished by
Lonely Planet Publications
Head Office: PO Box 617, Hawthorn, Vic 3122, Australia
Branches: 150 Linden Street, Oakland CA 94607, USA
              10a Spring Place, London NW5 3BH, UK
              1 rue du Dahomey, 75011 Paris, France

Printed by
The Bookmaker International Ltd
Printed in China

Cover Illustration
Tokyo Nights by Mic Looby

Published
November 1998

National Library of Australia Cataloguing in Publication Data

Abe, Yoshi
    Japanese phrasebook
    3rd ed.
    Includes index.
    ISBN 0 86442 616 X.

    1. Japanese language – Conversation and phrase books – English. I.
Title. (Series : Lonely Planet language survival kit).

    495.68421

About the Author

Yoshi Abe was born and educated in Japan. He has spent time in Canada and Indonesia, and has been living in Australia for more than 10 years. He holds a Bachelor of Arts in Anthropology and Linguistics and gained a Masters Degree in Anthropology at the University of Melbourne in 1996. Yoshi has six years of experience teaching Japanese at tertiary level and has also worked as a translator. He is currently undertaking research towards a PhD degree on Maritime Anthropology in eastern Indonesia.

From the Author

My thanks to Leonie Boxtel for providing me with many observations and advice. As an English speaker with much experience living in Japan her support was invaluable and made this work possible.

From the Publisher

Peter D'Onghia edited this book while becoming alarmingly sumo-like. Fabrice Rocher managed to knock out a passable karaoke version of *Bohemian Rhapsody* while laying out the book and designing the cover. Sally Steward oversaw production and proofread despite having a close shave with the local yakuza. Penelope Richardson's canary yellow kimono didn't detract from her fine eagle eye for detail during proofing. Elizabeth Swan proofread and decided that the tea ceremony could be done just as well with coffee. Mic Looby drew the witty illustrations and the cover illustration while discovering the finer points of manga.

Thanks to Kevin Chambers who wrote the first edition of the Lonely Planet Japanese phrasebook and to Kam Y Lau who wrote the second edition, from which this book developed. Thanks to both these authors for acting as readers for this edition.

CONTENTS

Cor...

INTRODUCTION

The Japanese language is relatively easy to pronounce for English-speaking people as it has a simple syllabic structure and is non-tonal. Although there are many local dialects in Japan, almost all of the population of 125 million speak standard Japanese. The basic word order is subject-object-verb, unlike English which is subject-verb-object. Some readers may find this a little difficult to adjust to at first. Nevertheless it is easy to communicate with Japanese people if you master some simple sentence structures and basic vocabulary.

There were three different languages spoken in Japan until the beginning of the 19th century; Japanese, the widest spoken language in Japan, Ainu, the language spoken in Hokkaidō in the north, and Ryūkyū, the language spoken in Okinawa, the southern most group of islands close to Taiwan. Older Okinawan residents still speak Ryūkyū, but there are almost no fluent Ainu speakers left in Hokkaidō.

From the 19th century until the end of WW II Japanese was taught in various Asian countries occupied by Imperial Japanese forces such as China, Taiwan, Korea and Indonesia. As a result, some of the older generation still speak some Japanese in these countries. There are also large Japanese-speaking populations in Hawaii and Brazil, made up mostly of descendants of Japanese immigrants.

The origin of Japanese is still under debate. It's thought that Japanese as it's known today is a combination of proto-Japanese (resembling Ainu) and Austronesian languages from Taiwan. Japanese has strong similarities to Korean in grammatical structure and bears some resemblance to Altaic languages such as Mongolian and Turkish.

Although Japanese is grammatically unrelated to Chinese, the original written language was adopted from the Chinese writing system over 1500 years ago. These characters, known as kanji, are ideographic (symbols which represent ideas rather than sounds).

INTRODUCTION

By the 10th century, the Japanese had devised two syllabic writing systems, katakana and hiragana, which are used in combination with Chinese characters. Nowadays hiragana is normally used to represent grammatical particles and verb, adjective and adverb endings, and katakana is used for foreign words, most of which have been imported since the 19th century when Japan opened up after a period of complete isolation. Japan adopted many aspects of western culture, administration and technology around this time, and introduced thousands of foreign words into the Japanese language. Many came from English, such as kōhī, 'coffee', chokorēto, 'chocolate', jūsu, 'juice', and later terebi, 'TV'. Often a native word and a borrowed word coexist – for example, 'toilet' can be called either toire or o-tearai

This phrasebook focuses on spoken Japanese rather than the written language, as writing takes some time to master. However, Japanese orthography is included in addition to the Romanised representation of words and phrases.

ABBREVIATIONS

f	feminine
inf	informal
lit	literally
m	masculine
pol	polite
v	verb

HOW TO USE THIS PHRASEBOOK
You Can Speak Another Language

It's true – anyone can speak another language. Don't worry if you haven't studied languages before, or that you studied a language at school for years and can't remember any of it. It doesn't even matter if you failed English grammar. After all, that's never affected your ability to speak English! And this is the key to picking up a language in another country. You don't need to sit down and memorise endless grammatical details and you don't need to memorise long lists of vocabulary. You just need to start speaking. Once you start, you'll be amazed how many prompts you'll get to help you build on those first words. You'll hear people speaking, pick up sounds from TV, catch a word or two that you think you know from the local radio, see something on a billboard – all these things help to build your understanding.

Plunge In

There's just one thing you need to start speaking another language – courage. Your biggest hurdle is overcoming the fear of saying aloud what may seem to you to be just a bunch of sounds.

The best way to start overcoming your fear is to memorise a few key words. These are the words you know you'll be saying again and again, like 'hello', 'thank you' and 'how much?'. Here's an important hint though: right from the beginning, learn at least one phrase that will be useful but not essential. Such as 'good morning' or 'good afternoon', 'see you later' or even a conversational piece like 'lovely day, isn't it?' or 'it's cold today' (people everywhere love to talk about the weather). Having this extra phrase (just start with one, if you like, and learn to say it really well) will enable you to move away from the basics, and when you get a reply and a smile, it'll also boost your confidence. You'll find that people you speak to will like it too, as they'll understand that at least you've tried to learn more of the language than just the usual essential words.

Ways to Remember

There are several ways to learn a language. Most people find they learn from a variety of these, although people usually have a preferred way to remember. Some like to see the written word and remember the sound from what they see. Some like to just hear it spoken in context (if this is you, try talking to yourself in Japanese, but do it in the car or somewhere private, to give yourself confidence, and so others don't wonder about your sanity!).

INTRODUCTION

Others, especially the more mathematically inclined, like to analyse the grammar of a language, and piece together words according to the rules of grammar. The very visually inclined like to associate the written word and even sounds with some visual stimulus, such as from illustrations, TV and general things they see in the street. As you learn, you'll discover what works best for you – be aware of what made you really remember a particular word, and if it sticks in your mind, keep using that method.

Kicking Off

Chances are you'll want to learn some of the language before you go. The first thing to do is to memorise those essential phrases and words. Check out the basics (pages 35–36) ... and don't forget that extra phrase (see Plunge In!). Try the sections on making conversation or greeting people for a phrase you'd like to use. Write some of these words down on a separate piece of paper and stick them up around the place. On the fridge, by the bed, on your computer, as a bookmark – somewhere where you'll see them often. Try putting some words in context – the 'How much is it?' note, for instance, could go in your wallet.

Finally

Don't be concerned if you feel you can't memorise words. On the inside front and back covers are the most essential words and phrases you'll need. You could also try tagging a few pages for other key phrases, or use the notes pages to write your own reminders.

PRONUNCIATION

Japanese pronunciation offers few difficulties for English speakers. It has no tones, unlike other languages in the region, and many of its sounds are found in English. The few points to watch are explained below.

VOWELS

a   as the 'a' in 'father'
e   as the 'e' in 'get'
i   as the 'i' in 'pin'
o   as the 'o' in 'lot'
u   as the 'u' in 'put', not the 'yu' sound as in 'use'

Long Vowels

Long vowels in this book are represented by double notations or the vowel with a line written above it (macrons). In both instances the vowel must be pronounced twice as long as a short vowel. This is important as vowel length can change the meaning of a word: suki means 'to like', while sukī means 'ski'.

Reduced Vowels

The vowel u is sometimes not pronounced. The most common instances are: between k and s (eg gakusei, 'student', sounds like *gaksei*). It's also dropped in the verb endings -desu and -masu (ii desu, 'it's good', sounds like ii des).

PRONUNCIATION

CONSONANTS

Most consonant sounds are similar to English, with the following important exceptions:

r   made with a single flap of the tip of the tongue against the ridge behind your front teeth. It's almost a cross between English 'r' and 'l'.

f   before u – 'fu' is pronounced by releasing the vowel 'u' while the lips are held as if you were trying to whistle. If you find this difficult you can also pronounce the 'f' like an English 'f'.

g   always hard as in 'good', never soft as in 'general'

ts   as the 'ts' in 'cats' even at the start of a word

Double Consonants

There is a slight pause between double consonants, as in the English word 'part-time': For example, gakkō, 'school', is pronounced ga (pause) kō.

Apostrophes

You should pause slightly between an apostrophe and the following syllables. The apostrophe is only found after n and it gives a different pronunciation and meaning to a word.

kinen   commemoration
kin'en   non-smoking

DID YOU KNOW...   Fuji-san (Mt Fuji), is Japan's tallest mountain at 3776 m. In fact, it's a dormant volcano and last erupted in 1707. Its majestic symmetrical slopes have been depicted in many works of art, including woodblock prints in the late Edo Period.

READING JAPANESE

Japanese is usually written vertically and from right to left. However, occasionally it is written horizontally like English, especially when text involves numbers, Romanised Japanese, or English (as in this book).

Written Japanese is actually a combination of three different scripts. The first, kanji, consists of ideographic characters. The other two, hiragana and katakana, are 'syllabic' scripts – that is, each character represents a syllable.

Kanji

Kanji are ideographs borrowed from Chinese that represent both meaning and pronunciation. Each kanji may be made up of anything from one to over 20 strokes. The Japanese have developed various ways of pronouncing words with kanji in them, so that there may be two or more ways of pronouncing any given kanji depending on the context. For example, the kanji 水, 'water', alone is pronounced mizu, but as part of a word, such as 水分, 'moisture', it's pronounced sui. A large number of kanji are common to both Japan and China. Some have been simplified by the Chinese over time and are no longer used by both languages. Over 2000 of these characters are still in everyday use in Japan.

Hiragana

Hiragana is used to represent particles and grammatical endings particular to Japanese. These characters are placed alongside the ideographic characters. Therefore, a single Japanese word may contain both scripts:

(I) drank water.   mizu o nomimashita
                               水を飲みました。

In this sentence, particle o, を, and the verb ending mimashita みました, are all written in hiragana.

PRONUNCIATION

HIRAGANA

あ a	い i	う u	え e	お o
か ka	き ki	く ku	け ke	こ ko
さ sa	し shi	す su	せ se	そ so
た ta	ち chi	つ tsu	て te	と to
な na	に ni	ぬ nu	ね ne	の no
は ha	ひ hi	ふ fu	へ he	ほ ho
ま ma	み mi	む mu	め me	も mo
や ya		ゆ yu		よ yo
ら ra	り ri	る ru	れ re	ろ ro
わ wa				を o
ん n				

きゃ kya	きゅ kyu	きょ kyo
しゃ sha	しゅ shu	しょ sho
ちゃ cha	ちゅ chu	ちょ cho
にゃ nya	にゅ nyu	にょ nyo
ひゃ hya	ひゅ hyu	ひょ hyo
みゃ mya	みゅ myu	みょ myo

りゃ rya	りゅ ryu	りょ ryo

が ga	ぎ gi	ぐ gu	げ ge	ご go
ざ za	じ ji	ず zu	ぜ ze	ぞ zo
だ da	ぢ ji	づ zu	で de	ど do

ぎゃ gya	ぎゅ gyu	ぎょ gyo
じゃ ja	じゅ ju	じょ jo

ば ba	び bi	ぶ bu	べ be	ぼ bo
ぱ pa	ぴ pi	ぷ pu	ぺ pe	ぽ po

びゃ bya	びゅ byu	びょ byo
ぴゃ pya	ぴゅ pyu	ぴょ pyo

KATAKANA

ア a	イ i	ウ u	エ e	オ o
カ ka	キ ki	ク ku	ケ ke	コ ko
サ sa	シ shi	ス su	セ se	ソ so
タ ta	チ chi	ツ tsu	テ te	ト to
ナ na	ニ ni	ヌ nu	ネ ne	ノ no
ハ ha	ヒ hi	フ fu	ヘ he	ホ ho
マ ma	ミ mi	ム mu	メ me	モ mo
ヤ ya		ユ yu		ヨ yo
ラ ra	リ ri	ル ru	レ re	ロ ro
ワ wa				ヲ o
ン n				

キャ kya	キュ kyu	キョ kyo
シャ sha	シュ shu	ショ sho
チャ cha	チュ chu	チョ cho
ニャ nya	ニュ nyu	ニョ nyo
ヒャ hya	ヒュ hyu	ヒョ hyo
ミャ mya	ミュ myu	ミョ myo

リャ rya	リュ ryu	リョ ryo

ガ ga	ギ gi	グ gu	ゲ ge	ゴ go
ザ za	ジ ji	ズ zu	ゼ ze	ゾ zo
ダ da	ヂ ji	ヅ zu	デ de	ド do

ギャ gya	ギュ gyu	ギョ gyo
ジャ ja	ジュ ju	ジョ jo

バ ba	ビ bi	ブ bu	ベ be	ボ bo
パ pa	ピ pi	プ pu	ペ pe	ポ po

ビャ bya	ビュ byu	ビョ byo
ピャ pya	ピュ pyu	ピョ pyo

Katakana

It's worth becoming familiar with these characters, as they are
used to indicate the many recent borrowings from other languages
and will also be useful when writing your name in Japanese:

I'm John. I'm Canadian.   jon desu. kanadajin desu
                                 ジョンです。カナダ人です。

Here, the word 'John', ジョン and 'Canada', カナダ are
written in katakana.

PRONUNCIATION

GRAMMAR

Knowing how to put a simple sentence together in Japanese will make communication quite a bit easier.

Japanese show different levels of formality by choosing particular words and often changing the forms of verbs. This phrasebook uses standard polite (-masu) forms which will be suitable for most situations you will encounter. The grammatical points listed are intended to enable the beginner to grasp language in a short time. Please note that the listings are not exhaustive.

WORD ORDER

Unlike in English, where the word order is *subject-verb-object*, the order of a Japanese sentence is subject-object-verb. Instead of saying 'I bought this book', a Japanese person will say the equivalent of 'I this book bought'. In addition, Japanese often omit the subject of a sentence if it is obvious or unimportant. The previous example can also end up as 'This book bought' ('I' being obvious from the context).

I bought this book.　　(watashi ga) kono hon o kaimashita
　　　　　　　　　　　(lit: I-*ga* this book-*o* bought)

ARTICLES

Japanese does not have words equivalent to 'a' and 'the':

This is a/the book.　　kore wa hon desu
　　　　　　　　　　　(lit: this-*wa* book is)

However, if you want to point out a specific item, you can use the word sono (that):

that book　　　　　　sono hon
　　　　　　　　　　　(lit: that book)

PARTICLES

A Japanese noun or pronoun is almost always followed by a particle. Each particle has at least one function relating to the preceding noun or pronoun. These small but important particles show us whether the preceding word is the subject (who or what is doing something) or object (the person or thing that is having something done to it). At other times they are equivalent to English prepositions such as 'in' or 'to'. Some examples of particles you will come across often in Japanese are: ga, wa, o, no, ni and e.

Subject Particle

The particle ga marks the subject:

This person is Mr Suzuki.	kono hito ga Suzuki-san desu (lit: this person-*ga* Suzuki-Mr is)
Petrol is expensive.	gasorin ga takai desu (lit: petrol-*ga* expensive is)

Here, ga indicates that the preceding nouns kono hito (this person) and gasorin (petrol) are the subject.

Topic Particle

The particle wa marks the topic or the focal point of the sentence. wa is often used when clarifying or stressing a particular point.

This person is Mr Suzuki.	kono hito wa Suzuki-san desu (lit: this person-*wa* Suzuki-Mr is)
Gasoline is expensive. (as opposed to diesel or LPG)	gasorin wa takai desu (lit: petrol-*wa* expensive is)

Object Particle

The particle o marks the object.

I ate a hamburger.	watashi wa hambāgā o tabemashita (lit: I-*wa* hamburger-*o* ate)
Sue saw a movie.	sue-san wa eiga o mimashita (lit: Sue-Ms-*wa* movie-*o* saw)

Possessive Particle

The particle no shows that something belongs to someone. It's like the English possessive 's' (poss):

Mr Tanaka's car	tanaka-san no kuruma
	(lit: Tanaka-Mr-*no* poss car)
my book	watashi no hon
	(lit: I-*no* book)
the Australian flag	ōsutoraria no hata
	(lit: Australia-*no* flag)
schoolteacher	gakkō no sensei
	(lit: school-*no* teacher)

Ni Particle

The particle ni is used in three different ways.

- the year/month/day or time

on Tuesday	kayō-bi ni
	(lit: Tuesday-*ni*)
at three o'clock	san-ji ni
	(lit: three-o'clock-*ni*)
in 1987	sen kyū hyaku hachi jūnana nen ni
	(lit: 1987 in)

- where something is:

at home	uchi ni
	(lit: home-*ni*)
in Japan	nihon ni
	(lit: Japan-*ni*)

- destination

(I'm) going to Japan.	nihon ni ikimasu
	(lit: Japan-*ni* to go)

Direction Particle

The particle e indicates direction. It's very similar to the destination function of ni:

to Tokyo	tōkyō e
	(lit: Tokyo-*e* towards)

GRAMMAR

De **Particle**

The particle de is used in two different ways.

- where something happens or happened

    I'll make a call at the hotel.   hoteru de denwa shimasu
    (lit: hotel-*de* telephone do)

- the means or instrument used to accomplish the verb

    (I'm) going by train.   .densha de ikimasu
    (lit: train-*de* go)

    Please write in pen.   pen de kaite kudasai
    (lit: pen-*de* write please)

Prefixes (o-, go-)

The prefixes o- and go- are added to certain nouns to indicate politeness or reverence.

rice/meal	go-han
letter	o-tegami
Japanese rice-cake	o-mochi
I'll introduce you.	go-shōkai shimasu
	(lit: *go*-introduction do)

On some occasions, the prefix indicates 'your honourable ...'. It's important not to use the prefixes o- and go- when talking about yourself or your situation.

your husband	go-shujin
my husband	shujin
What's your name?	o-namae wa nan desu ka?
	(lit: *go*-name-*wa* what is *ka*)
(My) name is Fabrice.	namae wa Faburisu desu
	(lit: name-*wa* Fabrice is)
How do (you) do?	o-genki desu ka?
	(lit: *go*-healthy is *ka*)
(I'm) fine.	genki desu
	(lit: healthy is)

This & That/Here & There

Japanese has three degrees indicating distance. The prefix ko-refers to something or someone close to the speaker. so- refers to something close to the listener: and a- refers to something far from both the speaker and the listener:

near speaker		near listener		far from both	
here	koko	there	soko	over there	asoko
this way	kochira	that way	sochira	that way over there	achira
this	kore	that	sore	that over there	are
this (book)	kono (hon)	that (book)	sono (hon)	that (book) over there	ano (hon)

NOUNS

Japanese nouns have no gender or plural forms but you must always use a particle after a noun. (See page 156 for an explanation of numeral counters.) There are three main types of nouns:

- kango
    These words are of Chinese origin and are written in kanji
    taiyō   the sun
    shimbun   newspaper

- wago
    These are Japanese nouns and may or may not use kanji
    mono   thing
    umi   sea

- gairaigo
    These words are borrowed from other languages and are written in katakana
    arubaito   part-time job
    kompyūta   computer

GRAMMAR

KEY VERBS

	-masu form	plain form	-te form	special form
buy	kaimasu	kau	katte	kawa
climb	noborimasu	noboru	nobotte	nobora
come	kimasu	kuru	kite	ko
cut	kirimasu	kiru	kitte	kira
do	shimasu	suru	shite	shi
drink	nomimasu	nomu	nonde	noma
eat	tabemasu	taberu	tabete	tabe
enter	hairimasu	hairu	haitte	haira
exit	demasu	deru	dete	de
find	mitsukemasu	mitsukeru	mitukete	mitsuke
get up	okimasu	okiru	okite	oki
go	ikimasu	iku	itte	ika
hear	kikimasu	kiku	kiite	kika
live	sumimasu	sumu	sunde	suma
make	tsukurimasu	tsukuru	tsukutte	tsukura
read	yomimasu	yomu	yonde	yoma
run	hashirimasu	hashiru	hashitte	hashira
search	sagashimasu	sagasu	sagashite	sagasa
see	mimasu	miru	mite	mina
send	okurimasu	okuru	okutte	okura
sit	suwarimasu	suwaru	suwatte	suwara
sleep	nemasu	neru	nete	nena
speak	hanashimasu	hanasu	hanashite	hanas
stay/stop	tomarimasu	tomaru	tomatte	tomara
teach	oshiemasu	oshieru	oshiete	oshie
understand	wakarimasu	wakaru	wakatte	wakara
walk	arukimasu	aruku	aruite	aruka
work	hatarakimasu	hataraku	hataraite	hataraka
write	kakimasu	kaku	kaite	kaka

GRAMMAR

PRONOUNS

The first person pronoun watashi has no gender and can therefore be used by females and males. However, there are some first person pronouns that are gender specific – boku, and ore are male terms for 'I' and 'me'. Women always use watashi. Men also use the word kimi, meaning 'you' (singular), towards subordinates who they know well. In formal cases, normally the word watakushi is used for 'I/me'.

Remember that a subject pronoun is often omitted when the person is obvious from the context.

I/me	watashi
I/me (formal)	watakushi
I/me (m)	boku/ore
you (singular)	anata
you (to subordinates)	kimi
she/her	kanojo
he/him	kare
we/us	watashi tachi
you (plural)	anata tachi
they/them (m)	kare ra
they/them (f)	kanojo tachi

GRAMMAR

VERBS

Japanese verbs don't change according to the subject: kaimasu can mean 'I buy' or 'she buys'. Japanese has only two basic tenses: present and past. The present tense is also used to express the future.

Verbs change their form in contexts we might not expect. For example verb forms alter when making requests and with words meaning 'can' and 'must'. Remember that the verb goes at the end of the sentence.

Present

If you look up a verb in a Japanese dictionary, you'll find the 'plain form' of the verb. The plain form is not appropriate for most conversations and you should use the polite form, or -masu form. Unfortunately, it is difficult to work out the -masu form from the plain form. For this reason, all the verbs found in the dictionary at the end of this book are given in the -masu form.

	-masu form	plain form
write	kakimasu	kaku
buy	kaimasu	kau
eat	tabemasu	taberu
do	shimasu	suru
come	kimasu	kuru
stay	tomarimasu	tomaru

(I) eat western food and Japanese food.
   yōshoku to washoku o tabemasu
   (lit: western-food and Japanese-food-*o* eat)

(I) go to work by car everyday.
   mainichi kuruma de shigoto ni ikimasu
   (lit: everyday car-*de* work to go)

Future

In Japanese, the future tense is expressed by using the same form as the present tense. To make it clear that you are talking about the future, you can use a time word such as ashita 'tomorrow'.

(I'll) stay in a youth hostel tonight.
   komban yūsu-hosuteru ni tomarimasu
   (lit: tonight youth-hostel-*ni* stay)

He won't come tomorrow.
   ashita kare wa kimasen
   (lit: tomorrow he-*wa* come-neg)

Past

To form the past tense, replace the polite ending -masu with -mashita:

I will go to the station.	eki ni ikimasu (lit: station to go)
I went to the station.	eki ni ikimashita (lit: station to go-past)

There Is/Are

There are two ways of expressing that something exists in Japanese. For animate objects the verb imasu is used. For inanimate objects arimasu is used.

She is in the hotel.	kanojo wa hoteru ni imasu (lit: she top hotel in *imasu*)
The book is in the bag.	hon wa kaban no naka ni arimasu (lit: book-*wa* bag-*no* inside at *imasu*)

To Be

The word desu is the rough translation of the English verb 'to be'. The past tense and negative forms of 'to be' don't follow the common conjugation for verbs, and are listed below. When you use 'to be' in any form, particles such as wa and ga are dropped:

Present desu	Present Negative ja arimasen
Past deshita	Past Negative ja arimasendeshita

(I'm) a student.	gakusei desu (lit: student am)

GRAMMAR

Requests

To ask someone to do something, you use what is called the -te form of the verb, plus the word kudasai 'please'. Unfortunately, there's no straightforward pattern of -te verbs so you just have to learn them.

Please come in.	haitte kudasai (lit: come-in please)
Please write that down.	kaite kudasai (lit: write please)

Negation

- To make a verb negative, replace the ending -masu with -masen

(I) don't eat meat.	niku o tabemasen (lit: meat-*o* eat-*masen*)
(I) don't go to church.	kyōkai ni ikimasen (lit: church-*ni* go-*masen*)

- To make the past tense negative, replace -masu with -masen deshita:

(I) didn't go to the station.	eki ni iki masen deshita (lit: station to go neg past)

MODAL WORDS
Must

- To say someone 'must' or 'has to' do something, add the words nakereba narimasen to the special form of the verb. (See page 24 for some examples of the special form of the verb.)

(You) have to pay.	harawa nakereba narimasen (lit: pay must)
(We) must wait.	mata nakereba narimasen (lit: wait must)

GRAMMAR

ADJECTIVES

As in English, adjectives come before the noun they describe. There are two types of adjectives:

- '-i adjectives' – those that end in a vowel and '-i'

expensive	takai
cheap	yasui
hot	atsui
cold	samui

(I) rented an expensive car. takai kuruma o karimashita
(lit: expensive car-*o* rented)

(I) had a hot bath. atsui o-furo ni harimashita
(lit: hot *o*-bath-*ni* entered)

- 'na-adjectives' – those that take the ending '-na'

convenient/useful	benrina
simple	kantanna
complicated	fukuzatsuna
regrettable	zannenna

This is a useful book. kore wa benrina hon desu
(lit: this-*wa* useful book is)

I solved a complicated problem. watashi wa fukuzatsuna
mondai o kaiketsu shimashta
(lit: I-*wa* complicated
problem-*o* solve-n did)

DOUBLE TROUBLE

Remember that double vowels and vowels with a line written above them (macron) are pronounced twice as long as normal vowels.

ADVERBS

Many adverbs exist as words in their own right. (ashita, 'tomor-row')

I eat slowly.	*yukkuri* tabemasu
	(lit: slowly eat)
I'll do it tomorrow.	*ashita* yarimasu
	(lit: tomorrow do)

You can also change an i-adjective into an adverb by replacing the '-i' with '-ku'.

late	osoi
He came back late.	kare wa oso*ku* kaerimashita
	(lit: he-*wa* late came-back)
quickly	hayai
He ran quickly.	kare wa haya*ku* hashirimashita
	(lit: he-*wa* quickly ran)

QUESTIONS

To ask a yes/no question, just add ka to the end of the sentence. Your voice should rise at the end of the sentence when forming a question.

This is a ticket.	kore wa kippu desu
	(lit: this-*wa* ticket is)
Is this a ticket?	kore wa kippu desu ka?
	(lit: this-*wa* ticket is *ka*)
(I'm) going.	ikimasu
	(lit: go)
(Are you) going?	ikimasu ka?
	(lit: go *ka*)

To find out specific information, you can use the Japanese equivalents of 'where', 'when', 'why' etc.

QUESTION WORDS

where?	doko	Where is it? doko desu ka? (lit: where is *ka*)
when?	itsu	When is it? itsu desu ka? (lit: when is *ka*)
who?	donata	Who is it? donata desu ka? (lit: who is *ka*)
why?	naze	Why? naze desu ka (lit: why is *ka*)
how?	dō	How is it? dō desu ka? (lit: how is *ka*)
	ikutsu	How many are there? kutsu desu ka? (lit: many is *ka*)
	ikura	How much is it? kura desu ka? (lit: much is *ka*)
what?	nan	What is it? nan desu ka? (lit: what is *ka*)

GRAMMAR

Note that these come towards the end of a sentence:

Where is the library?   toshokan wa doko desu ka?
(lit: library-*wa* where is *ka*)

What is this building?   kono biru wa nan desu ka?
(lit: this building-*wa* what is *ka*)

YES & NO

yes	hai/ee
Yes, certainly.	hai, wakarimashita (lit: yes understood)
Yes, it is.	hai, sō desu (lit: yes so is)
no	iie
No, it's not.	iie, sō ja arimasen (lit: no so is-*masen*)

MEETING PEOPLE

FIRST ENCOUNTERS

When meeting someone for the first time, Japanese people normally exchange the greeting hajime mashite, meaning 'How do you do?', followed by the name of the person being greeted. The expression hajime mashite is only used at first encounters. When meeting someone you have met previously the appropriate response is 'good morning', 'good day' or 'good evening'.

Japanese people don't often shake hands unless they are well-travelled overseas. Bowing or nodding is more common and is used when greeting other people, saying 'goodbye', apologising and showing gratitude. Nodding is a more informal way of acknowledging others. A bow or a nod is normally reciprocated, although there's no need to go overboard.

You Should Know

How do you do?	hajime mashite
	はじめまして。
Good morning.	ohayō
	おはよう。
	ohayō gozaimasu (pol)
	おはようございます。
Good day/afternoon.	konnichi wa
	こんにちは。
Good evening.	komban wa
	こんばんは。
Goodbye.	sayōnara
	さようなら。
Bye. (inf)	ja, mata
	じゃ、また。
Goodnight.	o-yasumi nasai
	おやすみなさい。
Yes.	hai
	はい。

No.	iie いいえ。
Excuse me/Sorry.	sumimasen すみません。
Please. (offering something)	dōzo どうぞ。
Thank you.	arigatō gozaimasu ありがとうございます。
Thank you very much (pol).	dōmo arigatō gozaimasu どうもありがとうございます。
You're welcome.	dō itashimashite どういたしまして。

FORMS OF ADDRESS

Close friends and children often call each other by their first names, but a new Japanese acquaintance will normally just tell you their surname. When addressing a person, follow their surname with san, equivalent to any of the English titles Mr, Mrs, Miss and Ms. For example, Ms Suzuki becomes Suzuki san

As san shows respect, it's never used to refer to yourself, your family, or even colleagues from work when talking about them to outsiders. For example, if someone is asking for your colleague Mr Tanaka and he's not around, you would say 'Tanaka (instead of Tanaka san) is not here'. This applies even when talking about your boss!

Sama is a very respectful form of san: for example, 'Honourable Guest' is o-kyaku sama, and 'God' is kami sama

You can also replace san with a more specific word referring to a person's occupation. For example, sensei is used for professionals such as teachers, doctors and lawyers. Mr Yamada, the lawyer, can be called Yamada sensei. It's also quite acceptable to address someone as sensei without their surname. Other titles used in a similar way include:

company president	kai chō	会長
divisional chief	bu chō	部長

general manager	sha chō	社長
manager	ka chō	課長
married woman	okusan/okusama	奥さん／奥様

Small children are often addressed by their first name plus chan

INTRODUCTIONS

(Excuse me,) what's your name?	(shitsurei desu ga,) o-namae wa nan desu ka? (失礼ですが、）お名前は何でか?
My name is (Smith).	watashi no namae wa (Sumisu) desu わたしの名前は（スミス）です。
I'd like to introduce you to (Mr. Tanaka).	(Tanaka-san) ni go-shōkai shimasu （田中さん）にご紹介します。
I'm pleased to meet you. (lit. I look forward to your assistance.)	dōzo yoroshiku どうぞよろしく。
How are you?	o-genki desu ka? お元気ですか?
Fine, and you (Mr Tanaka)?	hai, genki desu (Tanaka san) wa? はい、元気です。（田中さん）は?
May I/Do you mind?	yoroshii desu ka? よろしいですか?

BODY LANGUAGE

Japanese people rarely express their emotions openly in public. Outbursts of emotion such as anger or distress may be met with surprise as a result. Older people may still frown upon couples showing affection for each other in public, although young Japanese have changed considerably in this regard.

MEETING PEOPLE

Pointing at others is considered rude and you should use an upturned hand when indicating another person. Always pass objects directly to others – don't throw them. Avoid blowing your nose in public where possible as Japanese would rather sniff incessantly than blow into a dirty handkerchief.

Pointing to your nose indicates yourself, 'me' or 'my'. When someone waves their hand up and down with the palm down they are signalling 'come here' and not 'go away' as is sometimes interpreted by travellers.

MAKING CONVERSATION

Do you live here?	koko ni sunde imasu ka?
	ここに住んでいますか？
Where are you going?	doko ni ikimasu ka?
	どこに行きますか？
What are you doing?	nani o shimasu ka?
	何をしますか？
What do you think (about ...)?	(... o) dō omoimasu ka?
	(...を) どう思いますか？
Can I take a photo?	shashin o totte mo ii desu ka?
	写真を撮ってもいいですか？
What's this called?	kore wa nan to iimasu ka?
	これは何といいますか？

Beautiful, isn't it!	kirei desu ne!
	きれいですね！
It's very nice here.	koko wa totemo ii tokoro desu
	ここはとてもいいところす。
We love it here.	koko ga totemo ki ni irimashita
	ここがとても気に入りました。
What a cute baby!	kawaii aka-chan desu ne!
	かわいい赤ちゃんですね！
Are you waiting too?	anata mo koko de matte iru no desu ka?
	あなたもここで待っているのですか？
That's funny (amusing).	are wa omoshiroi desu
	あれはおもしろいです。
Did you come here on holiday?	kyūka de koko ni kimashita ka?
	休暇でここに来ましたか？

I came here ...	... kokoni kimashita	... ここに来た。
for a holiday	kyūka de	休暇で
on business	shigoto de	仕事で
to study	benkyō ni	勉強に

VISITING SOMEONE

It's customary in Japan to bring a small gift when visiting someone's home. Cakes, fruit or flowers are common and relatively safe gifts. When entering a Japanese home take your shoes off in the entrance hall. Check that your socks don't have holes in them! Slippers are usually provided to guests but remember that it is strictly socks only on the straw tatami matting.

It's polite to wait until your host indicates where to sit before being seated. If sitting on tatami matting women are advised to sit with legs to one side rather than cross-legged.

MEETING PEOPLE

How long are you here for?	itsu made koko ni imasu ka? いつまでここにいますか？
(I'm/We're) here for ... weeks/days.	... shūkan/nichikan koko ni imasu ... (週間／日間) ここにいます。
Do you like it here?	kokoga suki desu ka? ここが好きですか？
(I/We) like it here very much.	kokoga totemo suki desu ここがとても好きです。

Useful phrases

Sure.	mochiron もちろん。
Just a minute.	chotto matte kudasai ちょっと待ってください。
It's OK.	daijōbu desu だいじょうぶです。
It's important.	taisetsu/jūyō desu (大切／重要) です。
It's not important.	taisetsu/jūyō ja arimasen (大切／重要) じゃありません。
It's possible.	dekimasu できます。
It's not possible.	dekimasen できません。
Look!	mite! 見て！
Listen (to this)!	(kore o) kiite! (これを) 聞いて！
I'm ready.	jumbi ga dekimashita 準備ができました。
Are you ready?	jumbi ga dekimashita ka? 準備ができましたか？
Good luck!	gambatte! がんばって！

NATIONALITIES

Conversations often start with discussions on where you're all from. Unfortunately we can't list all countries here but you'll find that many country names in Japanese are similar to English but with Japanese pronunciation of course. Listed here are some that differ considerably.

Where are you from?	dochira kara kimashita ka? どちらから来ましたか？	
I'm from ...	... kara kimashita	... から来ました。
Australia	ōsutoraria	オーストラリア
England	igirisu	イギリス
Europe	yōroppa	ヨーロッパ
India	indo	インド
Ireland	airurando	アイルランド
the USA	amerika	アメリカ

I come from ...	... kara kimashita	... から来ました。
I live in (the) ...	... ni sunde imasu	... に住んでいます。
city	toshi	都市
countryside	inaka	田舎
mountains	yama	山
seaside	kaigan	海岸
suburbs of ...	... no kōgai	... の郊外
a village	mura	村

CULTURAL DIFFERENCES

How do you do this in your country?	o-kuni de wa kore o dō shimasu ka?
	お国ではこれをどうしますか?
Is this a local custom?	kore wa kono chihō no shūkan desu ka?
	これはこの地方の習慣ですか?
Is it a national custom?	sore wa zenkoku kyōtsū no shūkan desu ka?
	それは全国共通の習慣ですか?
I don't want to offend you.	shitsurei ni naranakereba ii no desuga
	失礼にならなければいいのですが。
I'm sorry, it's not the custom in my country.	sumimasen, watashi no kuni no shūkan dewa arimasen
	すみません、わたしの国の習慣ではありません。
I'm not accustomed to this.	watashi wa kore ni narete imasen
	私はこれに慣れていません。
I don't mind watching, but I'd prefer not to participate.	miru no wa kamaimasen ga, sanka wa enryo shimasu
	見るのはかまいませんが、参加は遠慮します。

THEY MAY SAY ...

Japanese people often say o-tsukare sama deshita or go-kurō sama deshita when they leave work. These lines express the gratitude towards the work done by the other and yourself.

MEETING PEOPLE

AGE

How old are you (to a child)?	o-ikutsu/nan-sai?
	おいくつ？/何歳？
How old are you (to an adult)?	o-ikutsu desuka/nan-sai desu ka?
	おいくつですか？/何歳ですか？
How old is your son/daughter?	musuko-san/ojō-san wa o-ikutsu desuka?
	(息子さん／お嬢さん) はおいくつですか？
I'm ... years old.	watashi wa ... sai desu
	私は ... 歳です。

(See Numbers & Amounts, page 155, for your age.)

OCCUPATIONS

What (work) do you do?	o-shigoto wa nan desu ka?
	お仕事は何ですか？
I'm unemployed.	watashi wa mushoku desu
	私は無職です。

I'm a/an ...	watashi wa ... desu	私は ... です。
artist	geijutsuka	芸術家
businessperson	sararīman	サラリーマン
doctor	isha	医者
engineer	enjinia	エンジニア
farmer	nōmin	農民
journalist	jānarisuto	ジャーナリスト
lawyer	bengoshi	弁護士
mechanic	seibishi	整備士
nurse (f)	kangofu	看護婦
nurse (m)	kangoshi	看護士
office worker	kaishain	会社員
scientist	kagakusha	科学者
student	gakusei	学生
teacher	kyōshi	教師
writer	sakka	作家

I'M HOME

Before a family member leaves home for work, school, or travel, they say ittekimasu (lit: 'I'll be back') to those remaining. Family members who remain respond by saying itterasshai (lit: 'Please return').

When a member comes home from being out they say tadaima (lit: 'I'm home!') in the entrance hall of the house. Those at home to greet the returned member reply okaeri (lit: 'Welcome back'). These may sound very formal, but are commonly used greetings which have now lost their original literal meaning.

STUDENT LIFE

What are you studying?	nani o benkyō shite imasu ka? 何を勉強していますか?
I'm studying ...	... o benkyō shiteimasu ... を勉強しています。

art	bijutsu	美術
arts/humanities	jimbungaku	人文学
business	shōgaku	商学
education	kyōikugaku	教育学
engineering	kōgaku	工学
Japanese	nihongo	日本語
languages	gengo	言語
law	hōgaku	法学
medicine	igaku	医学
science	kagaku	科学

FEELINGS

I'm ...	watashi wa ...	私は ...
Are you ...?	anata wa ... ka?	あなたは ... か?
grateful	kansha shite imasu	感謝しています
afraid	kowai desu	恐いです

angry	okotte imasu	怒っています
cold	samui desu	寒いです
happy	ureshii/shiawase desu	(うれしい／幸せ)です
hot	atsui desu	暑いです
hungry	onaka ga sukimashita	お腹が空きました
in a hurry	isoide imasu	急いでいます
keen to ...	... ni nesshin desu	... に熱心です
lonely	sabishii desu	寂しいです
right	tadashii desu	正しいです
sad	kanashii desu	悲しいです
sleepy	nemui desu	眠いです
sorry (condolence)	kinodoku ni omotte imasu	気の毒に思っています
sorry (regret)	zannen desu	残念です
thirsty	nodo ga kakimashita	喉が乾きました
tired	tsukaremashita	疲れました
well	genki desu	元気です
worried	shimpai desu	心配です

| I'm fed up! | unzari shimashita! | うんざりしました！ |

LANGUAGE DIFFICULTIES

Do you speak English?	eigo ga dekimasu ka?
	英語ができますか？
Yes, I do.	hai, dekimasu
	はい、できます。
No, I don't.	iie, dekimasen
	いいえ、できません。
Does anyone speak English?	donata ka, eigo ga dekimasu ka?
	どなたか、英語ができますか？
I speak a little.	sukoshi dekimasu
	少しできます。
Do you understand?	wakarimasu ka?
	分かりますか？
I understand.	wakarimasu
	分かります。

I don't understand.	wakarimasen 分かりません。
Could you speak more slowly?	motto yukkuri hanashite kudasaimasen ka? もっとゆっくり話してくだ さいませんか？
Could you repeat that?	mōichido hanashite kudasaimasen ka? もう一度話してください ませんか？
Please write it down.	kaite kudasai 書いてください。
How do you say ...?	... wa nanto iimerse ka? ... は何といいますか？
What does ... mean?	... wa dōiu imi desu ka? ... はどういう意味ですか？

GETTING AROUND

Public transport in Japan is clean, punctual and safe. All stations are announced by the driver which is handy for foreigners and those thousands of Japanese who fall asleep on their way home after a long working day. Most information in English about destinations, timetables and maps is provided free at information booths at train stations and Japan Railways booking counters (midori no mado-guchi).

FINDING YOUR WAY

Where's the ...?	... wa doko desu ka?	... はどこですか？
bus station	basu-tei	バス停
train station	eki	駅
road to ...	... e iku michi	... へ行く道

What time does the ... leave/arrive?	... wa nan-ji ni demasu/tsukimasu ka? ... は何時に（出ます／着きます）か？	
aeroplane	hikōki	飛行機
boat	bōto	ボート
bus	basu	バス
train	densha	電車

How do we get to ...?
... e wa dō ikeba iidesu ka?
... へはどう行けばいいですか？

Is it far from/near here?
sore wa koko kara chikai desu ka?
それはここから近いですか？

Can we walk there?
aruite ikemasu ka?
歩いて行けますか？

Can you show me (on the map)?
(chizu de) oshiete kuremasen ka?
（地図で）教えてくれませんか？

Are there other means of getting there?
hoka no ikikata ga arimasu ka?
他の行きかたがありますか？

GETTING AROUND

What ... is this?	kore wa nan to iu ... desu ka?	
	これは何という ... ですか？	
street	michi/dōro	道/道路
city	shi/machi	市/街
village	mura	村

DIRECTIONS

Turn ...	... o magatte kudasai	... 曲がって下さい。
at the next corner	tsugi no kado o	次のかどを
at the traffic lights	shingō o	信号を

Straight ahead.   massugu itte kudasai
まっすぐ行って下さい。

To the right.   migi ni magatte kudasai
右に曲がって下さい。

To the left.   hidari ni magatte kudasai
左に曲がって下さい。

north	kita	北
south	minami	南
east	higashi	東
west	nishi	西

behind	ushiro	後ろ
in front of	mae	前
far	tōku	遠く
near	chikaku	近く
opposite	mukai-gawa	向い側
here	koko	ここ
there	asoko	あそこ

ADDRESSES

A Japanese address might look like this:

> Ms Kimiko Ogawa
> 1-21-16 Minami Kotobuki-cho
> Shinjuku-ku TOKYO　〒160

Japanese streets normally have no names. Instead, areas and blocks within an area are numbered. The first number '1' denotes an area of blocks, (chōme); the second number '21' is the number of the individual block; the third number is the number of the house or building. The number after the sign '〒' is a postal code. Finding locations is difficult even for Japanese and most people have to ask a number of times to find their way to a specific address.

When written in Japanese, addresses list items from the largest unit to the smallest. That is, 'Tokyo' is written first, then the district and so on, with the person's name written last.

Police stands are common throughout Japan and are good places to check local maps and ask directions.

BUYING TICKETS

Where can I buy a ticket?	kippu wa doko de kau koto ga dekimasu ka?
	切符はどこで買うことが
	できますか？
We want to go to ...	... e ikitai no desuga
	... へ行きたいのですが。

GETTING AROUND

Do I need to book?	yoyaku ga hitsuyō desu ka? 予約が必要ですか？
I'd like to book a seat to ...	... yuki no seki o yoyaku shitai no desu ga ... 行きの席を予約した いのですが。
It's full.	man'in desu 満員です。
Can I get a stand-by ticket?	sutando-bai no chiketto ga hoshii no desu ga スタンドバイのチケットが 欲しいのですが。
I'd like two tickets.	kippu o ni-mai kudasai 切符を2枚ください。

I'd like ...	... o kudasai.	... をください。
a one-way ticket	katamichiken	片道券
a return ticket	ōfukuken	往復券
a student's fare	gakusei waribiki	学生割引
	gaku-wari	学割
a child's fare	kodomo ryōkin	子供料金
2nd class seat	nitōseki	2等席
unreserved seat	jiyūseki	自由席
reserved seat	shiteiseki	指定席
1st class seat	gurīnseki	グリーン席
non-smoking seat	kin'enseki	禁煙席
smoking seat	kitsuenseki	喫煙席
window side seat	mado-gawa no seki	窓側の席
aisle side seat	tsūro-gawa no seki	通路側の席

IT'S ALWAYS GOOD

Be aware that 'g' is always 'hard' as in 'good' and never 'soft' as in 'giant'.

AIR

Is there a flight to (Sapporo)?	(sapporo) yuki no bin wa arimasu ka? (札幌) 行きの便はありますか?
When is the next flight to (Osaka)?	tsugi no (ōsaka) yuki no bin wa nan-ji desu ka? 次の (大阪) 行きの便は何時ですか?
How many hours does the flight take to (Fukuoka)?	kono bin wa (fukuoka) made nan-jikan kakarimasu ka? この便は福岡まで何時間かかりますか?
What time do I have to check in at the airport?	nan-ji ni kūko de chekku-in shinakereba narimasen ka? 何時に空港でチェックインしなければなりませんか?
Where's the baggage claim?	baggēji-kurēmu wa doko desu ka? バッゲージクレームはどこですか?

AT CUSTOMS

I have nothing to declare.	shinkoku suru mono wa arimasen 申告するものはありません。
I have something to declare.	shinkoku suru mono ga arimasu 申告するものがあります。
Do I have to declare this?	kore wa shinkoku shinakereba narimasen ka? これは申告しなければなりませんか?
This is all my luggage.	watashi no nimotsu wa kore de zembu desu 私の荷物はこれで全部です。
I didn't know I had to declare it.	kore o shinkoku shikakereba naranai koto o shirimasen deshita これを申告しなければならないことを知りませんでした。

GETTING AROUND

BUS

Buses aren't used as commonly as trains because the train services are so good. They can also be sluggish due to the heavy traffic.

Highway buses run between major cities and are cheaper than trains. They normally depart from major train stations and seats should be booked in advance.

Where's the bus stop?	basŭ-tei wa doko desu ka? バス停はどこですか？
Which bus goes to ...?	... yuki no basu wa dore desu ka? ... 行きのバスはどれですか？
Does this bus go to ...?	kono basu wa ... ni ikimasu ka? このバスは ... に行きますか？
How often do buses come?	basu wa ichi-jikan ni nam-bon kimasu ka? バスは1時間に何本来ますか？
What time is the ... bus?	... no basu wa nan-ji desu ka? ... のバスは何時ですか？

next	tsugi	つぎ
first	shihatsu	始発
last	saishu	最終

THEY MAY SAY ...

oke	OK. (inf)
ii desu yo	OK. (standard)
mochiron	Sure.
ikimashō	Let's go.
matte	Wait. (inf)
chotto matte	Just a minute. (inf)
jumbi ga dekimashita ka?	Are you ready?
jumbi ga dekimashita	I'm ready.

Could you let me know when we get to ...?	... ni tsuitara oshiete moraemasen ka?
	... に着いたら教えてもらえませんか？
Where do I get the bus for ...?	doko ni ikeba ... yuki no basu ni noru koto ga dekimasu ka?
	どこに行けば ... 行きのバスに乗ることができますか？

TRAIN

The Japanese railway system is very accurate, reliable, clean and safe. The system is comprised of the National Railway (JR), municipally operated subways and many smaller private lines. Most commuters to Tokyo use trains because traffic jams and limited parking space make car travel extremely problematic. Rush hour – 7.30 to 9.30 am – is the most chaotic time for train travel. It's better to avoid this period whenever possible, especially if travelling with large luggage.

There are many train types in Japan; the very fast bullet train, known as the shinkansen, monorails, electro-magnetic trains, ultra-smooth ride rubber-tyre lines and driverless trains. Shinkansen join most major cities around Japan and trains leave Tokyo for Osaka every 10 minutes during peak hour. It may be worth reserving seats on longer journeys as many trains are often full. This is especially true between Tokyo and Osaka.

The Tokyo subway system is complicated. If you're planning to stay in Tokyo English maps are available at the Japan National Tourist Organisation, information counters at large stations such as Tokyo, Ueno and Shinjuku.

What station is this?	koko wa nani-eki desu ka?
	ここは何駅ですか？
What's the next station?	tsugi wa nani.eki desu ka?
	つぎは何駅ですか？
Does this train stop at (Shibuya)?	kono densha wa (shibuya) ni tomarimasu ka?
	この電車は渋谷に停まりますか？

GETTING AROUND

How long will it be delayed?	dono kurai okurete imasu ka? どのくらい遅れていますか？
How long does the trip take?	kono kōtei wa donokurai kakarimasu ka? この行程はどのくらいかかりますか？
Is it a direct route?	kore wa chokkō rūto desu ka? これは直行ルートですか。
Is this seat free?	kono seki wa aite imasu ka? この席は空いていますか？
I want to get off at ...	... de oritai no desu ga. ... で降りたいのですが。

> mamonaku (hassha/tōchaku) shimasu
> The train is about to (depart/arrive).
> まもなく（発車／到着）します。

TAXI

Taxis run on a metered basis in Japan. They can be expensive if you have to travel on toll roads (of which there are many) because you must pay these costs also.

taxi	takushī	タクシー

Is this taxi free?	kono takushī wa kūsha desu ka? このタクシーは空車ですか？
Please take me to ...	... made onegai shimasu. ... までお願いします。
How much does it cost to go to ...?	... made ikura desu ka? ... までいくらですか？
How much is the fare?	ryōkin wa ikura desu ka? 料金はいくらですか？
Do we pay extra for luggage?	nimotsu wa betsu-ryōkin desu ka? 荷物は別料金ですか？

Instructions

Go straight!/Continue!	kono mama massugu! このまま まっすぐ！
The next street to the left/right.	tsugi no michi o hidari/migi ni magatte kudasai つぎの道を (左／右) に曲がっ て下さい。
Please wait here.	koko de matte ite kudasai ここで待っていて下さい。
Stop here!	koko de tomatte kudasai ここで止まって下さい。
Stop at the corner.	sono kado de tomatte kudasai そのかどで止まって下さい。

BOAT

| Where does the boat
leave from? | fune wa dokokara demasu ka?
船はどこから出ますか？ |
| What time does the boat arrive? | fune wa nan-ji ni tōchaku
shimasu ka?
船は何時に到着しますか？ |

| pier | sambashi | 桟橋 | boat | bōto | ボート |
| ferry | ferī | フェリー | | | |

CAR

Japanese drive on the left-side of the road. Parking is a serious problem in urban areas and can prove very expensive. Toll roads in Japan can make long-distance travel expensive also.

| Where can I rent a car? | renta-kā wa doko de kariru
koto ga dekimasu ka?
レンタカーはどこで借りるこ
とができますか？ |
| How much is it daily/weekly? | ichi-nichi/isshūkan ikura
desu ka?
(一日／一週間) いくらですか |

Does that include insurance?　hoken-ryō komi desu ka?
　　　　　　　　　　　　　　保険料込みですか？

Where's the next petrol station?　tsugi no gasorin-sutando wa
　　　　　　　　　　　　　　　doko desu ka?
　　　　　　　　　　　　　　つぎのガソリンスタンドはど
　　　　　　　　　　　　　　こですか？

Please fill the tank.　　　　man-tan ni shite kudasai
　　　　　　　　　　　　満タンにして下さい。

I'd like ... litres.　　　　　... rittoru onegai shimasu
　　　　　　　　　　　　... リットルお願いします。

I want (2000 yen) worth　　(ni-sen yen) bun onegai
of petrol.　　　　　　　　shimasu
　　　　　　　　　　　　（2000円）分おねがいします。

Please check the ...　　　... no tenken o onegai shimasu
　　　　　　　　　　　... の点検をお願いします。

oil	oiru	オイル
water	mizu	水
tyre pressure	taiya no kūki-atsu	タイヤの空気圧

Does this road lead to ...?　kono michi wa ... ni ikimasu ka?
　　　　　　　　　　　　この道は ... に行きますか？

Can I park here?　　　　　koko ni chūsha shite mo ii
　　　　　　　　　　　　desu ka?
　　　　　　　　　　　　ここに駐車してもいいですか？

How long can we park here?　dono kurai koko ni chūsha
　　　　　　　　　　　　　dekimasu ka?
　　　　　　　　　　　　どのくらいここに駐車できますか？

air	kūki	空気
battery	batterī	バッテリー
brakes	burēki	ブレーキ
clutch	kuracchi	クラッチ
driver's licence	(unten) menkyoshō	（運転）免許証

engine	enjin	エンジン
garage	shūri kōjō	修理工場
indicator	uinkā	ウインカー
leaded/regular	yūen/regyurā	有鉛／レギュラー
lights	raito	ライト
oil	oiru	オイル
puncture	panku	パンク
radiator	rajietā	ラジエター
roadmap	dōro chizu	道路地図
seatbelt	shīto beruto	シートベルト
self-service	serufu sābisu	セルフサービス
speed limit	seigen sokudo	制限速度
tyres	taiya	タイヤ
unleaded	muen	無鉛
windscreen	furonto garasu	フロントガラス

Car Problems

We need a mechanic.	seibishi wa imasu ka?
	整備士はいますか？
The car broke down at ...	... de kuruma ga kowaremashita
	... で車がこわれました。
The battery's flat.	batterī ga nakunarimashita
	バッテリーがなくなりました。
The radiator's leaking.	rajietā ga morete imasu
	ラジエターが漏れています。
I have a flat tyre.	taiya ga panku shimashita
	タイヤがパンクしました。
It's overheating.	ōbāhīto shimashita
	オーバーヒートしました。
I've lost my car keys.	kuruma no kagi o nakushimashita
	車の鍵をなくしました。
It's not working.	ugokimasen	動きません。
I've run out of petrol.	gasu-ketsu desu.	ガス欠です。

GETTING AROUND

BICYCLE

Is it within cycling distance?	jitensha de ikeru kyori desu ka?	自転車で行ける距離ですか？
Where can I hire a bicycle?	jitensha wa doko de kariru koto ga dekimasu ka?	自転車はどこで借りることができますか？
Where can I find second-hand bikes for sale?	chūko no jitensha wa doko de kau koto ga dekimasu ka?	中古の自転車はどこで買うことができますか？

How much is it for ...?	... ikura desu ka?	... いくらですか？
an hour	ichi-jikan	1時間
the day	nicchū	日中
the morning/afternoon	gozen-chū/gogo	午前中／午後

bike	jitensha	自転車
brakes	burēki	ブレーキ
to cycle	saikuringu shimasu	サイクリングします
handlebars	handoru	ハンドル
helmet	herumetto	ヘルメット
inner tube	chūbu	チューブ
lights	raito	ライト
mountain bike	maunten-baiku	マウンテン・バイク
padlock	kagi	鍵
pump	pompu	ポンプ
puncture	panku	パンク
racing bike	supōtsu jitensha	スポーツ自転車
tandem	futari-nori-yō jitensha	2人乗り用自転車
wheel	sharin	車輪

ACCOMMODATION

Western-style hotels, or hoteru, range in price and standard. Most have English-speaking staff. Capsule hotels, or kapuseru hoteru are cheap and offer a coffin-sized space to sleep and often excellent bathing facilities. Check first, as many are for men only. Japanese youth hostels, or yūsu hosuteru also provide reasonably priced accommodation, but regulations such as curfews may curb your activities.

FINDING ACCOMMODATION

I'm looking for a ...   ... o sagashite imasu
        ... をさがしています。

camping ground	kyampu-jō	キャンプ場
guesthouse	minshuku	民宿
Japanese-style inn	ryokan	旅館
hotel	hoteru	ホテル
capsule hotel	capuseru hoteru	カプセルホテル
youth hostel	yūsu hosuteru	ユースホステル

Where can I find a ...?   ... wa doko ni arimasu ka?
        ... はどこにありますか?

good hotel	ii hoteru	良いホテル
nearby hotel	chikaku no hoteru	近くのホテル
clean hotel	seiketsuna hoteru	清潔なホテル

Where's the ... hotel?   ... hoteru wa doko desu ka?
        ... ホテルはどこですか。

best	ichiban ii	いちばん良い
cheapest	ichiban yasui	いちばん安い

What's the address?   jūsho wa nan desu ka?
        住所は何ですか?

Could you write the address,   jūsho o kaite itadakemasen ka?
please?   住所を書いていただけませんか?

ACCOMMODATION

BOOKING AHEAD

I'd like to book a room, please.	heya o yoyaku shitai no desuga 部屋を予約したいのですが。
For one/two/three night/s.	ippaku/nihaku/sampaku 一泊／二泊／三泊
How much for a week/ two people?	isshūkan/futari de ikura desu ka? (一週間／二人) でいくらですか?
We'll be arriving at ...	... ni tsukimasu ... に着きます。
My name is ...	watashi no namae wa ... desu 私の名前は ... です。

CHECKING IN

Do you have any rooms available?	akibeya wa arimasu ka? 空部屋はありますか?
Sorry, we're full.	sumimasen ga, manshitsu desu すみませんが、満室です。
Do you have a room with two beds?	tsuin-rūmu wa arimasu ka? ツインルームはありますか?
Do you have a room with a double bed?	daburu-rūmu wa arimasu ka? ダブルルームはありますか?
Can I see it?	misete itadakemasen ka? 見せていただけませんか?
Are there any others?	hoka ni arimasen ka? ほかにありませんか?
Where's the bathroom?	o-furo wa doko desu ka? お風呂はどこですか?
Is there hot water all day?	ichinichi-jū oyu ga arimasu ka? 一日中お湯がありますか?

How much for ...?	... de ikura desu ka?	... でいくらですか?
one night	ippaku	一泊
a week	isshūkan	一週間
two people	futari	二人

I'd like ...	... o onegai shimasu	... をお願いします。
to share a dorm	aibeya	相部屋
a single room	shinguru-rūmu	シングルルーム

We want a room with a ...	... tsuki no heya o onegai shimasu.	... 付きの部屋をお願いします。
bathroom	o-furo	お風呂
shower	shawā	シャワー
TV	terebi	テレビ
window	mado	窓

Is there a discount for children/students?
(kodomo-/gakusei-) waribiki wa arimasu ka?
(子供／学生)割引はありますか?

It's fine. I'll take this/ that room.
iidesu ne. kono/sono heya ni shimasu.
いいですね。(この／その) 部屋 にします。

ACCOMMODATION

THEY MAY SAY ...

go-yoyaku wa gozaimasu ka?
　Have you made a booking?
shinguru ni itashimashō ka, daburu ni itashimashō ka?
　Would you like single room, or double room?
nam-mei sama desu ka?
　How many people?
nam-paku saremasu ka?
　How many nights are you staying?
nan-ji ni go-shuppatsu desu ka?
　What time are you leaving?

REQUESTS & COMPLAINTS

I need a (another) ...	(hoka no) ... ga hoshiidesu (ほかの) ... が欲しいです。
Do you have a safe where I can leave my valuables?	anzen kinko ga arimasu ka? 安全金庫がありますか？
Could I have a receipt for them?	reshīto o itadake masen ka? レシートをいただけませんか？
Is there somewhere to wash clothes?	fuku o sentaku dekiru tokoro ga arimasu ka? 服を洗濯できるところがありますか？
Can we use the telephone?	denwa o tsukatte mo ii desu ka? 電話を使ってもいいですか？
My room's too dark	watashi no heya wa kura sugi masu 私の部屋は暗すぎます。
It's too cold/hot.	samu/atsu sugi masu (寒/暑) すぎます
It's too noisy.	urusa sugi masu うるさすぎます。
I can't open/close the window.	mado o akeru/shimeru koto ga dekimasen 窓を (開ける／閉める) ことができません。
This ... isn't clean.	kono ... wa kirei dewa arimasen この ... はきれいではありません。
blanket/sheet	mōfu/shītsu 毛布／シーツ
pillow case	makura-kabā 枕カバー
pillow	makura 枕
Please change them/it.	torikaete kudasai 取り替えて下さい。

CHECKING OUT

Can I pay with a travellers' cheque.

toraberāzu-chekku de harau koto ga dekimasu ka?

トラベラーズチェックで 払うことができますか?

Could I have the bill please?

seikyūsho o itadakemasen ka?

請求書をいただけませんか?

There's a mistake in the bill.

seikyūsho ni machigai ga arimasu

請求書に間違いがあります。

USEFUL WORDS

air-conditioning	eakon	エアコン
clean	kirei	きれい
key	kagi	鍵
hand towel	otefuki	お手ふき
bottle of water	bin iri no mizu	びん入りの水
lamp	rampu	ランプ
lock	jō	錠
mosquito coil	katori-senkō	蚊取り線香
soap	sekken	石鹸
toilet	toire	トイレ
toilet paper	toiretto-pēpā	トイレットペーパー
towel	taoru	タオル
cold water/hot water	mizu/oyu	水/お湯

PAPERWORK

name	namae	名前
address	jūsho	住所
date of birth	seinen-gappi	生年月日
place of birth	shussheichi	出身地
age	nenrei	年齢
gender	seibetsu	性別
nationality	kokuseki	国籍
religion	shūkyō	宗教
profession/work	shokugyō	職業
reason for travel	ryokō no mokuteki	旅行の目的
marital status	kekkon no umu	結婚の有無
single	mikon	未婚
married	kikon	既婚
divorced	rikon	離婚
identification	mibun shōmei	身分証明
passport number	ryoken-bangō;	旅券番号／
	pasupōto nambā	パスポートナンバー
visa	biza	ビザ
driving licence	(unten) menkyo-shō	(運転) 免許証
customs	zeikan	税関
Immigration Office	imin-kyoku	移民局
purpose of visit	taizai no mokuteki	滞在の目的
holiday	kyūka	休暇
business	shigoto	仕事
visiting relatives	sinseki hōmon	親戚訪問
visiting the homeland	shussheichi no hōmon	出身地の訪問

AROUND TOWN

LOOKING FOR ...

Where's a/an ...?	... wa doko desu ka?	... はどこですか？
bank	ginkō	銀行
consulate	ryōjikan	領事館
embassy	taishikan	大使館
museum	hakubutsukan	博物館
police	kōban	交番
post office	yūbinkyoku	郵便局
public telephone	kōshū denwa	公衆電話
public toilet	kōshū toire	公衆トイレ
nearest station	ichiban chikai eki	いちばん近い駅
tourist information office	kankō annai-jo	観光案内所

AT THE BANK

All banks have a guide stationed in the foyer to direct you to the correct counter. Most are very helpful, even if they have limited knowledge of English. Banking transactions can be very slow so allow yourself plenty of time.

You can change cash or travellers' cheques at major hotels and authorised foreign exchange banks. Although credit cards are becoming more commonly used, cash is still most popular and credit facilities may not be available in rural areas.

Can I use my credit card to withdraw cash.

kurejitto-kādo de genkin o orosu koto ga dekimasu ka?
クレジットカードで現金をおろすことができますか？

Can I exchange money here?

koko de ryōgae dekimasu ka?
ここで両替できますか？

How many yen per (dollar)?

(ichi doru) nan-en desu ka?
（1ドル）何円ですか？

Please write it down.	kaite kudasai 書いて下さい。	
Can I have smaller notes?	o-kane o kuzushite moraemasu ka? お金をくずしてもらえますか?	
The automatic teller swallowed my card.	eitīemu kara kādo ga dete kimasen ATMからカードが出てき ません。	
I want to change ...	... o kaetai no desu ga ... を換えたいのですが。	
cash/money	genkin/o-kane	現金/お金
a cheque	kogitte	小切手
a travellers' cheque	toraberāzu-chekku	トラベラーズ チェック

What time does the bank open?	ginkō wa nan-ji ni akimasu ka? 銀行は何時に開きますか?
Where can I cash a travellers' cheque?	doko de toraberāzu-chekku o genkin ni kaeru koto ga dekimasu ka? どこでトラベラーズチェック を現金に換えることがで きますか?
What's the exchange rate?	kawase rēto wa ikura desu ka? 為替レートはいくらですか?
Can I transfer money here from my bank?	kokokara watashi no ginkō ni sōkin dekimasu ka? ここから私の銀行に送金でき ますか?
How long will it take to arrive?	tōchaku suru made donokurai jikan ga kakarimasu ka? 到着するまでどのくらい時間 がかかりますか?

balance	zandaka	残高
sign	sain	サイン
banknote	o-satsu	お札
small change	kozeni	小銭
cash card	kyasshu kādo	キャッシュカード
deposit	yokin	預金
passbook	tsūchō	通帳
handling charge	tesūryō	手数料
account	kōza	口座
account number	kōza bangō	口座番号
amount	kingaku	金額

SIGNS

熱い／冷たい	HOT/COLD
入口	ENTRANCE
出口	EXIT
立入禁止	NO ENTRY
禁煙	NO SMOKING
営業中／準備中	OPEN/CLOSED
禁止	PROHIBITED
トイレ／お手洗い	TOILETS
男	MEN
女	WOMEN
危険	DANGER
手を触れないで下さい	DO NOT TOUCH
非常口	EMERGENCY EXIT
案内所	INFORMATION
駐車禁止	NO PARKING
受付	RECEPTION
土足厳禁	TAKE OFF SHOES
工事中	UNDER CONSTRUCTION
火気厳禁	USE OF FIRE STRICTLY PROHIBITED

AROUND TOWN

AT THE POST OFFICE

Most Japanese post offices also serve as a type of credit union, so be sure to check for the appropriate counters, normally coloured red and marked 'Letters' or 'Parcels' in English. Boxes for parcels sold at post offices also have pre-cut tape enclosed and are very reasonably priced.

air mail	kōkūyūbin	航空郵便
contents	nakami	中身
domestic mail	kokunai yūbin	国内郵便
envelope	fūtō	封筒
express mail	sokutatsu	速達
GPO	chūō yūbinkyoku	中央郵便局
letter box	yūbin bako	郵便箱
mail box	yūbin posuto	郵便ポスト
New Year's greeting card	nengajō	年賀状
pen	pen	ペン
PO box	shisho bako	私書箱
poste restante	tomeoki	留置き
postcode	yūbin bangō	郵便番号
printed matter	insatsubutsu	印刷物
registered cash mail	genkin kakitome	現金書留
registered mail	kakitome yūbin	書留郵便
surface mail	funabin	船便

I want to buy postcards/   hagaki/kitte o kudasai.
    stamps.   (はがき／切手) をください。

I want to send a/an ...   ... o okuritai no desuga.
                  ... を送りたいのですが。

aerogram	kōkūshokan	航空書簡
letter	tegami	手紙
parcel	kozutsumi	小包
telegram	dempō	電報

Please send it by ...   ... de okutte kudasai.
                  ... で送って下さい。

How much does it cost to send this to ...?	kore o ... ni okuru ni wa ikura kakarimasu ka? これを ... に送るにはいくら かかりますか？	
Are there any restrictions regarding ...?	... no seigen wa arimasu ka? ... の制限はありますか？	
size	saizu/ōkisa	サイズ／大きさ
thickness	atsusa	厚さ
weight	jūryō/omosa	重量／重さ

TELECOMMUNICATIONS

Public phones in Japan take telephone cards and coins. All calls are charged by the minute. Telephone cards can be bought at kiosks at train stations and vending machines often located inside telephone booths. International calls can be made from some telephones which are marked clearly in English. Most operators for international calls speak English.

Could I please use the telephone?	denwa o tsukatte mo ii desu ka? 電話を使ってもいいですか？
I want to call ...	... ni denwa shitai no desu ga ... に電話したいのですが。
The number is ...	denwa bangō wa ... -ban desu 電話番号は ... 番です。
How much does a three-minute call cost?	sampun kan ikura desu ka? ３分間いくらですか？
I want to make a call to Australia.	ōsutoraria ni denwashitai no desu ga オーストラリアに電話したいの ですが。
I want to make a collect call.	korekuto-kōru o shitai no desuga コレクトコールをしたいのですが。
What's the area code for ...?	... no shigai-kyokuban wa namban desu ka? ... の市外局番は何番ですか？

It's engaged.	o-hanashi-chū desu お話し中です。
I've been cut off.	denwa ga tochū de kiremashita 電話が途中で切れました。
Is there a local Internet café?	intānetto-kafe ga arimasu ka? インターネットカフェがあ りますか?
I need to get Internet access.	intānetto ni akusesu suru hitsuyō ga arimasu. インターネットにアクセスする 必要があります。
I need to check my email.	ī-mēru o minakereba narimasen E−メールを見なければなり ません。

country code	kunibangō	国番号
international phone call	kokusai denwa	国際電話
local call	shinai denwa	市内電話
long-distance call	chōkyori denwa	長距離電話
mobile phone	keitai denwa	携帯電話
operator	kōkanshu/operētā	交換手／オペレーター
phone book	denwachō	電話帳
phone box	denwa bokkusu	電話ボックス
phonecard	terefon kādo	テレフォンカード
telephone	denwa	電話
urgent	kinkyū	緊急
wrong number	machigai denwa	間違い電話

Making a Call

Hello, is ... there?	moshi-moshi, ... -san wa irasshaimasu ka? もしもし、... さんはいらっしゃ いますか。
Hello. (answering a call)	moshi-moshi もしもし
May I speak to ...?	... -san o onegaishimasu ... さんをお願いします。

Who's calling?	dochira-sama desu ka? どちらさまですか？
It's ...	... desu ... です。
Yes, he/she is here.	hai, imasu. はい、います。
One moment, please.	shōshō o-machi kudasai 少々お待ち下さい。
I'm sorry, ... is not here.	sumimasen ga, ... wa imasen すみませんが、... はいません。
What time will Mr. Suzuki be back?	Suzuki-san wa nan-ji ni kaerimasu ka? 鈴木さんは何時に帰りますか？
Can I leave a message?	dengon o onegai shimasu 伝言をお願いします。
Please tell her/him I called.	watashi ga denwashita to kanojo/kare ni tsutaete kudasai 私が電話したと（彼女／彼）に伝えて下さい。
I'll call back later.	mata ato de denwashimasu また後で電話します。

CHOTTO

You may often hear the word chotto in Japan, for example, chotto matte kudasai, 'Wait a minute'. chotto literary means 'a little', but Japanese people use it when they want to attract someone's attention, to soften the meaning and often just out of habit:

chotto, chotto
'Excuse me.' (attracting someone's attention)

chotto onegai ga arimasu
'I have a small favour to ask.'
(this can sometimes be a big favour)

SIGHTSEEING

Where's the tourist office?	kankō annai-jo wa doko desu ka?	
	観光案内所はどこですか？	
Do you have a local map?	kono atari no chizu wa arimasu ka?	
	この辺りの地図はありますか？	
I'd like to see ...	... o mitai no desu ga.	
	... を見たいのですが。	
What time does it open?	nan-ji ni akimasu ka?	
	何時に開きますか？	
What time does it close?	nan-ji ni shimarimasu ka?	
	何時に閉りますか？	
What's that building?	ano tatemono wa nan desu ka?	
	あの建物は何ですか？	
What's this monument?	kono kinen-hi wa nan desu ka?	
	この記念碑は何ですか？	
May we take photographs?	shashin o tottemo ii desu ka?	
	写真を撮ってもいいですか？	
I'll send you the photograph.	shashin o okurimasu	
	写真を送ります。	
Could you take a photograph of me?	shashin o totte moraemasu ka?	
	写真を撮ってもらえますか？	

art gallery	bijutsukan	美術館
castle	o-shiro	お城
church/cathedral	kyōkai	教会
cinema	eigakan	映画館
concert	konsāto	コンサート
crowded	konde imasu	込んでいます
museum	hakubutsukan	博物館
park	kōen	公園
statue	zō	像
university	daigaku	大学

AROUND TOWN

WHERE TO GO

I feel like going to ...	... ni ikitai desu	... に行きたいです。
a bar/cafe	bā/kafe	バー／カフェ
the cinema	eiga	映画
a concert	konsāto	コンサート
a disco	disuko	ディスコ
the opera	opera	オペラ
a restaurant	resutoran	レストラン
a night club	naito kurabu	ナイトクラブ
shopping	kaimono	買い物

ARRANGING TO MEET

Where shall we meet?	doko de aimashō ka?
	どこで会いましょうか？
What time shall we meet?	nan-ji ni aimashō ka?
	何時に会いましょうか？
Let's meet at (7 o'clock) in (Shibuya Station)	(shibuya-eki) de (shichi-ji) ni aimashō
	(渋谷駅) で (7時) に会いましょう。
OK, see you then.	wakarimashita. soko de aimashō
	わかりました。そこで会いましょう。

INVITES

Are you free this (Saturday night)?	(doyōbi no yoru) wa hima desu ka?
	(土曜日の夜) は暇ですか？
What are you doing this evening/weekend?	(komban/konshū no shūmatsu) nani o shimasu ka?
	(今晩／今週の週末) 何をしますか？
Would you like to go somewhere?	doko ka ikimashō ka?
	どこか行きましょうか？

Do you know a good restaurant (that's cheap)?	(yasukute) ii resutoran o shitte imasu ka? (安くて) いいレストランを知っていますか？
We're having a party.	pātī o shimasu. パーティーをします。
Would you like to come to my home?	watashi no ie ni kimasen ka? 私の家に来ませんか？
Would you like to go for a drink/meal?	nomi/tabe ni ikimasen ka? (飲み／食べ) に行きませんか？
Do you want to come to	issho ni konsāto ni ikimasen ka? いっしょにコンサートに行きませんか？

ON THE STREETS

What's this?	kore wa nan desu ka? これは何ですか？
What's happening?	nani ga okite imasu ka? 何が起きていますか？
What happened?	nani ga okitan desu ka? 何が起きたんですか？
What is she/he doing?	kare/kanojo wa nani o shite irun desu ka? (彼／彼女) は何をしているんですか？
Can I have one please?	hitotsu kudasai. 一つください。
How much?	ikura? いくら？
How do you read those kanji?	ano kanji wa dō yomun desu ka? あの漢字はどう読むんですか？

PEOPLE YOU SEE

advertisement distributors	chirashi kubari	チラシ配り
busker	daidōgeinin	大道芸人
demonstrator	demo	デモ
fortune teller	uranaishi	占師
homeless	hōmuresu	ホームレス
lottery ticket seller	takara kuji uriba	宝くじ売り場
magician	tejinashi	手品師

Responding to Invites

Sure.	mochiron	もちろん。
Yes, sounds good.	ii desu ne	いいですね。
Let's go!	ikimashō!	行きましょう！
Yes, let's go. Where shall we go?	hai, sō shimashō. doko ni ikimashō ka?	はい、そうしましょう。どこに行きましょうか？
No, I'm afraid I can't. What about tomorrow?	chotto tsugō ga warui desu. ashita wa dō desu ka?	ちょっと都合が悪いです。明日はどうですか？
I have other commitments.	hoka ni yōji ga arimasu	他に用事があります。

AT THE CLUB

Would you like to drink something?	nani ka nomimasen ka?	何か飲みませんか？
Shall we dance?	odorimasen ka?	踊りませんか？
I'm sorry, I'm a terrible dancer.	sumimasen, dansu wa nigate desu	すみません、ダンスは苦手です。

SWEARING

Bad language is not infused into the Japanese language to the degree that it occurs in English. In addition, swear words are less colourful than those in English. The words below can have a far greater impact than they might have in English, and care must be taken when using them.

Shit!	kuso!	くそ
You fool/idiot!	baka/aho	ばか／アホ
Goddamm it!	chikushō	畜生
This bastard!/	koitsu/aitsu	こいつ／あいつ
That son of a bitch!		

What type of music do you prefer?	donna taipu no ongaku ga suki desu ka? どんなタイプの音楽が好きですか？
What would you like to drink?	nani o nomimasu ka? 何を飲みますか？
This place is great!	koko wa suteki desu ne! ここは素敵ですね！
I'm having a great time!	totemo tanoshii desu! とても楽しいです！
I don't like the music here.	koko no ongaku wa amari suki ja arimasen ここの音楽はあまり好きじゃありません。
Shall we go somewhere else?	doko ka chigau tokoro ni ikimashō ka? どこか違うところに行きましょうか？

KARAOKE

Enjoy karaoke? The Japanese do – karaoke (literally 'empty orchestra') is extremely popular among the young and old alike in Japan. You can enjoy karaoke in small bars belting out songs with complete strangers – the shy can hire their own room and have a private sing-a-long. Most have some English songs in their listings though you might want to have a go at some Japanese classics.

Let's sing together.	issho ni utaimashō
	いっしょに歌いましょう。
Are there English songs?	eigo no uta ga arimasu ka?
	英語の歌がありますか？
I don't know this song.	kono uta o shirimasen
	この歌を知りません。
I'm not good at singing.	watashi wa uta ga jōzu ja arimasen
	私は歌が上手じゃありません。

INVITATIONS

- When inviting someone to do something with you, the negative -masu form of the verb is often used.

Would you like to go to a film?	eiga ni ikimasen ka? (lit: film to not-go question)

- You can reply to this with one of two options:

Let's go.	ikimashō
I'm sorry, but it's not convenient with me.	sumimasen, chotto tsugō ga warui desu

- You should avoid using very direct expressions such as 'I don't want to' when responding, unless you wish to stress the point.

I don't want to go.	ikitaku nai desu

GOING OUT

TRADITIONAL ENTERTAINMENT

Traditional performances are considered as much art as they are entertainment.

Bunraku

This is musical puppet drama accompanied by a shamisen, a lute-like instrument with three strings.

jōruri   浄瑠璃
  musical accompaniment

ningyō   人形
  puppet

omo zukai; ashi zukai; hidari zukai   面遣い／足遣い／左遣い
  trio of puppeteers operating the performance

Kabuki

Spectacular musical drama in which both the male and female roles are played by men.

hana michi   花道
  elevated section in front of the stage

mawari butai   まわり舞台
  revolving stage

STRESSING OUT

To qualify or stress a particular point you can use the topic particle wa:

> This person is Mr. Suzuki.
> kono hito wa suzuki-san desu
> (lit: this person top Suzuki-Mr is)

Nō

These are a type of play involving stylised movement, chanting and elaborate costumes and masks.

atoza 後座
  space for the orchestra

hayashi はやし
  musical accompaniment

kyōgen/aikyōgen 狂言/間狂言
  comic interlude between acts

mai 舞
  dance

men/kamen 面/仮面
  mask

shite 仕手
  principal actor

yōkyoku/utai 謡曲/謡
  chorus

IT'S AMAZING

raishū no butai wa ... desu ka?	Is the performance next week ... ?
kono butai wa ... desu	This performance is ...

... desu	It's ...
sugoi	amazing
subarashii	brilliant
ii	good
māmā	so so
omoshiroi	fun/interesting
tsumaranai	boring
mechamecha	crap
hidoi	terrible

GOING OUT

Yose

This is popular theatre.

kōdan　　　　　講談
　historical storytelling

manzai/kōshaku　漫才/講釈
　comic dialogue

rōkyoku　　　　浪曲
　story-telling and singing

rakugo　　　　落語
　comic story-telling

Traditional Music

biwa　　　　　琵琶
　four-stringed lute

dōyō　　　　　童謡
　children's songs

ga gaku　　　　雅楽
　court music

hō gaku　　　　邦楽
　traditional Japanese music

komori uta　　　子守り歌
　lullaby

koto/o-koto　　琴/お琴
　13-stringed zither

ko uta　　　　　小唄
　short popular song

min yō　　　　　民謡
　folk song

naga uta　　　　長唄
　epic song

shaku hachi　　尺八
　five-holed bamboo flute

sō kyoku　　　そう曲
　music played on a koto

taiko　　　　　太鼓
　drum

COMMON INTERESTS

What do you do in your spare time?	himana toki nani o shimasu ka? 暇なとき何をしますか？
What's your favourite hobby?	shumi wa nan desu ka? 趣味は何ですか？

I like ...   ... ga suki desu
... が好きです。

I don't like ...   ... ga suki ja arimasen
... が好きじゃありません。

Do you like ...?   ... ga suki desu ka?   ... が好きですか？

art	bijutsu	美術
classical music	kurashikku	クラシック
cooking	ryōri	料理
dancing	dansu	ダンス
film	eiga	映画
going out	gaishutsu	外出
golf	gorufu	ゴルフ
karaoke	karaoke	カラオケ
music	ongaku	音楽
photography	shashin	写真
popular music	poppu myūjikku	ポップミュージック
playing baseball	yakyū	野球
playing games	gēmu	ゲーム
playing soccer	sakkā	サッカー
playing sport	supōtsu	スポーツ
reading books	dokusho	読書
shopping	kaimono	買い物
talking	oshaberi	おしゃべり
the theatre	geki	劇
travelling	ryokō	旅行
TV	terebi	テレビ

INTERESTS

SPORT

Baseball has been a very popular sport in Japan for decades, and teams from the two national leagues attract major corporate sponsors and are based in various cities throughout Japan. There are many baseball fans who follow their favourite team and study the game in detail. In spring and summer the high school baseball competition is broadcast nationally and attracts millions of viewers.

Interest in soccer has grown significantly in recent years. Popular among the young, soccer has developed its own professional league, and, like baseball, imports overseas players to supplement local talent.

Do you like sport?	supōtsu ga suki desu ka? スポーツが好きですか?
I like playing sport.	supōtsu o suru no ga suki desu スポーツをするのが好きです。
(I) prefer to watch rather than play sport.	supōtsu wa suru yori miru hō ga suki desu スポーツは、するより見るほうが好きです。
Do you play ...?	... o shimasu ka? ... をしますか?
Would you like to play ...?	... o shimasen ka? ... をしませんか?

Useful Words

baseball	yakyū	野球
basketball	basuketto bōru	バスケットボール
boxing	bokushingu	ボクシング
cricket	kuriketto	クリケット
diving	daibingu	ダイビング
football	futto bōru	フットボール
hockey	hokkē	ホッケー
keeping fit	karada o kitaeru koto	体を鍛えること
martial arts	budō	武道
rugby	ragubī	ラグビー
soccer	sakkā	サッカー
surfing	sāfin	サーフィン

swimming	suiei	水泳
tennis	tenisu	テニス
gymnastics	taisō	体操
skiing	sukī	体操

SUMO

Sumo wrestling is Japan's national sport. It's linked to the Shintō religion and originated as a religious rite to obtain the blessings of the gods for the year's harvest. Sumo incorporates many ritualistic elements from Shintō such as the throwing of salt – purification – and clapping of hands – blessing of the ring.

Although sumo attracts the attention of many non-Japanese due to the size of the wrestlers, the most exciting element of the sport for local fans is the skill and strategy employed to oust competitors from the ring.

Six ōzumō tournaments are held each year across different cities. Competetion is limited to 38, each striving to become a yokozuna, 'grand champion' – a title held for life.

The wrestlers build up their gigantic frames with a staple diet of fattening stew called chanko nabe . The wrestlers touch their starting lines with their fists to indicate that they're ready. The referee signals the start of the match with the call hakkeyoi! and the wrestlers attack, attempting to throw their opponent onto the ground or out of the ring.

Sumo Talk

arena	dohyō	土俵
loincloth	mawashi	まわし
program	banzuke hyō	番付表
referee	gyōji	行司
school	heya	部屋
stomping	shiko	四股
tactics	waza	技
tournament	basho	場所
wrestler	rikishi	力士

MORE SUMO TERMS

chanko nabe　　　ちゃんこ鍋
a rich and hearty stew to fatten up the wrestlers

dohyōiri　　　　土俵入り
an opening ceremony

ginōshō　　　　技能賞
a prize awarded for skill

gumbai　　　　軍配
a fan held by the referee as a symbol of his authority

hiki otoshi　　　引き落し
to pull down an opponent

higashi　　　　東
the east end of the arena

kantōshō　　　　敢闘賞
a prize awarded for fighting spirit

matta!　　　　　まった
the cry to 'Wait!'

nishi　　　　　西
the west end of the arena

nokotta　　　　のこった
the cry to 'Continue!'

oshi taoshi　　　押し倒し
to knock or throw down the opponent

oshi dashi　　　押し出し
to push the opponent out of the arena

senshūraku　　　千秋楽
the final day of the tournament

shukunshō 殊勲章
a prize for distinguished achievement

sunakaburi 砂かぶり
front-row seats

tachi mochi 太刀持ち
a sword bearer in the opening ceremony

tennōhai 天皇杯
the Emperor's Cup – this is only awarded to the
grand champion

tsuri dashi つり出し
to carry the opponent out of the arena

yori kiri 寄り切り
to drive the opponent out of the arena

INTERESTS

FAMILY

Are you married?	kekkon shite imasu ka?
	結婚していますか？
I'm single.	dokushin desu
	独身です。
I'm married.	kekkon shite imasu
	結婚しています。
How many children do you have?	kodomo wa nan-nin imasu ka?
	子供は何人いますか？
I have two sons/daughters.	musuko/musume ga futari imasu
	(息子／娘) が2人います。
We don't have any children.	kodomo wa imasen
	子供はいません。
How many siblings do you have?	kyōdai wa nan-nin imasu ka?
	きょうだいは何人いますか？
Is your husband/wife here?	go-shujin/oku-san wa koko ni imasu ka?
	(ご主人／奥さん) はここにいますか？
Do you have a boyfriend/ girlfriend?	bōi/gāru furendo wa imasu ka?
	(ボーイ／ガール) フレンドはいますか？

DIALECTS

There are many dialects in Japan. People who come from outside Tokyo often speak their own dialect within the home region, and are also fluent in standard Japanese. As standard Japanese is based on Yamanote dialect in Tokyo, most people in Tokyo speak standard Japanese only. Osaka and Kyoto dialects are commonly spoken in those areas and are linked to a sense of pride in one's hometown. Many young people chose to speak standard Japanese instead of their regional dialect and some have lost their fluency.

INTERESTS

family	kazoku	家族
husband/wife	otto/ tsuma	夫/妻
child	kodomo	子供
daughter/son	musume/ musuko	娘／息子

(my/our) mother	haha	母
(your/his/her/their) mother	okāsan	お母さん
(my/our) father	chichi	父
(your/his/her/their) father	otōsan	お父さん

sister	shimai	姉妹
(my/our) older sister	ane	姉
(your/his/her/their) older sister	onēsen	お姉さん
younger sister	imōto	妹

brother	kyōdai	兄弟
(my/our) older brother	ani	兄
(your/his/her/their) older brother	onīsan	お兄さん
younger brother	otōto	弟

POLITICS

Heated discussion is not looked upon favourably among Japanese people. As a result, the Japanese tend to avoid showing their political inclination or debating political issues. After-hours drinking sessions are the most conducive places for open discussion.

Did you hear about ...?	... ni tsuite kikimashita ka? ... について聞きましたか？
I read in (Asahi Newspaper) today that ...	kyō no (asahi shimbun) de ... ni tsuite yomimashita 今日の (朝日新聞) で ... について読みました。
What do you think of the current government?	ima no seifu o dō omoimasu ka? 今の政府をどう思いますか？

INTERESTS

What will happen to the Japanese economy?	nihon no keizai wa dō naru no deshō ka? 日本の経済はどうなるのでしょうか?

I'm against/in favour of ...	... seisaku ni hantai/sansei shimasu. ... 政策に (反対/賛成) します。
education	kyōiku	教育
environment	kankyō	環境
military affairs	gunji	軍事
social welfare	shakai fukushi	社会福祉
tax	zeikin	税金

I support the ...	watashi wa ... o shiji shimasu 私は ... を支持します。
Communist Party	kyōsantō	共産党
Conservative Party	hoshutō	保守党
Democratic Party	minshutō	民主党
Liberal Democratic Party	jimintō	自民党
Social Democratic Party	shakai-minshu tō	社会民主党

Politicians are all the same.	seiji-ka wa minna onaji desu 政治家はみんな同じです。
Politicians can never be trusted.	seiji-ka wa shinjiraremasen 政治家は信じられません。
In my country we have a labour/conservative government.	watashi no kuni de wa rōdōtō/hoshutō ga seiken o nigitte imasu 私の国では (労働党/保守党) が政権を握っています。
Do you support the royal family?	kōshitsu o shiji shimasu ka? 皇室を支持しますか?

SHOPPING

LOOKING FOR ...

Where can I buy ...?	... wa doko de kau koto ga dekimasu ka? ... はどこで買うことができますか?
Where's the nearest ...?	ichiban chikai ... wa doko desu ka? いちばん近い ... はどこですか?

barber	tokoya	床屋
beauty salon	biyōin	美容院
bookshop	hon-ya	本屋
camera shop	kamera-ya	カメラ屋
chemist/pharmacy	yakkyoku	薬局
clothing store	fuku-ya	服屋
department store	depāto	デパート
general store	sutoa	ストア
coin laundry	koin randorī	コインランドリー
market	ichiba	市場
souvenir shop	miyagemono-ya	土産物屋

MAKING A PURCHASE

I'd like to buy ...	... o kudasai ... をください。
How much is this?	kore wa ikura desu ka? これはいくらですか?
Do you have others?	hoka ni arimasu ka? 他にありますか?
I don't like it.	sore wa amari suki ja arimasen それはあまり好きじゃありません。
Can I look at it?	sore o mite mo ii desu ka? それを見てもいいですか?
I'm just looking.	mite iru dake desu 見ているだけです。

Can you write down the price?	nedan o kaite moraemasu ka? 値段を書いてもらえますか?
Do you accept credit cards?	kurejitto-kādo de mo ii desu ka? クレジットカードでもいいですか?
Please wrap it.	tsutsunde kudasai 包んで下さい。

BARGAINING

I think it's too expensive.	taka sugimasu 高すぎます。
It's too much for us.	watashi-tachi ni wa taka sugimasu 私達には高すぎます。
Can you lower the price?	yasuku shite moraemasen ka? 安くしてもらえませんか?

ESSENTIAL GROCERIES

Where can I find?		... wa doko ni arimasu ka? ... はどこにありますか?
I'd like ...	... o kudasai.	... をください。
batteries	denchi	電池
bread	pan	パン
butter	batā	バター
cheese	chīzu	チーズ
chocolate	chokorēto	チョコレート
eggs	tamago	たまご
flour	komugiko	小麦粉
gas cylinder	gasu shirindā	ガスシリンダー
ham	hamu	ハム
honey	hachimitsu	蜂蜜
margarine	māgarin	マーガリン
matches	macchi	マッチ
milk	gyūnyū/miruku	牛乳／ミルク

pepper	koshō	胡椒
salt	shio	塩
shampoo	shampū	シャンプー
soap	sekken	石鹸
sugar	satō	砂糖
toilet paper	toiretto-pēpā	トイレットペーパー
toothpaste	hamigaki	ハミガキ
washing powder	sentaku senzai	洗濯洗剤
yoghurt	yōguruto	ヨーグルト

SOUVENIRS

kimono style bathrobe	yukata	浴衣
happi coat	happi	法被

(a traditional brightly coloured festival coat normally made from cotton)

cloisonné	shippōyaki	七宝焼き
antique	kottōhin	骨董品
doll	ningyō	人形
fan (folding)	sensu	扇子
fan (round)	uchiwa	団扇
chinaware	setomono	瀬戸物
furniture	kagu	家具
food	shokuryōhin	食料品
jewellery	hōseki	宝石
kimono	kimono	着物
lacquerware	shikki	漆器
painting (Japanese)	nihon-ga	日本画
painting (oil)	abura-e	油絵
painting/picture	e	絵
paper (Japanese)	washi	和紙
pearl	shinju	真珠
personal seal	inkan/hanko	印鑑／はんこ
postcard	e-hagaki	絵葉書
pottery	tōki	陶器
umbrella	kasa	傘

SHOPPING

CLOTHING

jacket	jaketto	ジャケット
jumper (sweater)	sētā	セーター
trousers	zubon	ズボン
raincoat	reinkōto	レインコート
shirt	shatsu	シャツ
shoes	kutsu	靴
socks	kutsushita	靴下
swimsuit	mizugi	水着
T-shirt	tīshatsu	Tシャツ
underwear	shitagi	下着

COLOURS

dark ...	kurai ...	暗い ...
light ...	akarui ...	明るい ...
black	kuro	黒
blue	ao	青
brown	cha-iro	茶色
green	midori	緑
grey·	hai-iro	灰色
orange	orenji-iro	オレンジ色
pink	pinku	ピンク
purple	murasaki	紫
red	aka	赤
white	shiro	白
yellow	ki-iro	黄色

TOILETRIES

condoms	kondōmu	コンドーム
deodorant	deodoranto	デオドラント
moisturising cream	kurīmu	クリーム
razor	kamisori	剃刀
sanitary napkins	napukin	ナプキン
shampoo	shampū	シャンプー

shaving cream	shēbingu-kurīmu	シェービング クリーム
soap	sekken	石鹸
sunblock	hiyakedome	日焼け止め
tampons	tampon	タンポン
toilet paper	toiretto-pēpā	トイレット ペーパー

FOR THE BABY

canned baby food	kanzume no yōjishoku	缶詰の幼児食
baby powder	bebī-paudā	ベビーパウダー
bib	yodarekake	よだれ掛け
disposable nappies	kami-omutsu	紙おむつ
dummy/pacifier	oshaburi	おしゃぶり
feeding bottle	honyūbin	哺乳びん
nappy/diaper	omutsu	おむつ
nappy rash cream	kabure-dome kurīmu	かぶれ止めクリーム
powdered milk	kona miruku	粉ミルク

STATIONERY & PUBLICATIONS

Is there an English-language bookshop near here?	kono chikaku ni eigo no hon-ya ga arimasu ka? この近くに英語の本屋があり ますか?
Is there an English-language section?	eigo no sekushon ga arimasu ka? 英語のセクションンがあり ますか?
Is there a local entertainment guide?	kono chiiki no goraku jōhō gaido ga arimasu ka? この地域の娯楽情報ガイドが ありますか?

Do you sell ...?	... ga arimasu ka?	... がありますか?
magazines	zasshi	雑誌
newspapers	shimbun	新聞
postcards	ehagaki	絵葉書
dictionary	jisho	辞書
envelope	fūtō	封筒
... map	... chizu	... 地図
city	shigai	市街
regional	chiiki	地域
road	dōro	道路
newspaper in English	eiji-shimbun	英字新聞
paper	kami	紙
pen (ballpoint)	pen (bōrupen)	ペン (ボールペン)
stamp	kitte	切手

NEW ORDER

Remember that word order in Japanese is *subject-object-verb* unlike English which is *subject-verb-object*. This means that the verb comes after the object.

MUSIC

I'm looking for a ... CD.	... no shīdī o sagasite imasu. ... のＣＤを探しています。
Do you have any ...?	... wa arimasu ka? ... はありますか？
What's his/her best recording?	kare/kanojo no ichiban ii rekōdo wa nan desu ka (彼／彼女)の一番いいレコードは何ですか？
I heard a band/singer called ...	... to iu namae no bando/kashu o kiita no desu ga ... という名前の (バンド／歌手) を聞いたのですが。
Can I listen to this CD here?	koko de kono shīdī o kiite mo ii desu ka? ここでこのＣＤを聞いてもいいですか？
I need a blank tape.	kara no tēpu ga hoshii no desu ga 空のテープが欲しいのですが。

SHOPPING

THEY MAY SAY ...

irasshai mase	May I help you?
nani ka osagashi desu ka?	Are you looking for something?
kochira wa ikaga de shō ka?	How about this one?
o-tsutsumi shimashō ka?	Would you like me to wrap it?
(sanzen) en desu	It's (3000) yen.
arigatō gozaimashita	Thank you very much.

PHOTOGRAPHY

How much is it to process this film?	kono firumu no genzōryō wa ikura desu ka? このフィルムの現像料はいくらですか。
When will it be ready?	itsu dekiagarimasu ka? いつ出来上がりますか？
I'd like a film for this camera.	kono kamera no firumu o kudasai このカメラのフィルムをください。

battery	denchi	電池
B&W film	shiro-kuro firumu	白黒フィルム
camera	kamera	カメラ
colour film	karā firumu	カラーフィルム
film	firumu	フィルム

IS THAT SO?

It is important when speaking with Japanese people to frequently acknowledge the speaker verbally. It isn't polite to stand and say nothing when having a conversation. This is why you'll often hear the listener using terms such as a, sō (desu ka)?

This well known expression literally means 'Oh, is that so?', and is used to acknowledge the speaker's utterances. It's an easy expression to remember, but try not to overuse it. Other expressions you can use to show acknowledgment are:

hontō (desu ka)?	Really?
hai	Yes.
ee	Yes.
un	Yep.

flash (bulb)	sutorobo (no denkyū)	ストロボ(の電球)
lens	renzu	レンズ
light meter	sokkōki	測光器
slides	suraido	スライド
videotape	bideo tēpu	ビデオテープ

SMOKING

70 percent of Japanese men and 35 percent of Japanese women are smokers. Smoking is allowed in most restaurants and public places in Japan.

(A packet of) cigarettes, please.	tabako o (hito-hako) kudasai たばこを（一箱）ください。
Are these cigarettes strong or mild?	kono tabako wa tsuyoi desu ka, yowai desu ka? このたばこは強いですか、弱いですか？
Do you have a light?	raitā ga arimasu ka? ライターがありますか？
Do you mind if I smoke?	tabako o sutte mo ii desu ka? たばこを吸ってもいいですか？
Please don't smoke.	tabako o suwanaide kudasai たばこを吸わないで下さい。
I'm trying to give up.	kin'en shite imasu 禁煙しています。

cigar	hamaki	葉巻
cigarettes	tabako	たばこ
cigarette papers	maki-tabako no kami	巻き煙草の紙
filtered	firutā tsuki	フィルター付き
lighter	raitā	ライター
matches	macchi	マッチ
menthol	mensōru	メンソール
pipe	paipu	パイプ
tobacco	kizami tabako	刻み煙草

SIZES & COMPARISONS

small	chiisai	小さい
big	ōkii	大きい
heavy	omoi	重い
light	karui	軽い
more	motto	もっと
little (amount)	sukoshi	少し
too much/many	ōsugimasu.	多すぎます。
many	ōi	多い
enough	jūbun	じゅうぶん
a little bit	sukoshi dake	少しだけ

Restaurants in Japan tend to specialise in a particular type of food, such as Japanese-style noodles, sushi, pot cooking or Korean barbeque. In this section dishes are grouped together with others that you're likely to find in one type of restaurant, so that you can refer to a particular page and find most foods in one attempt. Be careful of restaurants that don't list prices on the menu because they can be extremely expensive.

breakfast	chōshoku/asa-gohan	朝食／朝ご飯
lunch	chūshoku/hiru-gohan/ ranchi	昼食／昼ご飯／ ランチ
dinner	yūshoku/ban-gohan	夕食／晩ご飯
supper	yashoku	夜食
banquet	enkai	宴会
party	pātī	パーティー

VEGETARIAN & SPECIAL MEALS

There are very few vegetarian restaurants in Japan. While many Japanese dishes don't include meat, fish is used as a stock base or flavouring for many vegetable dishes. Ask the staff when in doubt.

I'm a vegetarian.
watashi wa bejitarian desu
私はベジタリアンです。

I don't eat meat.
niku wa tabemasen
肉は食べません。

I don't eat chicken, fish or ham.
toriniku to sakana to hamu wa tabemasen
鶏肉と魚とハムは食べません。

I can't eat dairy products.
nyūseihin o taberu koto ga dekimasen
乳製品を食べることができません。

Do you have any vegetarian dishes?
bejitarian no ryōri ga arimasu ka?
ベジタリアンの料理がありますか？

Does this dish have meat?	kono ryōri ni niku ga haitte imasu ka? この料理に肉が入っていますか？
Can I get this without meat?	kore o niku nashi de onegai dekimasu ka? これを肉なしでお願いできますか？
Does it contain eggs?	tamago ga haitte imasu ka? たまごが入っていますか？
I'm allergic to (peanuts).	watashi wa (pīnattsu) arerugī desu 私は（ピーナッツ）アレルギーです。
Is this organic?	kore wa yūki saibai desu ka? これは有機栽培ですか？

EATING OUT

Popular restaurants will often have a line of customers waiting outside for a table. Most restaurants display the menu or plastic models of dishes in the front of the restaurant, making it possible to point to what you want to order.

A table for two/five people, please.	futari/go-nin onegai shimasu （2人／5人）お願いします。
Can we see the menu?	menyū o misete kudasai メニューを見せて下さい。

FOOD

BUT WHO'LL FOOT THE BILL?

watashi no ogori desu

This commonly heard Japanese phrase means 'I'll pay'. The expression warikan means 'pay Dutch'. Japanese people do not start drinking before saying kampai, 'cheers' to each other at the beginning of the party.

Do you have an English menu?	eigo no menyū ga arimasu ka?	英語のメニューがありますか？
Can you recommend any dishes?	osusume no ryōri ga arimasu ka?	お勧めの料理がありますか？
Is this self-service?	koko wa serufu sābisu desu ka?	ここはセルフサービスですか？
Is service included in the bill?	sābisu ryō wa komi desu ka?	サービス料は込みですか？

Please bring (a/an) ...	... o onegai shimasu.	... をお願いします。
ashtray	haizara	灰皿
the bill	o-kanjō/o-aiso	お勘定／おあいそ
chopsticks	hashi	箸
fork	fōku	フォーク
glass (of water)	koppu (ippai no mizu)	コップ（一杯の水）
knife	naifu	ナイフ
plate	sara	皿
soy sauce	shōyu	醤油
spoon	supūn	スプーン
toothpick	yōji	楊枝

Useful Words & Phrases

This is ...	kore wa ... desu	これは ... です。
cold	tsumetai	冷たい
delicious	oishii	おいしい
fresh	shinsen	新鮮
horrible	mazui	まずい
hot (taste)	karai	辛い
hot (temperature)	atsui	熱い
not very nice	oishikunai	おいしくない
old	furui	古い
salty	shoppai/shiokarai	しょっぱい／塩辛い
smelly	kusai	臭い
spicy	supaishī	スパイシー
sweet	amai	甘い

FOOD

chef for Japanese food	itamae	板前
chef for western food	kokku/shefu	コック／シェフ
waiter	weitā	ウェイター
waitress	weitoresu	ウェイトレス
Japanese cuisine	washoku	和食
	yōshoku	洋食
Korean cuisine	kankoku/	（韓国／朝鮮）
	chōsen ryōri	料理
Chinese cuisine	chūka ryōri	中華料理
(... style) cuisine	(...) ryōri	(...) 料理

WHERE TO EAT

kappō 割烹
   expensive Japanese restaurant – generally quite small
ryōtei 料亭
   very expensive and classy Japanese restaurant
soba-ya そば屋
   Japanese buckwheat noodle shop

sushi-ya	寿司屋	sushi bar
kaiten-zushi	回転寿司	rotating sushi bar
tachi-gui soba	立ち食いそば	quick soba stand
chūka ryōri ten	中華料理店	Chinese restaurant
rāmen-ya	ラーメン屋	Chinese style noodle shop
resutoran	レストラン	western restaurant

FOOD

MAY OR MAY NOT

The simplest way of giving permission is to say ii
desu 'you may'.

To refuse a request you can use dame desu 'you
may not'.

WHERE TO DRINK

There are many different types of drinking spots. Japanese bars (bā/sunakku) are normally small in scale, offer limited food only and focus on karaoke. Some charge just to sit down regardless of what you drink, so always check first. Cheap places like izakaya offer a variety of food and drinks, but can be a bit noisy.

bar	bā	バー
night club	kurabu	クラブ
beer garden	biya-gāden	ビヤガーデン
licenced snack bar	sunakku	スナック
Japanese-style bar	nomi-ya	飲み屋
Japanese-style pub	izaka-ya	居酒屋

FOOD

TYPICAL DISHES

Rice Dishes

hayashi-raisu	ハヤシライス
meat and vegetables with rice	
karē-raisu	カレーライス
Japanese-style curry and rice	

donburi

This is a bowl of rice with a topping of meat, seafood or vegetables. The following donburi are common:

katsu-don	カツ丼
fried pork cutlet on rice	
oyako-don	親子丼
chicken and egg on rice	
gyū-don	牛丼
thinly sliced cooked beef on rice	
ten-don	天丼
battered shrimp on rice	
una-don	うな丼
grilled eel on rice	

FOOD

Noodle Dishes

soba; udon

Japanese style noodle dishes: soba is made of buckwheat, udon is made of flour.

kake soba/udon	かけそば／うどん
plain noodles in broth	
kitsune soba/udon	きつねそば／うどん
noodles with fried tofu	
tempura soba/udon	天ぷらそば／うどん
noodles with tempura	

tsukimi soba/udon 月見そば/うどん
   noodles with raw egg

zaru-soba ざるそば
   cold noodles with seaweed strips served on a bamboo tray

rāmen

These are Chinese-style noodles. It is in shops specialising in these noodles where you'll normally find the following dishes:

rāmen ラーメン
   soup and noodles with a slice of meat and some vegetables

chāshū-men チャーシュー麺
   rāmen topped with slices of roast pork

wantan-men ワンタン麺
   rāmen with meat dumplings

miso-rāmen みそラーメン
   rāmen with miso-flavoured broth

gomoku soba 五目そば
   rāmen with assorted vegetables (sometimes includes meat)

hiyashi-chūka 冷やし中華
   cold noodles

gyōza ぎょうざ
   fried dumplings

chāhan/yaki-meshi チャーハン／焼き飯
   fried rice

izakaya

These popular dishes are available at izakaya-Japanese pubs:

agedashi-dōfu 揚げ出し豆腐
   deep fried tofu in fish stock

jaga-batā ジャガバター
   baked potatoes with butter

niku-jaga 肉じゃが
   pork and potato stew

yaki-zakana 焼き魚
   grilled fish

FOOD

yaki-onigiri 焼きおにぎり
  grilled rice ball
poteto-furai ポテトフライ
  fried potatoes
hiya-yakko 冷奴
  cold bean curd
tsuna-sarada ツナサラダ
  salad with tinned tuna
sashimi mori-awase 刺身盛り合せ
  assorted raw fish and seafood
umeboshi 梅干し
  pickled plums (very sour)
tsukemono 漬物
  pickled or salted vegetables

hot plates

Noodles and pancakes made on hot plates:

okonomi-yaki お好み焼き
  standard savoury pancake
modan-yaki モダン焼き
  savoury pancake with noodles
yaki-soba 焼きそば
  fried noodles
kata-yaki-soba 堅焼きそば
  crunchy fried noodles

yakitori

Skewered chicken meat:

yakitori やきとり
  served with tare (a sweet soy based sauce) or shio (salt)
  plain, grilled white chicken meat
negima/hasami ねぎま/はさみ
  pieces of white chicken meat alternating with long onions
sasami ささみ
  skinless chicken breast pieces

hatsu	ハツ	chicken heart
kawa	かわ	chicken skin
tsukune	つくね	chicken meat balls
reba	レバ	chicken liver
shiro	シロ	intestine
shītake	しいたけ	Japanese mushrooms
pīman	ピーマン	small green peppers
negi	ネギ	long onions
ginnan	銀杏	ginko nuts

Sushi & Sashimi

Sushi is generally raw seafood arranged on vinegared rice and Japanese horseradish, wasabi. Sometimes it's rolled in a thin sheet of dried nori – a type of seaweed – and then sliced.

At sushi bars you can either sit at the counter and order directly from the chef, or sit at a table and order from the waiter. The cheapest type of sushi is kaiten-zushi, where you choose from plates of sushi rotating along the counter on a conveyor belt. Sashimi is thinly sliced raw fish.

ama-ebi	甘海老	sweet shrimp
awabi	あわび	abalone
ebi	海老	prawn/shrimp
hamachi	はまち	yellowtail
ika	いか	squid
ikura	イクラ	salmon roe
kaibashira/hotate-gai	貝柱／ホタテ	scallop
kani	かに	crab
katsuo	かつお	bonito
maguro	まぐろ	tuna
tai	鯛	snapper
tamago	たまご	sweetened egg
toro	とろ	fatty tuna belly (this is very expensive)
unagi	うなぎ	eel with a sweet sauce
uni	うに	sea urchin roe

FOOD

tako	たこ	octopus
kappa-maki	かっぱ巻き	cucumber sushi rolled in sea weed
futo-maki	太巻き	various ingredients rolled in seaweed (large rolls)
tekka-maki	鉄火巻き	tuna rolled in seaweed
te-maki	手巻き	special hand-rolled sushi
chirashi-zushi	ちらし寿司	bowl of vinegared rice topped with raw fish and vegetables
wasabi	わさび	wasabi (horseradish)
gari	がり	pickled ginger

Winter Family Food

chanko-nabe　ちゃんこ鍋
  sumō wrestler's stew of meat and vegetables

oden　おでん
  fish cake, beancurd, rolls of kelp, konnyaku (gelatine-like
  ingredient) and vegetables in fish broth

suki-yaki　すき焼き
  beef, bean curd, vegetables, shirataki (gelatine-like) noodles
  in an iron pan with soy sauce base, served with raw eggs

shabu-shabu　しゃぶしゃぶ
  various kinds of meat and vegetables simmered in broth

yose-nabe　寄せ鍋
  seafood and chicken stew with vegetables

yudōfu　湯豆腐
  bean curd in broth

Bento Box

obentō　お弁当
  lunch boxes obentō are sold in small takeaway shops at
  stations and convenient stores. They normally contain rice
  with different vegetables, meats, fish and sometimes fruit.

FOOD

SELF-CATERING

bread	pan	パン
butter	batā	バター
cheese	chīzu	チーズ
chocolate	chokorēto	チョコレート
eggs	tamago	たまご
flour	komugiko	小麦粉
ham	hamu	ハム
honey	hachimitsu	蜂蜜
jam	jamu	ジャム
margarine	māgarin	マーガリン
milk	gyūnyū/miruku	牛乳／ミルク
pepper	koshō	胡椒
salt	shio	塩
sugar	satō	砂糖
yoghurt	yōguruto	ヨーグルト

FOOD

AT THE MARKET
Meat

Beef is very expensive in Japan, but in recent times it has become more accessible due to imports from Australia and the USA. Prices are normally displayed in units of 100gms, not kgs. Beef is most often sold pre-sliced, and you'll need to order larger cuts of beef from the butcher.

meat	niku	肉
beef	gyū-niku/bīfu	牛肉／ビーフ
chicken	tori-niku/chikin	鶏肉／チキン
pork	buta-niku/pōku	豚肉／ポーク

Seafood

English	Romaji	Japanese
clams	hamaguri	はまぐり
cod	tara	たら
crab	kani	かに
eel	unagi	うなぎ
fish	sakana	魚
flounder	karei	カレイ
herring	nishin	ニシン
lobster/crayfish	robusutā/ise-ebi	ロブスター／伊勢海老
mackerel	saba	サバ
mullet	bora	ボラ
mussels	mūru-gai	ムール貝
octopus	tako	たこ
oyster/s	kaki	カキ
perch	suzuki	スズキ
prawn/shrimp	ebi	エビ
salmon	sake	鮭
sardine	iwashi	イワシ
scallop	hotate-gai	ホタテ貝
shrimp	ebi	海老
snapper	tai	タイ
sole	hirame	ヒラメ
squid	ika	イカ
trout	masu	マス
tuna	maguro	マグロ
whiting	kisu	キス

FOOD

DID YOU KNOW... Thrillseekers might want to try the deadly pufferfish, fugu. This delicacy is surprisingly bland given its high cost and although the danger is negligible you might want to let someone else try it first.

Vegetables

asparagus	asuparagasu	アスパラガス
bamboo shoots	takenoko	たけのこ
bean sprouts	moyashi	モヤシ
beans	mame	豆
broccoli	burokkorī	ブロッコリー
cabbage	kyabetsu	キャベツ
Chinese cabbage	hakusai	白菜
capsicum	pīman	ピーマン
carrot	ninjin	にんじん
cauliflower	karifurawā	カリフラワー
celery	serori	セロリ
Chinese radish	daikon	大根
corn	tōmorokoshi	とうもろこし
cucumber	kyūri	キュウリ
eggplant	nasu	なす
green peas	gaurīn pīsu	グリーンピース
lettuce	retasu	レタス
mushroom	kinoko	キノコ
shitake mushroom	shītake	しいたけ
onion	tamanegi	たまねぎ
long onion	negi	ネギ
parsely	paseri	パセリ
potato	jagaimo	ジャガイモ
pumpkin	kabocha	カボチャ
seaweed (dried sheets)	nori	海苔
seaweed (for soup)	wakame	わかめ
soy bean	daizu	大豆
spinach	hōrensō	ほうれん草
sweet potato	satsumaimo	サツマイモ
tomato	tomato	トマト
vegetables	yasai	野菜

FOOD

Fruit

apple	ringo	リンゴ
avocado	abogado	アボガド
banana	banana	バナナ

grape	budō	ぶどう
mandarine	mikan	ミカン
orange	orenji	オレンジ
pear	nashi	なし
persimmon	kaki	柿
pineapple	painappuru	パイナップル

Spices & Condiments

bean paste	miso	味噌
chilli	tōgarashi	唐辛子
garlic	ninniku	ニンニク
ginger	shōga	ショウガ
ketchup	kechappu	ケチャップ
mayonnaise	mayonēzu	マヨネーズ
MSG	aji no moto	味の素
mustard	karashi	からし
oil	abura	油
pepper	koshō	胡椒
Japanese rice wine	sake	酒
salt	shio	塩
sauce	sōsu	ソース
soy sauce	shōyu	醤油
sugar	satō	砂糖
sweet rice cooking wine	mirin	みりん
vinegar	su	酢

FOOD

ITADAKIMASU

Japanese people say itadakimasu before a meal when the meal is shared with family, friends, guests or colleagues. After a meal, before leaving the table, they say gochisōsama to show appreciation for the meal. You can also say gochisōsama to restaurant staff when leaving to show your gratitude.

DRINKS
Tea

bancha tea	ban cha	番茶
Chinese tea	chūgoku cha	中国茶
fresh tea	shin cha	新茶
green tea	ryoku cha	緑茶
gyokuro tea	gyokuro	玉露
Japanese green tea	o-cha	お茶
oolong tea	ūron-cha	烏龍茶
powdered green tea	maccha	抹茶
sencha tea	sen cha	煎茶
tea	kōcha	紅茶
tea powder	kona cha	粉茶
tea with milk	miruku tī	ミルクティー
western tea	kōcha	紅茶
wheat tea	mugi cha	麦茶

Other Drinks

café au lait	kafe ōre	カフェオーレ
coffee	kōhī	コーヒー
coffee/tea with milk	miruku iri kōhī/ kōcha	ミルク入り (コーヒー／紅茶)
coffee/tea with sugar	satō iri kōhī/ kōcha	砂糖入り (コーヒー／紅茶)
lemonade	remonēdo	レモネード
orange juice	orenji jūsu	オレンジジュース
water (cold)	mizu	水
mineral water	mineraru-wōtā	ミネラルウォーター
boiled water	sayu	白湯

FOOD

Alcoholic Drinks

The legal age to drink alcohol in Japan is 20. Alcoholic drinks can be bought from bottleshops, supermarkets, many convenience stores and the hundreds of vending machines scattered around both urban and residential areas.

beer	bīru	ビール
Japanese rice wine	sake	酒
distilled spirit made from various grains and potatoes	shōchū	焼酎
highball with soda and lemon	chūhai	酎ハイ
wine	wain	ワイン
whisky	wisukī	ウィスキー
whisky with ice	on za rokku (on the rocks)	オンザロック

FOOD

IN THE COUNTRY

CAMPING

Camping is an increasingly popular form of leisure for Japanese families. Facilities at campsites are well established and you can often rent camping gear from the campsite office. Make sure that you book sites well in advance during school holidays. Caravan touring is reasonably popular, however onsite vans are rare.

Do you have any sites available?	tento o haru basho wa arimasu ka?
	テントを張る場所はありますか？
How much is it per person/tent?	(hitori/tento hito-hari) ikura desu ka?
	（1人／テント一張り）いくらですか？
Where can I hire a tent?	tento wa doko de kariru koto ga dekimasu ka?
	テントはどこで借りることができますか？
Can we camp here?	koko de kyampu shite mo ii desu ka?
	ここでキャンプしてもいいですか？
Are there shower facilities?	shawā no setsubi ga arimasu ka?
	シャワーの設備がありますか？
Where's the water facility?	mizu-ba wa doko desu ka?
	水場はどこですか？

backpack	bakkupakku	バックパック
camping	kyampu	キャンプ
campsite	kyampu jō	キャンプ場
can opener	kankiri	缶切り
canvas	kyambasu	キャンバス
compass	kompasu/hōi jishaku	コンパス／方位磁石

firewood	maki/takigi	まき／たきぎ
gas cartridge	gasu-bombe	ガスボンベ
hammer	hammā	ハンマー
hammock	hammokku	ハンモック
mat	matto	マット
pocket knife	poketto naifu	ポケットナイフ
rope	rōpu	ロープ
sleeping bag	surīpingu baggu/ nebukuro	スリーピングバッグ／ 寝袋
stove	konro	コンロ
tent	tento	テント
tent pegs	pegu	ペグ
torch (flashlight)	kaichū dentō	懐中電灯
water bottle	suitō	水筒

HIKING

Japanese hikers are well equipped and very well prepared. The most popular mountains (the Japan Alps, Mt Fuji and Yatsugatake) are well signposted and have toilets and simple hut accommodation. Many peaks can be dangerous during winter due to heavy snow and extreme conditions. It's better to climb peaks over 2000 metres with experienced climbers who know the area well.

Are there any tourist attractions near here?	kono chikaku ni kankōmeisho ga arimasu ka? この近くに観光名所がありますか？
Where's the nearest village?	ichiban chikai mura wa doko desu ka? いちばん近い村はどこですか？
Is it safe to climb this mountain?	kono yama wa anzen ni noboremasu ka? この山は安全に登れますか？
Is there a hut up there?	ue ni yama-goya ga arimasu ka? 上に山小屋がありますか？

Do we need a guide?	gaido ga hitsuyō desu ka? ガイドが必要ですか?
Where can I find out about hiking trails in this region?	kono chiiki no tozan-dō annai wa doko ni arimasu ka? この地域の登山道案内はどこにありますか?
Are there guided treks?	gaido tsuki no torekkingu ga arimasu ka? ガイド付きのトレッキングがありますか?
I'd like to talk to someone who knows this area.	kono chiiki ni kuwashii hito to hanashitai desu この地域に詳しいひとと話したいです。
How long is the trail?	kono tozan-dō no kōtei wa donokurai desu ka? この登山道の行程はどのくらいですか?
Is the track well marked?	tozandō no mejirushi wa wakariyasui desu ka? 登山道の目印はわかりやすいですか?
How high is the climb?	hyōkō-sa wa donokurai desu ka? 標高差はどのくらいですか?
Which is the shortest/ easiest route?	ichiban mijikai/rakuna rūto wa dore desu ka? いちばん（短い／楽な）ルートはどれですか?
Is the path open?	kono michi wa kaitsū shite imasu ka? この道は開通していますか?
What time does it get dark?	nan-ji goro kuraku narimasu ka? 何時ごろ暗くなりますか?
Is it very scenic?	keshiki ga ii desu ka? 景色がいいですか?

Where can I hire mountain gear?	doko de tozan-yōgu o kariru koto ga dekimasu ka? どこで登山用具を借りることができますか？
Where can we buy supplies?	doko de hitsuju-hin o kau koto ga dekimasu ka? どこで必需品を買うことができますか？

On the Path

Where have you come from?	dochira kara kimashita ka? どちらから来ましたか？
How long did it take you?	koko made donokurai jikan ga kakarimashita ka? ここまでどのくらい時間がかかりましたか？
Does this path go to ...?	kono michi wa ... made ikimasu ka? この道は ... まで行きますか？
I'm lost.	michi ni mayoimashita 道に迷いました。
Where can we spend the night?	doko de tomaremasu ka? どこで泊まれますか？
Can I leave some things here for a while?	chotto koko ni nimotsu o oite mo ii desu ka? ちょっとここに荷物を置いてもいいですか？

altitude	hyōkō	標高
binoculars	sōgankyō	双眼鏡
compass	kompasu/hōi-jishaku	コンパス／方位磁石
downhill	kudari-zaka	下り坂
first-aid kit	kyūkyū-bako	救急箱
gloves	tebukuro	手袋
guide	gaido/annai-nin	ガイド／案内人
guided trek	gaido-tsuki no torekkingu	ガイド付きのトレッキング

hiking	haikingu	ハイキング
hiking boots	tozan-gutsu	登山靴
ledge	iwa-dana	岩棚
lookout	miharashi-dai	見晴台
map	chizu	地図
mountain climbing	tozan	登山
pick	pikkeru	ピッケル
provisions	shokuryō	食料
rock climbing	rokku kuraimingu/ iwanobori	ロッククライミング／岩登り
rope	rōpu/zairu	ロープ／ザイル
signpost	dōhyō/ michi-shirube	道標／道しるべ
steep slope	kyūna saka	急な坂
to climb	noborimasu	登ります
to walk	arukimasu	歩きます
uphill	nobori-zaka	上り坂

AT THE BEACH

Many of the beaches around Tokyo, Nagoya and Osaka are overcrowded and not always picturesque. Avoiding public holidays is wise if you want to enjoy the sea breeze and water without fighting for space over other holidaymakers. Resort destinations such as Okinawa offer golden sands, tropical coral reefs and good diving facilities.

Can we swim here?	koko de oyoide mo ii desu ka?
	ここで泳いでもいいですか?
Is it safe here?	koko wa anzen desu ka?
	ここは安全ですか?
What time is high/low tide?	manchō/kanchō wa nan-ji desu ka?
	(満潮/干潮) は何時ですか?

coast	kishi	岸
fishing	tsuri	釣
reef	anshō	暗礁
rock	iwa	岩
sand	suna	砂
sea	umi	海
snorkelling	shunōkeringu	シュノーケリング
sunblock	hiyake-dome	日焼け止め
sunglasses	sangurasu	サングラス
surfboard	sāfubōdo	サーフボード
surfing	sāfin	サーフィン
swimming	suiei	水泳
towel	taoru	タオル
waterskiing	suijōsukī	水上スキー
waves	nami	波
windsurfing	windosāfin	ウィンドサーフィン

IN THE COUNTRY

Scuba Diving

The most popular places for divers are the southern islands of Okinawa Prefecture, ōshima in Tokyo and Wakayama, south of Osaka. Diving tours, which include the supply of diving gear, are available at all of the above destinations.

scuba diving	sukyūba daibingu スキューバダイビング
Are there good diving sites here?	ii daibingu no basho ga arimasu ka? いいダイビングの場所がありますか?
Can we hire a diving boat?	daibingu-yō no bōto o kariru koto ga dekimasu ka? ダイビング用のボートを借りることができますか?
Is there a diving guide?	daibingu no gaido ga imasu ka? ダイビングのガイドがいますか?
We'd like to hire diving equipment.	daibingu no dōgu ga karitai no desu ga ダイビングの道具が借りたいのですが。
I'm interested in exploring wrecks.	nampa-sen o mitai no desu ga 難破船を見たいのですが。

WEATHER

What's the weather like?	tenki wa dō desu ka?	
	天気はどうですか?	
It's raining heavily.	doshaburi desu	
	土砂降りです。	
It's raining lightly.	ame wa koburi desu	
	雨は小降りです。	

It's ... today.	kyō wa ... desu	今日は ... です
cloudy	kumori	曇り
cold	samui	寒い
fine	hare	晴
hot	atsui	暑い
rainy	ame	雨
warm	atatakai	温かい
windy	kaze ga tsuyoi	風が強い

storm	arashi	嵐
sun	taiyō	太陽
typhoon	taifū	台風

SEASONS

spring	haru	春
summer	natsu	夏
autumn	aki	秋
winter	fuyu	冬

dry season	kanki	乾季
rainy season	uki	雨季
monsoon season	tsuyu	梅雨

YES OR NO

To ask a yes/no question, just add ka to the end of the sentence. Your voice should also rise at the end of the sentence when forming a question.

IN THE COUNTRY

GEOGRAPHICAL TERMS

beach	kaigan	海岸
bridge	hashi	橋
cave	dōkutsu	洞窟
cliff	gake	崖
earthquake	jishin	地震
forest	mori/hayashi	森／林
harbour	minato	港
hill	oka	丘
hot spring	onsen	温泉
island	shima	島
lake	mizuumi	湖
mountain	yama	山
mountain path	yama-michi	山道
pass	ko-michi	小道
peak	sanchō/chōjō	山頂／頂上
river	kawa	川
sea	umi	海
valley	tani	谷
waterfall	taki	滝

FAUNA

bird	tori	鳥
cat	neko	猫
chicken	niwatori	ニワトリ
cow	ushi	牛
dog	inu	犬
fish	sakana	魚
fly	hae	ハエ
horse	uma	馬
leech	hiru	ヒル
monkey	saru	猿
mosquito	ka	蚊
pig	buta	ブタ
snake	hebi	蛇
spider	kumo	クモ

IN THE COUNTRY

FLORA & AGRICULTURE

agriculture	nōgyō	農業
corn	tōmorokoshi	とうもろこし
crops	sakumotsu	作物
flower	hana	花
harvest (verb)	shūkaku shimasu	収穫します
irrigation	kangai	潅漑
leaf	ha	葉
plant/sow	uemasu/makimasu	植えます／播きます
rice field	ta/tambo	田／田んぼ
sugar cane	satōkibi	サトウキビ
terraced land	daichi	台地
tobacco	tabako	たばこ
tree	ki	木

AT THE DOCTOR

Treatment in Japan can be very expensive for travellers who are not part of the national health system. There's no system of small general practitioners, and most people visit public hospitals or smaller private clinics. Neither have a system of appointments, so it's important to arrive as early as possible to minimise the waiting time (this can be hours). Doctors can often understand written English and some hospitals provide treatment for foreigners in English. English receipts can usually be produced if required for insurance.

Where's the ...?	... wa doko desu ka?	... はどこですか？
doctor	isha/o-isha-san	医者／お医者さん
hospital	byōin	病院
chemist/ pharmacy	yakkyoku	薬局
dentist	ha-isha	歯医者

I'm ill.	kibun ga warui desu 気分が悪いです。
My friend is sick.	tomodachi ga byōki desu 友達が病気です。
Is there a doctor who speaks English?	eigo ga dekiru o-isha-san wa imasu ka? 英語ができるお医者さんはいますか？
It hurts here.	koko ga itai desu ここが痛いです。
I feel nauseous.	hakike ga shimasu 吐き気がします。
I feel better/worse.	kibun ga yoku/waruku narimashita 気分が（良く／悪く）なりました。

HEALTH

THE DOCTOR MAY SAY ...

dō shimashita ka?	What's the matter?
kibun wa dō desu ka?	How are you feeling?
itami ga arimasu ka?	Do you feel any pain?
doko ga itai desu ka?	Where does it hurt?
seiri-chu desu ka?	Are you menstruating?
netsu ga arimasu ka?	Do you have a temperature?
itsu kara kono yōna jōtai desu ka?	Since when have you been like this?
mae ni mo kono yō ni narimashita ka?	Have you had this before?
nani ka kusuri o nonde imasu ka?	Are you on some medication?
tabako o suimasu ka?	Do you smoke?
o-sake o nomimasu ka?	Do you drink?
kusuri o shiyōshite imasu ka?	Do you take drugs?
arerugī ga arimasu ka?	Are you allergic to anything?
ninshin shite imasu ka?	Are you pregnant?
... nonde kudasai (ichi/ni)-jo ichi-nichi (san/yon)-kai shokuzen/shokugo	Please take ... one/two tablet/s three/four times a day before meal/after meals

AILMENTS

I'm ill.	watashi wa byōki desu	私は病気です。
I've been vomiting	modoshite imasu	もどしています。
I can't sleep.	nemuremasen	眠れません。

I ...	watashi wa ...	私は ...
feel dizzy	memai ga shimasu めまいがします	
feel shivery	samuke ga shimasu 寒気がします	
have a headache	zutsū ga shimasu 頭痛がします	
have a stomachache	fukutsū ga shimasu 腹痛がします	
have a migraine	henzutsū ga shimasu 偏頭痛がします	
feel weak	tairyoku ga arimasen 体力がありません	
have an allergy	arerugī desu アレルギーです	
have anaemia	hinketsu-shō desu 貧血症です	
have cancer	gan desu 癌です	
have a cold	kaze desu 風邪です	
have constipation	bempi desu 便秘です	
have cystitis	bōkōen desu 膀胱炎です	
have diarrhoea	geri o shite imasu 下痢をしています	
have a fever	netsu ga arimasu 熱があります	
have gastroenteritis	ichōen desu 胃腸炎です	
have a heart condition	shinzōbyō desu 心臓病です	
have indigestion	shōka furyō desu 消化不良です	

HEALTH

HEALTH

have lice	shirami ga imasu
	しらみがいます
have a runny nose	hana-mizu ga demasu
	鼻水が出ます
have a cough	seki ga demasu
	せきが出ます
have no appetite	shokuyoku ga arimasen
	食欲がありません
feel tired	tsukare ga arimasu
	疲れがあります

I have a pain in ...	... ga itai desu
	... が痛いです
I have a sore throat	nodo ga itai desu
	のどが痛いです。
My ... is itchy.	... ga kayui desu
	... がかゆいです。
I burned my ...	... ni yakedo o shimashita
	... にやけどをしました。

a sprain	nenza	捻挫
a stomachache	fukutsū	腹痛
sunburn	hiyake	日焼け
a toothache	haita	歯痛
travel sickness	norimono yoi	乗物酔
a urinary infection	nyōdōen	尿道炎
venereal disease	seibyō	性病
worms	kiseichū	寄生虫

Useful Phrases

I feel better/worse.	kibun ga yoku/waruku narimashita
	気分が（良く／悪く）なりました。
I've been vaccinated.	yobō chūsha o shimasita
	予防注射をしました。
I don't want a blood transfusion.	yuketsu o shinaide kudasai
	輸血をしないでください。

This is my usual medicine.	kore wa watashi ga itsumo tsukatte iru kusuri desu これは私がいつも使っている薬です。
Can I have a receipt for my insurance?	hoken no tame no reshīto o kudasai 保険のためのレシートをください。

HEALTH

WOMEN'S HEALTH

Could I see a female doctor?	josei no o-isha-san o onegai shimasu 女性のお医者さんをお願いします。
I'm pregnant.	ninshin shite imasu 妊娠しています。
I think I'm pregnant.	ninshin shite iru to omoimasu 妊娠していると思います。
I'm on the pill.	piru/hinin-yaku o nonde imasu （ピル／避妊薬）を飲んでいます。
I haven't had my period for ... weeks.	... shūkan seiri ga arimasen. ... 週間生理がありません。
I'd like to use contraception.	hinin shitai no desu ga 避妊したいのですが。

SCOUT'S HONOUR

You shouldn't use the 'honourable' prefixes o- and go- when you're talking about yourself or your situation. Only use them when talking about other people:

your husband	go-shujin (lit: hon-husband)
my husband	shujin (lit: husband)

abortion	datai/chūzetsu	堕胎／中絶
cystic fibrosis	nōhōsei sen'i shō	嚢胞性繊維症
cystitis	bōkōen	膀胱炎
diaphragm	ōkakumaku	横隔膜
IUD	aiyūdī/hinin ringu	ＩＵＤ／避妊リング
mammogram	nyūbō ekkusu sen shashin	乳房Ｘ線写真
menstruation	gekkei	月経
miscarriage	ryūzan	流産
pap smear	papu-sumia-tesuto	パプスミアテスト
the Pill	piru/hinin-yaku	ピル／避妊薬
period pain	seiri-tsū	生理痛
premenstrual tension	gekkei zen kinchō	月経前緊張
thrush	kōkū kanjida-shō	口腔カンジダ症
ultrasound	chōompa	超音波

SPECIAL HEALTH NEEDS

I'm ...	watashi wa ... desu	私は ... です。
asthmatic	zensoku	喘息
anaemic	hinketsu-shō	貧血症
diabetic	tōnyōbyō	糖尿病

I have a skin allergy.
watashi wa hifu arerugī desu
私は皮膚アレルギーです。

I've had my vaccinations.
yobō-chūsha o shimashita
予防注射をしました。

I'm on medication for ...
... no tame no kusuri o nonde imasu
... のための薬を飲んでいます。

I need a new pair of glasses/ contact lens.
atarashii (megane; kontakuto renzu) ga hitsuyō desu
新しい (眼鏡；コンタクト レンズ) が必要です。

HEALTH

I'm allergic to ...	watashi wa ... arerugī desu	
	私は ... アレルギーです。	
antibiotics	kōsei busshitsu	抗生物質
aspirin	asupirin	アスピリン
bees	hachi	ハチ
codeine	kodein	コデイン
dairy products	nyūseihin	乳製品
MSG	ajimomoto	味の素
penicillin	penishirin	ペニシリン
pollen	kafun	花粉

addiction	chūdoku	中毒
blood test	ketsueki kensa	血液検査
contraceptive	hinin	避妊
injection	chūsha	注射
injury	kega	けが
insect bite	mushi sasare	虫刺され
vitamins	bitamin-zai	ビタミン剤
wound	kizu	傷

ALTERNATIVE TREATMENTS

acupuncture	hari ryōhō	鍼療法
aromatherapy	aromaterapī	アロマテラピー
Chinese medicine	kampō-yaku	漢方薬
herbalist	hābu dokutā	ハーブドクター
massage	massāji/amma	マッサージ／按摩
meditation	meisō	瞑想
naturopath	shizen ryōhō	自然療法
yoga	yoga	ヨガ

HEALTH

PARTS OF THE BODY

ankle	ashikubi	足首
appendix	mōchō	盲腸
arm	ude	腕
artery	dōmyaku	動脈
back	senaka	背中
bladder	bōkō	膀胱
blood	ketsueki/chi	血液／血
bone	hone	骨
chest	mune	胸
ears	mimi	耳
eye	me	目
finger	yubi	指
foot/legs	ashi	足
hand	te	手
head	atama	頭
heart	shinzō	心臓
kidney	jinzō	腎臓
knee	hiza	膝
liver	kanzō	肝臓
lungs	hai	肺
mouth	kuchi	口
muscle	kinniku	筋肉
ribs	rokkotsu	肋骨
shoulder	kata	肩
skin	hifu/kawa	皮膚／皮
stomach	i	胃
teeth	ha	歯
throat	nodo	喉
vein	jōmyaku	静脈

PRONOUNS

Remember that while men can use watashi boku and ore for 'I/me', women can only use watashi

VISITING HOME

When visiting someone at home, Japanese say ojama
shimasu when entering the house. When entering and
leaving someone's work office, shitsurei shimasu is
used. Each expression literally means 'I'm sorry to
bother your territory'.

AT THE CHEMIST

I need something for ...	... no tame no kusuri o kudasai
	... のための薬をください。
Do I need a prescription for ...?	... wa shohōsen ga hitsuyō desu ka?
	... は処方箋が必要ですか？
How many times a day?	ichi-nichi nan-kai desu ka?
	一日何回ですか？

antiseptic	shōdoku	消毒
aspirin	asupirin	アスピリン
Band-aids	bandoeido	バンドエイド
bandage	hōtai	包帯
condoms	kondōmu	コンドーム
cotton balls	dasshimen	脱脂綿
cotton buds	menbō	綿棒
cough medicine	sekidome	咳止め
gauze	gāze	ガーゼ
laxatives	gezai	下剤
painkillers	itamidome/chintsūzai	痛み止め／鎮痛剤
rubbing alcohol	shōdoku yō arukōru	消毒用アルコール
sanitary napkins	napukin	ナプキン
sleeping pills	suimin-yaku	睡眠薬
tampons	tampon	タンポン
thermometer	taionkei	体温計

HEALTH

AT THE DENTIST

I have a toothache.	ha ga itai desu 歯が痛いです。
I have a hole/cavity.	mushi-ba ga arimasu 虫歯があります。
I've lost a filling.	tsumemono o nakushimashita 詰め物をなくしました。
I've broken my tooth.	ha ga kakemashita 歯が欠けました。
My gums hurt.	haguki ga itai desu 歯茎が痛いです。
I don't want it extracted.	nukanai de kudasai 抜かないで下さい。
Please give me an anaesthetic.	masui o shite kudasai 麻酔をして下さい。

IT MAY HURT ...

Ouch!   itai!   痛い！

SPECIFIC NEEDS

DISABLED TRAVELLERS

Japanese cities are generally not well designed for disabled people.
Footpaths are often uneven and the many light poles and signs
create significant hazards. Overhead pedestrian crossings make
crossing the road difficult for wheelchair users. Special tiles to
assist blind people are placed along many Japanese streets and train
stations. The Japanese rail system is notorious for its lack of elevators, although many stations are currently being upgraded and
railway staff will always assist.

I'm disabled/handicapped.	watashi wa shōgaisha desu 私は障害者です。
I need assistance.	te o kashite kudasai 手を貸して下さい。
What services do you have for disabled people?	shōgaisha no tame ni donna setsubi ga arimasu ka? 障害者のためにどんな設備が ありますか?
Is there wheelchair access?	kuruma-isu de deiri dekimasu ka? 車椅子で出入りできますか?
I'm deaf/blind.	watashi wa (chōkaku shōgai)/ (shikaku shōgai) ga arimasu 私は (聴覚障害／視覚障害) があります。
Speak more loudly, please.	mō sukoshi ōkii koe de hanashite kudasai もう少し大きい声で話して 下さい。
I can lipread.	dokushinjutsu ga dekimasu 読唇術ができます。
I have a hearing aid.	hochōki o shite imasu 補聴器をしています。

135

SPECIFIC NEEDS

USEFUL ABBREVIATIONS

There are many words in Japanese that are abbreviations of compound nouns. Many such words are originally from English. These abbreviations tend to be made up of four syllables.

rajikase	radio cassette tape recorder
kāsute	car stereo system
pasokon	personal computer
famikon	family computer
yondabu	4WD car (yon: 'four'and dabu: the letter 'w')
kara oke	kara: empty and oke: orchestra

Does anyone here know sign language?	donata ka shuwa ga dekimasu ka?	
	どなたか手話ができますか?	
Are guide dogs permitted?	mōdōken wa kyoka sarete imasu ka?	
	盲導犬は許可されていますか?	
Is there a guide service for blind people?	shikaku shōgaisha no tame no gaido no setsubi ga arimasu ka?	
	視覚障害者のためのガイドの設備がありますか?	
Is there any information in braille?	tenji no infomēshon wa arimasu ka?	
	点字のインフォメーションはありますか?	

braille library	tenji toshokan	点字図書館
disabled person	shōgaisha	障害者
guide dog	mōdōken	盲導犬
wheelchair	kuruma-isu	車椅子

GAY TRAVELLERS

It's rare for gays to meet with violence in Japan. People may stare at gay couples but in general will not threaten or intimidate them. However, gay couples may find it difficult to find accommodation. There are many gay bars and meeting places in large cities such as Tokyo, Osaka and Kyoto, and these places are often excellent sources of information about the gay community.

Where are the gay hangouts?	gei ga atsumaru basho wa doko desu ka? ゲイが集まる場所はどこですか？
Is there a predominantly gay street/district?	gei dōri/chiiki ga arimasu ka? ゲイ（通り／地域）がありますか？
Are we/Am I likely to be harassed (here)?	(koko de) iyagarase saresō desu ka? （ここで）嫌がらせされそうですか？
Is there a gay bookshop/ bar around here?	kono chikaku ni (gei no tame no hon-ya; gei-bā) ga arimasu ka? この近くに（ゲイのための本屋／ゲイバー）があり ますか？
Is there a local gay guide?	kono chiiki no gei no tame no gaido ga arimasu ka? この地域のゲイのためのガイドがありますか？
Is there a gay telephone hotline?	gei no denwa sōdan ga arimasu ka? ゲイの電話相談がありますか？

SPECIFIC NEEDS

THAT'S THE WAY

Japanese doesn't have exact equivalents to 'a' and 'the' so to point out a specific item you should use sono 'that':

sono hon (lit: that book)

TRAVELLING WITH THE FAMILY

Are there facilities for babies?
yōji no tame no setsubi ga arimasu ka?
幼児のための設備がありますか?

Do you have a child minding service?
takuji shisetsu ga arimasu ka?
託児施設がありますか?

Where can I find a (English-speaking) babysitter?
(eigo ga dekiru) bebī-shittā wa doko de mitsukarimasu ka?
(英語ができる) ベビーシッターはどこで見つかりますか?

Can you put an extra bed/cot in the room?
mōhitotsu (beddo; yōji yō beddo) o heya ni irete moraemasu ka?
もう一つ (ベッド/幼児用ベッド) を部屋に入れてもらえますか?

I need a car with a child seat.
yōji yō shīto tsuki no kuruma ga hitsuyō desu
幼児用シート付きの車が必要です。

Is it suitable for children?
kodomo muki desu ka?
子供向けですか?

Is there a family discount?
kazoku-waribiki ga arimasu ka?
家族割引がありますか?

How much is children's fare?
kodomo-ryōkin wa ikura desu ka?
子供料金はいくらですか?

Are children allowed?
kodomo wa kyoka sarete imasu ka?
子供は許可されていますか?

Do you have a children's menu?
kodomo yō no menyū ga arimasu ka?
子供用のメニューがありますか?

Is there a playground around here?
chikaku ni asobiba wa arimasu ka?
近くに遊び場はありますか?

LOOKING FOR A JOB

I'm looking for a job.	shigoto o sagashite imasu 仕事を探しています。
Where can I find local job advertisements?	kono chiiki no shūshoku jōhō wa doko ni arimasu ka? この地域の就職情報はどこにありますか？
Do I need a work permit?	rōdōkyoka ga hitsuyō desu ka? 労働許可が必要ですか？
I've had experience.	watashi wa keiken ga arimasu 私は経験があります。
I can teach English.	eigo o oshieru koto ga dekimasu 英語を教えることができます。
I've come about the position advertised.	kōbo sareta shigoto ni tsuite kimashita 公募された仕事について来ました。
I'm ringing about the position advertised.	kōkoku de mita shigoto ni tsuite denwa shite imasu 広告で見た仕事について電話しています。
What's the wage?	kyūryō wa ikura desu ka? 給料はいくらですか？
Do I have to pay tax?	zeikin o harawanakereba narimasen ka? 税金を払わなければなりませんか？

casual	rinji/kajuaru	臨時／カジュアル
employee	jūgyōin	従業員
employer	koyōnushi	雇用主
full-time	jōkin	常勤
job	shigoto	仕事
occupation/trade	shokugyō	職業
part-time	pāto/arubaito	パート／アルバイト
resumé/CV	rirekisho	履歴書
traineeship	minarai	見習い
work experience	shokuba taiken	職場体験

When can I start?

itsu kara hajimeraremasu ka?
いつから始められますか？

What are the working hours?

kimmu-jikan wa nan-ji kara nan-ji made desu ka?
勤務時間は何時から何時まで ですか？

I can start ...

... kara hajimeraremasu.
... から始められます。

today	**kyō**	今日
tomorrow	**ashita**	明日
next week	**raishū**	来週

SPECIFIC NEEDS

DID YOU KNOW...

Business card (meishi) exchange is a very important part of business dealings in Japan. Keep your cards in a place where they won't get creased or dirty – buying a business card holder is a good idea. When exchanging cards, face the writing so that the receiver can read it, and preferably pass it over with both hands. Always read the card you are given, and treat them with care. Never write on the card, fold it or leave it behind as this is interpreted as a sign of disrespect.

ON BUSINESS

We're attending a ...	... ni sanka shimasu	... に参加します。
conference	gakkai/kaigi	学会／会議
meeting	kaigi	会議
trade fair	mihon-ichi	見本市

I'm on a course.
kōsu ni kayotte imasu
コースに通っています。

I have an appointment with ...
... to apointo ga arimasu
... とアポイントがあります。

Here's my business card.
watashi no meishi desu
私の名刺です。

I need an interpreter.
tsūyaku ga hitsuyō desu
通訳が必要です。

I need to use a computer.
kompyūta ga hitsuyō desu
コンピュータが必要です。

I want to send a fax/an email.
(fakkusu; ī mēru) o okuritai
no desu ga
(ファックス／e−メール)
を送りたいのですが。

SPECIFIC NEEDS

cellular/mobile phone	keitai denwa	携帯電話
client	kokyaku	顧客
colleague	dōryō	同僚
distributor	oroshiuri gyōsha	卸売業者
email	ī mēru	e−メール
exhibition	tenrankai	展覧会
loss	sonshitsu	損失
manager	manējā	マネージャー
profit	rijun	利潤
proposal	teian	提案

ON TOUR

We're part of a group.
dantai de kite imasu
団体で来ています。

We're on tour.
tsuā-chū desu
ツアー中です。

SPECIFIC NEEDS

I'm with the ...	... to issho desu	... といっしょです。
group	dantai/gurūpu	団体／グループ
team	chīmu	チーム
band	bando	バンド
crew	kurū	クルー

We sent equipment on this ...		kono ... de kizai o okurimashita この ... 器材を送りました。
flight	hikōbin	飛行便
train	densha	電車
bus	basu	バス

Please speak with our manager.
watashi no manējā to hanashite kudasai
私のマネージャーと話して下さい。

We've lost our equipment.
kizai o nakushimashita
器材をなくしました。

We're taking a break of ... days.
... nichikan kyūka o torimasu
... 日間休暇をとります。

We're playing on ...
... ni ensō shimasu
... に演奏します。

DID YOU KNOW...

The Japanese are the world's biggest consumers of comics, manga, in the world. Manga range from children's to educational to soft-porn. Some of the most popular are also the biggest and are the size of small telephone books.

Film & TV Crews

We're on location.	roke ni imasu	
	ロケにいます	
We're filming!	satsuei chū desu	
	撮影中です	
May we film here?	koko de satsuei shimashō ka?	
	ここで撮影しましょうか？	
We're making a ...	... o seisaku shite imasu.	
	... を制作しています	
film	eiga	映画
documentary	dokyumentarī	ドキュメンタリー
TV series	terebi bangumi	テレビ番組

PILGRIMAGE & RELIGION

Shintoism is the indigenous religion of Japan, but Buddhism has the largest following. At large temples you can sometimes find evidence of a mixing of the two religions from the architecture and religious symbols displayed. The mixing of religious practices is also common. Weddings follow Shinto rituals, whereas funerals are conducted in accordance with Buddhist practices. Many Japanese say that their family belongs to one branch of Buddhism, but they don't practise it in everyday life. A small percentage of the population is Christian and many new religions have emerged in recent years.

What's your religion?	anata no shyūkyō wa nan desu ka?	
	あなたの宗教は何ですか？	
I'm ...	watashi wa ... desu.	
	私は ... です	
Buddhist	bukkyōto	仏教徒
Christian	kirisutokyōto	キリスト教徒
Hindu	hinzūkyōto	ヒンズー教徒
Jewish	yudayakyōto	ユダヤ教徒
Muslim	isuramukyōto	イスラム教徒

I'm not religious.	**watashi wa mushūkyō desu.** 私は無宗教です。
I'm (Catholic), but not practising.	**watashi wa (katorikkukyōto) desu ga, amari misa ni ikimasen** 私は (カトリック教徒) ですが、あまりミサに行きません。
I believe in God.	**watashi wa kami o shinjite imasu** 私は神を信じています。
I think I believe in God.	**watashi wa kami o shinjite iru to omoimasu** 私は神を信じていると思います。
I believe in destiny/fate.	**watashi wa ummei ronja desu.** 私は運命論者です。
I'm interested in astrology/philosophy.	**watashi wa hoshiuranai/ tetsugaku ni kyōmi ga arimasu** 私は (星占い／哲学) に興味があります。
I'm an atheist.	**watashi wa mushinronja desu** 私は無神論者です
I'm agnostic.	**watashi wa fukachironja desu** 私は不可知論者です。
Can I pray here?	**koko de oinori shitemo ii desu ka?** ここでお祈りしてもいいですか?

SPECIFIC NEEDS

WHO SAID THAT?

Remember that the subject of a sentence is often left out if it's obvious or not important. 'I bought this book' can be simply said as 'bought this book'.

kono hon o kaimashita
(lit: this book obj bought)

Can I attend this service/ mass?
: kono reihai/misa ni sanka shitemo ii desu ka?
この (礼拝/ミサ) に参加しても いいですか？

Where can I pray/worship?
: doko de oinori dekimasu ka?
どこでお祈りできますか？

Where can I make confession (in English)?
: doko de (eigo de) zange dekimasu ka?
どこで (英語で) 懺悔できますか？

Can I receive communion here?
: koko de seisan/seitai ga ukeraremasu ka?
ここで (聖餐/聖体) が受けら れますか？

baptism/christening	senrei	洗礼
church	kyōkai	教会
communion	seisan/seitai	聖餐/聖体
confession	zange/kokukai	懺悔/告悔
funeral	sōshiki	葬式
god	kami	神
monk (Christian)	shūdōshi	修道士
monk (Buddhist)	oshō	和尚
prayer	oinori	お祈り
priest	shisai	司祭
religious procession	gyōretsu seika	行列聖歌
sabbath	ansokubi	安息日
saint	seija	聖者
shrine	jinja	神社
temple	tera	寺

TRACING ROOTS & HISTORY

I think my ancestors came
from this area.

watashi no senzo wa koko kara
kita to omoimasu
私の先祖はここから来たと思い
ます。

I'm looking for my relatives.

watashi wa shinseki o sagashite
imasu
私は親戚を探しています。

I have/had a relative who
lives around here.

watashi no shinseki wa kono
atari ni sunde imasu/
imashita
私の親戚はこのあたりに住んで
（います／いました）。

Is there anyone here by
the name of ...?

koko ni ... to iu namae no hito
ga imasu ka?
ここに ... という名前の人がい
ますか？

I'd like to go to the
cemetery/burial ground.

ohaka ni ikitai desu
お墓に行きたいです。

TIME, DATES & FESTIVALS

TELLING THE TIME

To specify an hour, add the number (see Numbers & Amounts page 155) to the word ji 'o'clock':

| five o'clock | go-ji | 5時 |

four o'clock is an exception: yo-ji (not shi-ji). 4時

To say 'half past' use -ji han:

| half past five | go-ji han | 5時半 |

Combining numbers with minutes produces some special forms:

one minute	ip-pun	1分
two minutes	ni-fun	2分
three minutes	sam-pun	3分
four minutes	yom-pun	4分
five minutes	go-fun	5分
six minutes	rop-pun	6分
seven minutes	nana-fun	7分
eight minutes	hap-pun	8分
nine minutes	kyū-fun	9分
10 minutes	jip-pun	10分
20 minutes	ni-jip-pun	20分

5:20	go-ji ni-jip-pun	5時20分
AM	gozen	午前
PM	gogo	午後

What time is it?	ima nan-ji desu ka?	今何時ですか？
(It's) one o'clock.	ichi-ji desu.	1時です。
(It's) ten o'clock.	jū-ji desu.	10時です。
Half past one.	ichi-ji han desu.	1時半です。
3:10 PM.	gogo san-ji jip-pun desu	午後3時10分です。

DAYS OF THE WEEK

Sunday	nichi-yōbi	日曜日
Monday	getsu-yōbi	月曜日
Tuesday	ka-yōbi	火曜日
Wednesday	sui-yōbi	水曜日
Thursday	moku-yōbi	木曜日
Friday	kin-yōbi	金曜日
Saturday	do-yōbi	土曜日

MONTHS

January	ichi-gatsu	1 月
February	ni-gatsu	2 月
March	san-gatsu	3 月
April	shi-gatsu	4 月
May	go-gatsu	5 月
June	roku-gatsu	6 月
July	shichi-gatsu	7 月
August	hachi-gatsu	8 月
September	ku-gatsu	9 月
October	jū-gatsu	１０月
November	jūichi-gatsu	１１月
December	jūni-gatsu	１２月

DATES

What date it is today?	kyō wa nan-nichi desu ka? 今日は何日ですか?
It's (18) October.	jū-gatsu (jūhachi-nichi) desu １０月（１８日）です。

The regular form of dates in Japanese is a cardinal number plus -nichi (日). For example 12th is jūni-nichi, and 25th is nijūgo-nichi From 1st to 10th, 14th, 20th and 24th have irregular forms. The followings are the list of irregular dates:

1st	tsuitachi	1 日
2nd	futsuka	2 日
3rd	mikka	3 日

4th	yokka	4日
5th	itsuka	5日
6th	muika	6日
7th	nanoka/nanuka	7日
8th	yōka	8日
9th	kokonoka	9日
10th	tōka	10日
14th	jūyokka	14日
20th	hatsuka	20日
24th	nijūyokka	24日

PRESENT

today	kyō	今日
this morning	kesa	今朝
tonight	kon'ya	今夜
this week	konshū	今週
this year	kotoshi	今年
now	ima	今

PAST

yesterday	kinō	きのう
day before yesterday	ototoi	おととい
yesterday morning	kinō no asa	きのうの朝
yesterday afternoon	kinō no gogo	きのうの午後
last night	yūbe	ゆうべ
last week	senshū	先週
last year	kyonen	去年

FUTURE

tomorrow	ashita	明日
day after tomorrow	asatte	あさって
tomorrow morning	ashita no asa	明日の朝
tomorrow afternoon	ashita no gogo	明日の午後
tomorrow evening	ashita no yoru	明日の夜
next week	raishū	来週
next year	rainen	来年

TIME, DATES & FESTIVALS

DURING THE DAY

afternoon	gogo	午後
dawn	akegata	明け方
daytime	nicchū	日中
early	hayai	早い
midnight	mayonaka/shin'ya	真夜中／深夜
morning	asa	朝
night	yoru	夜
noon	hiru	昼
sunrise	hinode	日の出
sunset	hinoiri	日の入り

FESTIVALS
Christmas & New Year

Christmas is not a public holiday in Japan but some families give gifts to children on Christmas day. Offices normally begin the New Year break from around 28 December until 3 or 4 January. Special foods are eaten at this time and people return home to their families. It's a Japanese tradition to visit a shrine in the first few days of the New Year. Thousands visit shrines on the evening of 31 December to see the New Year in.

National Celebrations

New Year	oshōgatsu	お正月
Doll's Festival (early March)	hina matsuri	ひな祭り
Blossom Viewing (April)	hanami	花見
Children's Day (early May)	kodomoni hi	子供の日
Star Festival (early July)	tanabata	七夕
Festival of the Dead (mid August)	obon	お盆
7-5-3 Festival (mid November)	shichigosan	七五三

National Holidays

1 January	New Year	gantan
15 January	Adults' Day	seijin no hi
11 February	National Foundation Day	kenkoku kinen no hi

21 March	Vernal Equinox Day	shumbun no hi
29 April	Green Day	midori no hi
3 May	Constitution Day	kempō kinem-bi
5 May	Children's Day	kodomo no hi
20 July	Sea Day	umi no hi
15 September	Respect for the Aged Day	keirō no hi
23 September	Autumnal Equinox Day	shūbun no hi
10 October	Sports Day	taiiku no hi
3 November	Culture Day	bunka no hi
23 November	Labour Thanksgiving Day	kinrō kansha no hi
23 December	Emperor's Birthday	tennō tanjōbi

Regional Festivals

Sapporo Snow Festival (Sapporo) – early February
   a spectacular display of statues, and replicas of famous buildings and icons made of ice and snow that are lit up at night. The festival was started by high school students in the 1950s.

Nebuta Festival (Aomori) – first week of August
   an impressive parade of giant lanterns, shaped into various figures, which are pulled through the streets at night as thousands of locals dance and join in the festivities

TIME, DATES & FESTIVALS

DID YOU KNOW... Japan is one of the most seismically active regions of the world. About 1000 earthquakes a year shake Japan, although most of them are only noticed by scientists and their expensive equipment.

Sendai Tanabata Festival (Sendai) – early August

Spring Festival of Tōshōgū (Nikkō) – mid May
the Spring Festival celebrates the completion of the Tōshōgū Shrine at Nikko, dedicated to Shōgun Tokugawa Ieyasu, which was built in 1617. More than a thousand people dress up annually in costumes of the Edo period and parade to the Shrine.

Kanda Matsuri Festival (Kanda Myōjin Shrine, Tōkyō) – mid May
young locals from downtown Tokyo carry portable shrines (**mikoshi**) through the crowded streets to shouts of encouragement. The brilliant golden lion heads display at this time is also famous.

Sanja Matsuri Festival (Asakusa, Tōkyō) – late May
portable shrines are carried to Asakusa Kannon Shrine by traditionally dressed local men. On the last day of the festival the three main shrines are carried from Asakusa Shrine through thousands of cheering spectators lining the streets. The shrine-bearers normally wear loincloths, so the festival is also an opportunity to view some amazing body tattoos.

TIME, DATES & FESTIVALS

DID YOU KNOW... Kondō Hall and Gojū-no-tō Pagoda in Hōryūji Temple in Nara is the world's oldest wooden structure, believed to have been built in 607 AD. These structures have miraculously survived many earthquakes, wars and fires.

Yabusame Festival (Kamakura) – mid September
  men in traditional hunting gear shoot arrows at three targets
  while galloping on horseback. This festival has a history dating
  back to 1185, when Shōgun Minamoto no Yoritomo
  established the event.

Ombashira Festival (Suwa)
  this unusual festival is held every seven years (the most recent
  being 1998) from early April to mid May. The festival
  originated in the tradition of replacing sacred pillars of the Suwa
  shrines, which was conducted every seven years. Locals haul
  large logs from the mountains down to the shrines, travelling
  through narrow streets, down dangerous slopes and across rivers.
  They are accompanied by local criers, trumpeters and thousands
  of high spirited well wishers.

Gion Matsuri Festival (Kyōto) – July
one of the most famous Japanese festivals held each summer in Kyōto with a history dating back over 1000 years. Impressive two-storey decorated floats carrying traditionally dressed locals are pulled along the streets to the sounds of 'gion bayashi' music.

Awa Odori Festival (Tokushima) – mid August

Wakakusayama Turf Burning Festival (Nara) – mid January
participants burn turf dressed in monk-warrior attire

Omizutori (Nara) – mid March
monks bearing giant torches purify the Nigatsudō temple on the evening of March 12 by running along the external balcony of the temple. Spectators below believe that fallen ash will bring good luck to those it lands on.

Daimon-ji Yaki (Kyōto) – mid August

Tenjin Matsuri (Ōsaka) – late July
two days of festivities, based at the Temmangū Shrine, culminates in a huge parade of lantern-lit boats down the Yodo River

Yamagasa Festival (Hakata) – the first two weeks of July

Nagasaki Okunchi (Nagasaki) – early October
based at the Suwa Shrine, this Festival reflects the city's early contact with China and the Netherlands. Chinese dragons, firecracker displays, and three golden portable shrines are some of the many attractions.

floors (of buildings)	-kai/gai	階
objects (small)	-ko	こ
people	-nin	人
time	-ji	時
vehicles	-dai	台
age	-sai	歳

- The counter for animals -hiki changes to -piki and -biki according to the preceding number.

1 animal	ip-piki	1匹
2 animals	ni-hiki	2匹
3 animals	sam-biki	3匹
4 animals	yon-hiki	4匹
5 animals	go-hiki	5匹
6 animals	rop-piki	6匹
7 animals	nana-hiki	7匹
8 animals	hap-piki/ hachi-hiki	8匹
9 animals	kyū-hiki	9匹
10 animals	jupī-piki/jip-piki	10匹

- Similarly the counter for long objects -hon changes to -pon and -bon

1 bottle	ip-pon	1本
2 bottles	ni-hon	2本
3 bottles	sam-bon	3本
4 bottles	yon-hon	4本
5 bottles	go-hon	5本
6 bottles	rop-pon	6本
7 bottles	nana-hon	7本
8 bottles	hap-pon/hachi-hon	8本
9 bottles	kyū-hon	9本
10 bottles	jup-pon/jip-pon	10本

Generic Counters

The following counters can be used to count most objects. However they can't be used for people and animals. Remember that you put the counter after the cardinal number.

1	hitotsu	一つ
2	futatsu	二つ
3	mittsu	三つ
4	yottsu	四つ
5	itsutsu	五つ
6	muttsu	六つ
7	nanatsu	七つ
8	yattsu	八つ
9	kokonotsu	九つ
10	tō	十

Numbers after 10 take the suffix -ko with Japanese cardinal numbers, eg 12 is jūni-ko.

Help!	tasukete!	助けて！
Stop!	tomare!	止まれ！
Stop it!	yamero!	やめろ！
Go away!	acchi e ike!	あっちへ行け！
Thief!	dorobō!	どろぼう！
Fire!	kaji da!	火事だ！
Watch out!	ki o tsukete!	気を付けて！

It's an emergency.	kinkyū jitai desu 緊急事態です。
Call a doctor!	oishasan o yonde! お医者さんを呼んで！
Call an ambulance!	kyūkyūsha o yonde! 救急車を呼んで！
Call the police!	keisatsu o yonde! 警察を呼んで！

Where's the police station?	kōban wa doko desu ka? 交番はどこですか？
Could you help us please?	tetsudatte kuremasen ka? 手伝ってくれませんか？
Could I please use the telephone?	denwa o karitai no desu ga 電話を借りたいのですが。
I'm lost.	michi ni mayoi mashita 道に迷いました。

| Where are the toilets? | toire wa doko desu ka? トイレはどこですか？ |

DEALING WITH THE POLICE

| police | keisatsu | 警察 |

| We want to report an offence. | hanzai o hōkoku shitai no desu ga 犯罪を報告したいのですが。 |

THE POLICE MAY SAY ...

anata wa ... de kokuhatsu saremasu
あなたは ... で告発されます。
You will be charged with ...

kanojo/kare wa ... de kokuhatsu saremasu
(彼女／彼) は ... で告発されます。
She/He will be charged with ...

han-seifu undō 反政府運動	anti-government activity
bōkō 暴行	assault
chian bōgai 治安妨害	disturbing the peace
fuhō nyūkoku 不法入国	illegal entry
satsujin 殺人	murder
biza nashi ビザなし	having no visa
fuhō taizai 不法滞在	overstaying your visa
(ihōna busshitsu no) shoji (違法な物質の) 所持	possession (of illegal substances)
reipu/gōkan レイプ／強姦	rape
gōtō/tōnan 強盗／盗難	robbery/theft
mambiki 万引き	shoplifting
kōtsū ihan 交通違反	traffic violation
fuhō rōdō 不法労働	working with no permit

I've been raped/assaulted.	reipu/bōkō saremashita	
	(レイプ／暴行) されました。	
I've been robbed.	gōtō ni aimashita	
	強盗にあいました。	

My ... was/were stolen.	watashi no ... ga nusumaremashita	
	私の ... が盗まれました。	
backpack	bakku pakku	バックパック
bags	nimotsu	荷物
handbag	handobaggu	ハンドバッグ
money	o-kane	お金
papers	shorui	書類
travellers' cheques	toraberāzu chekku	トラベラーズ チェック
passport	pasupōto	パスポート
wallet	saifu	財布

My possessions are insured.	watashi no shoyūbutsu wa hoken ni kakete arimasu
	私の所有物は保険にかけてあります。
I didn't realise I was doing anything wrong.	ihōkōi o shiteiru tsumori wa nakatta no desu ga
	違法行為をしているつもりはなかったのですが。
I didn't do it.	watashi wa yatte imasen
	私はやっていません。
We're innocent.	watashitachi wa keppaku desu
	私達は潔白です。
We're foreigners.	watashitachi wa gaikoku-jin desu
	私達は外国人です。
I wish to contact my embassy/consulate.	taishikan/ryōjikan ni renraku shitai no desu ga
	(大使館／領事館) に連絡したいのですが。
Can I call someone?	chijin ni denwa shi te mo ii desu ka
	知人に電話してもいいですか？

EMERGENCIES

I want a lawyer who speaks English.	eigo ga dekiru bengoshi o onegai shimasu	英語ができる弁護士をお願いします。
Can we pay an on-the-spot fine?	kono ba de bakkin o harau koto ga dekimasu ka?	この場で罰金を払うことができますか?
I understand.	wakarimashita	わかりました。
I don't understand.	wakarimasen	わかりません。
What am I accused of?	donna riyū de kokuso sareru no desu ka	どんな理由で告訴されるのですか?
I know my rights.	watashi ni kenri ga aru no o shitteimasu	私に権利があるのを知っています。

to arrest	taiho shimasu	逮捕します。
embassy/consulate	taishikan/ryōjikan	大使館／領事館
fine (payment)	bakkin	罰金
guilty	yūzai	有罪
lawyer	bengoshi	弁護士
not guilty	muzai	無罪
police officer	keisatsukan	警察官
police station	kōban	交番
prison	keimusho	刑務所
trial	saiban	裁判

HEALTH EMERGENCIES

I'm ill.	watashi wa byōki desu 私は病気です。
My friend's ill.	tomodachi ga byōki desu 友達が病気です。
I have medical insurance.	iryō hoken ga arimasu 医療保険があります。

A

able (to be); can	dekimasu	できます
Can I ...?	... mo ii desu ka?	... もいいですか?
Can I take a photo?	shashin o totte mo ii desu ka?	写真を撮ってもいいですか?
Can I ...? (asking for favour)	... kuremasen ka?	... くれませんか?
Can you show me on the map?	chizu de oshiete kuremasen ka?	地図で教えてくれませんか?
aboard	notte	乗って
abortion	chūzetsu	中絶
about	yaku	約
above	ue ni	上に
abroad	kaigai	海外
to accept	uketorimasu	受け取ります
accident	jiko	事故
accommodation	shukuhaku setsubi	宿泊設備
activist	katsudōka	活動家
addiction	chūdoku	中毒
address	jūsho	住所
to admire	homemasu	誉めます
admission	nyūjō	入場
to admit	mitomemasu	認めます
adult	otona	大人
advantage	yūri	有利
advice	adobaisu/jogen	アドバイス／助言
aeroplane	hikōki	飛行機
to be afraid of	kowagarimasu	恐がります
after	ato	後
again	mata	また
against	hantai	反対
age	toshi/nenrei	歳／年齢
agency	dairiten	代理店
aggressive	kōgekiteki na	攻撃的な
to agree	dōi shimasu	同意します
I don't agree.	sansei shimasen	賛成しません。
Agreed!	sansei!	賛成!
agriculture	nōgyō	農業
ahead	mukō ni	向こうに
aid (help)	enjo	援助
AIDS	eizu	エイズ

air	kūki	空気
air mail	kōkūbin	航空便
air-conditioned	eakon	エアコン
airport (tax)	kūkō (zei)	空港 (税)
alarm clock	mezamashi-dokei	目覚まし時計
all	subete	すべて
allergy	arerugī	アレルギー
to allow	kyoka shimasu	許可します
It's allowed.	kyoka sarete imasu	許可されています。
It's not allowed.	kyoka sarete imasen	許可されていません。
almost	hotondo	ほとんど
alone	hitori de	独りで
already	sude ni	すでに
also	mata	また
altitude	hyōkō	標高
always	itsumo	いつも
amateur	shirōto	素人
ambassador	taishi	大使
among	uchi de	うちで
anarchist	anākisuto/	アナーキスト／
	museifu-shugisha	無政府主義者
ancient	ōmukashi no	大昔の
and	soshite/sorekara/to	そして／それから／と
to get angry	okorimasu	怒ります
animal	dōbutsu	動物
annual	ichi-nen no	1年の
to answer	kotaemasu	答えます
answering machine	rusuban denwa	留守番電話
antibiotics	kōseibusshitsu	抗生物質
antinuclear	han-kaku	反核
antiques	kottōhin/antiku	骨董品／アンティーク
antiseptic	shōdoku	消毒
any time	itsu de mo	いつでも
anything	nan de mo	何でも
anywhere	doko de mo	どこでも
appointment	yoyaku	予約
April	shi-gatsu	4月
archaeological	kōkogakuteki na	考古学的な
architect	sekkeishi	設計士
architecture	kenchikubutsu	建築物
to argue	hanron shimasu	反論します
arm	ude	腕
arrival	tōchaku	到着

to arrive	tōchaku shimasu/tsukimasu	到着します／着きます
art	bijutsu	美術
art gallery	bijutsukan	美術館
artist	geijutsuka	芸術家
artwork	geijutsuhin	芸術品
ashamed	hazukashii	恥ずかしい
ashtray	haizara	灰皿
to ask (a question)	kikimasu/tazunemasu	聞きます／たずねます
to ask (for something)	tanomimasu	頼みます
to be asleep	nemutte imasu	眠っています
aspirin	asupirin	アスピリン
asthma	zensoku	喘息
at the back (behind)	ushiro	後ろ
atmosphere	fun'iki	雰囲気
August	hachi-gatsu	8月
aunt	oba/obasan	おば／おばさん
Australia	ōsutoraria	オーストラリア
automatic teller (ATM)	genkin jidō shiharai ki; ētiemu	現金自動支払機／ＡＴＭ
autumn	aki	秋
avenue	ōdōri	大通り
awful	hidoi	ひどい

B

B&W (film)	shirokuro (firumu)	白黒 (フィルム)
baby	akachan	赤ちゃん
baby food	rinyūshoku	離乳食
baby powder	bebīpaudā	ベビーパウダー
baby-sitter	bebī shittā/komori	ベビーシッター／子守り
back	ushiro	後
back (body)	senaka	背中
backpack	bakkupakku	バックパック
bad	warui	悪い
bag	baggu	バッグ
baggage	tenimotsu	手荷物
baggage claim	baggēji kurēmu	バッゲージクレーム
bakery	pan'ya	パン屋
balcony	barukonī	バルコニー
ball	bōru	ボール
ballet	barē	バレエ
band (music)	bando	バンド
bandage	hōtai	包帯

bank	ginkō	銀行
banknote	ginkōken	銀行券
banquet	enkai	宴会
a bar	bā	バー
bargain	bāgen	バーゲン
basket	kago	かご
basketball	basuketto	バスケット
bath	furo	風呂
bathing suit	mizugi	水着
bathroom	furoba	風呂場
battery	denchi	電池
to be	desu	です
beach	hamabe/bīchi	浜辺／ビーチ
beautiful	kirei na; utsukushii	きれいな／美しい
because	dakara/kara	だから／から
bed	beddo	ベッド
bedroom	shinshitsu	寝室
before	mae	前
beggar	kojiki	乞食
to begin	hajimarimasu	始まります
behind	ushiro	後
below	shita	下
beside	yoko	横
best	saikō	最高
a bet	kake	賭け
between	aida	間
Bible	seisho	聖書
bicycle	jitensha	自転車
big	ōkii	大きい
bike	jitensha	自転車
bill	kanjō	勘定
binoculars	sōgankyō	双眼鏡
biodegradable	seibutsu bunkai	生物分解
biography	denki	伝記
bird	tori	鳥
birth certificate	shussei shōmeisho	出生証明書
birthday	tanjōbi	誕生日
birthday cake	bāsudē kēki	バースデーケーキ
to bite (dog)	kamimasu	噛みます
to bite (insect)	sashimasu	刺します
bitter	nigai	苦い

B

black	kuro	黒
blanket	mōfu	毛布
to bleed	chi ga demasu	血が出ます
blind	me no fujiyū na hito;	目の不自由な人／
	shikaku shōgaisha	視覚障害者
blood	chi	血
blood group	ketsueki-gata	血液型
blood pressure	ketsuatsu	血圧
blood test	ketsueki kensa	血液検査
blue	ao	青
to board (ship, etc)	norimasu	乗ります
boarding pass	tōjōken	搭乗券
boat	bōto	ボート
body	karada	からだ
Bon appétit!	meshiagare	召し上がれ
Bon voyage!	saraba/sayōnara	さらば／さようなら
bone	hone	骨
book	hon	本
to book	yoyaku shimasu	予約します
booking	yoyaku	予約
book shop	hon'ya	本屋
boots	būtsu	ブーツ
border	kokkyō	国境
bored	taikutsu na	退屈な
boring	tsumaranai	つまらない
to borrow	karimasu	借ります
botanic garden	shokubutsuen	植物園
both	ryōhō	両方
bottle	bin	ビン
bottle opener	sennuki	栓抜き
box	hako	箱
boxing	bokushingu	ボクシング
boy	otoko no ko	男の子
boyfriend	bōifurendo	ボーイフレンド
branch (company)	shiten	支店
branch (tree)	eda	枝
brave	yūkan na	勇敢な
bread	pan	パン
to break	kowashimasu	壊します
breakfast	chōshoku/asagohan	朝食／朝御飯
to breathe	iki o shimasu	息をします
a bribe	wairo	賄賂
to bribe	shūwai shimasu	収賄します
bridge	hashi	橋

**D
I
C
T
I
O
N
A
R
Y**

bright	akarui	明るい
brilliant	subarashii	素晴らしい
to bring	motte kimasu	持って来ます
broken	kowareta/koshō shita	壊れた／故障した
brother	kyōdai	兄弟
brown	chairo	茶色
a bruise	uchimi	打ち身
bucket	baketsu	バケツ
Buddhist	bukkyōto	仏教徒
bug	mushi	虫
to build	tatemasu	建てます
building	tatemono	建物
bullet train	shinkansen	新幹線
bus	basu	バス
bus (city)	shi-basu/to-basu	市バス／都バス
bus (intercity)	chōkyori-basu	長距離バス
bus station	basutei	バス停
bus terminal	basu-tāminaru	バスターミナル
business	bijinesu	ビジネス
businessman	bijinesu man	ビジネスマン
businesswoman	kyaria ūman	キャリアウーマン
busker	daidō geinin	大道芸人
busy	isogashii	忙しい
but	shikashi/demo	しかし／でも
butterfly	chō	蝶
buttons	botan	ボタン
to buy	kaimasu	買います
I'd like to buy ...	... o kudasai	... をください。

C

a café	kafe/kissaten	カフェ／喫茶店
calendar	karendā	カレンダー
camera	kamera	カメラ
camera shop	kamerya	カメラ屋
to camp	kyampu shimasu	キャンプします
Can we camp here?	koko de kyampu shite mo ii desu ka?	ここでキャンプしてもいいですか？
campsite	kyampujō	キャンプ場
can (aluminium)	(arumi) kan	（アルミ）缶
can (to be able)	dekimasu	できます
I can't do it.	watashi wa dekimasen	私はできません。

We can do it.	watashi-tachi wa dekimasu	私達はできます。
can opener	kankiri	缶切り
cancel (n)	torikeshi/kyanseru	取り消し／キャンセル
to cancel	torikeshimasu; kyanseru shimasu	取り消します／キャンセルします
candle	rōsoku	ろうそく
car	kuruma	車
car park	chūshajō	駐車場
car registration	jidōsha tōroku	自動車登録
cards	kādo	カード
to care (about)	shimpai shimasu	心配します
to care (for someone)	mendō o mimasu	面倒を見ます
Careful!	ki o tsukete!	気を付けて！
caring	mendōmi ga ii	面倒見がいい
to carry	hakobimasu	運びます
carton	danbōru	ダンボール
cartoons	manga	漫画
cash	genkin	現金
cash register	reji	レジ
cashier	reji-gakari	レジ係
cassette	kasetto	カセット
castle	shiro	城
casual dress	fudangi	普段着
cat	neko	ねこ
cathedral	daiseidō	大聖堂
Catholic	katorikku	カトリック
caves	dōkutsu	洞窟
CD	shīdī	ＣＤ
to celebrate	iwaimasu	祝います
centimetre	senchi	センチ
ceramic	tōjiki/seramikku	陶磁器／セラミック
certificate	shōmeisho	証明書
chair	isu	椅子
champagne	shampen	シャンペン
championships	championshippu	チャンピオンシップ
chance	kikai/chansu	機会／チャンス
change (coins)	otsuri	おつり
change over	norikae	乗り換え
to change	kaemasu	代えます
changing rooms	kōishitsu	更衣室
charming	chāmingu na	チャーミングな
to chat up	shaberimasu	喋ります
cheap (hotel)	yasui (hoteru)	安い (ホテル)

a cheat	zuru	ずる
Cheat!	zurui!	ずるい！
to check	shirabemasu	調べます
check-in (desk)	chekku-in	チェックイン
Checkmate!	tsumi!	詰み！
checkpoint	chekku-pointo	チェックポイント
cheese	chīzu	チーズ
chemist	yakkyoku	薬局
cheque	kogitte	小切手
cherry blossom	sakura	桜
chess	chesu	チェス
chessboard	chesuban	チェス盤
chest	mune	胸
chewing gum	chūingamu	チューインガム
chicken	niwatori	ニワトリ
child	kodomo	子供
childminding	komori	子守り
children	kodomo tachi	子供たち
chinaware	setomono	瀬戸物
Chinese food	chūka ryōri	中華料理
Chinese tea	chūgoku cha	中国茶
chocolate	chokorēto	チョコレート
to choose	erabimasu	選びます
Christian	kirisuto kyōto	キリスト教徒
christian (first) name	senrei mei	洗礼名
Christmas card	kurisumasu kādo	クリスマスカード
Christmas Day	kurisumasu	クリスマス
Christmas Eve	kurisumasu ibu	クリスマスイブ
chrysanthemum	kiku	菊
church	kyōkai	教会
cigarette papers	tabako no makigami	たばこの巻き紙
cigarettes	tabako	たばこ
cinema	eiga kan	映画館
citizenship	shiminken	市民権
city	shi/toshi	市／都市
civil rights	shiminken	市民権
class	kurasu	クラス
class system	kaikyū seido	階級制度
classical art	koten bijutsu	古典美術
classical music	kurashikku	クラシック
classical theatre	koten geinō	古典芸能
clean (hotel)	seiketsu na (hoteru)	清潔な（ホテル）
cleaning	sōji	掃除
client	kokyaku	顧客

cliff	gake	崖
to climb	noborimasu	登ります
cloak	gaitō	外套
cloakroom	keitaihin azukarijo	携帯品預所
clock	tokei	時計
to close	shimemasu	閉めます
closed	heiten	閉店
clothing	irui	衣類
clothing store	yōfukuya	洋服屋
cloud	kumo	雲
cloudy	kumori	曇り
clown	piero	ピエロ
coast	kaigan	海岸
coat	kōto	コート
cocaine	kokain	コカイン
coffee	kōhī	コーヒー
coins	koin	コイン
a cold	kaze	風邪
to have a cold	kaze o hikimasu	風邪をひきます。
cold (object)	tsumetai	冷たい
It's cold. (object)	tsumetai desu	冷たいです。
cold (weather)	samui	寒い
It's cold. (weather)	samui desu	寒いです。
cold water	mizu	水
colleague	dōryō	同僚
college	karejji	カレッジ
colour	iro	色
comb	kushi	櫛
to come	kimasu	来ます
comedy	komedī	コメディー
comfortable	kokochi yoi	心地よい
comics	manga	漫画
communion	seisan/seitai	聖餐／聖体
communist	kyōsan shugisha	共産主義者
companion	nakama	仲間
company	kaisha	会社
compass	hōi jishaku	方位磁石
computer games	kompyūta gēmu	コンピュータゲーム
a concert	konsāto	コンサート
condom	kondōmu	コンドーム
confession	kokkai/zange	告解／懺悔
to confirm (a booking)	kakunin shimasu	確認します
Congratulations!	omedetō!	おめでとう！
conservative	hoshuteki na	保守的な

to be constipated	bempi shimasu	便秘します
constipation	bempi	便秘
construction work	kensetsu sagyō	建設作業
consulate	ryōji kan	領事館
contact lenses	kontakuto renzu	コンタクトレンズ
contraception	hinin	避妊
contraceptive	hininyaku	避妊薬
contract	keiyaku	契約
convent	shūdōin	修道院
to cook	ryōri shimasu	料理します
cool [colloquial]	kūru	クール
corner	kado	かど
corruption	oshoku	汚職
cosmetics	keshōhin	化粧品
to cost	kakarimasu	かかります
How much does it cost to go to ...?	... made ikura desu ka?	... までいくらですか?
It costs a lot.	takai desu	高いです。
cotton	wata/men	綿
a cough	seki	せき
to count	kazoemasu	数えます
counter	kauntā	カウンター
country	kuni	国
countryside	inaka	田舎
coupon	kūpon	クーポン
court (legal)	saibansho	裁判所
court (tennis)	kōto	コート
cow	ushi	牛
crab	kani	かに
crafts	kōgei hin	工芸品
crafty	zurui	ずるい
crag; wall of rock	iwa yama	岩山
crane	tsuru	鶴
crazy	kichigai	気違い
credit card	kurejitto kādo	クレジットカード
creep (slang)	zotto suru	ぞっとする
cricket	kuriketto	クリケット
cross (angry)	fukigen na	不機嫌な
cross (religious)	jūjika	十字架
cross country	kurosu kantorī	クロスカントリー
to cuddle	dakimasu	抱きます
cup	kappu	カップ
cupboard	shokkidana	食器棚
curator	kanchō	館長

D

current affairs	jiji	時事
cushions	zabuton/kusshon	座布団／クッション
customs	shūkan	習慣
to cut	kirimasu	切ります
cuttlefish	ika	イカ
to cycle	jitensha ni norimasu	自転車に乗ります
cycling	saikuringu	サイクリング
cyclist	saikurisuto	サイクリスト
cystitis	bōkōen	膀胱炎

D

dad	otōsan	お父さん
daily	mainichi	毎日
dairy products	nyūseihin	乳製品
dance	dansu	ダンス
to dance	dansu shimasu	ダンスします
Danger!	abunai!	危ない！
dangerous	kiken na	危険な
dark	kurai	暗い
date (appointment)	dēto	デート
date (time)	hizuke	日付
date of birth	seinengappi	生年月日
to date (someone)	dēto shimasu	デートします
daughter	musume	娘
dawn	akegata/yoake	明け方／夜明け
day	nicchū	日中
day after tomorrow	asatte	あさって
day before yesterday	ototoi	おととい
dead	shitai	死体
deaf	mimi no fujiyū na hito/ chōkaku shōgaisha	耳の不自由な人／聴覚障害者
to deal	kubarimasu	配ります
death	shi	死
December	jūni-gatsu	１２月
to decide	kimemasu	決めます
deck (of cards)	torampu hitokumi	トランプ１組
deep	fukai	深い
deer	shika	鹿
deforestation	shinrin bassai	森林伐採
degree	teido	程度
to delay	enki shimasu/ okuremasu	延期します／遅れます

delicatessen	derikatessen	デリカテッセン
delicious	oishii	おいしい
democracy	minshu shugi	民主主義
demonstration	demo	デモ
dental floss	ito yōji	糸楊枝
dentist	haisha	歯医者
to deny	hitei shimasu	否定します
deodorant	deodoranto	デオドラント
to depart (leave)	shuppatsu shimasu	出発します
department stores	depāto	デパート
departure	shuppatsu	出発
descendent	shison	子孫
desert	sabaku	砂漠
design	dezain	デザイン
destination	mokuteki-chi	目的地
to destroy	hakai shimasu	破壊します
detail	shōsai	詳細
diabetic	tōnyōbyō	糖尿病
dial tone	daiaru tōn	ダイアルトーン
dialect	hōgen	方言
diaper	omutsu	おむつ
diarrhoea	geri	下痢
diary	nikki	日記
dice/die	saikoro	サイコロ
dictionary	jisho	辞書
to die	shinimasu	死にます
different	chigau/kotonaru	違う／異なる
difficult	muzukashii	難しい
dining car	shokudōsha	食堂車
dinner	yūshoku/bangohan	夕食／晩ごはん
direct	chokusetsu	直接
direction	hōkō	方向
director	kanrishoku/shidōsha	管理職／指導者
directory	denwa chō	電話帳
dirty	kitanai	汚い
disabled	shōgai sha	障害者
disadvantage	furi	不利
disco	disuko	ディスコ
discount	waribiki	割引
to discover	hakken shimasu	発見します
discrimination	sabetsu	差別
disease	byōki	病気
dismissal	kaiko	解雇
distributor	oroshiuri gyōsha	卸売業者
diving	daibingu	ダイビング

diving equipment	daibingu no sōbi	ダイビングの装備
divorce	rikon	離婚
dizzy	memai	めまい
to do	shimasu/yarimasu	します／やります
I didn't do it.	watashi wa yarimasen deshita	私はやりませんでした。
doctor	isha	医者
a documentary	dokyumentarī	ドキュメンタリー
dog	inu	犬
dole	shitsugyō teate	失業手当
doll	ningyō	人形
Don't worry!	shimpai shinai de!	心配しないで！
door	doa	ドア
dope (drugs)	marifana	マリファナ
double	ni bai	2倍
a double bed	daburu beddo	ダブルベッド
drama	dorama	ドラマ
dramatic	gekiteki na/ doramachikku na	劇的な／ドラマチックな
a double room	daburu rūmu	ダブルルーム
to dream	yume o mimasu	夢を見ます
dress	doresu	ドレス
a drink	nomimono	飲物
to drink	nomimasu	飲みます
to drive	unten shimasu	運転します
driver	unten shu	運転手
drivers' licence	unten menkyo	運転免許
drug (medicine)	kusuri	薬
drug addiction	mayaku chūdoku	麻薬中毒
drug dealer	mayaku no bainin	麻薬の売人
drums	taiko	太鼓
to be drunk	yopparaimasu	酔っ払います
to dry (clothes)	kawakashimasu	乾かします
dummy (pacifier)	oshaburi	おしゃぶり

E

each	sorezore/kaku	それぞれ／各
ear	mimi	耳
early	hayai	早い
It's early.	hayai desu	早いです。
to earn	kasegimasu	稼ぎます
earrings	iyaringu	イヤリング
Earth	chikyū	地球

earth (soil)	tsuchi	土
earthquake	jishin	地震
east	higashi	東
Easter	fukkatsu sai	復活祭
easy	kantan na	簡単な
to eat	tabemasu	食べます
economy	keizai	経済
editor	henshūsha	編集者
education	kyōiku	教育
egg	tamago	たまご
elbow	hiji	ひじ
elections	senkyo	選挙
electorate	yūkensha	有権者
electricity	denki	電気
elevator	erebētā	エレベーター
embarassed	kihazukashii	気恥ずかしい
embassy	taishikan	大使館
emergency	kinkyū	緊急
emergency exit	hijō guchi	非常口
employee	jūgyōin	従業員
employer	yatoinushi	雇い主
empty	kara no	空の
end	owari	終わり
to end	owarasemasu	終わらせます
endangered species	zetsumetsu no kiki ni hinshita seibutsu	絶滅の危機に瀕した生物
engagement	kon'yaku	婚約
engine	enjin	エンジン
engineer	enjinia/gijutsusha	エンジニア／技術者
engineering	kōgaku	工学
English	eigo	英語
to enjoy (oneself)	tanoshimimasu	楽しみます
enough	jūbun na	十分な
Enough!	mō takusanda!	もうたくさんだ！
to enter	hairimasu	入ります
entertaining	yukai na/omoshiroi	愉快な／おもしろい
entrance	iriguchi	入口
envelope	fūtō	封筒
environment	kankyō	環境
epileptic	tenkan	癲癇
equal opportunity	byōdō koyō	平等雇用
equality	byōdō	平等
equipment	sōbi	装備
European	yōroppajin	ヨーロッパ人

euthanasia	anraku shi	安楽死
evening	ban/yūgure	晩／夕暮れ
every day	mainichi	毎日
example	rei	例
For example, ...	tatoeba, ...	例えば、 ...
excellent	subarashii	素晴らしい
to exchange	kōkan shimasu	交換します
exchange rate	kawase rēto	為替レート
excluded	nozokarete	除かれて
Excuse me.	sumimasen	すみません
to exhibit	tenji shimasu	展示します
exhibition	tenrankai	展覧会
exit	deguchi	出口
expensive	takai	高い
exploitation	kaihatsu	開発
express	kyūkō no	急行の
express mail	sokutatsu	速達
eye	me	目

F

face	kao	顔
factory	kōjō	工場
factory worker	kōin	工員
fall (autumn)	aki	秋
to fall	ochimasu	落ちます
family	kazoku	家族
famous	yūmei na	有名な
fan (folding)	sensu	扇子
fan (machine)	sempūki	扇風機
fan (round)	uchiwa	団扇
fans (of a team)	fan	ファン
far	tōi	遠い
farm	nōjō	農場
farmer	nōmin	農民
fast	hayai	速い
fat	shibō	脂肪
father (my)	chichi	父
father (your)	otō san	お父さん
father-in-law	giri no otōsan	義理のお父さん
fault (someone's)	machigai	間違い

faulty	kekkan hin	欠陥品
favourite	konomi	好み
fax	fakkusu	ファックス
fear	osore	恐れ
February	ni-gatsu	2月
fee	ryōkin	料金
to feel	kanjimasu	感じます
feelings	kimochi	気持ち
fencing	fenshingu	フェンシング
festival	matsuri	祭り
fever	netsu	熱
few	sukoshi	少し
fiancé/fiancée	kon'yakusha/fianse	婚約者／フィアンセ
fiction	fikushon/shōsetsu	フィクション／小説
field	bun'ya	分野
fight	kenka	けんか
to fight	tatakaimasu	戦います
figures	sūji	数字
to fill	ippai ni shimasu	いっぱいにします
film (cinema)	eiga	映画
film (for camera)	firumu	フィルム
a film (negatives)	firumu (nega)	フィルム（ネガ）
film speed/ASA	āsa	ASA
to find	mitsukemasu	見つけます
a fine	bakkin	罰金
finger	yubi	指
to finish	owarasemasu	終わらせます
fire (disaster)	kaji	火事
fire (general)	hi	火
fire extinguisher	shōkaki	消火器
firewood	maki/takigi	薪／たきぎ
first	ichiban	一番
first time	hajimete	はじめて
first-aid kit	kyūkyūbako	救急箱
fish (shop)	sakana (ya)	魚（屋）
flag	hata	旗
flash	furasshu	フラッシュ
flashlight	kaichū dentō	懐中電灯
flat (land, etc)	taira na	平らな
flea	nomi	蚤
flight	hikōbin	飛行便
flood	kōzui	洪水
floor	yuka	床
floor (storey)	kai	階

F

florist	hanaya	花屋
flour	komugiko	小麦粉
flower	hana	花
flower arrangement	ikebana	生け花
fly	hae	ハエ
fog	kiri	霧
It's foggy.	kiri ga dete imasu	霧が出ています。
folding screen	byōbu	屏風
to follow	shitagaimasu	従います
food	tabemono	食べ物
foot	ashi	足
football (soccer)	sakkā	サッカー
footpath	hodō	歩道
foreign	gaikoku no	外国の
foreign country	gaikoku	外国
foreign currency	gaika	外貨
foreign language	gaikoku go	外国語
foreigner	gaikoku/gaijin	(外国／外) 人
forest	mori	森
forever	eien ni	永遠に
to forget	wasuremasu	忘れます
I forget.	wasuremashita	忘れました。
to forgive	yurushimsu	許します
fork	fōku	フォーク
fortnight	ni-shūkan	2週間
fortune teller	uranaishi	占師
foyer	robī	ロビー
free (not bound)	jiyū na	自由な
free (of charge)	muryō	無料
freeway	kōsoku dōro	高速道路
to freeze	kōrasemasu	凍らせます
Friday	kin'yōbi	金曜日
friend	tomodachi	友達
from	kara	から
frozen	reitō	冷凍
fruit (shop)	kudamono (ya)	果物 (屋)
full	ippai	いっぱい
fun	tanoshii	楽しい
to make fun of	karakaimasu	からかいます
to have fun	tanoshimimasu	楽しみます
funeral	sōshiki	葬式
future	shōrai	将来

D I C T I O N A R Y

G

game (sport)	gēmu	ゲーム
a game show	kuizu bangumi	クイズ番組
garage	garēji/shako	ガレージ／車庫
garbage	gomi	ごみ
gardening	niwa-zukuri	庭造り
gardens	niwa	庭
gas cartridge	gasu kātorijji	ガスカートリッジ
gate	mon/gēto	門／ゲート
gay	gei	ゲイ
general	ippan no	一般の
to get	te ni iremasu	手に入れます
Get lost!	usero!	失せろ！
to get off	orimasu	降ります
to get on	norimasu	乗ります
geyser	kanketsu sen	間欠泉
gift	okuri mono	贈り物
girl	onna no ko	女の子
girlfriend	gārufurendo	ガールフレンド
to give	agemasu	あげます
Could you give me ...?	... o kudasai.	... をください。
glass	gurasu	グラス
glasses	megane	眼鏡
to go	ikimasu	行きます
Go straight ahead.	massugu itte kudasai	まっすぐ行って下さい。
to go out with ...	... to dekakemasu	... と出かけます。
goal	gōru/mokuteki	ゴール／目的
goalkeeper	gōrukīpā	ゴールキーパー
goat	yagi	やぎ
God	kami	神
of gold	kin no	金の
good	yoi/ii	良い／いい
Good afternoon.	konnichi wa	こんにちは。
Good evening/night.	komban wa	こんばんは。
Good health!; Cheers!	kampai!	乾杯！
good hotel	ii hoteru	いいホテル
Good luck!	gambatte!	がんばって！
Good morning.	ohayō (gozaimasu)	おはよう（ございます）。
Good night.	oyasumi (nasai)	おやすみ（なさい）。
Goodbye.	sayōnara	さようなら。
goods	shinamono	品物
government	seifu	政府

gram	guramu	グラム
grandchild	mago	孫
grandfather	ojī san	おじいさん
grandmother	obā san	おばあさん
grapefruit	gurēpu furūtsu	グレープフルーツ
graphic art	gurafikku āto	グラフィックアート
grass	kusa	草
grave	haka	墓
great	idai na	偉大な
Great!	subarashii!/ sugoi!	すばらしい！／すごい！
green	midori	緑
greengrocer	yaoya	八百屋
grey	haiiro	灰色
to guess	atemasu	当てます
guest	o-kyaku	お客
guide (audio)	annai hōsō	案内放送
guide (person)	gaido	ガイド
guidebook	ryokō annaisho;	旅行案内書／
	gaidobukku	ガイドブック
guided trek	gaido tsuki torekkingu	ガイド付きトレッキング
guide dog	mōdōken	盲導犬
guinea pig	morumotto	モルモット
guitar	gitā	ギター
gym	jimu/taiikukan	ジム／体育館
gymnastics	taisō	体操

H

hair	kaminoke/ke	髪の毛／毛
hairbrush	heaburashi	ヘアブラシ
half	hambun	半分
half-price	hangaku	半額
to hallucinate	genkaku o mimasu	幻覚をみます
ham	hamu	ハム
hammer	kana-zuchi	金槌
hammock	hammokku	ハンモック
hand	te	手
handbag	handobaggu	ハンドバッグ
handicrafts	hankachi	ハンカチ
handmade	tezukuri	手作り
handsome	hansamu	ハンサム
happy	ureshii	うれしい
Happy birthday!	o-tanjōbi omedetō!	お誕生日おめでとう！
harassment	iyagarase	嫌がらせ

harbour	minato	港
hard/solid	katai	固い
hash	hasshisshi	ハッシッシ
hat	bōshi	帽子
to have	mochimasu	持ちます
Do you have ...?	... ga arimasu ka?	... がありますか？
I have ...	... o motte imasu	... を持っています。
hayfever	kafunshō	花粉症
he	kare	彼
head	atama	頭
a headache	zutsū	頭痛
health	kenkō	健康
health food	kenkō shoku	健康食
to hear	kikimasu	聞きます
hearing aid	hochōki	補聴器
heart	shinzō	心臓
heat	netsu	熱
heater	hītā	ヒーター
heating	dambō	暖房
heavy	omoi	重い
Hello (telephone)	moshi-moshi	もしもし
Hello.	konnichi wa	こんにちは。
helmet	herumetto	ヘルメット
to help	tasukemasu	助けます
Help!	tasukete!	助けて！
herbalist	kampōi/ hābui	漢方医／ハーブ医
herbs	hābu	ハーブ
here	koko	ここ
heroin (addict)	heroin (chūdoku)	ヘロイン (中毒)
high	takai	高い
high blood pressure	kōketsuatsu	高血圧
high school (senior)	kōkō	高校
high school (junior)	chūgaku	中学
to hike	haikingu shimasu	ハイキングします
hiking	haikingu	ハイキング
hiking routes	haikingu no rūto	ハイキングのルート
hill	oka	丘
Hindu	hinzū kyō	ヒンズー教
to hire	karimasu	借ります
to hitchhike	hicchihaiku shimasu	ヒッチハイクします
HIV positive	eizu kansensha	エイズ感染者
holiday	kyūjitsu	休日
home	ie/uchi	家／うち
homeless	hōmuresu	ホームレス
homeopathy	homeopashī	ホメオパシー

homosexual	homo	ホモ
honey	hachimitsu	**蜂蜜**
honeymoon	hanemŭn	ハネムーン
horrible	hidoi	ひどい
horse	uma	馬
horse riding	jōba	乗馬
horseradish	wasabi	わさび
hospital	byōin	病院
hot (spicy)	karai	辛い
hot (object)	atsui	熱い
hot (weather)	atsui	暑い
It's hot.	atsui desu	暑いです。
hot spring	onsen	温泉
hot water	o-yu	お湯
to be hot	atsuku narimasu	熱くなります
hotel	hoteru	ホテル
house	ie	家
housework	kaji	家事
how	dōyatte	どうやって
How do I get to …?	… e wa dō ikimasu ka?	… へはどう行きますか?
How do you say …?	… wa nan to iimasu ka?	… は何といいますか?
to hug	dakimasu	抱きます
human rights	jinken	人権
a hundred	hyaku	百
to be hungry	onakaga sukimasu	お腹が空きます
husband	otto	夫

I

I (any gender)	watashi	私
I (male)	boku	僕
ice	kōri	氷
ice water	kōri mizu	氷水
icecream	aisukurimu	アイスクリーム
identification	shōmeisho	証明書
identification card	mibun shōmeisho	身分証明書
idiot	baka	ばか
if	moshi	もし
ill	byōki	病気
immediately	sugu	すぐ
immigration	imin	移民
Immigration Office	iminkyoku	移民局

important	taisetsu na	大切な
It's important.	taisetsu desu	大切です。
It's not important.	taisetsu ja arimasen	大切じゃありません。
in a hurry	isoide	急いで
in five minutes	go-fun kan ni	5分間に
in front of	no mae ni	の前に
in six days	muika kan ni	6日間に
included	komi	込み
income tax	shotoku-zei	所得税
indicator	hyōshiki	標識
indigestion	shōka furyō	消化不良
industry	sangyō	産業
inequality	fu-byōdō	不平等
ingredient	zairyō	材料
to inject	chūsha shimasu	注射します
injection	chūsha	注射
injury	kega	けが
inn	ryokan	旅館
inside	naka ni	中に
instructor	insutorakutā/kyōshi	インストラクター／教師
insurance	hoken	保険
intense	hageshii	激しい
interesting	omoshiroi	おもしろい
international (call)	kokusai (denwa)	国際 (電話)
interpreter	tsūyaku	通訳
interview	mensetsu/intabyū	面接／インタビュー
iron (clothes)	airon	アイロン
island	shima	島
itch	kayui	かゆい
itinerary	yoteihyō	予定表

J

jail	rōya	牢屋
January	ichi-gatsu	1月
Japan	nihon/nippon	日本
Japanese food	nihon shoku	日本食
Japanese garden	nihon teien	日本庭園
jar	jā	ジャー
jealousy	netami	妬み
jeans	jīnzu	ジーンズ
jewellery	hōseki	宝石
Jewish	yudayajin	ユダヤ人
job	shigoto	仕事

job advertisement	shūshoku kōkoku	就職広告
job centre	shokugyō annaijo	職業案内所
job description	shokumu naiyō setsumeisho	職務内容説明書
jockey	keiba no kishu	競馬の騎手
joke	jōdan	冗談
to joke	jōdan o iimasu	冗談を言います
journalist	kisha	記者
journey	tabi	旅
judge	saibankan	裁判官
juice	jūsu	ジュース
July	shichi-gatsu	7月
to jump	tobimasu	飛びます
jumper (sweater)	sētā	セーター
junction	kōsaten	交差点
June	roku-gatsu	6月
Just a minute.	chotto matte kudasai	ちょっと待って下さい。
justice	kōsei	公正

K

karaoke	karaoke	カラオケ
kelp	kombu	昆布
key	kagi	鍵
keyboard	kībōdo	キーボード
to kick	kerimasu	蹴ります
kick off	kikku ofu	キックオフ
to kill	koroshimasu	殺します
kilogram	kiro-guramu	キログラム
kilometre	kiro-mētoru	キロメートル
kind	yasashii/shinsetsu na	優しい／親切な
kindergarten	yōchi-en	幼稚園
king	osama	王様
kiosk	baiten	売店
kiss	kisu	キス
to kiss	kisu shimasu	キスします
kitchen	daidokoro	台所
kitchen (restaurant)	chūbō	厨房
kitten	koneko	子猫
knee	hiza	膝
knife	naifu/hōchō	ナイフ／包丁
to know (someone)	shitte imasu	知っています
to know (something)	wakarimasu	わかります
I don't know.	wakarimasen	わかりません。

L

lace	rēsu	レース
lacquerware	shikki/urushi nuri	漆器／漆塗り
lake	mizūmi	湖
land	riku	陸
language	kotoba/gengo	言葉／言語
large	ōkii	大きい
last	saigo no	最後の
last month	sengetsu	先月
last night	yūbe	ゆうべ
last week	senshū	先週
last year	kyonen	去年
late	osoi	遅い
to laugh	waraimasu	笑います
launderette	koin randorī	コインランドリー
law	hōritsu	法律
lawn	shibafu	芝生
lawyer	bengoshi	弁護士
laxatives	bempiyaku	便秘薬
lazy	taida na	怠惰な
leaded (petrol/gas)	yūen gasorin	有鉛ガソリン
leader	ridā/shidōsha	リーダー／指導者
leaf	ha	葉
to learn	naraimasu	習います
leather	kawa	皮
leathergoods	kawa seihin	革製品
ledge	iwadana	岩棚
left (not right)	hidari	左
left luggage office	tenimotsu azukarijo	手荷物預所
to be left (behind/over)	nokosaremasu	残されます
left-wing	sayoku	左翼
leg	ashi	足
leg (in race)	kukan	区間
legalisation	gōhōka	合法化
legislation	rippō	立法
lens	renzu	レンズ
lesbian	rezu	レズ
less	sukunai	少ない
Let's go.	ikimashō	行きましょう。
letter	tegami	手紙
lettuce	retasu	レタス
liar	usotsuki	うそつき
library	toshokan	図書館

lice	shirami	シラミ
to lie	uso o tsukimasu	うそをつきます
life	jinsei	人生
lift (elevator)	erebētā	エレベーター
light (adj)	karui	軽い
light (n)	raito	ライト
light (sun/lamp)	hikari	光
light bulb	denkyū	電球
light meter	kōdokei	光度計
lighter	raitā	ライター
to like	suki ni narimasu	好きになります
lips	kuchibiru	唇
lipstick	kuchibeni	口紅
to listen	kikimasu	聞きます
little (small)	chiisai	小さい
a little bit	sukoshi	少し
to live (somewhere)	sumimasu	住みます
to live (life)	ikimasu	生きます
local	chihō no	地方の
local call	shinai denwa	市内電話
local/city bus	shi-basu/to-basu	市バス／都バス
location	ichi	位置
lock	jō	錠
to lock	kagi o kakemasu	鍵をかけます
lonely	sabishii	寂しい
long	nagai	長い
long distance	chōkyori	長距離
Long live ...!	... banzai!	... 万歳！
long-distance bus	chōkyori basu	長距離バス
long-distance call	chōkyori denwa	長距離電話
to look	mimasu	見ます
to look after	mendō o mimasu	面倒を見ます
to look for	sagashimasu	探します
lookout	miharashi dai	見晴台
loose change	kozeni	小銭
to lose	nakushimasu	なくします
loser	haisha/makeinu	敗者／負け犬
loss	sonshitsu	損失
a lot	takusan	たくさん
loud	urusai	うるさい
lounge	raunji	ラウンジ
love	ai	愛
to love	ai shimasu	愛します

lovely	kawaii	かわいい
lover	koibito	恋人
low	hikui	低い
low blood pressure	teiketsuatsu	低血圧
loyal	chūjitsu na	忠実な
luck	un	運
lucky	kōun na	幸運な
luggage (lockers)	nimotsu (rokkā)	荷物 (ロッカー)
lump	kobu	こぶ
lunch	hiru gohan; ranchi; chūshoku	昼御飯／ランチ／昼食
lunch box	o-bentō	お弁当
lunchtime	hiru yasumi	昼休み
luxury	gōka na	豪華な

M

machine	kikai	機械
mad	kichigai	気違い
made (of)	sei	製
magazine	zasshi	雑誌
magic show	tejina shō	手品ショー
magician	tejinashi	手品師
mahjong	mājan	麻雀
mail	yūbin	郵便
mailbox	yūbin-bako	郵便箱
main road	kansen dōro	幹線道路
main square	chūō hiroba	中央広場
majority	daitasū	大多数
to make	tsukurimsu	作ります
make-up	mēkyappu	メーキャップ
man (human)	ningen/hito	人間／人
man (male)	otoko	男
manager	manējā	マネージャー
manual worker	nikutai rōdōsha	肉体労働者
many	takusan no	たくさんの
map	chizu	地図
March	san-gatsu	3 月
marijuana	marifana	マリファナ
marital status	kekkon no umu	結婚の有無
market	ichiba	市場
marriage	kekkon	結婚
to marry	kekkon shimasu	結婚します

marvellous	subarashii	素晴らしい
mass (Catholic)	misa	ミサ
massage	massāji/amma	マッサージ／按摩
mat	matto	マット
match	macchi	マッチ
mattress	mattoresu	マットレス
May	go-gatsu	5月
maybe	moshika suru to	もしかすると
mayor	shichō	市長
mechanic	seibishi/kikaikō	整備士／機械工
medal	medaru	メダル
medicine (drug)	kusuri	薬
medicine (study)	igaku	医学
meditation	meisō	瞑想
to meet	aimasu	会います
member	membā/kaiin	メンバー／会員
menstruation	gekkei	月経
menu	menyū	メニュー
message	messēji/dengon	メッセージ／伝言
metal	kinzoku	金属
meteor	nagareboshi	流れ星
metre	mētoru	メートル
in the middle	man-naka ni/chūō ni	真ん中に／中央に
midnight	mayonaka/shin'ya	真夜中／深夜
migraine	henzutsū	偏頭痛
military service	heieki	兵役
milk	miruku/gyūnyū	ミルク／牛乳
millimetre	mirimētoru	ミリメートル
million	hyaku man	百万
mind (n)	kokoro	心
mineral water	mineraru wōtā	ミネラルウォーター
mini bar	mini bā	ミニバー
a minute	ippun	1分
mirror	kagami	鏡
miscarriage	ryūzan	流産
to miss (feel absence)	natsukashiku omoimasu	懐かしく思います
mistake	machigai	間違い
mobile phone	keitai denwa	携帯電話
model	moderu	モデル
modem	modemu	モデム
moisturising cream	kurīmu	クリーム
monastery	shūdōin	修道院

Monday	getsuyōbi	月曜日
money	o-kane	お金
monk (Christian)	shūdōshi	修道士
monk (Buddhist)	oshō	和尚
monorail	monorēru	モノレール
month	tsuki	月
monument	kinenhi	記念碑
moon	tsuki	月
more	motto	もっと
morning (5 - 11am)	asa	朝
mosque	mosuku	モスク
mother (my/your)	haha/okāsan	母／お母さん
mother-in-law	giri no haha	義理の母
motorboat	mōtābōto	モーターボート
motorcycle	ōtobai	オートバイ
motorway (tollway)	kōsoku dōro	高速道路
mountain	yama	山
mountain bike	maunten baiku	マウンテンバイク
mountain hut	yama goya	山小屋
mountain path	yama michi	山道
mountain range	sammyaku	山脈
mountaineering	tozan	登山
mouse	nezumi	ネズミ
mouth	kuchi	口
movie	eiga	映画
MSG	aji no moto	味の素
mud	doro	泥
Mum	okāsan	お母さん
muscle	kinniku	筋肉
museum	hakubutsukan	博物館
music	ongaku	音楽
musical instrument	gakki	楽器
musician	ongakuka	音楽家
Muslim	musurimu;	ムスリム／
	isuramu kyōto	イスラム教徒
mute	rōasha	聾唖者

N

nail clippers	tsume kiri	爪切り
name	namae	名前
nappy (rash)	omutsu (kabure)	おむつ（かぶれ）
national park	kokuritsu kōen	国立公園
nationality	kokuseki	国籍
nature	shizen	自然

ENGLISH – JAPANESE

N

naturopath	shizen ryōhō	自然療法
nausea	hakike	吐き気
near	chikai	近い
nearby hotel	chikaku no hoteru	近くのホテル
necessary	hitsuyō na	必要な
necklace	nekkuresu	ネックレス
need	hitsuyō	必要
needle (sewing)	hari	針
needle (syringe)	chūsha-bari	注射針
net	ami	網
new	atarashii	新しい
New Year's Day	gantan	元旦
New Year's Eve	ōmisoka	大晦日
New Zealand	nyū jīrando	ニュージーランド
news	nyūsu	ニュース
newsagency	shimbun no baiten	新聞の売店
newspaper	shimbun	新聞
newspaper in English	eiji shimbun	英字新聞
next	tsugi no	次の
next month	raigetsu	来月
next to	tonari	となり
next week	raishū	来週
next year	rainen	来年
nice	suteki na	素敵な
nickname	adana	あだ名
night	yoru	夜
nightclub	kurabu	クラブ
noise	zatsuon	雑音
noisy	urusai	うるさい
non-direct	kansetsuteki	間接的
none	nani mo nai	何もない
noon	shōgo	正午
north	kita	北
nose	hana	鼻
not yet	mada	まだ
notebook	nōto	ノート
nothing	nani mo nai	何もない
novel (book)	shōsetsu	小説
November	jūichi-gatsu	11月
now	ima	今
nuclear energy	kaku enerugī	核エネルギー
nuclear testing	kaku jikken	核実験
nun	shūdōjo	修道女
nurse (f)	kangofu	看護婦
nurse (m)	kangoshi	看護士

D
I
C
T
I
O
N
A
R
Y

O

obvious	meikaku na	明確な
occupation	shokugyō	職業
ocean	umi	海
October	jū-gatsu	10月
offence	hanzai	犯罪
office	jimusho	事務所
office worker	jimuin	事務員
offside	ofusaido	オフサイド
often	yoku	よく
oil (cooking)	abura	油
oil (crude)	sekiyu	石油
oil (engine)	oiru	オイル
OK	ōkē	OK
old	furui	古い
old city	koto	古都
old person	nempai no hito	年配の人
olive oil	oribu oiru	オリーブオイル
olives	oribu	オリーブ
Olympic Games	orimpikku	オリンピック
on	ue ni	上に
on sale	yasu uri	安売り
on strike	sutoraiki chū	ストライキ中
on time	jikan-dōri	時間通り
once; one time	ichi-do	1度
one-way (ticket)	katamichi	片道
only	dake	だけ
open	aite imasu	開いています
to open	akemasu/hirakimasu	開けます／開きます
opening	kaikai	開会
opera	opera	オペラ
opera house	opera hausu	オペラハウス
operation	shujutsu/sakusen	手術／作戦
operator	kōkanshu	交換手
opinion	iken	意見
opposite	hantai	反対
opposite side	hantai gawa	反対側
or	mata wa	または
orange (colour)	orenji iro	オレンジ色
orchestra	ōkesutora	オーケストラ
order	chūmon	注文
to order	chūmon shimasu	注文します
ordinary	futsū no	普通の

to organise	seiri shima...	整理します
orgasm	ōgazumu	オーガズム
original	motomoto no	もともとの
other	hoka no	ほかの
out of order	koshō chū	故障中
out of stock	shinagire	品切れ
outgoing	sekkyokuteki na	積極的な
outside	soto	外
over	koete	越えて
overcoat	ōbā	オーバー
overdose	kusuri o nomisugimasu	薬を飲み過ぎます
to owe	kashi o tsukurimasu	貸しを作ります
owner	mochinushi	持ち主
oxygen	sanso	酸素

P

pacifier (dummy)	oshaburi	おしゃぶり
package	kozutsumi	小包
packet (cigarettes)	(tabako no) hako	(たばこの) 箱
padlock	jōmae	錠前
page	pēji	ページ
a pain	itami	痛み
painful	itai	痛い
painkillers	itami-dome	痛み止め
to paint	penki o nurimasu	ペンキを塗ります
painter	ekaki	絵かき
painting (Japanese)	nihonga	日本画
painting (the art)	kaiga	絵画
paintings	e	絵
pair (a couple)	pea/kappuru	ペア／カップル
palace	shiro	城
pan	nabe	鍋
pap smear	papu tomatsuhyōhon	パプ塗抹標本
paper	kami	紙
paper (Japanese)	washi	和紙
paraplegic	hanshin fuzui	半身不随
parcel	kozutsumi	小包
parents	ryōshin	両親
a park	kōen	公園
to park	chūsha shimasu	駐車します
parliament	kokkai	国会
part	bubun	部分
party	pātī	パーティー

pass	pasu	パス
passenger	jōkyaku	乗客
passport	pasupōto	パスポート
passport number	pasupōto bangō	パスポート番号
past	kako	過去
path	komichi	小道
patient (adj)	gaman-zuyoi	我慢強い
to pay	haraimasu	払います
payment	shiharai	支払い
peace	heiwa	平和
peak	chōjō	頂上
pearl	shinju	真珠
pedestrian	hokōsha	歩行者
pen (ballpoint)	bōru-pen	ボールペン
pencil	empitsu	鉛筆
peninsula	hantō	半島
penis	inkei	陰茎
penknife	pen-naifu	ペンナイフ
pensioner	nenkinsha	年金者
people	hito	人
pepper	koshō	胡椒
percent	pāsento	パーセント
performance	engi	演技
performance art	pafōmansu āto	パフォーマンスアート
period pain	seiritsū	生理痛
permanent	eikyū no	永久の
permission	kyoka	許可
permit	kyokashō	許可証
person	hito	人
personality	seikaku	性格
to perspire	ase o kakimasu	汗をかきます
petition	seigansho	請願書
petrol (gasoline)	gasorin	ガソリン
petrol station	gasorin sutando	ガソリンスタンド
pharmacy	yakkyoku	薬局
phone book	denwachō	電話帳
phone box	denwa bokkusu	電話ボックス
phonecard	terefon kādo	テレホンカード
photo	shashin	写真
photographer	shashinka	写真家
to take photographs	shashin o torimasu	写真を撮ります
to pick up	hiroimasu	拾います
pick (pickaxe)	tsuruhashi	つるはし

P

picnic	pikunikku	ピクニック
pie	pai	パイ
piece	kire	切れ
pig	buta	ブタ
the pill	piru	ピル
pillow	makura	枕
pillowcase	makura kabā	枕カバー
pine	matsu	松
pink	pinku	ピンク
pipe	paipu	パイプ
place	basho	場所
place of birth	shusseichi	出生地
plan	keikaku	計画
plane	taira na	平らな
planet	wakusei	惑星
plant (n)	shokubutsu	植物
to plant	uemasu	植えます
plastic	purasuchikku	プラスチック
plate	sara	皿
platform	purattofōmu	プラットフォーム
play (theatre)	geki	劇
to play cards	torampu o shimasu	トランプをします
to play (a game)	(gēmu o) shimasu	(ゲームを)します
to play (music)	ensō shimasu	演奏します
player (sports)	senshu	選手
plug (bath)	sen	栓
plug (electricity)	puragu	プラグ
pocket	poketto	ポケット
poetry	shi	詩
point (games)	tokuten	得点
point (tip)	saki	先
to point	sashimasu	指します
poker	pōkā	ポーカー
police	keisatsu	警察
police box	kōban	交番
politicians	seijika	政治家
politics	seiji	政治
polls	tōhyō	投票
pollution	kōgai	公害
pool (game)	tama tsuki	玉突き
pool (swimming)	pūru	プール
poor	mazushii/bimbō na	貧しい／貧乏な
popular	ninki ga arimasu	人気があります
popular music	poppu myūjikku	ポップミュージック

**D
I
C
T
I
O
N
A
R
Y**

port	minato	港
porter	pōtā	ポーター
portrait sketcher	jimbutsuga no gaka	人物画の画家
possible	kanō na	可能な
It's (not) possible.	(fu-)kanō desu	(不)可能です。
post code	yūbinbangō	郵便番号
post office	yūbinkyoku	郵便局
postage	yūbin ryōkin	郵便料金
postcard	hagaki	はがき
poster	posutā	ポスター
pot (ceramic)	tsubo	壷
pottery	tōgei	陶芸
poverty	hinkon	貧困
power	chikara	力
prayer	o-inori	お祈り
prayer book	kitōsho	祈祷書
premenstrual tension	gekkeimae kinchō	月経前緊張
to prefer	konomimasu	好みます
pregnant	ninshin	妊娠
prehistoric art	senshi geijutsu	先史芸術
to prepare	jumbi shimasu	準備します
present (gift)	okurimono/purezento	贈り物／プレゼント
present (time)	genzai	現在
presenter (TV, etc)	anaunsā	アナウンサー
president (company)	shachō	社長
president (national)	daitōryō	大統領
pretty	utsukushii/kirei na	美しい／きれいな
to prevent	yobō shimasu	予防します
price	nedan	値段
price tag	nefuda	値札
pride	puraido/hokori	プライド／誇り
priest	shisai	司祭
prime minister	sōri daijin	総理大臣
to print	insatsu shimasu	印刷します
printed matter	insatsu butsu	印刷物
prison	rōya	牢屋
prisoner	shūjin	囚人
private	kojinteki na	個人的な
private hospital	shiritsu byōin	私立病院
privatisation	kigyōka	企業化
to produce	sakusei shimasu	作製します
producer	purodyūsā/seisakusha	プロデューサー／製作者
profession	semmon	専門
profit	rieki	利益

profitability	rijunritsu	利潤率
program	puroguramu	プログラム
projector	purojekutā	プロジェクター
promise	yakusoku	約束
proposal	teian	提案
to protect	hogo shimasu	保護します
protected forest	hogo sareta shinrin	保護された森林
protected species	hogo sareta seibutsu	保護された生物
to protest	hantai shimasu	反対します
public phone	kōshū denwa	公衆電話
public toilet	kōshū toire	公衆トイレ
to pull	hikimasu	引きます
pump	pompu	ポンプ
puncture	panku	パンク
to punish	basshimasu	罰します
puppy	koinu	小犬
pure	junsui na	純粋な
purple	murasaki	紫
to push	oshimasu	押します
to put	okimasu	置きます

Q

qualifications	shikaku	資格
quality	hinshitsu	品質
quarantine	ken'eki	検疫
quarrel	kenka	けんか
quarter	yon-bun no ichi	4分の1
queen	joō	女王
question (n)	shitsumon	質問
to question	shitsumon shimasu	質問します
queue	gyōretsu	行列
quick	subayai	すばやい
quickly	subayaku	すばやく
quiet	shizuka na	静かな
to quit	yamemasu	やめます

R

rabbit	usagi	ウサギ
race (breed)	jinshu	人種
race (sport)	rēsu	レース
racing bike	rēshingu baiku	レーシングバイク
racism	jinshu sabetsu	人種差別
racquet	raketto	ラケット

radiator	rajietā	ラジエター
radio	rajio	ラジオ
railway station	eki	駅
rain	ame	雨
It's raining.	ame ga futte imasu	雨が降っています。
rainbow	niji	虹
rainy season	tsuyu/uki	梅雨／雨季
rally	rari	ラリー
rape	reipu/gōkan	レイプ／強姦
rare	mezurashii	めずらしい
a rash	hasshin	発疹
rat	nezumi	ネズミ
rate of pay (hourly)	jikyū	時給
raw	nama no	生の
razor (blades)	kamisori (no ha)	剃刀 (の刃)
to read	yomimasu	読みます
to be ready	yōi ga dekimasu	用意ができます
to realise	ki ga tsukimasu	気が付きます
rear	ushiro	後
reason	riyū	理由
receipt	reshito/ryōshūsho	レシート／領収書
to receive	ukemasu	受けます
recent	saikin no	最近の
recently	saikin	最近
receptionist	uketsuke-kakari	受付係
to recognise	ninshiki shimasu	認識します
to recommend	suisen shimasu	推薦します
recording	rokuon	録音
recyclable	risaikuru dekiru	リサイクルできる
recycling	risaikuru	リサイクル
red	aka	赤
referee	shimpan	審判
reference	sankōbunken	参考文献
reflection (thinking)	han'ei	反映
refrigerator	reizōko	冷蔵庫
refugee	nammin	難民
refund (n)	haraimodoshi	払い戻し
to refund	haraimodoshi shimasu	払い戻しします
to refuse	kyohi shimasu	拒否します
regional	chiiki no	地域の
register	reji	レジ
registered mail	kakitome yūbin	書留郵便
to regret	kōkai shimasu	後悔します

R

relationship	kankei	関係
relative	shinseki	親戚
to relax	rirakkusu shimasu	リラックスします
religion	shūkyō	宗教
religious	shūkyōteki na	宗教的な
to remember	omoidashimasu	思い出します
remote	hanareta	離れた
remote control	rimo kon	リモコン
rent (of a house)	yachin	家賃
to rent	kashimasu	貸します
rent-a-car	rentakā	レンタカー
to repeat	kurikaeshimasu	繰り返します
replacement	kōkan	交替
republic	kyōwasei	共和制
reservation	yoyaku	予約
to reserve	yoyaku shimasu	予約します
resignation	jinin	辞任
respect	sonkei	尊敬
rest (relaxation)	yasumi	休み
to rest	yasumimasu	休みます
restaurant	resutoran	レストラン
resume	rirekisho	履歴書
retired	taishoku	退職
return ticket	ōfukuken	往復券
to return	modorimasu	戻ります
review	kensa/hihyō	検査／批評
rhythm	rizumu	リズム
rich (food)	shitsukoi	しつこい
rich (wealthy)	yūfuku na	裕福な
rich people	kanemochi	金持ち
to ride (a horse)	norimasu	乗ります
right (correct)	tadashii	正しい
right (not left)	migi	右
right now	tatta ima	たった今
to be right	atatte imasu	当たっています
You're right.	sonotōri	そのとおり。
right-wing	uyoku	右翼
ring (of phone)	(denwa no) yobirin	(電話の) 呼び鈴
I'll give you a ring.	denwa shimasu	電話します。
ring (on finger)	yubiwa	指輪
ring (sound)	rinrin	リンリン
to rip-off	borimasu	ぼります
to ripe	jukushimasu	熟します
risk	kiken	危険

D I C T I O N A R Y

river	kawa	川
road (main)	dōro	道路
road map	dōro chizu	道路地図
roadworks	dōro kōji	道路工事
to rob	gōtō shimasu	強盗します
rock	iwa	岩
rock climbing	iwa nobori;	岩登り／
	rokku kuraimingu	ロッククライミング
rock group	rokku gurūpu	ロックグループ
romance	romansu	ロマンス
room	heya	部屋
room number	heya bangō	部屋番号
rope	nawa	縄
round	marui	丸い
to row	kogimasu	漕ぎます
rubbish	gomi	ごみ
rug	shikimono	敷物
ruins	iseki	遺跡
rules	rūru/kimari	ルール／決まり
to run	hashirimasu	走ります

S

sad	kanashii	悲しい
safe	anzen na	安全な
safe sex	anzen na sekkusu	安全なセックス
saint	seijin	聖人
salary	kyūryō	給料
sales department	hambai bumon	販売部門
salt	shio	塩
same	onaji	同じ
sand	suna	砂
sandals (Japanese)	zōri	草履
sanitary napkins	seiriyō napukin	生理用ナプキン
Saturday	doyōbi	土曜日
sauna	sauna	サウナ
to save	setsuyaku shimasu	節約します
to say	iimasu	言います
to scale/climb	noborimasu	登ります
scared	kowai	恐い
scarves	sukāfu	スカーフ
school	gakkō	学校
science	kagaku	科学
scientist	kagakusha	科学者

scissors	hasami	はさみ
to score	ten o kasegimasu	点を稼ぎます
screen	sukurīn	スクリーン
script	daihon	台本
scriptwriter	kyakuhonka	脚本家
sculptor	chōkokuka	彫刻家
sculpture	chōkoku	彫刻
sea	umi	海
seasick	funayoi	船酔い
seaside	kaigan-zoi	海岸沿い
season	kisetsu	季節
seat	zaseki/shīto	座席／シート
seatbelt	shīto-beruto	シートベルト
second	ni-ban	2番
second (n)	byō	秒
secretary	hisho	秘書
to see	mimasu	見ます
See you later.	ja, mata	じゃ、また。
See you tomorrow.	ja, mata ashita	じゃ、また明日。
I see. (understand)	wakarimashita	わかりました。
self-employed	jieigyō	自営業
self-service	serufu sābisu	セルフサービス
selfish	rikoteki na	利己的な
to sell	urimasu	売ります
to send	okurimasu	送ります
sensible	funbetsu no aru	分別のある
sentence (prison)	hanketsu	判決
sentence (words)	bun	文
to separate	wakemasu	分けます
separated	bekkyo	別居
September	ku-gatsu	9月
series	shirīzu/renzoku	シリーズ／連続
serious	majime na	真面目な
service (assistence)	sābisu	サービス
service (religious)	reihai	礼拝
service charge	sābisu ryō	サービス料
several	ikutsuka no	いくつかの
to sew	nuimasu	縫います
sex	sei/sekkusu	性／セックス
sexism	sei sabetsu	性差別
sexy	sekushī na	セクシーな
shade (shadow)	kage	陰
shame	haji	恥
shampoo	shampū	シャンプー

shape	katachi	形
to share (with)	wakeaimasu	分けあいます
to share a house	ie o shea shimasu	家をシェアします
to shave	sorimasu	剃ります
she	kanojo	彼女
sheep	hitsuji	羊
sheet (bed)	shītsu	シーツ
a sheet (of paper)	ichi-mai (no kami)	1枚 (の紙)
shelves	tana	棚
ship	fune	船
to ship	funabin de okurimasu	船便でおくります
shirt	shatsu	シャツ
shoe shop	kutsuya	靴屋
shoes	kutsu	靴
to shoot	uchimasu	撃ちます
shop	mise	店
shopping	kaimono	買い物
to go shopping	kaimono ni ikimasu	買い物に行きます
short (height/length)	hikui/mijikai	低い／短い
short films	tampen eiga	短編映画
short stories	tampen shōsetsu	短編小説
short-sighted	kingan	近眼
shortage	fusoku	不足
shorts	han zubon	半ズボン
shoulders	kata	肩
to shout	donarimasu	怒鳴ります
a show	shō	ショー
to show	misemasu	見せます
shower	shawā	シャワー
shrine	jinja	神社
to shut	shimemasu	閉めます
shy	hazukashii	恥ずかしい
sick	byōki	病気
a sickness	byōki	病気
side	gawa	側
sightseeing	kankō	観光
a sign	hyōshiki	標識
to sign	sain shimasu	サインします
signature	sain	サイン
silk	kinu	絹
of silver	gin no	銀の
similar	dōyō no	同様の
simple	tanjun na	単純な
sin	tsumi	罪

since (May)	(go-gatsu) kara	（5月）から
to sing	utaimasu	歌います
singer	kashu	歌手
singing	uta	歌
single (person)	dokushin	独身
single (unique)	tatta hitotsu no	たったひとつの
single room	shinguru rūmu	シングルルーム
sister	shimai	姉妹
sister (older) my	ane	姉
sister (older) your	onēsan	お姉さん
sister (younger)	imōto	妹
to sit	suwarimasu	座ります
size (clothes)	saizu	サイズ
size (of anything)	ōkisa	大きさ
to ski	sukī o shimasu	スキーをします
skiing	sukī	スキー
sky	sora	空
to sleep	nemurimasu	眠ります
sleeping bag	nebukuro	寝袋
sleeping pill	suimin yaku	睡眠薬
sleepy	nemui	眠い
slide (film)	suraido	スライド
slippers	surippa	スリッパ
slow/slowly	yukkuri	ゆっくり
small	chiisai	小さい
small change	kozeni	小銭
a smell	nioi	におい
to smell	kagimasu	嗅ぎます
to smile	waraimasu	笑います
to smoke	tabako o suimasu	たばこを吸います
snow	yuki	雪
soap	sekken	石鹸
soap opera	terebi dorama	テレビドラマ
soccer	sakkā	サッカー
social sciences	shakai kagaku	社会科学
social security	shakai hoshō	社会保障
social welfare	shakai fukushi	社会福祉
social-democratic	shakai minshu shugi	社会民主主義
socialist	shakai shugisha	社会主義者
socks	kutsushita	靴下
soldier	heishi/gunjin	兵士／軍人
solid	katai	固い
some	ikutsuka no	いくつかの
somebody/someone	dareka	誰か

S

something	nanika	何か
sometimes	tokidoki	ときどき
son	musuko	息子
song	uta	歌
soon	sugu	すぐ
I'm sorry.	gomennasai	ごめんなさい。
sound	oto	音
sour	suppai	酸っぱい
south	minami	南
souvenir (shop)	o-miyage (ya)	お土産 (屋)
soy sauce	shōyu	醤油
space	kūkan	空間
to speak	hanashimasu	話します
special	tokubetsu	特別
specialist	semmonka	専門家
spectacles	megane	眼鏡
speed	supido/sokudo	スピード／速度
speed limit	seigen sokudo	制限速度
spicy (hot)	karai	辛い
sport	supōtsu	スポーツ
sportsperson	supōtsu-man	スポーツマン
a sprain	nenza	捻挫
spring (coil)	bane/supuringu	ばね／スプリング
spring (season)	haru	春
square (in town)	hiroba	広場
square (shape)	seihōkei	正方形
stadium	sutajiamu	スタジアム
stage	butai	舞台
stairway	kaidan	階段
stamps	kitte	切手
standard (usual)	hyōjun	標準
standard of living	seikatsu suijun	生活水準
stars	hoshi	星
to start	hajimemasu	始めます
station	eki	駅
stationers	bunbōgu	文房具
statue	zō	像
to stay (remain)	todomarimasu	留まります
to stay (somewhere)	taizai shimasu	滞在します
to steal	nusumimasu	盗みます
steam	jōki	蒸気
steep	kyū na	急な
step	kaidan	階段
stomach	i/onaka	胃／お腹

D I C T I O N A R Y

stomachache	fukutsū	腹痛
stone	ishi	石
stop	tomarimasu/yamemasu	止まります／やめます
Stop!	tomare!	止まれ！
storm	arashi	嵐
story	hanashi	話
stove	sutōbu/renji	ストーブ／レンジ
straight	massugu na	まっすぐな
strange	hen na	変な
stranger	yosomono	よそもの
street	michi	道
strength	tsuyosa	強さ
a strike	sutoraiki	ストライキ
string	himo	紐
to stroll/walk	arukimasu	歩きます
strong	tsuyoi	強い
stubborn	ganko na	頑固な
student	gakusei	学生
student discount	gaku wari	学割
studio	sutajio	スタジオ
style	sutairu	スタイル
subtitles	jimaku	字幕
suburb	chiiki	地域
suburbs of ...	... no chiiki	... の地域
subway (station)	chikatetsu (no eki)	地下鉄 (の駅)
success	seikō	成功
to suffer	kurushimimasu	苦しみます
sugar	satō	砂糖
suitcase	sūtsu kēsu	スーツケース
summer	natsu	夏
sun	taiyō	太陽
sunblock	hiyake-dome	日焼け止め
sunburn	hiyake	日焼け
Sunday	nichiyōbi	日曜日
sunglasses	sangurasu	サングラス
sunny	hare	晴れ
sunrise	nikkō	日光
sunset	nichibotsu	日没
supermarket	sūpā	スーパー
supper	yashoku	夜食
Sure.	mochiron	もちろん
surface mail	funabin	船便
surfboard	sāfu bōdo	サーフボード
surfing	sāfin	サーフィン

surname	myōji	名字
a surprise	odoroki	驚き
to survive	ikinokorimasu	生き残ります
sweat	ase	汗
sweet	amai	甘い
to swim	oyogimasu	泳ぎます
swimming	suiei	水泳
swimming pool	pūru	プール
swimsuit	mizugi	水着
sword	katana	刀
sympathy	dōjō	同情
synagogue	yudaya kyōkai	ユダヤ教会
synthetic	gōsei	合成
syringe	chūshaki	注射器

T

T-shirt	tīshatsu	Tシャツ
table	tēburu	テーブル
table tennis	takkyū/pimpon	卓球／ピンポン
tail	shippo/o	尻尾／尾
to take (away)	hakobi (sari) masu	運び(去り)ます
to talk	hanashimasu	話します
tall	takai	高い
tampons	tampon	タンポン
tasty	oishii	おいしい
taxi	takushī	タクシー
taxi stand	takushī noriba	タクシー乗り場
tea (Japanese)	o-cha	お茶
tea (Western)	kōcha	紅茶
tea ceremony	sadō	茶道
teacher	sensei/kyōshi	先生／教師
teaching	kyōiku	教育
team	chīmu	チーム
teapot	kyūsu	急須
tear (crying)	namida	涙
technique	gijutsu	技術
teeth	ha	歯
telegram	dempō	電報
telephone	denwa	電話
telephone booth	denwa bokkusu	電話ボックス
telephone card	terefon kādo	テレホンカード
telephone charge	denwa ryōkin	電話料金
telephone number	denwa bangō	電話番号

telephone operator	denwa kōkanshu	電話交換手
to telephone	denwa shimasu	電話します
television	terebi	テレビ
to tell	hanashimasu	話します
temperature (fever)	taion	体温
temperature (weather)	kion	気温
temple	tera	寺
tennis	tenisu	テニス
tennis court	tenisu kōto	テニスコート
tent	tento	テント
tent pegs	pegu	ペグ
tenth	jūban	10番
term of office	ninki	任期
terminal	tāminaru	ターミナル
terrible	hidoi	ひどい
test	tesuto/shiken	テスト／試験
to thank	kansha shimasu	感謝します
Thank you.	arigatō	ありがとう。
that	are/ano	あれ／あの
theatre	gekijō	劇場
theft	tōnan	盗難
thermometer	ondokei	温度計
they	karera	彼ら
thick	atsui	厚い
thief	dorobō	どろぼう
thin	usui	薄い
to think	kangaemasu	考えます
third	sam-ban	3番
thirsty	nodo no kawaki	のどのかわき
this	kore/kono	これ／この
this afternoon	kyōno gogo	今日の午後
this month	kongetsu	今月
this week	konshū	今週
this year	kotoshi	今年
thought	shisō	思想
throat	nodo	のど
thunder	kaminari	雷
Thursday	mokuyōbi	木曜日
ticket	kippu	切符
ticket collector	shashō	車掌
ticket machine	kippu no jidō hambaiki	切符の自動販売機
ticket office	hakkenjo	発券所
tide	shio no michihiki	潮の満ち引き
tiger	tora	トラ

T

tight	kitsui	きつい
time	jikan	時間
timetable	jikokuhyō	時刻表
tin (can)	kan	缶
tin opener	kankiri	缶切り
tip (gratuity)	hinto	ヒント
tip (money)	chippu	チップ
to be tired	tsukaremasu	疲れます
tissues	tisshu	ティッシュ
toast	tōsuto	トースト
tobacco	tabako	たばこ
tobacco kiosk	tabakoya	たばこ屋
today	kyō	今日
together	issho	一緒
together with	issho ni	一緒に
toilet	toire	トイレ
toilet paper	toiretto pēpā	トイレットペーパー
tomorrow	ashita/asu	明日／明日
tomorrow afternoon	ashita no gogo	明日の午後
tomorrow evening	ashita no ban	明日の晩
tomorrow morning	ashita no gozen chū	明日の午前中
tonight	kon'ya/komban	今夜／今晩
too (as well)	mo	も
too expensive	takasugimasu	高すぎます
too much/many	ōsugimasu	多すぎます
tooth (back)	okuba	奥歯
tooth (front)	maeba	前歯
toothache	haita	歯痛
toothbrush	ha burashi	歯ブラシ
toothpaste	ha migaki	歯磨き
torch (flashlight)	kaichū dentō	懐中電灯
total (amount)	gōkei	合計
to touch	sawarimasu	触ります
tour (guide)	tsuā (gaido)	ツアー (ガイド)
tourist	kankōkyaku	観光客
tourist information office	kankō annaijo	観光案内所
towards	hō e	方へ
towel	taoru	タオル
tower	tō/tawā	塔／タワー
track (car-racing)	rēsu kōsu	レースコース
track (footprints)	ashiato	足跡
track (path)	komichi	小道
track (sports)	torakku	トラック
trade union	rōdō kumiai	労働組合

traffic	kōtsū	交通
traffic light	shingō	信号
trail/route	rūto	ルート
train	densha	電車
train station	eki	駅
tram	shiden	市電
transit lounge	machiai shitsu	待ち合い室
to translate	hon'yaku shimasu	翻訳します
travel	ryokō	旅行
to travel	ryokō shimasu	旅行します
travel agency	ryokō dairiten	旅行代理店
travel sickness	norimono yoi	乗物酔
travel sickness pill	yoi dome	酔い止め
travellers' cheques	toraberāzu chekku	トラベラーズチェック
tree	ki	木
trek	torekkingu	トレッキング
trendy (person)	torendīna	トレンディーな
trip	tabi	旅
trousers	zubon	ズボン
truck	torakku	トラック
to trust	shin'yō shimasu	信用します
truth	hontō/shinjitsu	本当/真実
It's true.	hontō desu	本当です。
to try (attempt)	tameshimasu	試します
Tuesday	kayōbi	火曜日
tune	senritsu	旋律
Turn left/right.	hidari/migi ni magatte kudasai	(左/右) に曲がって ください。
TV	terebi	テレビ
twice	nikai	2回
twin beds	tsuin beddo	ツインベッド
twins	futago	双子
to type	taipu shimasu	タイプします
typical	tenkeiteki na	典型的な
tyres	taiya	タイヤ

U

ugly	minikui	醜い
umbrella	kasa	傘
uncle	oji/ojisan	おじ/おじさん
underpants	pantsu	パンツ

to understand	rikai shimasu	理解します
unemployed	shitsugyōsha	失業者
unemployment	shitsugyō	失業
unions	kumiai	組合
universe	uchū	宇宙
university	daigaku	大学
unleaded	muen	無鉛
unsafe	kiken na	危険な
until (June)	(roku-gatsu) made	(6月) まで
unusual	mezurashii	珍しい
up	ue	上
uphill	nobori-zaka	上り坂
upstairs	ue no kai	上の階
urgent	kinkyū	緊急
useful	benri na	便利な

V

vacant	akibeya	空部屋
vacation	kyūka	休暇
vaccination	yobō chūsha	予防注射
valley	tani	谷
valuable	kichōhin	貴重品
value (price)	kachi	価値
van	ban	バン
vegetable	yasai	野菜
vegetarian	bejitarian	ベジタリアン
I'm vegetarian.	watashi wa bejitarian desu	私はベジタリアンです。
vegetation	shokubutsu	植物
vein	jōmyaku	静脈
vending machine	jidō hambaiki	自動販売機
venereal disease	seibyō	性病
very	totemo/taihen	とても／たいへん
via	keiyu	経由
video tape	bideo tēpu	ビデオテープ
view	nagame	眺め
village	mura	村
vineyard	budō-batake	ぶどう畑
virus	uirusu	ウイルス
visa	biza	ビザ
to visit	hōmon shimasu	訪問します
vitamins	bitamin	ビタミン
voice	koe	声
voltage	den'atsu	電圧

| volume | boryūmu | ボリューム |
| to vote | tōhyō shimasu | 投票します |

W

to wait	machimasu	待ちます
Wait!	matte!	待って！
waiter	ueitā	ウエイター
waiting room	machiai shitsu	待ち合い室
to walk	arukimasu	歩きます
wall	kabe	壁
wallet	saifu	財布
to want	hoshigarimasu	欲しがります
We'd like to go to ...	... ni iki tai desu	... に行きたいです。
war	sensō	戦争
wardrobe	tansu	たんす
warm	atatakai	暖かい
to warm up	atatamemasu	温めます
to warn	keikoku shimasu	警告します
to wash (clothes)	sentaku shimasu	洗濯します
to wash (oneself)	araimasu	洗います
washing machine	sentakki	洗濯機
a watch	ude-dokei	腕時計
to watch	mimasu	見ます
water	mizu	水
water bottle	suitō	水筒
waterfall	taki	滝
wave	nami	波
way	michi	道
Please tell me the way to ...	... ni iku michi o oshiete kudasai	.... に行く道を教えて下さい。
Way Out	deguchi	出口
we	watashi tachi	私達
weak	yowai	弱い
wealthy	yūfuku na	裕福な
to wear	kimasu	着ます
weather	tenki	天気
wedding	kekkonshiki	結婚式
Wednesday	suiyōbi	水曜日
week	shū	週
weekend	shūmatsu	週末
to weigh	omosa o hakarimasu	重さを計ります
welcome	yōkoso	ようこそ
welfare	fukushi	福祉

well	yoi/ii	良い／いい
west	nishi	西
western food	seiyō ryōri	西洋料理
wet	nurete iru	ぬれている
what	nani	なに
What are you doing?	nani o shite imasu ka?	何をしていますか?
What's he saying?	kare wa nan to itte imasu ka?	彼は何と言っていますか?
What time is it?	ima, nan-ji desu ka?	今、何時ですか?
wheel	sharin	車輪
wheelchair	kuruma isu	車椅子
when	itsu	いつ
When does it leave?	itsu shuppatsu shimasu ka?	いつ出発しますか?
where	doko	どこ
Where can I buy a ticket?	doko de kippu ga kaemasu ka?	どこで切符が買えますか?
Where is the bank?	ginkō wa doko desu ka?	銀行はどこですか?
Which way?	dochira desu ka?	どちらですか?
white	shiro	白
who	dare	誰
Who are they?	karera wa dare desu ka?	彼らは誰ですか?
Who is it?	donata desu ka?	どなたですか?
whole	subete	すべて
why	naze/nande	なぜ／なんで
wide	hiroi	広い
wife (my)	tsuma	妻
wife (your)	okusan	奥さん
wild animal	yasei dōbutsu	野生動物
to win	kachimasu	勝ちます
wind	kaze	風
window	mado	窓
window seat	mado gawa	窓側
windscreen	furonto garasu	フロントガラス
wine	wain	ワイン
wine (Japanese)	sake	酒
wine glass	wain gurasu	ワイングラス
wine list	wain risuto	ワインリスト
winery	wainarī	ワイナリー
winter	fuyu	冬
wire	waiyā/harigane	ワイヤー／針金
wise	kashikoi	賢い

to wish	kibōshimasu	希望します
with	to	と
within	naka de	中で
within an hour	ichi-jikan inai ni	1時間以内に
without	nashi de	なしで
without filter	firutā nashi de	フィルターなしで
woman	onna no hito	女の人
wonderful	subarashii	素晴らしい
wood	ki	木
woodblock print	hanga	版画
wool	yōmō	羊毛
word	kotoba	言葉
word processor	wāpuro	ワープロ
work	shigoto	仕事
to work	hatarakimasu	働きます
work permit	rōdō kyoka	労働許可
workout	renshū	練習
workshop	wāku shoppu	ワークショップ
world	sekai	世界
World Cup	wārudo kappu	ワールドカップ
worried	shimpai shimasu	心配します
worry	shimpai	心配
worship	sūhai	崇拝
worth	kachi ga aru	価値がある
wound	kega	けが
to write	kakimasu	書きます
writer	sakka	作家
wrong	chigaimasu	違います
I'm wrong. (my fault)	watashi no sei desu	私のせいです。
I'm wrong. (not right)	watashi ga machigaemashita	私が間違えました。
wrong number	machigai denwa	間違い電話

Y

yacht	yotto	ヨット
year	toshi	年
yellow	kiiro	黄色
yellowtail	hamachi	ハマチ
yen	en	円
yesterday	kinō	きのう

yet	mada	まだ
you (pol)	anata	あなた
young	wakai	若い
youth (collective)	wakamono	若者

Z

zebra	shima uma	シマウマ
zodiac	seiza	星座
zoo	dōbutsuen	動物園

A

āsa	ＡＳＡ	film speed/ASA
abunai!	危ない！	Danger!
abura	油	oil (cooking)
adana	あだ名	nickname
adobaisu	アドバイス	advice
agemasu	あげます	to give
ai	愛	love
ai shimasu	愛します	to love
aida	間	between
aimasu	会います	to meet
airon	アイロン	iron (for pressing clothes)
aisu	アイス	ice
aisukurimu	アイスクリーム	icecream
aji	味	taste/flavour
aji no moto	味の素	MSG
aka	赤	red
akachan	赤ちゃん	baby
akarui	明るい	bright
akegata	明け方	dawn
akemasu	開けます	to open
aki	秋	autumn
akibeya	空部屋	vacant room
amai	甘い	sweet
ame	雨	rain
ame ga futte imasu	雨が降って。います	It's raining.
ami	網	net
amma	按摩	massage
anata	あなた	you (pol)
anaunsā	アナウンサー	presenter (TV, etc)
ane	姉	sister (older)
annai	案内	guidance
ano	あの	that
anraku shi	安楽死	euthanasia
antiku	アンティーク	antiques
anzen	安全	safe (n)
anzen na	安全な	safe (adj)
anzen na sekkusu	安全なセックス	safe sex
ao	青	blue

araimasu	洗います	to wash (oneself)
arashi	嵐	storm
are	あれ	that
arerugī	アレルギー	allergy
ari	アリ	ant
arigatō	ありがとう。	Thank you.
arimasu	あります	there is/are
... ga arimasu ka?	... がありますか？	Do you have ...? [at a shop]
arukimasu	歩きます	to stroll/walk
asa	朝	morning (5am - 11pm)
asagohan	朝ごはん	breakfast
asatte	あさって	day after tomorrow
ase	汗	sweat
ase o kakimasu	汗をかきます	to perspire
ashi	足	foot/leg
ashiato	足跡	track (footprints)
ashita/asu	明日	tomorrow
asupirin	アスピリン	aspirin
atama	頭	head
atarashii	新しい	new
atatakai	暖かい	warm
atatamemasu	温めます	to heat up
atatte imasu	当たっています	to be right
atemasu	当てます	to guess
ato	後	after
atsui	暑い	hot (weather)
atsui	厚い	thick
atsui	熱い	hot (object)
atsuryoku	圧力	pressure

B

bā	バー	a bar
bāgen	バーゲン	bargain
baggu	バッグ	bag
bagu	馬具	harness (for horse)
baiten	売店	kiosk
baka	馬鹿	stupid
baketsu	バケツ	bucket
bakkin	罰金	a fine
bakkupakku	バックパック	backpack
ban	バン	van
ban	晩	evening
bando	バンド	band (music)

bane	ばね	spring (coil)
bangohan	晩ごはん	dinner
banzai!	万歳！	Hurray!
barē	バレエ	ballet
barukonī	バルコニー	balcony
basho	場所	place
basshimasu	罰します	to punish
basu	バス	bus/bath
bāsudē kēki	バースデーケーキ	birthday cake
(ni) bai	（2）倍	double
basu-tāminaru	バスターミナル	bus terminal
basuketto	バスケット	basket
basutei	バス停	bus station
bebī shittā	ベビーシッター	baby-sitter
bebīpaudā	ベビーパウダー	baby powder
beddo	ベッド	bed
bejitarian	ベジタリアン	vegetarian
bekkyo	別居	separated
bempi	便秘	constipation
bempi shimasu	便秘します	to be constipated
bempi yaku	便秘薬	laxatives
bengoshi	弁護士	lawyer
benri na	便利な	useful
bīchi	ビーチ	beach
bideo tēpu	ビデオテープ	video tape
bijinesu	ビジネス	business
bijinesu man	ビジネスマン	businessman
bijutsu	美術	art
bijutsukan	美術館	art gallery
bimbō na	貧乏な	poor
bin	ビン	bottle
bitamin	ビタミン	vitamins
biza	ビザ	visa
bōenkyō	望遠鏡	telescope
bōifurendo	ボーイフレンド	boyfriend
bōkōen	膀胱炎	cystitis
boku	僕	I, me (male)
bokushingu	ボクシング	boxing
borimasu	ぼります	to rip-off
bōru	ボール	ball
bōru pen	ボールペン	pen (ballpoint)
boryūmu	ボリューム	volume
bōshi	帽子	hat
botan	ボタン	buttons

bōto	ボート	boat
būtsu	ブーツ	boots
bubun	部分	part
budō	ぶどう	grapes
budō-batake	ぶどう畑	vineyard
bukkyōto	仏教徒	Buddhist
bumbōgu	文房具	stationers
bun	文	sentence (words)
bun'ya	分野	field
buta	ブタ	pig
butai	舞台	stage
byō	秒	second (n)
byōbu	屏風	folding screen
byōdō	平等	equality
byōdō koyō	平等雇用	equal opportunity
byōin	病院	hospital
byōki	病気	disease/sick/a sickness

C

chāmingu na	チャーミングな	charming
chairo	茶色	brown
championshippu	チャンピオンシップ	championships
chansu	チャンス	chance
chekku in	チェックイン	check-in (desk)
chesu	チェス	chess
chi	血	blood
chi ga demasu	血が出ます	to bleed
chichi	父	father (my)
chigaimasu	違います	wrong/different
chihō no	地方の	local
chiiki no	地域の	regional
chiisai	小さい	little (small)
chikai	近い	near
chikaku no hoteru	近くのホテル	nearby hotel
chikara	力	power
chikatetsu	地下鉄	subway
chikatetsu no eki	地下鉄の駅	subway station
chikyū	地球	Earth
chīmu	チーム	team
chippu	チップ	tip (gratuity)
chizu	地図	map
chizu de oshiete kuremasen ka?	地図で教えてくれませんか?	Can you show me on the map?

D

chīzu	チーズ	cheese
chō	蝶	butterfly
chōjō	頂上	peak
chōkaku shōgai sha	聴覚障害者	deaf
chōkoku	彫刻	sculpture
chōkokuka	彫刻家	sculptor
chōkyori	長距離	long distance
chōkyori basu	長距離バス	long-distance bus
chōkyori denwa	長距離電話	long-distance call
chōshoku	朝食	breakfast
chokorēto	チョコレート	chocolate
chokusetsu	直接	direct
chotto	ちょっと	a bit
chotto matte kudasai	ちょっと待って下さい。	Just a minute.
chūbō	厨房	kitchen (restaurant)
chūdoku	中毒	addiction
chūgoku	中国	China
chūin gamu	チューインガム	chewing gum
chūjitsu na	忠実な	loyal
chūka ryōri	中華料理	Chinese food
chūmon	注文	order
chūmon shimasu	注文します	to order
chūō hiroba	中央広場	main square
chūō ni	中央に	in the middle
chūsha	注射	injection
chūsha shimasu	注射します/駐車します	to inject/to park
chūsha-bari	注射針	needle (syringe)
chūshajō	駐車場	car park
chūshoku	昼食	lunch
chūzetsu	中絶	abortion

D

daburu beddo	ダブルベッド	a double bed
daburu rūmu	ダブルルーム	a double room
daiaru	ダイアル	dial
daibingu	ダイビング	diving
daidō geinin	大道芸人	busker
daidokoro	台所	kitchen
daigaku	大学	university
daihon	台本	script
dairiten	代理店	agency

daiseidō	大聖堂	cathedral
daitasū	大多数	majority
daitōryō	大統領	president (of a country)
dakara	だから	because
dake	だけ	only
dakimasu	抱きます	to cuddle/hug
dambō	暖房	heating
dambōru	段ボール	carton
dansu	ダンス	dance
dansu shimasu	ダンスします	to dance
dare	誰	who
dareka	誰か	somebody/someone
(ichi) -dāsu	(1) ダース	(a) dozen
deguchi	出口	exit/way out
dekakemasu	出かけます	to go out
dekimasu	できます	able (to be); can
demo	でも	but
dempō	電報	telegram
den'atsu	電圧	voltage
denchi	電池	battery
denki	伝記	biography
denki	電気	electricity
denkyū	電球	light bulb
densha	電車	train
denwa	電話	telephone
denwa bangō	電話番号	telephone number
denwa bokkusu	電話ボックス	telephone booth
denwa kōkanshu	電話交換手	telephone operator
denwa kyoku	電話局	telephone office
denwa ryōkin	電話料金	telephone charge
denwa shimasu	電話します	to telephone
denwachō	電話帳	phone book
deodoranto	デオドラント	deodorant
depāto	デパート	department stores
derikatessen	デリカテッセン	delicatessen
desu	です	to be
dēto	デート	date (appointment)
dēto shimasu	デートします	to date (someone)
dezain	デザイン	design
disuko	ディスコ	disco
(ichi) -do	(1) 度	once; one time
dō	どう	how
... e wa dō ikimasu ka?	...へはどう 行きますか？	How do I get to ...?

dōro	道路	road (main)
doa	ドア	door
dōbutsu	動物	animal
dōbutsuen	動物園	zoo
dochira	どちら	which way
dochira sama	どちらさま	who (pol)
dōi shimasu	同意します	to agree
dōjō	同情	sympathy
doko	どこ	where
doko de kippu ga kaemasu ka?	どこで切符が買えますか?	Where can I buy a ticket?
doku	毒	poison
dokushin	独身	single (person)
dokyumentarī	ドキュメンタリー	a documentary
donarimasu	怒鳴ります	to shout
donata	どなた	who
dorama	ドラマ	drama
doresu	ドレス	dress
dōro chizu	道路地図	road map
dorobō	どろぼう	thief
dōryō	同僚	colleague
dōshite	どうして	why
dōyatte	どうやって	how
dōyō no	同様の	similar
doyōbi	土曜日	Saturday

E

e	絵	paintings
eakon	エアコン	air-conditioned
eda	枝	branch (tree)
eien ni	永遠に	forever
eiga	映画	movie
eiga kan	映画館	cinema
eigo	英語	English
eiji shimbun	英字新聞	newspaper in English
eikyū no	永久の	permanent
eizu	エイズ	AIDS
eizu kansensha	エイズ感染者	HIV positive
ekaki	絵かき	painter
eki	駅	train station
empitsu	鉛筆	pencil
en	円	yen

engi	演技	performance
enjin	エンジン	engine
enjo	援助	aid (help)
enkai	宴会	banquet
enki shimasu	延期します	to delay
ensō shimasu	演奏します	to play (music)
ensōkai	演奏会	gig
erabimasu	選びます	to choose
erebētā	エレベーター	elevator/lift

F

fakkusu	ファックス	fax
fan	ファン	fans (of a team)
fenshingu	フェンシング	fencing
fensu	フェンス	fence
fianse	フィアンセ	fiance
fikushon	フィクション	fiction
firumu	フィルム	film (for camera)
firutā	フィルター	filter
fōku	フォーク	fork
fu-byōdō	不平等	inequality
fu-kigen na	不機嫌な	angry
fuda	札	tag
fudangi	普段着	casual dress
fukai	深い	deep
fukanō na	不可能な	impossible
fukkatsu sai	復活祭	Easter
fukushi	福祉	welfare
fukutsū	腹痛	stomachache
fumbetsu no aru	分別のある	sensible
fumikiri	踏み切り	rail crossing
fun	分	minute
fun'iki	雰囲気	atmosphere
funabin	船便	surface mail
funayoi	船酔い	seasick
fune	船	ship/boat
furasshu	フラッシュ	flash
furo	風呂	bath
furoba	風呂場	bathroom
furonto garasu	フロントガラス	windscreen
furui	古い	old
fusoku	不足	shortage
futago	双子	twins

fūtō	封筒	envelope
futotte iru	太っている	fat
futsū no	普通の	ordinary
fuyu	冬	winter

G

gaikoku	外国	foreign country
gaido	ガイド	guide (person)
gaido tsuki torekkingu	ガイド付き トレッキング	guided trek
gaijin	外人	foreigner
gaika	外貨	foreign currency
gaikoku go	外国語	foreign language
gaikokujin	外国人	foreigner
gaikoku no	外国の	foreign
gaitō	外套	cloak
gake	崖	cliff
gakki	楽器	musical instrument
gakkō	学校	school
gaku wari	学割	student discount
gakusei	学生	student
gama	ガマ	toad
gaman	我慢	endurance/patience
gaman-zuyoi	我慢強い	patient (adj)
gambarimasu!	がんばります！	I'll do my best!
gambatte!	がんばって！	Good luck!
gantan	元旦	New Year's Day
gara	柄	pattern
garēji	ガレージ	garage
gārufurendo	ガールフレンド	girlfriend
gasorin	ガソリン	petrol
gasorin sutando	ガソリンスタンド	petrol station
gasu kātorijji	ガスカートリッジ	gas cartridge
gei	ゲイ	gay
geijutsu	芸術	art
geijutsuka	芸術家	artist
geki	劇	play (theatre)
gekijō	劇場	theatre
gekiteki na	劇的な	dramatic
gekkei	月経	menstruation
gekkeimae kinchō	月経前緊張	premenstrual tension
gēmu	ゲーム	game (sport)
gengo	言語	language

genkaku o mimasu	幻覚をみます	to hallucinate
genkin	現金	cash
genkin jidō shiharai ki	現金自動支払機	automatic teller (ATM)
genzai	現在	present (time)
geri	下痢	diarrhoea
getsuyōbi	月曜日	Monday
gijutsu	技術	technique
gijutsusha	技術者	engineer
gin	銀	silver
ginkō	銀行	bank
ginkō wa doko desu ka?	銀行はどこですか?	Where's the bank?
ginkōken	銀行券	banknote
giri no chichi	義理の父	father-in-law
giri no haha	義理の母	mother-in-law
gitā	ギター	guitar
go-gatsu	5月	May
gōhōka	合法化	legalisation
gohan	ごはん	(cooked) rice/meal
gōka na	豪華な	luxury
gōkei	合計	total (amount)
gōru kīpā	ゴールキーパー	goalkeeper
gōsei	合成	synthetic
gōtō shimasu	強盗します	to rob
gomennasai	ごめんなさい。	I'm sorry.
gomi	ごみ	garbage/rubbish
gunjin	軍人	soldier
guramu	グラム	gram
gurasu	グラス	glass
gurēpu furūtsu	グレープフルーツ	grapefruit
gyōretsu	行列	queue
gyūnyū	牛乳	milk

H

ha	葉/歯	leaf/teeth
ha burashi	歯ブラシ	toothbrush
ha migaki	歯磨き	toothpaste
hābu	ハーブ	herbs
hachi-gatsu	8月	August
hachimitsu	蜂蜜	honey
hae	ハエ	fly
hagaki	はがき	postcard
hageshii	激しい	intense

haha	母	mother (my)
hai	灰	ash
hai iro	灰色	grey
haikingu	ハイキング	hiking
hairimasu	入ります	to enter
haisha	歯医者	dentist
haisha	敗者	loser
haita	歯痛	toothache
haizara	灰皿	ashtray
haji	恥	shame
hajimemasu	始めます	to start
haka	墓	grave
hakai shimasu	破壊します	to destroy
hakike	吐き気	nausea
hakken shimasu	発見します	to discover
hakkenjo	発券所	ticket office
hako	箱	box
hakobimasu	運びます	to carry
hakubutsukan	博物館	museum
hakuchō	白鳥	swan
hamabe	浜辺	beach
hamachi	ハマチ	yellowtail
hambai	販売	sales
hambun	半分	half
hammokku	ハンモック	hammock
hamu	ハム	ham
han zubon	半ズボン	shorts
han'ei	反映	reflection (thinking)
han-kaku	反核	antinuclear
hana	花	flower
hana	鼻	nose
hanareta	離れた	remote
hanashi	話	story
hanashimasu	話します	to speak/talk/tell
hanaya	花屋	florist
hando baggu	ハンドバッグ	handbag
hanemūn	ハネムーン	honeymoon
hanga	版画	woodblock print
hangaku	半額	half-price
hankachi	ハンカチ	handicrafts
hanketsu	判決	sentence (prison)
hanko	はんこ	personal seal
hanron shimasu	反論します	to argue
hansamu	ハンサム	handsome

hansha	反射	reflection (mirror)
hanshin fuzui	半身不随	paraplegic
hantai	反対	against/opposite
hantai gawa	反対側	opposite side
hantai shimasu	反対します	to protest
hantō	半島	peninsula
hanzai	犯罪	offence
happyō	発表	presentation
harai modoshi	払い戻し	refund
harai modoshi shimasu	払い戻しします	to refund
haraimasu	払います	to pay
hare	晴	sunny
hari	針	needle (sewing)
harigane	針金	wire
haru	春	spring (season)
hasami	はさみ	scissors
hashi	橋	bridge
hashirimasu	走ります	to run
hasshin	発疹	a rash
hasshisshi	ハッシッシ	hash
hata	旗	flag
hatarakimasu	働きます	to work
hayai	早い /速い	early/fast
hazukashii	恥ずかしい	ashamed/shy
heaburashi	ヘアブラシ	hairbrush
hei	塀	fence
heieki	兵役	military service
heishi	兵士	soldier
heiten	閉店	closed
heiwa	平和	peace
hen na	変な	strange
henshūsha	編集者	editor
henzutsū	偏頭痛	migraine
heroin	ヘロイン	heroin
heroin chūdoku	ヘロイン中毒	heroin addict
herumetto	ヘルメット	helmet
heya	部屋	room
heya bangō	部屋番号	room number
hi	火	fire
hicchihaiku shimasu	ヒッチハイクします	to hitchhike
hidari	左	left (not right)
hidari ni magatte kudasai	左に曲がってください。	Turn left please
hidoi	ひどい	awful/horrible

226

higashi	東	east
hiji	ひじ	elbow
hijō-guchi	非常口	emergency exit
hikari	光	light (sun/lamp)
hikimasu	引きます	to pull
hikōbin	飛行便	flight
hikōki	飛行機	aeroplane
hikui	低い	low/short (height)
himo	ひも	string
hinin	避妊	contraception
hinin yaku	避妊薬	contraceptive
hinkon	貧困	poverty
hinshitsu	品質	quality
hinto	ヒント	tip (gratuity)
hinzūkyō	ヒンズー教	Hindu
hirakimasu	開きます	to open
hiroba	広場	square (in town)
hiroi	広い	wide
hiroimasu	拾います	to pick up
hiru gohan	昼ごはん	lunch
hiru yasumi	昼休み	lunchtime
hisho	秘書	secretary
hitei shimasu	否定します	to deny
hītā	ヒーター	heater
hito	人	people/person
hitori de	独りで	alone
hitsuji	羊	sheep
hitsuyō	必要	need
hiyake	日焼け	sunburn
hiyake-dome	日焼け止め	sunblock
hiza	膝	knee
hizuke	日付	date (time)
hōchō	包丁	knife
hochōki	補聴器	hearing aid
hodō	歩道	footpath
hōgen	方言	dialect
hogo	保護	protection
hogo shimasu	保護します	to protect
hōi jishaku	方位磁石	compass
hoken	保険	insurance
hōkō	方向	direction
hokōsha	歩行者	pedestrian
hokori	誇り	pride
homemasu	誉めます	to admire

homeopashī	ホメオパシー	homeopathy
homo	ホモ	homosexual
hōmon shimasu	訪問します	to visit
hōmuresu	ホームレス	homeless
hon	本	book
hon'yaku shimasu	翻訳します	to translate
hone	骨	bone
hontō	本当	truth
hontō desu	本当です。	It's true.
hon'ya	本屋	bookshop
hōritsu	法律	law
hōseki	宝石	jewellery
hoshi	星	stars
hoshigarimasu	欲しがります	to want
hoshuteki na	保守的な	conservative
hōtai	包帯	bandage
hoteru	ホテル	hotel
hotondo	ほとんど	almost
hyaku	百	a hundred
hyaku man	百万	million
hyōjun	標準	standard (usual)
hyōkō	標高	altitude
hyōshiki	標識	a sign/indicator

I

i	胃	stomach
ichi	位置	location
ichi-gatsu	1月	January
ichiba	市場	market
idai na	偉大な	great
ie	家	house
igaku	医学	medicine (study)
ii	いい	good/OK
ii hoteru	いいホテル	good hotel
iimasu	言います	to say
iken	意見	opinion
iki	息	breath
ikimasu	行きます	to go
ikimasu	生きます	to live (life)
ikinokorimasu	生き残ります	to survive
ikura	いくら	how much
... made ikura desu ka?	...までいくらですか?	How much does it cost to go to ...?

ikutsuka no	いくつかの	several/some
ima	今	now
imin	移民	immigration
iminkyoku	移民局	Immigratiion Office
imōto	妹	sister (younger)
inaka	田舎	countryside
inkei	陰茎	penis
insutorakutā	インストラクター	instructor
intabyū	インタビュー	interview
inu	犬	dog
ippai	いっぱい	full
ippan no	一般の	general
ippun	1分	a minute
iriguchi	入口	entrance
iro	色	colour
irui	衣類	clothing
iseki	遺跡	ruins
isha	医者	doctor
ishi	石	stone
isogashii	忙しい	busy
isoide	急いで	in a hurry
issho	一緒	together
isu	椅子	chair
isuramukyō	イスラム教	Islam
itai	痛い	painful
itami	痛み	a pain
itami-dome	痛み止め	painkillers
ito yōji	糸楊枝	dental floss
itsu	いつ	when
itsu de mo	いつでも	any time
itsumo	いつも	always
iwa	岩	rock
iwa nobori	岩登り	rock climbing
iwa yama	岩山	crag; wall of rock
iwadana	岩棚	ledge
iwaimasu	祝います	to celebrate
iyagarase	嫌がらせ	harassment
iyaringu	イヤリング	earrings

J

ja!	じゃ！	See ya!
ja, mata	じゃ、また。	See you later.

jā	ジャー	jar
jidō hambaiki	自動販売機	vending machine
jidōsha	自動車	car
jidōsha tōroku	自動車登録	car registration
jieigyō	自営業	self-employed
jiji	時事	current affairs
jikan	時間	time/hour
jikan-dōri	時間通り	on time
jikokuhyō	時刻表	timetable
jiko	事故	accident
jikyū	時給	rate of pay (hourly)
jimaku	字幕	subtitles
jimbutsuga	人物画	portrait
jimu	事務	office work
jimu	ジム	gym
jimuin	事務員	office worker
jimusho	事務所	office
jinin	辞任	resignation
jinja	神社	shrine
jinken	人権	human rights
jinsei	人生	life
jinshu	人種	race (breed)
jinshu sabetsu	人種差別	racism
jīnzu	ジーンズ	jeans
jishin	地震	earthquake
jisho	辞書	dictionary
jitensha	自転車	bicycle
jitensha ni norimasu	自転車に乗ります	to cycle
jiyū na	自由な	free (not bound)
jō	錠	lock
jōdan	冗談	joke
jōdan o iimasu	冗談を言います	to joke
jogen	助言	advice
jōki	蒸気	steam
jōkyaku	乗客	passenger
jōmae	錠前	padlock
jōmyaku	静脈	vein
joō	女王	queen
jūbun na	十分な	enough
jū-gatsu	1 0月	October
jūgyōin	従業員	employee
jūichi-gatsu	1 1月	November
jūjika	十字架	cross (religious)
jūni-gatsu	1 2月	December

jūsho	住所	address
jūsu	ジュース	juice
jumbi shimasu	準備します	to prepare
junsui na	純粋な	pure

K

kabe	壁	wall
kachi	価値	value (price)
kachimasu	勝ちます	to win
kado	かど	corner
kādo	カード	cards
kaemasu	代えます	to change
kafe	カフェ	a cafe
kafunshō	花粉症	hayfever
kagaku	科学	science
kagakusha	科学者	scientist
kagami	鏡	mirror
kage	陰	shade/shadow
kagi	鍵	key
kagi o kakemasu	鍵をかけます	to lock
kai	階	floor (storey)
(san) -kai	(3) 回	(3) times
kaichū dentō	懐中電灯	flashlight
kaidan	階段	stairway/step
kaiga	絵画	painting (the art)
kaigai	海外	abroad
kaigan	海岸	coast
kaigan-zoi	海岸沿い	seaside
kaigara	貝殻	shell
kaihatsu	開発	exploitation
kaiin	会員	member
kaikai	開会	opening
kaiko	解雇	dismissal
kaimasu	買います	to buy
kaimono	買い物	shopping
kaisha	会社	company
kaji	火事	fire (disaster)
kaji	家事	housework
kakarimasu	かかります	to cost
kake	賭け	a bet
kakimasu	書きます	to write
kakitome yūbin	書留郵便	registered mail
kako	過去	past

kaku	各	each
kaku (enerugî)	核 (エネルギー)	nuclear (energy)
kaku jikken	核実験	nuclear testing
kakunin shimasu	確認します	to confirm (a booking)
kamera	カメラ	camera
kameraya	カメラ屋	camera shop
kami	神	God
kami	紙	paper
kamimasu	噛みます	to bite (dog)
kaminari	雷	thunder
kaminoke	髪の毛	hair
kamisori (no ha)	剃刀(の刃)	razor (blades)
kampai!	乾杯！	Good health!; Cheers!
kampôi	漢方医	herbalist
kan	缶	can (aluminium)
kanashii	悲しい	sad
kana-zuchi	金槌	hammer
kanchô	館長	curator
kanemochi	金持ち	rich people
kangaemasu	考えます	to think
kangofu	看護婦	nurse (f)
kangoshi	看護士	nurse (m)
kani	かに	crab
kanjimasu	感じます	to feel
kanjô	勘定	bill
kankei	関係	relationship
kanketsu sen	間欠泉	geyser
kankiri	缶切り	can tin opener
kankô	観光	sightseeing
kankô annaijo	観光案内所	tourist information office
kankôkyaku	観光客	tourist
kankyô	環境	environment
kanô na	可能な	possible
kanojo	彼女	she/girlfriend
kanrishoku	管理職	director/management
kansen dôro	幹線道路	main road
kansetsuteki	間接的	non-direct
kansha shimasu	感謝します	to thank
kantan na	簡単な	easy
kao	顔	face
kappu	カップ	cup
kappuru	カップル	pair (a couple)
kara no	空の	empty
kara	から	from/because

karada	からだ	body
karai	辛い	hot (spicy)
karakaimasu	からかいます	to make fun of
karaoke	カラオケ	karaoke
kare	彼	he/boyfriend
karejji	カレッジ	college
karendā	カレンダー	calendar
karera	彼ら	they
karimasu	借ります	to borrow/hire
karui	軽い	light (adj)
kasa	傘	umbrella
kasegimasu	稼ぎます	to earn
kasetto	カセット	cassette
kashikoi	賢い	wise
kashimasu	貸します	to rent
kashu	歌手	singer
kata	肩	shoulders
katachi	形	shape
katai	固い	hard/solid
katamichi	片道	one-way (ticket)
katana	刀	sword
katorikku	カトリック	Catholic
katsudōka	活動家	activist
kauntā	カウンター	counter
kawa	皮	leather
kawa	川	river
kawaii	かわいい	lovely
kawakashimasu	乾かします	to dry (clothes)
kawase rēto	為替レート	exchange rate
kayōbi	火曜日	Tuesday
kayui	かゆい	itch
kaze	風	wind
kaze (o hikimasu)	風邪(をひきます)	(to have) a cold
kazoemasu	数えます	to count
kazoku	家族	family
ke	毛	hair
kega	けが	injury/wound
keiba no kishu	競馬の騎手	jockey
keikaku	計画	plan
keikoku shimasu	警告します	to warn
keisatsu	警察	police
keitai denwa	携帯電話	mobile phone
keitaihin azukarijo	携帯品預所	cloakroom
keiyaku	契約	contract

keiyu	経由	via
keizai	経済	economy
kekkan hin	欠陥品	faulty
kekkon	結婚	marriage
kekkon no umu	結婚の有無	marital status
kekkon shimasu	結婚します	to marry
kekkonshiki	結婚式	wedding
ken'eki	検疫	quarantine
kenchikubutsu	建築物	architecture
kenka	けんか	fight/quarrel
kenkō	健康	health
kenkō shoku	健康食	health food
kensa	検査	review
kensetsu sagyō	建設作業	construction work
kerimasu	蹴ります	to kick
keshō	化粧	make up
keshōhin	化粧品	cosmetics
ketsuatsu	血圧	blood pressure
ketsueki	血液	blood
ketsueki-gata	血液型	blood group
ketsueki kensa	血液検査	blood test
ki	木	tree/wood
ki ga tsukimasu	気が付きます	to realise
ki o tsukete!	気を付けて！	Careful!
kibōdo	キーボード	keyboard
kibōshimasu	希望します	to wish
kichigai	気違い	mad
kichōhin	貴重品	valuable
kigyōka	企業化	privatisation
kihazukashii	気恥ずかしい	embarassed
kiiro	黄色	yellow
kikai	機械	machine
kikai	機会	chance
kikaikō	機械工	mechanic
kiken	危険	risk/danger
kiken na	危険な	dangerous
kikimasu	聞きます	to hear/listen; ask (a question)
kikku ofu	キックオフ	kick off
kiku	菊	chrysanthemum
kimari	決まり	rules
kimasu	来ます	to come
kimasu	着ます	to wear
kimemasu	決めます	to decide

kimochi	気持ち	feelings
kin	金	gold
kin'yōbi	金曜日	Friday
kinenhi	記念碑	monument
kingan	近眼	short-sighted
kinkyū	緊急	emergency/urgent
kinniku	筋肉	muscle
kinō	きのう	yesterday
kinu	絹	silk
kinzoku	金属	metal
kion	気温	temperature (weather)
kippu	切符	ticket
kire	切れ	piece
kirei na	きれいな	beautiful/clean/pretty
kiri	霧	fog
kiri ga dete imasu	霧が出ています。	It's foggy.
kirimasu	切ります	to cut
kirisuto kyōto	キリスト教徒	Christian
kiro guramu	キログラム	kilogram
kiro mētoru	キロメートル	kilometre
kisetsu	季節	season
kisha	記者	journalist
kisu	キス	kiss
kita	北	north
kitanai	汚い	dirty
kitōsho	祈祷書	prayer book
kitsui	きつい	tight
kitte	切手	stamps
kiyomemasu	清めます	to bless
kobu	こぶ	lump
kōban	交番	police box
kōcha	紅茶	tea (western)
kōdokei	光度計	light meter
kodomo	子供	child/children
koe	声	voice
kōen	公園	a park
kōgai	公害	pollution
kōgaku	工学	engineering
kōgei hin	工芸品	crafts
kōgekiteki na	攻撃的な	aggressive
kōgen	高原	plateau
kogimasu	漕ぎます	to row
kogitte	小切手	cheque
kōhī	コーヒー	coffee
kōin	工員	factory worker

koibito	恋人	lover
koin	コイン	coins
koin randorī	コインランドリー	launderette
koinu	小犬	puppy
kōishitsu	更衣室	changing rooms
kōji	工事	construction
kojiki	乞食	beggar
kojinteki na	個人的な	private
kōjō	工場	factory
kōkai shimasu	後悔します	to regret
kokain	コカイン	cocaine
kōkan shimasu	交換します	to exchange
kōkanshu	交換手	operator
kōketsuatsu	高血圧	high blood pressure
kokkai	国会	parliament
kokkyō	国境	border
koko	ここ	here
kōkō	高校	high school
kokochi yoi	心地よい	comfortable
kōko-gaku	考古学	archaeology
kokoro	心	mind (n)
kōkūbin	航空便	air mail
kokuritsu	国立	national
kokusai	国際	international
kokusai denwa	国際電話	international call
kokuseki	国籍	nationality
kokyaku	顧客	client
komban	今晩	tonight
kombanwa	こんばんは。	Good evening.
kombu	昆布	kelp
komedī	コメディー	comedy
komi	込み	included
komichi	小道	path/track
komori	子守り	childminding
kompyūta	コンピュータ	computer
komugiko	小麦粉	flour
kon'ya	今夜	tonight
kon'yaku	婚約	engagement
kon'yakusha	婚約者	fiance
kondōmu	コンドーム	condom
kongetsu	今月	this month
konnichiwa	こんにちは。	Good afternoon; Hello.
kono	この	this
konomimasu	好みます	to prefer

konsāto	コンサート	a concert
konshū	今週	this week
kontakuto renzu	コンタクトレンズ	contact lenses
kore	これ	this
kōri	氷	ice
kōrimasu	凍ります	to be frozen
kōri mizu	氷水	ice water
koroshimasu	殺します	to kill
kōsaten	交差点	junction
kōsei	公正	justice
kōseibusshitsu	抗生物質	antibiotics
koshō	胡椒	pepper
koshō	故障	out of order
kōshū denwa	公衆電話	public phone
kōshū toire	公衆トイレ	public toilet
kōsoku dōro	高速道路	freeway/motorway
kotae	答	answer
kotaemasu	答えます	to answer
koten	古典	classical
kōto	コート	coat
kotoba	言葉	word/language
kotonarimasu	異なります	to differ
kotoshi	今年	this year
kōtsū	交通	traffic
kottōhin	骨董品	antiques
kōun na	幸運な	lucky
kowagarimasu	恐がります	to be afraid of
kowai	恐い	scared
kowareta	壊れた	broken
kowashimasu	壊します	to break
kozeni	小銭	small change
kōzui	洪水	flood
kozutsumi	小包	parcel/package
ku-gatsu	9月	September
kubarimasu	配ります	to deal
kuchi	口	mouth
kuchibeni	口紅	lipstick
kuchibiru	唇	lips
kudamono	果物	fruit
kudamonoya	果物屋	fruit shop
... o kudasai	...をください。	I'd like to buy ...
kuizu bangumi	クイズ番組	a game show
kukan	区間	leg (in race)
kūkan	空間	space

K

kūki	空気	air
kūkō	空港	airport
kūkō zei	空港税	airport tax
kumiai	組合	unions
kumo	雲	cloud
kumori	曇り	cloudy
kuni	国	country
kūpon	クーポン	coupon
kurabu	クラブ	nightclub
kurai	暗い	dark
kurashikku	クラシック	classical music
kurasu	クラス	class
kaikyū seido	階級制度	class system
kurejitto kādo	クレジットカード	credit card
kurīmu	クリーム	moisturising cream/cream
kurikaeshimasu	繰り返します	to repeat
kuriketto	クリケット	cricket
kurisumasu	クリスマス	Christmas Day
kurisumasu ibu	クリスマスイブ	Christmas Eve
kurisumasu kādo	クリスマスカード	Christmas card
kuro	黒	black
kurosu-kantorī	クロスカントリー	cross-country
kūru	クール	cool [colloquial]
kuruma	車	car
kuruma isu	車椅子	wheelchair
kurushimimasu	苦しみます	to suffer
kusa	草	grass
kushi	櫛	comb
kusuri	薬	medicine (drug)
kutsu	靴	shoes
kutsushita	靴下	socks
kutsuya	靴屋	shoe shop
kyakuhonka	脚本家	scriptwriter
kyampu	キャンプ	camping
kyampu shimasu	キャンプします	to camp
kyampujō	キャンプ場	campsite
kyaria ūman	キャリアウーマン	businesswoman
kyō	今日	today
kyōdai	兄弟	brother
kyohi shimasu	拒否します	to refuse
kyōiku	教育	education
kyoka	許可	permission
kyōkai	教会	church
kyokashō	許可証	permit

DICTIONARY

238

kyonen	去年	last year
kyōsan shugisha	共産主義者	communist
kyōshi	教師	teacher
kyōwasei	共和制	republic
kyū	急	suddenly
kyū na	急な	steep
kyūjitsu	休日	holiday/vacation
kyūkei	休憩	intermission
kyūkō no	急行の	express (transport)
kyūkyū-ako	救急箱	first-aid kit
kyūkyūsha	救急車	ambulance
kyūryō	給料	salary
kyūsu	急須	teapot

M

mājan	麻雀	mahjong
macchi	マッチ	match
machiai shitsu	待合室	waiting room
machigai	間違い	mistake
machigai denwa	間違い電話	wrong number
machimasu	待ちます	to wait
made	まで	until
mado	窓	window
mado gawa	窓側	window seat
mae	前	before
maeba	前歯	tooth (front)
mago	孫	grandchild
mainichi	毎日	every day
majime na	真面目な	serious
make	負け	loser
maki	薪	firewood
makura	枕	pillow
makura kabā	枕カバー	pillowcase
manējā	マネージャー	manager
manga	漫画	comics
mannaka ni	真ん中に	in the middle
marifana	マリファナ	marijuana
marui	丸い	round
massāji	マッサージ	massage
massugu na	まっすぐな	straight

mata	また	again/also
mata wa	または	or
matsu	松	pine
matsuri	祭り	festival
matte!	待って！	Wait!
matto	マット	mat
mattoresu	マットレス	mattress
maunten baiku	マウンテンバイク	mountain bike
mayaku	麻薬	drug
mayaku chūdoku	麻薬中毒	drug addiction
mayonaka	真夜中	midnight
mazemasu	混ぜます	to mix
mazushii	貧しい	poor
me	目	eye
me-gusuri	目薬	eye drops
medaru	メダル	medal
megane	眼鏡	glasses (eye)
meikaku na	明確な	obvious
meisō	瞑想	meditation
mēkyappu	メーキャップ	make-up
memai	めまい	dizzy
membā	メンバー	member
men	綿	cotton
mendō o mimasu	面倒を見ます	to look after
mendōmi ga ii	面倒見がいい	caring
mendō na	面倒な	troublesome
mensetsu	面接	interview
mensōru	メンソール	menthol (cigarettes)
menyū	メニュー	menu
meshiagare	召し上がれ	Bon appétit!
messēji	メッセージ	message
mētoru	メートル	metre
mezamashi-dokei	目覚まし時計	alarm clock
mezurashii	めずらしい	rare
mibun shōmeisho	身分証明書	identification card
michi	道	street
midori	緑	green
migi	右	right (not left)
migi ni magatte kudasai	右に曲がってください。	Turn right please.
miharashi dai	見晴台	lookout
mijikai	短い	short (length)
mimasu	見ます	to look/see/watch

mimi	耳	ear
minami	南	south
minato	港	harbour
mineraru uōtā	ミネラルウォーター	mineral water
mini bā	ミニバー	mini bar
minikui	醜い	ugly
minshu shugi	民主主義	democracy
minto	ミント	mint
mirimētoru	ミリメートル	millimetre
miruku	ミルク	milk
misa	ミサ	mass (Catholic)
mise	店	shop
misemasu	見せます	to show
mitomemasu	認めます	to admit/acknowledge
mitsukemasu	見つけます	to find
mizu	水	water
mizugi	水着	swimming suit
mizūmi	湖	lake
mo	も	too (as well)
mō takusanda!	もうたくさんだ！	Enough!
mochimasu	持ちます	to have
... o motte imasu	…を持っています。	I have ...
mochinushi	持ち主	owner
mochiron	もちろん	Sure.
modemu	モデム	modem
moderu	モデル	model
mōdōken	盲導犬	guidedog
modorimasu	戻ります	to return
mōfu	毛布	blanket
mokuteki	目的	goal
mokutekichi	目的地	destination
mokuyōbi	木曜日	Thursday
momi	樅	fir
mon	門	gate
monorēru	モノレール	monorail
moraimasu	もらいます	to get/to be given
mori	森	forest
morumotto	モルモット	guinea pig
moshi	もし	if
moshi-moshi	もしもし	Hello. (answering telephone)
moshika suru to	もしかすると	maybe
mosuku	モスク	mosque

mōtābōto	モーターボート	motorboat
motomoto no	もともとの	original
motte kimasu	持って来ます	to bring
motto	もっと	more
muen	無鉛	unleaded
mukō ni	向こうに	across
mune	胸	chest
mura	村	village
murasaki	紫	purple
muryō	無料	free (of charge)
museifu shugisha	無政府主義者	anarchist
mushi	虫	bug
musuko	息子	son
musume	娘	daughter
muzukashii	難しい	difficult
myōji	名字	surname

N

nabe	鍋	pan
nagai	長い	long
nagame	眺め	view
nagareboshi	流れ星	meteor
naifu	ナイフ	knife
naka	なか	inside
nakama	仲間	companion
nakushimasu	なくします	to lose
nama no	生の	raw
namae	名前	name
nami	波	wave
namida	涙	tear (crying)
nammin	難民	refugee
nan de mo	何でも	anything
nande	なんで	why
nani	なに	what
nani o shite imasu ka?	何をしていますか?	What are you doing?
nani mo nai	何もない	none
nanika	何か	something
nan-ji	何時	what time
nan-ji desu ka?	何時ですか?	What time is it?
nappusakku	ナップサック	knapsack
naraimasu	習います	to learn
nashi de	なしで	without
natsu	夏	summer
natsukashiku omoimasu	懐かしく思います	to miss (feel absence)

nawa	縄	rope
naze	なぜ	why
nebukuro	寝袋	sleeping bag
nedan	値段	price
nefuda	値札	price tag
nega	ネガ	a film (negatives)
nekkuresu	ネックレス	necklace
neko	猫	cat
nempai	年配	old person
nemui	眠い	sleepy
nemurimasu	眠ります	to sleep
nenkan	年間	annual
nenkin	年金	pension
nenrei	年齢	age
nenza	捻挫	a sprain
netami	妬み	jealousy
netsu	熱	fever/heat
nezumi	ネズミ	mouse/rat
ni-gatsu	2月	February
nicchū	日中	daytime
nichi	日	day/date
nichibotsu	日没	sunset
nichiyōbi	日曜日	Sunday
nigai	苦い	bitter
nihon	日本	Japan
nihon shoku	日本食	Japanese food
nihon teien	日本庭園	Japanese garden
nihonga	日本画	Japanese painting
niji	虹	rainbow
nikki	日記	diary
nikkō	日光	sunlight
nikutai rōdōsha	肉体労働者	manual worker
nimotsu	荷物	luggage
ningen	人間	human
ningyō	人形	doll
ninki ga aru	人気がある	popular
ninshiki shimasu	認識します	to recognise
ninshin	妊娠	pregnant
nioi	におい	a smell
nioi o kagimasu	においを嗅ぎます	to smell
nippon	日本	Japan
nishi	西	west
niwa	庭	gardens
niwatori	ニワトリ	chicken

nōgyō	農業	agriculture
nōjō	農場	farm
nōmin	農民	farmer
nōto	ノート	notebook
nobori-zaka	上り坂	uphill
noborimasu	登ります	to climb
nodo	のど	throat
nodo ga kawakimasu	のどが渇きます	thirsty
nokori	残り	rest (what's left)
nokosaremasu	残されます	to be left (behind/over)
nomi	蚤	flea
nomimasu	飲みます	to drink
nomimono	飲物	a drink
norikae	乗り換え	change over
norimasu	乗ります	to get on/ride
norimono yoi	乗物酔	travel sickness
nozokimasu	除きます	to exclude
nuimasu	縫います	to sew
nurete imasu	ぬれています	wet
nusumimasu	盗みます	to steal
nyū-jirando	ニュージーランド	New Zealand
nyūjō	入場	admission
nyūseihin	乳製品	dairy products
nyūsu	ニュース	news

O

oba	おば	aunt
ōbā	オーバー	overcoat
obā san	おばあさん	grandmother; elderly woman
obasan	おばさん	aunt; middle age woman
o-bentō	お弁当	lunch box
o-cha	お茶	tea (Japanese)
ochimasu	落ちます	to fall
ōdōri	大通り	main street
odoroki	驚き	a surprise
ōfukuken	往復券	return ticket
ofusaido	オフサイド	offside
ogawa	小川	stream
ōgazumu	オーガズム	orgasm
ohayō (gozaimasu)	おはよう（ございます）。	Good morning.
o-inori	お祈り	prayer

O

oiru	オイル	oil (engine)
oishii	おいしい	delicious/tasty
oji	おじ	uncle
ojī san	おじいさん	grandfather/elderly man
ojisan	おじさん	uncle/middle age man
oka	丘	hill
o-kane	お金	money
okāsan	お母さん	mother
ōkē	OK	OK
ōkesutora	オーケストラ	orchestra
ōkii	大きい	large
okimasu	置きます	to put
ōkisa	大きさ	size (of anything)
okorimasu	怒ります	to get angry
okuba	奥歯	tooth (back)
okuremasu	遅れます	to be late
okuri mono	贈り物	gift
okurimasu	送ります	to send
okurimono	贈り物	present (gift)
omedetō!	おめでとう！	Congratulations!
o-kyaku	お客	guest
ōmisoka	大晦日	New Year's Eve
omiyage	お土産	souvenir
omoi	重い	heavy
omoidashimasu	思い出します	to remember
omosa	重さ	weight
omoshiroi	おもしろい	interesting/fun
ōmukashi no	大昔の	ancient
omutsu	おむつ	nappy/diaper
omutsu kabure	おむつかぶれ	nappy rash
onaji	同じ	same
onaka	お腹	stomach
onakaga sukimasu	お腹が空きます	to be hungry
ondo	温度	temperature
ondokei	温度計	thermometer
onēsan	お姉さん	sister (older) your
ongaku	音楽	music
ongakuka	音楽家	musician
onna	女	woman
onna no ko	女の子	girl
onsen	温泉	hot spring
opera	オペラ	opera
ore	俺	I (male: inf)
orenji	オレンジ	orange

orimasu	降ります	to get off
orimpikku	オリンピック	Olympic Games
oroshiuri gyōsha	卸売業者	distributor
ōsama	王様	king
oshaburi	おしゃぶり	dummy (baby's)
oshiemasu	教えます	to teach
oshimasu	押します	to push
oshoku	汚職	corruption
osoi	遅い	late
osore	恐れ	fear
ōsugimasu	多すぎます	too much; many
ōsutoraria	オーストラリア	Australia
oto	音	sound
otō san	お父さん	father (your)
ōtobai	オートバイ	motorcycle
otoko	男	man (male)
otoko no ko	男の子	boy
otona	大人	adult
ototoi	おととい	day before yesterday
otsuri	おつり	change (coins)
otto	夫	husband
owarasemasu	終わらせます	to finish
owari	終わり	end
oyamsumi (nasai)	おやすみ （なさい）。	Good night.
oyogimasu	泳ぎます	to swim
o-yu	お湯	hot water
ozonsō	オゾン層	ozone layer

P

paipu	パイプ	pipe
pan	パン	bread
panku	パンク	puncture
pantsu	パンツ	underpants
papu tomatsuhyōhon	パプ塗抹標本	pap smear
pāsento	パーセント	percent
pasu	パス	pass
pasupōto	パスポート	passport
pasupōto bangō	パスポート番号	passport number
pātī	パーティー	party
pegu	ペグ	tent pegs
pēji	ページ	page
pen	ペン	pen

penki	ペンキ	paint
pikkeru	ピッケル	ice axe
pikunikku	ピクニック	picnic
pinku	ピンク	pink
piru	ピル	the pill
pōkā	ポーカー	poker
poketto	ポケット	pocket
pun	分	minute
pompu	ポンプ	pump
poppu myūjikku	ポップミュージック	popular music
posutā	ポスター	poster
pōtā	ポーター	porter
pūru	プール	swimming pool
puragu	プラグ	plug (electricity)
puraido	プライド	pride
purasuchikku	プラスチック	plastic
purattohōmu	プラットホーム	platform
purezento	プレゼント	present (gift)
purinto	プリント	print
purodyūsā	プロデューサー	producer
puroguramu	プログラム	program
purojekutā	プロジェクター	projector

R

raigetsu	来月	next month
rainen	来年	next year
raishū	来週	next week
raitā	ライター	lighter
raito	ライト	light (n)
rajietā	ラジエター	radiator
rajio	ラジオ	radio
raketto	ラケット	racquet
ranchi	ランチ	lunch
rari	ラリー	rally
raunji	ラウンジ	lounge
rei	例	example
reihai	礼拝	service (religious)
reipu	レイプ	rape
reitō	冷凍	frozen
reizōko	冷蔵庫	refrigerator
reji	レジ	cash register
renji	レンジ	stove
renshū	練習	training
rentakā	レンタカー	rent-a-car

renzoku	連続	series
renzu	レンズ	lens
rēshingu baiku	レーシングバイク	racing bike
reshīto	レシート	receipt
rēsu	レース	lace/race
rēsu kōsu	レースコース	track (car-racing)
resutoran	レストラン	restaurant
retasu	レタス	lettuce
rezu	レズ	lesbian
ridā	リーダー	leader
rieki	利益	profit
rijun-ritsu	利潤率	profitability
rikai shimasu	理解します	to understand
rikon	離婚	divorce
rikoteki na	利己的な	selfish
riku	陸	land
rimo kon	リモコン	remote control
rinrin	リンリン	ring (sound)
rinyūshoku	離乳食	baby food
rippō	立法	legislation
rirakkusu shimasu	リラックスします	to relax
rirekisho	履歴書	resume
risaikuru	リサイクル	recycling
rittoru	リットル	litter
riyū	理由	reason
rizumu	リズム	rhythm
robī	ロビー	foyer
rōdō	労働	labour
rōdō kumiai	労働組合	trade union
rōdō kyoka	労働許可	work permit
rokasareta	濾過された	filtered
rokku	ロック	rock music
rokku kuraimingu	ロッククライミング	rock climbing
roku-gatsu	6月	June
rokuon	録音	audio recording
romansu	ロマンス	romance
rōsoku	ろうそく	candle
rōya	牢屋	jail
rūru	ルール	rules
rusu	留守	absense
rusuban	留守番	a person who stays at home and looks after the house
rusuban denwa	留守番電話	answering machine

248

rūto	ルート	trail/route
ryōhō	両方	both
ryōji kan	領事館	consulate
ryokan	旅館	inn
ryōkin	料金	fee
ryokō	旅行	travel
ryokō annaisho	旅行案内書	guidebook
ryokō dairiten	旅行代理店	travel agency
ryokō shimasu	旅行します	to travel
ryōri shimasu	料理します	to cook
ryōshin	両親	parents
ryōshūsho	領収書	receipt
ryūzan	流産	miscarriage

S

sabaku	砂漠	desert
sabetsu	差別	discrimination
sabishii	寂しい	lonely
sābisu	サービス	service (assistence)
sābisu ryō	サービス料	service charge
sadō	茶道	tea ceremony
sāfin	サーフィン	surfing
sāfu bōdo	サーフボード	surfboard
sagashimasu	探します	to look for
saiban	裁判	a trial
saibankan	裁判官	judge
saibansho	裁判所	court (legal)
saifu	財布	wallet
saigo	最後	last
saikin	最近	recently
saikō	最高	best
saikoro	サイコロ	dice/die
saikuringu	サイクリング	cycling
saikurisuto	サイクリスト	cyclist
sain	サイン	signature
sain shimasu	サインします	to sign
saizu	サイズ	size (clothes)
sakana	魚	fish
sakana (ya)	魚(屋)	fish (shop)
sākasu	サーカス	circus
sake	酒	wine (Japanese)
saki	先	point (tip)
sakka	作家	writer

sakkā	サッカー	football (soccer)
sakura	桜	cherry blossom
sakusei shimasu	作製します	to produce
sammyaku	山脈	mountain range
samui	寒い	cold (weather)
samui desu	寒いです。	It's cold. (weather)
san-gatsu	3月	March
sangurasu	サングラス	sunglasses
sangyō	産業	industry
sankōbunken	参考文献	reference (articles)
sansei shimasu	賛成します	to agree.
sanso	酸素	oxygen
sara	皿	plate
saraba!	さらば！	Bon voyage!
sashimasu	刺します	to bite (insect)/to pierce
sashimasu	指します	to point
satō	砂糖	sugar
sauna	サウナ	sauna
sawarimasu	触ります	to touch
sayōnara.	さようなら。	Goodbye.
sayoku	左翼	left-wing
sētā	セーター	jumper (sweater)
sei; ... sei	性／... 製	sex; made in ...
sei sabetsu	性差別	sexism
seibishi	整備士	mechanic
seibutsu bunkai	生物分解	biodegradable
seibyō	性病	venereal disease
seifu	政府	government
seigansho	請願書	petition
seigen sokudo	制限速度	speed limit
seihōkei	正方形	square (shape)
seiji	政治	politics
seiji enzetsu	政治演説	political speech
seijika	政治家	politicians
seijin	聖人	saint
seikaku	性格	personality
seikatsu	生活	life
seikatsu suijun	生活水準	standard of living
seiketsu na (hoteru)	清潔な（ホテル）	clean (hotel)
seikō	成功	success
seinengappi	生年月日	date of birth
seiri shimasu	整理します	to organise
seiritsū	生理痛	period pain
seiriyō napukin	生理用ナプキン	sanitary napkins

S

seisakusha	製作者	producer
seisan	聖餐	holy communion
seisho	聖書	the Bible
seitai	聖体	communion
seiyō ryōri	西洋料理	western food
seiza	星座	zodiac
sekai	世界	world
seki	せき	a cough
sekiyu	石油	oil (crude)
sekkeishi	設計士	architect
sekken	石鹸	soap
sekkyokuteki na	積極的な	outgoing
sekushī na	セクシーな	sexy
semmon	専門	profession
semmonka	専門家	specialist
sempūki	扇風機	fan (machine)
sen	栓	plug (bath)
senaka	背中	back (body)
senchi	センチ	centimetre
sengetsu	先月	last month
senkyo	選挙	elections
sennuki	栓抜き	bottle opener
senritsu	旋律	tune
sensei	先生	teacher
senshu	選手	player (sports)
senshū	先週	last week
sensō	戦争	war
sensu	扇子	fan (folding)
sentakki	洗濯機	washing machine
sentaku shimasu	洗濯します	to wash (clothes)
serufu sābisu	セルフサービス	self-service
setomono	瀬戸物	chinaware
setsuyaku shimasu	節約します	to save
shaberimasu	喋ります	to chat up
shachō	社長	president (of a company)
shakai	社会	society
shakai fukushi	社会福祉	social welfare
shakai hoshō	社会保障	social security
shakai kagaku	社会科学	social sciences
shakai minshu shugi	社会民主主義	social-democratic
shakai shugisha	社会主義者	socialist
shako	車庫	garage
shampen	シャンペン	champagne
shampū	シャンプー	shampoo

D I C T I O N A R Y

sharin	車輪	wheel
shashin	写真	photo
shashin o torimasu	写真を撮ります	to take photographs
shashinka	写真家	photographer
shashō	車掌	ticket collector
shatsu	シャツ	shirt
shawā	シャワー	shower
shi	死	death
shi	詩	poetry
shi	市	city
shi-basu	市バス	local; city bus
shi-gatsu	4月	April
shīdī	CD	CD
shīto beruto	シートベルト	seatbelt
shītsu	シーツ	sheet (bed)
shibafu	芝生	lawn
shichi-gatsu	7月	July
shichō	市長	mayor
shiden	市電	tram
shidōsha	指導者	leader
shigoto	仕事	job/work
shiharai	支払い	payment
shihyō	指標	indicator
shika	鹿	deer
shikaku	資格	qualifications
shikashi	しかし	but
shiken	試験	exam
shikimono	敷物	rug
shikki	漆器	lacquerware
shima	島	island
shima uma	シマウマ	zebra
shimai	姉妹	sister
shimasu	します	to do
shimbun	新聞	newspaper
shimemasu	閉めます	to close
shimin	市民	citizen
shiminken	市民権	citizenship
shimpai	心配	worry
shimpai shimasu	心配します	worried
shimpai shinai de!	心配しないで！	Don't worry!
shimpan	審判	referee
shin'ya	深夜	midnight
shin'yō	信用	trust
shin'yō shimasu	信用します	to trust

shinagire	品切れ	out of stock
shinai denwa	市内電話	local call
shinamono	品物	goods
shindai sha	寝台車	sleeping car
shingō	信号	traffic light
shinguru rūmu	シングルルーム	single room
shinimasu	死にます	to die
shinjitsu	真実	truth
shinju	真珠	pearl
shinkansen	新幹線	bullet train
shinrin bassai	森林伐採	deforestation
shinseki	親戚	relative
shinsetsu na	親切な	kind
shinshitsu	寝室	bedroom
shinzō	心臓	heart
shio	塩	salt
shio no michihiki	潮の満ち引き	tide
shippo	尻尾	tail
shirabemasu	調べます	to check
shirami	シラミ	lice
shirīzu	シリーズ	series
shiriai	知り合い	acquaintance
shiritsu (byōin)	私立（病院）	private (hospital)
shiro	城	castle
shiro	白	white
shirōto	素人	amateur
shirokuro (firumu)	白黒 (フィルム)	B&W (film)
shisai	司祭	priest
shisō	思想	thought
shison	子孫	descendent
shita	下	below
shitai	死体	dead
shitagaimasu	従います	to follow
shiten	支店	branch (company)
shitsugyō	失業	unemployment
shitsugyō teate	失業手当	dole
shitsugyōsha	失業者	unemployed
shitsumon	質問	question
shitsumon shimasu	質問します	to question
shitte imasu	知っています	to know (someone)
shizen	自然	nature
shizen ryōhō	自然療法	naturopath
shizuka na	静かな	quiet (adj)
shō	ショー	a show

shōdoku	消毒	antiseptic
shōgai sha	障害者	disabled
shōgo	正午	noon
shōka furyō	消化不良	indigestion
shōkaki	消火器	fire extinguisher
shokkidana	食器棚	cupboard
shokubutsu	植物	plant
shokubutsu en	植物園	botanic garden
shokudō	食堂	canteen
shokugyō	職業	occupation
shokugyō annaijo	職業案内所	job centre
shokuhin	食品	food
shōmeisho	証明書	certificate
shōrai	将来	future
shōsai	詳細	detail
shōsetsu	小説	novel (book)
shotoku	所得	income
shotoku zei	所得税	income tax
shōyu	醤油	soy sauce
shū	週	week
shūdōin	修道院	monastery
shūdōjo	修道女	nun
shūdōshi	修道士	monk
shūjin	囚人	prisoner
shujutsu	手術	operation
shūkan	習慣	customs
shukuhaku	宿泊	accommodation
shūkyō	宗教	religion
shūkyōteki na	宗教的な	religious
shūmatsu	週末	weekend
shuppatsu	出発	departure
shuppatsu shimasu	出発します	to depart (leave)
shūshoku shimasu	就職します	to get a job
shūshoku kōkoku	就職広告	job advertisement
shussei shōmeisho	出生証明書	birth certificate
shusseichi	出生地	place of birth
shūwai shimasu	収賄します	to bribe
sōbi	装備	equipment
sōgan kyō	双眼鏡	binoculars
sōgen	草原	grassy plains
sōji	掃除	cleaning
sokudo	速度	speed
sokutatsu	速達	express mail
sonkei	尊敬	respect

sonotōri	そのとおり。	You're right.
sonshitsu	損失	loss
sora	空	sky
sorekara	それから	and
sorezore	それぞれ	each
sōri daijin	総理大臣	prime minister
sorimasu	剃ります	to shave
sōshiki	葬式	funeral
soshite	そして	and
soto	外	outside
subarashii	素晴らしい	brilliant
subayai	すばやい	quick
subete	すべて	all
sude ni	すでに	already
sugoi!	すごい!	Great!
sugu	すぐ	immediately
sūhai shimasu	崇拝します	worship
suiei	水泳	swimming
suimin yaku	睡眠薬	sleeping pill
suisen shimasu	推薦します	to recommend
suitō	水筒	water bottle
suiyōbi	水曜日	Wednesday
sūji	数字	figures
suki ni narimasu	好きになります	to like
sukī	スキー	skiing
sukī o shimasu	スキーをします	to ski
sukoshi	少し	a little bit
sukunai	少ない	less
sukurīn	スクリーン	screen
sumimasen	すみません	Excuse me.
sumimasu	住みます	to live (somewhere)
suna	砂	sand
sūpā	スーパー	supermarket
supīdo	スピード	speed
supōtsu	スポーツ	sport
supōtsu man	スポーツマン	sportsperson
suppai	酸っぱい	sour
suraido	スライド	slide (film)
surippa	スリッパ	slippers
sutairu	スタイル	style
sutajiamu	スタジアム	stadium
sutajio	スタジオ	studio
suteki na	素敵な	nice
sutōbu	ストーブ	stove
sutoraiki	ストライキ	a strike

| sūtsu kēsu | スーツケース | suitcase |
| suwarimasu | 座ります | to sit |

T

tabako	たばこ	cigarettes
tabako o suimasu	たばこを吸います	to smoke
tabakoya	たばこ屋	tobacco kiosk
tabemasu	食べます	to eat
tabemono	食べ物	food
tabi	旅	trip
tadashii	正しい	right (correct)
taida na	怠惰な	lazy
taihen	たいへん	very
taiikukan	体育館	gym
taiko	太鼓	drums
taikutsu na	退屈な	bored
taion	体温	temperature (fever)
taipu shimasu	タイプします	to type
taira na	平らな	flat (land, etc)
taisetsu na	大切な	important
taishi	大使	ambassador
taishikan	大使館	embassy
taishoku	退職	retired
taisō	体操	gymnastics
taiya	タイヤ	tyres
taiyō	太陽	sun
taizai shimasu	滞在します	to stay (somewhere)
takai	高い	expensive/high/tall
takai desu	高いです。	It costs a lot.
takasugimasu	高すぎます	too expensive
taki	滝	waterfall
takigi	たきぎ	firewood
takkyū	卓球	table tennis
takusan no	たくさんの	many
takushī	タクシー	taxi
takushī noriba	タクシー乗り場	taxi stand
tama tsuki	玉突き	pool (game)
tamago	たまご	egg
tameshimasu	試します	to try (attempt)
tāminaru	ターミナル	terminal
tampon	タンポン	tampons
tana	棚	shelves
tani	谷	valley

tanjōbi	誕生日	birthday
o-tanjōbi omedetō!	お誕生日 おめでとう！	Happy birthday!
tanjun na	単純な	simple
tanomimasu	頼みます	to ask (for something)
tanoshii	楽しい	fun
tanoshimimasu	楽しみます	to enjoy (oneself)
tansu	たんす	wardrobe
taoru	タオル	towel
tasukemasu	助けます	to help
tasukete!	助けて！	Help!
tatakaimasu	戦います	to fight
tatemasu	建てます	to build
tatemono	建物	building
tatoeba, ...	例えば、...	For example, ...
tatta	たった	only
tazunemasu	たずねます	to ask (a question); visit (a person)
te	手	hand
te ni iremasu	手に入れます	to get
tēburu	テーブル	table
tegami	手紙	letter
teian	提案	proposal
teido	程度	degree
teiketsuatsu	低血圧	low blood pressure
tejina	手品	magic
tejinashi	手品師	magician
ten	点	point
tenimotsu	手荷物	baggage
tenimotsu azukarijo	手荷物預所	left luggage office
tenisu	テニス	tennis
tenisu kōto	テニスコート	tennis court
tenji shimasu	展示します	to exhibit
tenkan	癲癇	epileptic
tenkeiteki na	典型的な	typical
tenki	天気	weather
tenrankai	展覧会	exhibition
tento	テント	tent
tera	寺	temple
terebi	テレビ	television
terebi dorama	テレビドラマ	soap opera
terefon kādo	テレホンカード	telephone card
tesuto	テスト	test/exam
tezukuri	手作り	handmade
tīshatsu	Tシャツ	T-shirt

tisshu	ティッシュ	tissues
to	と	and
tō	塔	tower
tō	党	political party
tobimasu	飛びます	to jump
tōchaku	到着	arrival
tōchaku shimasu	到着します	to arrive
todomarimasu	留まります	to stay (remain)
tōgei	陶芸	pottery
tōhyō	投票	polls
tōhyō shimasu	投票します	to vote
tōi	遠い	far
toire	トイレ	toilet
toiretto pēpā	トイレットペーパー	toilet paper
tōjiki	陶磁器	ceramic
tōjōken	搭乗券	boarding pass
tokei	時計	clock
tokidoki	ときどき	sometimes
tokubetsu	特別	special
tokuten	得点	point (games)
tomare!	止まれ！	Stop!
tomarimasu	止まります	to stop
tomodachi	友達	friend
tōnan	盗難	theft
tōnyōbyō	糖尿病	diabetic
tora	虎	tiger
toraberāzu chekku	トラベラーズチェック	travellers' cheques
torakku	トラック	truck/track (sports)
torampu	トランプ	cards
torekkingu	トレッキング	trek
torendīna	トレンディーな	trendy (person)
tori	鳥	bird
torikeshi	取り消し	cancel
toshi	都市	city
toshi	年	year
toshokan	図書館	library
tōsuto	トースト	toast
totemo	とても	very
tozan	登山	mountaineering
tozan-gutsu	登山靴	hiking boots
tsūyaku	通訳	interpreter
tsuā (gaido)	ツアー(ガイド)	tour (guide)
tsubasa	翼	wings
tsubo	壷	pot (ceramic)
tsuchi	土	earth (soil)

tsugi no	次の	next
tsuin beddo	ツインベッド	twin beds
tsukaremasu	疲れます	to be tired
tsuki	月	month/moon
tsukimasu	着きます	to arrive
tsukurimsu	作ります	to make
tsuma	妻	wife
tsumaranai	つまらない	boring
tsume kiri	爪切り	nail clippers
tsumetai	冷たい	cold (object)
tsumi	罪	sin
tsuru	鶴	crane
tsuruhashi	つるはし	pick/pickaxe
tsuta	蔦	vine
tsuyoi	強い	strong
tsuyosa	強さ	strength
tsuyu	梅雨	rainy season

U

uchi	うち	home
uchimasu	撃ちます	to shoot
uchimi	打ち身	a bruise
uchiwa	団扇	fan (round)
uchū	宇宙	universe
ude	腕	arm
ude-dokei	腕時計	a watch
ue	上	up
no ue ni	の上に	above/on
ue no kai	上の階	upstairs
ueitā	ウエイター	waiter
uemasu	植えます	to plant
uirusu	ウイルス	virus
ukemasu	受けます	to receive
ukemiteki na	受け身的な	passive
uketorimasu	受け取ります	to accept
uketsuke kakari	受付係	receptionist
uki	雨季	rainy season
uma	馬	horse
umi	海	sea
un	運	luck
unten menkyo	運転免許	drivers' licence
unten shimasu	運転します	to drive
unten shu	運転手	driver

uranaishi	占師	fortune teller
ureshii	うれしい	happy
urimasu	売ります	to sell
urusai	うるさい	noisy
urushi nuri	漆塗り	lacquerware
usagi	ウサギ	rabbit
usero!	失せろ！	Get lost!
ushi	牛	cow
ushiro	後	behind/back
ushiro de	後ろで	at the back; behind
uso	うそ	lie
usotsuki	うそつき	liar
usui	薄い	thin
uta	歌	song
utaimasu	歌います	to sing
utsukushii	美しい	beautiful
uyoku	右翼	right-wing

W

wain	ワイン	wine
wain gurasu	ワイングラス	wine glass
wain risuto	ワインリスト	wine list
wainarī	ワイナリー	winery
wairo	賄賂	a bribe
wakai	若い	young
wakamono	若者	youth (collective)
wakarimasu	わかります	to know (something)
wakarimasen	わかりません。	I don't know.
wakarimashita	わかりました。	I see. (understand)
wakare	分かれ	a parting
wakemasu	分けます	to separate
wāku shoppu	ワークショップ	workshop
wakusei	惑星	planet
wāpuro	ワープロ	word processor
waraimasu	笑います	to laugh
waribiki	割引	discount
wārudo kappu	ワールドカップ	World Cup
warui	悪い	bad
wasabi	わさび	horseradish
washi	和紙	paper (Japanese)
wasuremasu	忘れます	to forget
wata	綿	cotton

| watashi | 私 | I, me |
| watashi tachi | 私達 | we, us |

Y

yachin	家賃	rent (of a house)
yakkyoku	薬局	chemist/pharmacy
yaku	約	about
yakusoku	約束	promise
yama	山	mountain
yama-goya	山小屋	mountain hut
yama michi	山道	mountain path
yamemasu	やめます	to stop/give up
yaoya	八百屋	greengrocer
yarimasu	やります	to do
yasai	野菜	vegetable
yasashii	優しい	kind
yasei	野生	wild
yashoku	夜食	supper
yasu uri	安売り	on sale
yasui	安い	cheap
yasumi	休み	rest (relaxation)
yasumimasu	休みます	to rest
yatoinushi	雇い主	employer
yoake	夜明け	dawn
yobō chūsha	予防注射	vaccination
yobō shimasu	予防します	to prevent
yōchi-en	幼稚園	kindergarten
yōfuku	洋服	western clothes
yoi	良い	good
yoi-dome	酔い止め	travel sickness pill
yói ga dekimasu	用意ができます	to be ready
yoi masu	酔います	to be drunk
yoko	横	beside
yōkoso	ようこそ	welcome
yoku	よく	often
yomimasu	読みます	to read
yōmō	羊毛	wool
yōroppajin	ヨーロッパ人	European
yoru	夜	night
yosomono	よそもの	stranger
yoteihyō	予定表	itinerary
yotto	ヨット	yacht
yowai	弱い	weak

Y

D
I
C
T
I
O
N
A
R
Y

yoyaku	予約	appointment/ booking
yoyaku shimasu	予約します	to reserve
yūbe	ゆうべ	last night
yubi	指	finger
yubiwa	指輪	ring (on finger)
yūbin	郵便	mail
yūbin-bako	郵便箱	mailbox
yūbinbangō	郵便番号	post code
yūbinryōkin	郵便料金	postage
yūbinkyoku	郵便局	post office
yūen gasorin	有鉛ガソリン	leaded (petrol/gas)
yudayajin	ユダヤ人	Jewish
yudayakyo	ユダヤ教	Judaism
yūfuku na	裕福な	wealthy
yuka	床	floor
yukai na	愉快な	entertaining
yūkan na	勇敢な	brave
yūkensha	有権者	electorate
yuki	雪	snow
yukkuri	ゆっくり	slow/slowly
yume o mimasu	夢を見ます	to dream
yūmei na	有名な	famous
yūri	有利	advantage
yurushimsu	許します	to forgive
yūshoku	夕食	dinner
yūsu hosuteru	ユースホステル	youth hostel

zabuton	座布団	Japanese-style cushions
zairyō	材料	ingredient
zange	懺悔	confession (religious)
zaseki	座席	seat
zasshi	雑誌	magazine
zatsuon	雑音	noise
zensoku	喘息	asthma
zetsumetsu	絶滅	extinct
zō	象	elephant
zō	像	statue
zōri	草履	sandals (Japanese)
zotto suru	ぞっとする	creep
zubon	ズボン	trousers
zuru	ずる	a cheat
zutsū	頭痛	a headache

INDEX

LONELY PLANET

Phrasebooks

L onely Planet phrasebooks are packed with essential words and phrases to help travellers communicate with the locals. With colour tabs for quick reference, an extensive vocabulary and use of script, these handy pocket-sized language guides cover day-to-day travel situations.

- handy pocket-sized books
- easy to understand Pronunciation chapter
- clear & comprehensive Grammar chapter
- romanisation alongside script to allow ease of pronunciation
- script throughout so users can point to phrases for every situation
- full of cultural information and tips for the traveller

'...vital for a real DIY spirit and attitude in language learning'
– *Backpacker*
'the phrasebooks have good cultural backgrounders and offer solid advice for challenging situations in remote locations'
– *San Francisco Examiner*

Arabic (Egyptian) • Arabic (Moroccan) • Australian *(Australian English, Aboriginal and Torres Strait languages)* • Baltic States *(Estonian, Latvian, Lithuanian)* • Bengali • Brazilian • Burmese • British • Cantonese • Central Asia • Central Europe *(Czech, French, German, Hungarian, Italian, Slovak)* • Eastern Europe *(Bulgarian, Czech, Hungarian, Polish, Romanian, Slovak)* • Ethiopian (Amharic) • Fijian • French • German • Greek • Hill Tribes • Hindi/Urdu • Indonesian • Italian • Japanese • Korean • Lao • Latin American Spanish • Malay • Mandarin • Mediterranean Europe *(Albanian, Croatian, Greek, Italian, Macedonian, Maltese, Serbian, Slovene)* • Mongolian • Nepali • Papua New Guinea • Pilipino (Tagalog) • Quechua • Russian • Scandinavian Europe *(Danish, Finnish, Icelandic, Norwegian, Swedish)* • South-East Asia *(Burmese, Indonesian, Khmer, Lao, Malay, Tagalog Pilipino, Thai, Vietnamese)* • Spanish (Castilian) *(also includes Catalan, Galician and Basque)* • Sri Lanka • Swahili • Thai • Tibetan • Turkish • Ukrainian • USA *(US English, Vernacular, Native American languages, Hawaiian)* • Vietnamese • Western Europe *(Basque, Catalan, Dutch, French, German, Greek, Irish)*

COMPLETE LIST OF LONELY PLANET BOOKS

AFRICA Africa – the South • Africa on a shoestring • Arabic (Egyptian) phrasebook • Arabic (Moroccan) phrasebook • Cairo • Cape Town • Central Africa • East Africa • Egypt • Egypt travel atlas • Ethiopian (Amharic) phrasebook • The Gambia & Senegal • Kenya • Kenya travel atlas • Malawi, Mozambique & Zambia • Morocco • North Africa • South Africa, Lesotho & Swaziland • South Africa, Lesotho & Swaziland travel atlas • Swahili phrasebook • Trekking in East Africa • Tunisia • West Africa • Zimbabwe, Botswana & Namibia • Zimbabwe, Botswana & Namibia travel atlas
Travel Literature: The Rainbird: A Central African Journey • Songs to an African Sunset: A Zimbabwean Story • Mali Blues: Traveling to an African Beat

AUSTRALIA & THE PACIFIC Australia • Australian phrasebook • Bushwalking in Australia • Bushwalking in Papua New Guinea • Fiji • Fijian phrasebook • Islands of Australia's Great Barrier Reef • Melbourne • Micronesia • New Caledonia • New South Wales & the ACT • New Zealand • Northern Territory • Outback Australia • Papua New Guinea • Papua New Guinea (Pidgin) phrasebook • Queensland • Rarotonga & the Cook Islands • Samoa • Solomon Islands • South Australia • Sydney • Tahiti & French Polynesia • Tasmania • Tonga • Tramping in New Zealand • Vanuatu • Victoria • Western Australia
Travel Literature: Islands in the Clouds • Sean & David's Long Drive

CENTRAL AMERICA & THE CARIBBEAN Bahamas and Turks & Caicos • Barcelona • Bermuda • Central America on a shoestring • Costa Rica • Cuba • Dominican Republic & Haiti • Eastern Caribbean • Guatemala, Belize & Yucatán: La Ruta Maya • Jamaica • Mexico • Mexico City • Panama
Travel Literature: Green Dreams: Travels in Central America

EUROPE Amsterdam • Andalucía • Austria • Baltic States phrasebook • Berlin • Britain • British phrasebook • Central Europe • Central Europe phrasebook • Croatia • Czech & Slovak Republics • Denmark • Dublin • Eastern Europe • Eastern Europe phrasebook • Edinburgh • Estonia, Latvia & Lithuania • Europe • Finland • France • French phrasebook • Germany • German phrasebook • Greece • Greek phrasebook • Hungary • Iceland, Greenland & the Faroe Islands • Ireland • Italian phrasebook • Italy • Lisbon • London • Mediterranean Europe • Mediterranean Europe phrasebook • Paris • Poland • Portugal • Portugal travel atlas • Prague • Provence & the Côte D'Azur • Romania & Moldova • Russia, Ukraine & Belarus • Russian phrasebook • Scandinavian & Baltic Europe • Scandinavian Europe phrasebook • Scotland • Slovenia • Spain • Spanish phrasebook • St Petersburg • Switzerland • Trekking in Spain • Ukrainian phrasebook • Vienna • Walking in Britain • Walking in Italy • Walking in Ireland • Walking in Switzerland • Western Europe • Western Europe phrasebook
Travel Literature: The Olive Grove: Travels in Greece

INDIAN SUBCONTINENT Bangladesh • Bengali phrasebook • Bhutan • Delhi • Goa • Hindi/Urdu phrasebook • India • India & Bangladesh travel atlas • Indian Himalaya • Karakoram Highway • Nepal • Nepali phrasebook • Pakistan • Rajasthan • South India • Sri Lanka • Sri Lanka phrasebook • Trekking in the Indian Himalaya • Trekking in the Karakoram & Hindukush • Trekking in the Nepal Himalaya